A NOVEL

Which Way From Here

Tim Bloomquist

To the ol' Coyote
Enjoy the ride!
Tim Bloomquist

NOSLO
PUBLISHING
Traverse City, Michigan

Published by
NOSLO PUBLISHING
P.O. Box 4015
Traverse City, Michigan 49685

PUBLISHER'S NOTE: This is a work of fiction, and is in no way autobiographical. Its characters, dialogue, incidents, and plot come from the author's imagination. References to, any depiction of, real people, places, or things are used fictitiously. Any resemblance to actual persons, companies, or events is purely coincidental.

Publisher's Cataloging-in-Publication Data
Bloomquist, Tim.
Which way from here: a novel / Tim Bloomquist. Traverse City, Mich.: Noslo Publishing, 2000.

p. cm.

ISBN 0-9674119-0-4
1. Businessmen—Fiction. 2. Corporate culture—Fiction.
I. Title.

PS3552 . L66 W55 2000 CIP
813'.54—dc21 99-64736

Printed in the United States of America

03 02 01 00 ✦ 5 4 3 2 1

To my family . . .

wife, Cheryl,
and daughters Elizabeth, Emily, and Esme
who weathered my moods, and my solitude, and never stopped
asking, "Are you almost finished, Dad?"

In memory of my grandparents
Charles & Helen Olson
Arthur & Cosetta Bloomquist

and my father
Clayton Bloomquist

ACKNOWLEDGMENTS

TRULY, NO ONE ACCOMPLISHES ANYTHING ALONE. AND with that profundity out of the way let me credit some folks.

Cheryl Bloomquist, my wife, my champion, my critic, and my financier. Thanks for allowing me to cut my work hours, and buy those Harley-Davidsons. This story wouldn't exist without you.

Beverly McMillan, my mother. Mothers should always be acknowledged. (Mom, the bad language and behaviors depicted within the body of this work are the responsibility of those characters, not that of your son.)

Angie Williams, my longtime friend, who actually volunteered to proofread those early rough drafts. The green pen was a gentle touch.

Matt, the computer guy at Inacomp, who rescued 200 pages of manuscript from the diabolical software that thought it would be funny to spew my young novel into hard-drive oblivion.

Theodora Keith, colleague and friend, who was courageous enough to read my manuscript, and then give me an honest opinion.

Nancy Sundstrom, a very talented and versatile woman with an endless schedule, who still found time to read my manuscript. And then took two hours on the afternoon of October 31st to advise me and to cheer me on, knowing there were three Halloween costumes to be made before dusk.

Phil Murphy, who told me like it was, and was right.

Mary Jo Zazueta, who made the final editorial recommendations, and thus convinced me to review my copy of *Elements of Style*.

The Jenkins Group (Susan, Nikki, Theresa, and Eric) who helped me get this first novel into a bookstore near you.

Big George, who kept telling me it's a damn good story.

Speedo, who's been there, and continues to fight back.

Friday, July 3

One

"Hey, how 'bout that Sammy Sosa?" The young man behind the bar smiled as he propped the Louisville Slugger on his shoulder. "Smackin' the hell out of the ball."

"How many is that now?"

Thoughtfully the bartender set the bat down on the bar. "Hit twenty last month! He's right up there with Griffey and McGwire, I know that."

Thatcher nodded agreeably as the distant whine of jet engines announced another late morning flight departing from O'Hare.

"So, whatta ya have?"

Sliding onto the stool, he said, "Coke."

As the bartender scooped ice into a glass, he asked, "Comin', or goin', or just passin' through?"

Thatcher glanced across the small bar toward the terminal walkway. He momentarily watched the ongoing parade of people passing by against the background of a Boeing jumbo jet slowly pulling away from the accordion arm of the concourse. He returned his attention to the bartender as the glass was placed in front of him.

"I'm not sure." He took a sip and nodded toward the baseball bat. "Sammy's autograph."

"Sure is. And it's gonna be worth something by the end of this season." He emphasized the last two words.

"Give you five hundred." Thatcher began to reach inside his Armani jacket.

"Not for sale."

"A thousand."

Without hesitation, "Nope."

Pulling out his wallet, Thatcher looked squarely at the young man. "You're a credit to baseball fans everywhere." He placed a hundred on the bar.

"Can't break that this early in the day."

"No need." He took another sip. "You have any classifieds around?"

"Sure." Excitedly the young man pulled out a rolled up newspaper from beneath the bar. "Yesterday's '*Trib*'."

Thatcher stuck the paper under his arm and picked up his glass. "Thanks."

The bartender slipped the large bill into his shirt pocket. "No problem," he said with a smile.

Thatcher turned and headed toward a booth adjacent to the entrance. As he spread the classifieds out in front of him, he noticed the jumbo jet was beginning its trek toward the runway. The self-acknowledgement that his jetting around days were over gave exuberance to his index finger as it traced rapidly along the first column of classifieds.

After scribbling down two phone numbers into his pocket-sized book, a large man in a dark suit, black shirt, white tie, and gold jewelry slid in beside him.

Without the slightest reaction, Thatcher closed his leatherbound planner and slipped it into the inside pocket of his jacket. Taking his time folding the newspaper, he neatly placed it between the seat and the wall.

"Mr. Burdick wants to talk with you." The voice was brusque and deep.

Unimpressed, Thatcher gave his boorish boothmate the once-over. "Is this good fella day at the office? Or did Mr. Burdick dress you up this morning to intimidate me?"

"I don't like you."

Thatcher looked the man in the eyes. "You've ruined my day."

JJ Burdick, CEO of Burdick Corporation, stepped into the bar. Another man, who was beside him, pointed in Thatcher's direction — as if JJ couldn't spot the only two patrons in the small air terminal bar. Within moments JJ was sitting across from Thatcher. The short, stout man with the keen sense of direction stood at attention beside the booth.

"Now that we're all present and accounted for," Thatcher tipped his glass in JJ's direction, "shall we order cocktails?" Taking a sip of soda, he looked back and forth between the three doleful gentlemen around him. "Or, are there more coming?"

JJ Burdick, a bald, humorless man of nearly seventy-five attempted to snarl; it sounded like an asthmatic Pomeranian. "Consider yourself fucked."

Thatcher grinned earnestly. "You know, the gentleman at the IRS made that very same innuendo in regards to your assets."

"This isn't finished, Thatcher." JJ snatched the inhaler from the extended hand of his stalwart assistant beside him.

Thatcher glanced up toward the standing man. "I know Mr. Gridly," he began, then turning toward the large man beside him, he added, "but I don't think I've been introduced to gangster-for-a-day."

JJ grinned as his oversized associate suddenly pinned Thatcher against the wall. He took two puffs from his inhaler. "Let me introduce," he sniggered, "my associate, Mr. Brogan."

"The pleasure is all mine," Thatcher replied, as he snatched Brogan's white tie and pulled. A quick push forward with his elbow to the back of the big man's extended neck resulted in a resounding collision with the table.

JJ watched in dismay as Brogan's forehead bounced off the tabletop with a dull thud.

Nudging JJ's fallen associate onto the floor on his way out of the booth, Thatcher straightened his own tie. "Give Mr. Brogan my apologies."

"This isn't finished!"

"You've said that." Thatcher stepped over the unconscious man. "You'll excuse me, I've things to do."

Mr. Gridly gave a wide berth as Thatcher walked past.

"Thirty-six!"

Everyone except Mr. Brogan looked in the direction of the young man behind the bar.

Disregarding the man on the floor, the bartender, with his prized autographed bat raised high above his head, addressed his exiting patron. "Sammy's got thirty-six... I think."

As Thatcher waved farewell and headed toward the door, he heard the young man call out. "Hey! Wait!"

Thatcher turned just in time to catch a fluttering blue Cubbies cap.

"I was wearing it when Sammy signed my bat. It's yours."

Inspecting the well-worn cap, he turned and smiled at the devout Cubbies fan. The young man smiled back as Thatcher respectfully slapped the cap hard against his hand. After stretching it vigorously, he put it on as if he was headed to the mound instead of the baggage claim.

"You were supposed to be here when my plane landed." Pulling off her Ray Bans, the stunning blonde raised her voice. She was dressed in a short, summer skirt with a matching black lycra top. "I've been trying to call you for forty-five minutes!"

With the luggage carousel at a standstill and his bag nowhere in sight, Thatcher turned his attention toward the theatrical vignette at the pay phone.

Restlessly running her fingers through her hair, she snapped, "Where have you been? You know I can't be late."

Sensing an audience, she turned to see an impeccably dressed man sporting a ratty baseball cap. Within milliseconds, she discerned he was the kind of guy women tend to look at just a little too long. The tailored suit, the gold cuff links, and the silk tie suggested he was important and undoubtedly full of himself. The oddly out-of-place cap, however, softened the image, giving him a boyish charm as irresistible as Swiss chocolate. She nervously shifted her weight from one leg to the other, and looked away as he glanced at his Rolex.

"Curtis," she whispered harshly as she stooped down to slip her sunglasses into her Gucci bag that was setting on the floor. "Curtis, come get me. Now!"

Thatcher wasn't a typical eavesdropper; he was a highly skilled professional. Although, at the moment he wasn't being clandestine and he wasn't particularly interested in the young woman's conversation. He wanted to use the phone. Amazingly, out of a half dozen pay phones, three were donning out-of-order signs, one had a foreign substance stuck to the receiver, and one had no receiver.

"It's your fucking job to pick me up." Her fingers raced through her hair. "I'm not taking a goddamn cab!" The onset of a few stray tears began to smudge her mascara. "Come get me," she moaned.

Thatcher had observed the performance long enough. He was quite certain she had no inclination of relinquishing the only phone any time soon, so he began his approach.

"Just do your job," she demanded.

Again, she ran her fingers through her hair.

That simple unconscious act seemed to disperse a subtle, beckoning fragrance in Thatcher's direction. He paused, ever so slightly, before easing beside her.

He was tempted to tap her lightly on the shoulder, just to touch her. She was the kind of woman, he thought, that men would contrive any reason to get close to, and if the moment presented itself, touch. Instead, Thatcher simply and deftly lifted the receiver from her hand without the slightest contact.

"Curtis," he said in a relaxed, encouraging voice as he adjusted the bill of his cap. "Come get her, now." Handing the receiver back, he smiled earnestly. "He's coming."

Curiously unabashed, she looked long and hard at him. She was drawn to the steel blue eyes that melded together sincerity and obscurity into a fatal draught of trust. She resisted the temptation to say something appreciative. Instead, she delicately wiped beneath each eye with her pinkie finger.

"I don't know," she whispered into the receiver.

As she pulled the receiver away from her ear, Thatcher held his hand out. "May I?"

Her eyes told him she did not understand.

"The phone, may I use it?"

She said nothing, and set the receiver in Thatcher's hand. She stooped abruptly to pick up her leather Gucci bag. She wanted to hurry and linger at the same time.

Admiring her long Coppertone legs as she walked away, Thatcher considered calling out a farewell. He thought better of it, and slipped two quarters into the slot.

Thatcher punched in the seven digits of the first number he had written down earlier.

It rang a half dozen times before going into a recorded message. "Get fucked, Marion." Obviously Marion had been a nuisance caller.

He tried the other number. It rang twice.

"Yeah." The voice was low and impatient.

The sudden clanking of the baggage carousel drew Thatcher's attention. "Hold on," he said as he glanced between the narrow breaches left by the scurrying baggage searchers.

"Who the fuck is this?"

"Thatcher."

"Who?"

"I have eighteen grand. Cash. For your merchandise."

There was a long pause. "Ain't enough."

Thatcher had anticipated the response. "I've got a list of six other sellers." Lying was so keenly honed, Thatcher himself lost track of the truth from time to time.

After a brief silence the voice said, "Wait a minute," followed by a raspy cough. "Cash?"

Leaning against the wall, he loosened his tie. "Little portraits of Ben Franklin all in a roll."

"I'll give ya directions..."

"No," Thatcher said calmly. "I'm no good at directions," he lied again. "I'm from out of town." This wasn't a great stretch of the truth; he never actually had an address in Chicago. "You deliver, I'll cover the expense."

"Wait a minute..." It was a slow mind thinking.

"I'm at O'Hare, United terminal."

A groan. "I'll send someone. Thirty minutes," the voice grumbled. "Wait outside. Black Chevy pickup with big fucking tires."

"Gate 23."

Thatcher hung the receiver in place as the carousel stopped its second roundabout. Watching the covey of United passengers swarm the carousel, he scanned the remains of the luggage. It seemed his black leather duffel bag may have been given passage elsewhere.

Checking his watch, he measured out the thirty minutes, and considered the prospect of being picked up at O'Hare by person or persons unknown of potentially questionable character. He wasn't overly enthused; he considered Mr. Brogan his quota of dubious personalities for one day. If up to him, he would have chosen to carry out the negotiations at the airport. It was public. It was convenient. And it was most expeditious. He preferred efficiency.

With some time to kill, Thatcher decided to call his answering service; a daily addiction he truly wanted to break. Punching in the numbers, he reached into his pants pocket and retrieved his last piece of bubble gum, another addiction.

"Call received, 3:43 P.M., Thursday, July second, twenty seconds. This is Jennifer. I'm calling on behalf of Dialing for Dollars..." Thatcher knew the spiel.

This was Friday. Without realizing it, he had missed an entire day of messages. Perhaps his addiction was manageable after all.

"Call received, 4:24 P.M., Thursday, July second, twenty seconds. This is Merry Maids Cleaning Service. Charlene went on a bender again. We won't be able to replace her 'til Friday, or until she sobers up. Sorry for the inconvenience."

He made a mental note to call Merry Maids and cancel their service. Everything in the Bloomfield Hills condo was indefinitely enshrouded with white sheets.

"Call received, 9:06 P.M., Thursday, July second, ten seconds. "Consider yourself fucked." It was JJ's buffoon using JJ's clever phrase. Snapping his gum generously, Thatcher smiled.

"Call received, 9:11 A.M., Friday, July third, twenty seconds. This is Dialing for Dollars . . ." Persistent.

"Call received, 11:56 A.M., Friday, July third, ten seconds. "This isn't finished!" Glancing at his watch (it was a couple minutes past noon), he smiled. It was JJ's way of having the last word via wireless technology.

Thatcher's first bubble was nearly perfect. Admiring the achievement was a six-year-old, wearing an oversized number twenty-one Cubbies jersey. He stood securely nestled between two older sisters. Thatcher winked. The boy winked back.

As he chewed and watched another round of luggage on parade, he imagined his bag in the cargo bay of a 747 heading west. And then, miraculously it seemed, the duffel bag appeared, nestled against a cardboard guitar case wrapped in red bungee cords. Things seemed to be looking up, he thought.

With a swipe of his right hand, he grabbed his bag and headed in the direction of his rendezvous point. The rushing masses around him reminded him of one reason he was walking away from his six-figure emolument; places to be instead of places to go.

It was much more than being tired of the places. Thatcher was tired of the game. He no longer wanted to play. The rules were degenerating. Wearied by the digressing code of conduct, Thatcher simply wanted to clear the board of his game pieces.

In the beginning it seemed so simple; there were the big fat cat corporations eager to swallow up the competition at first advantage. Without moral issue, Thatcher provided the resource. Information.

Thatcher infiltrated multimillion-dollar corporations under the guise of an ameliorator, and quickly befriended key figures through his charisma, cunning, and Machiavellian eclecticism. From these key corporate figures, he was contractually paid huge sums for his seemingly omniscient counsel, all the while collecting information (Wire Tapping 101 courtesy of the United States government) he later would provide to other corporations. It was a vicious food chain; the corporate world attempting to devour itself. Thatcher was the jackal living high off the scraps.

However, when his last employer, Mr. JJ Burdick and Corporation, began stalking a small, three-generation family business in Wheaton, Illinois, Thatcher decided he had had enough. Burdick was trampling on Thatcher's only rule; pick on somebody your own size.

Among the miles of audiotape that Thatcher had collected over several months at Burdick was a single, brief message that explained the impetus behind JJ's decree to gobble up a retail hardware chain consisting of three small stores.

The hardware store owner's granddaughter was in the second trimester of her pregnancy. She carried the first and last great-grandchild of the CEO of Burdick Corporation.

JJ Burdick's prodigal grandson recently left JJ without his chosen heir to the Burdick empire when he turned himself into a 160-miles-per-hour projectile while driving his Corvette convertible on the Dan Ryan Expressway. After serious reflection, JJ resolved not to leave his corporate creation to his thrice divorced daughter, who would undoubtedly turn it over to the next squandering drunk she married.

Shortly after his grandson's memorial it came to JJ's attention that the brief notorious life of JJ III had rendered a, yet unborn, biological heir. He was ecstatic. JJ Burdick never considered it would be another quarter century before his great-grandchild would be old enough for corporate rule.

However, when the young mother-to-be refused to relinquish custody of her yet unborn child despite JJ Burdick's outlandish monetary offer, JJ determined he would resort to extortion. When he found no basis for blackmail against Sam Brewster, he turned to the only option left. Reprisal. Consuming Brewster Hardware wouldn't be difficult for a fat cat with an inexhaustible appetite for power and control, and, in this case, mean-spirited vengeance.

The hardware Brewsters of Wheaton, Illinois, held together by their unwavering faith in the American way, prayed for a higher power to step forward to save Brewster Hardware for the next generation. That higher power turned out to be the Internal Revenue Service.

Dissolving his contractual arrangement with The Burdick Corporation, upon principle and regardless of the substantial personal financial loss, was one of Thatcher's more meritorious acts. Conveyance to the IRS of certain financial data from the personal files of JJ Burdick, for the express purpose of freezing Burdick Corporation assets and thus rescuing Brewster Hardware from subjugation, at the cost of his own esteemed professional reputation, was nothing less than one man's valorous cry of "Take this job and shove it."

Sam Brewster swore it was an act of God. It practically was.

Once outside, Thatcher moved with the flow of pedestrians as he made his way to the curb. It was the fragrance that announced her presence. Unexpected as it was, standing near the young blonde in the short skirt was a pleasant coincidence. He made no effort to be noticed. Instead he chose to watch from the corner of his eye, and to absorb her essence one last time. Within seconds a black limousine veered to the curb. He watched an unattractive burly fellow emerge from the driver's side door.

A light touch on his shoulder startled him. Turning, he found himself face to face with the young woman. Quickly pushing the bill of the cap out of the way, he began to excuse his intrusion, yet before he could speak, her lips brushed across his. Suddenly, somewhere in his brain, the brash, bustling sound of traffic, was transposed into a soft, sultry, sax solo of "Smoke Gets in Your Eyes."

As they parted, she smiled coyly and stroked the side of his face. She whispered, "Going my way?"

Thatcher was certain he wasn't, yet for a brief moment he considered the possibility. It was the hostile glare from her churlish driver that persuaded him to answer, "Another time, maybe."

Without taking her eyes from his, she slipped the strap of her bag over her shoulder, and replied demurely, "Another time."

The driver took no inclination to assist his passenger. Thatcher watched as she opened her own door and withdrew from the bright afternoon into the shadowy obscurity of the limousine.

Thatcher's eyes shifted from the departing limousine to an approaching black Chevy pickup set atop four giant tires. He glanced at his watch and determined twenty-five minutes had passed. He flipped his hand into the air, as if hailing a taxi. He waited to see if it would pull over. The truck grunted to an abrupt stop.

A petite, expressionless woman, with dark unruly hair, remarkably untouched by the slightest benevolence of beauty and uninhibited by etiquette, sneered through the open window, "Who the fuck you suppose to be?"

Thatcher never imagined he was supposed to be anybody. Sticking his hands into his pants pockets, he shrugged his shoulders, and said, "The man with the money."

With her right hand delicately holding a long slender cigarette, inches away from her cheek, and her left hand fixed firmly upon the oversized steering wheel, she gave him a quick once-over. "Yeah, the money man," she said tersely as she leaned over toward the passenger side door. Pushing open the door, she growled, "Fucking Cubs fan."

As the door swung open, Thatcher was greeted by an immodest exposition of unassuming cleavage from beneath a frayed denim vest. Undaunted, he adjusted the cap to purposely display the red "C" to the hostile driver, and with duffel bag in hand, he climbed in.

Turning away briskly to check traffic, she exclaimed through a nasally Midwestern drawl, "You look like a man with money."

He said nothing as the pickup sped away. Thatcher pulled the door shut and grabbed the seat belt.

"Hey." The woman turned in his direction.

Thatcher met her stare head-on. It was one of those haven't-I-seen-you-somewhere-before looks. He knew it was mistaken identity, but when she said, "FBI," he froze. The unexpected sound of those three letters momentarily unnerved him.

The woman glanced away as she changed lanes. "Yeah." She turned back and looked him up and down repeating, "Yeah." Breaking into a wide, chipped tooth grin, she announced, "You look like 'em."

Thatcher scanned his memory. The woman beside him was no one he had seen before. He was certain of that. In his brief and not-so-meritorious career at The Bureau, he worked the East Coast, never having set foot and badge into the Chicago region. That was nearly twenty years ago. He looked hard at her, and suddenly smiled sheepishly to himself. Twenty years ago she would have been steering a Big Wheel by Hasbro.

She delicately took a drag on her thin cigarette, held in the toxins for several seconds for maximum absorption, then tilted her head back exhaling a plume of smoke. It momentarily created an imperfect halo around her unbridled hair. Glancing again at her passenger she said with an edgy giddiness, "Yeah, you look like 'em a lot." Pausing, as if to collect a wayward thought, she said, "Say this for me, will ya?" She gathered herself for a moment, as if to get it just right. Then, in a dramatic rush of breath she said, "The truth is out there."

He casually ignored her unusual request and asked, "Where we going?"

The woman cast him a disgruntled glance as she shifted the truck into third. "Not far," she replied sullenly.

"What's 'not far'?"

The pickup zipped along the airport access boulevard as she shifted into fourth. She said sourly, "Not far is not far. What part of that don't you understand?"

Surmising he had thoughtlessly spurned his new acquaintance, he chose to let the conversation end. With nothing else to do, he stretched out his legs and rolled down the window. Leaning back, he tried to remember the last time he had ridden in a truck: maybe 1979.

Moments later the truck was hustling westbound on Interstate 90.

The woman drove fast. Tailgating: an amusement. Thatcher closed his eyes and tried to relax. He imagined long Coppertone legs.

The young woman sat stoically in the back of the limousine and stared out the tinted windows. She felt as if her entire life had been placed behind tinted windows; nothing seemed as clear and bright as it once did. Classical music played softly: another analgesic for the senses. She ached for the guidance of Alanis Morissette as she recalled the lyrics to "Mary Jane." "There's a few more bruises if that's the way you insist on heading . . ."

She noticed that Curtis was talking on the phone. It occurred to her he was speaking to Aaron. She felt a sudden chill come over her. She lowered the privacy window in time to hear his parting words.

"I don't know who he was, but they were real friendly."

She raised the window, closed her eyes, slumped into the cool leather seat, and remembered his steel blue eyes.

The black pickup rumbled down Melody Lane. Mobile homes lined either side in a discordant harmony. Thatcher noticed few people were about. He imagined the inhabitants of Melody Lane gazing into cable TV, or cruising the nearest strip mall, or simply being elsewhere in an effort to forget where they lived. And, then again, he didn't know these people. Maybe this was nirvana, maybe purgatory, or maybe... He quit thinking about it as the truck pulled into a short gravel driveway.

An immense brooding figure sat at a picnic table beside a rusting double-wide Marlette mobile home enshrouded by unkempt evergreen shrubbery. Through reflective sunglasses, he appeared to be staring and pondering. He wore black jeans and a chrome-studded, patch-ladened, black leather vest. The matrix of interconnecting tattoos across his back and down each massive arm suggested a Ray Bradbury character.

The woman got out of the truck quickly and walked over to her illustrated man, leaned into him, and kissed him on the cheek. She remained standing with her fingertips caressing the fire-breathing dragon lurking across his deltoid.

Thatcher removed his cap and tucked it into his duffel bag before pushing the door open. It creaked and buckled like an arthritic appendage. So much for making an entrance, he thought, as he clambered out of the truck. Shoving his hands into his pockets, he took his first step, then halted dead in his tracks. Remarkably, he hadn't noticed it until that moment: a shining oracle of chrome, steel, and customized paint. Set against the contrasting backdrop of the rusting Marlette it appeared surreal: a Van Gogh displayed with hubcaps on a garage wall, displaced, yet no less remarkable, no less entrancing to look at. Thatcher stood silently and admired the motorcycle's brilliant artistry.

The illustrated man spoke. "It's a fucking shame." Slowly rising, a voice of a prophet shattering the afternoon serenity, "A goddamn, fucking shame!" Getting up from the table, he slowly backed up to the customized Harley Davidson.

Thatcher began delineating a bargaining strategy.

"Let's see the cash." Caressing the handlebars tenderly, he eagerly eyed the prissy-ass chump with the big wad of cash. "No doubt you like what you see."

Thatcher took a seat at the picnic table. He decided to stand his ground sitting down. As Thatcher knew, in this type of negotiation force wasn't necessarily measured in muscle mass. Still, to be on the safe side, he'd do his very best not to piss him off... until the advantage was his. Reaching into his jacket pocket, he pulled out one-hundred-eighty hundred dollar bills, held together with a red rubber band. To make the sight of the money even more compelling, he slipped off the rubber band, neatly rolled the bills into a bundle, and re-secured it with the rubber band. He momentarily held the bundle in his fist to allow the seller time to contemplate the color of money, the initial touch of the smooth, crisp paper. Thatcher nodded casually toward the bike. "What color do you call that?"

The woman glared at him as she stepped beside her man once again. "Menstrual," she snarled.

Evidently she was still miffed about "the truth is out there." Whatever that was about. Perhaps, he thought, he should have humored her.

He smiled as he set the roll upright on the table. He picked up a small sprig of evergreen from the table and said coolly, "Eighteen." He inserted the sprig into the hole as if to demonstrate another use for a wad of money.

Unimpressed, the biker reached behind him and pulled out an excessively large stainless steel semi-automatic. "Forty-five," he said with the gushing self-satisfaction of a moron.

The woman gasped, "Phillip, what are you doin'?"

Thatcher hated guns, especially big ones pointed in his direction. Nonetheless, he was impressed. Phillip had taken him by complete surprise. His eyes went first to the safety; it was, indeed, in firing position.

"Smith & Wesson, 4500 Series. Eight rounds. How many you have in there, Phil?"

Thatcher's calm demeanor confounded the biker. Phillip furled his forehead as he confirmed the eight rounds.

"Safety's on, Phil."

Glancing down, Outlaw Phil made the adjustment quickly, as if he truly meant to fire the big gun in broad daylight in the middle of trailer town.

Relieved that the gun was no longer going to discharge accidentally, Thatcher inquired, "Phillip, what the hell are you doing?"

Idiots with guns murdered more people accidentally than on purpose. Thatcher knew it wasn't a proven statistic. In any case, he would do whatever it took to avoid being a statistic, of any kind.

The woman latched onto his left arm. "Are you crazy?"

He shook her off and said, without taking his eyes from Thatcher, "See if he's packin', Stella."

Her mouth hung open like a bemused Labrador Retriever. She cowered away.

"Go on, Stella." Motioning with his gun, he flashed an angry look at her. "Do it!"

Thatcher concluded this was an act equally sanctioned by spontaneity and stupidity. Curious as to how extensively Phillip had planned this armed robbery, Thatcher jovially encouraged him to sit back down as the woman awkwardly pawed at his clothing.

"Stella," Thatcher looked into her woeful expression. "What are the neighbors going to think?"

"They don't," she said nervously.

Turning to Phillip, he said, "Phil, sit down. Relax. Have a smoke."

A grin came over the biker. "Sure, why not?" He aimed the Smith & Wesson belligerently at Thatcher's chest as he stepped over to the table. "How much more cash you got?"

Looking into Phil's reflective sunglasses rather than the black hole of the .45, Thatcher shrugged his shoulders. "A C-note or two, maybe a fifty, a couple twenties, tens, fives." By his expression, Thatcher sensed Outlaw Phillip was attempting to add up his additional spoils, without much success.

Phillip motioned with the gun. "Lay it on the table." He said to the woman, "Stella, light me a smoke."

Stella lit a Marlboro from the pack setting on the table and placed it between his lips.

Reaching for his inside coat pocket, Thatcher continued looking into his opponent's eyes, even though he only saw his own reflection in the silver lenses. He pulled out the remaining bills from his wallet, and slowly slid them to the center of the table.

"This motorcycle is becoming more expensive all the time," he quipped as he slipped the wallet into his back pocket.

Phillip let out a roar and a whirl of smoke. "He thinks he's buyin' a fuckin' motorcycle." The big man plopped down at the table straight across from Thatcher. The table bounced, and the Smith & Wesson nudged Thatcher's chest.

Thatcher was thankful Outlaw Phil had unknowingly made the victim-friendly adjustment on his firearm.

Then, with a surprise move, the outlaw biker removed his glasses.

In front of Thatcher, wobbling like a pollywog trapped at the bottom of a Mason jar, was Phillip's left pupil struggling unsuccessfully to stay focused.

"Phil," he said amiably, "what's the bike worth to you?"

Phillip inhaled a draft of smoke and set the Marlboro down in a tuna fish can turned ashtray. Smoke oozed through his teeth, depicting a hygienist's worst nightmare. Phil genteelly wiped the spittle from the corner of his mouth with the back of his hand. "It's not for sale, ass wipe."

Manufacturing a confounded expression, Thatcher moved his attention from the pollywog eye to the silver thread of saliva dangling from the corner of Outlaw Phil's mouth.

"Well..." Thatcher was amazed at his self-control. He took a deep breath and exhaled slowly. "I'm confused, Phil." Feigning naivete, "Why am I here?" he asked.

Phil snatched the Marlboro from the tunafish can: the drool was inadvertently swept away. "To lose your fuckin' money." The barrel of the .45 poked Thatcher's chest.

Wondering how Phil had concluded a midday robbery in his own front yard was a good idea, Thatcher shook his head in mock despair. "You got me, Phil."

Thatcher snapped his gum vigorously and began rolling it around in his mouth.

Phil grinned as he reached for the roll of bills. The evergreen sprig tumbled out as he snatched up the money. Thatcher picked up the sprig.

As the tattooed biker attempted to count his loot, Thatcher slipped the gum from his mouth and stuck it to the sturdy end of the sprig.

"Stella," he said, "count this up for me."

As Phillip glanced away to hand the bills to his reluctant accomplice, Thatcher inserted the gummy end of the evergreen into the barrel of the gun.

At the sight of his weaponry sprouting a spruce, the biker became momentarily dumbfounded. This provided Thatcher the opportunity to seize the gun with his left hand. Turning it upward and away as he leaned forward, he jabbed the big man squarely between the eyes with the base of his right hand. Thatcher grimaced at the sound of the cracking nasal bone. As he twisted the gun from Phillip's hand, Thatcher pushed him backwards, and watched him tumble to the ground.

The woman screamed as she fell beside her man's crumpled body. His legs were over the top of the seat and wedged snugly beneath the table. Outlaw Phil groaned.

"You son-of-a-bitch!" she yelped.

"He'll be all right. His nose is going to smart for awhile," Thatcher consoled her as he extricated the magazine from the handgun, "but he'll be okay."

"You son-of-a-bitch!"

"No empathy for the victim?"

Thatcher looked curiously around to find no one particularly interested in Phillip's attempted armed robbery. As Thatcher emptied the magazine and tossed the bullets into the bushes beside the rusting Marlette home, two boys on skateboards whirred by, completely unconcerned about anything, except passing a cigarette back and forth without missing a stride.

"You son-of-a-bitch!" she repeated one more time.

Stella's redundancy, Thatcher felt, was obviously fueled by her scant vocabulary, and the distress of the moment. He consoled her. "You're right, I need to work on that."

Thatcher stepped over to his fallen opponent and knelt beside him. He really hated the sight of blood, and made a point not to look directly at the biker's face.

"He looks peaceful, don't you think?" he said to the woman.

Examining Phil's nose, she whispered, "It's bent sideways."

With minimal success she attempted to straighten it with a gentle push. Phillip groaned.

"What you gonna do?" she asked, looking up at the man in the fancy suit.

Thatcher knew what she meant. He said nothing.

"I mean, he's on parole. Something like this..."

"I came here to buy the bike." Thatcher read her expression. "I'm going to pay for it. But, I think the price has just gone down."

Clutching the bills in her right hand, she held them out to him. "Take what you want." The sound of her voice expressed remorse and gratitude.

Thatcher, still holding the .45, nodded toward Phillip, who was still wedged between the table and the bench. "Phil needs to sign off on the title," he said despairingly. "That could be a while."

"No." The woman sighed. "It's in my name." She sighed even louder. "He lost his last one with one roll of the dice."

Subduing his elation of not having to wait for the big guy to come around, he walked promptly over to a garbage can sitting next to the front steps and opened the lid. "Guess I won't need this after all." He dropped the Smith & Wesson onto a pile of macaroni and cheese, and suggested, "Gamblers Anonymous."

She shrugged her shoulders. "Yeah, he's a lousy gambler," she mumbled, as if Gamblers Anonymous was only for lousy gamblers.

Thatcher felt charitable. He left Phillip, the illustrated outlaw, with ten grand and a monumental headache. As it was, the market price for the chromed-out, customized "menstrual" Fat Boy with leather bags and gangster whitewalls, would surpass twenty Gs.

Before straddling the Harley-Davidson, he knelt beside it and ran his fingers lightly over the black script along the tank. *Wanderer.* It seemed appropriate. His reflection in the chrome air cover conveyed unequivocally the suit would have to go. He'd change later.

A tap on his shoulder brought him quickly to his feet. As he turned around, two keys and the signed title were presented to him.

"Here," she muttered.

Stella wasn't really a bad person, he thought, just kept bad company. As he inspected the scribbled signature, it occurred to him he would need to wait until after the weekend to get a Michigan plate. Tomorrow was a holiday.

Backing away, she asked earnestly, "You're sure he's gonna be okay? I mean, I don't need to take him to the hospital or nothin'?"

Thatcher glanced down and saw the eyelids fluttering. "Phil's tough, not overly acute, but tough."

Kneeling beside him, she whispered, "I don't like cute."

"As soon as he can swallow," he maintained an insightful sensibility, "you might want to slip him some ibuprofen."

"We ain't got any," she said, looking at Thatcher.

As he watched her contorted expression, Thatcher sensed that an idea was coming to her.

"I have a couple joints," she reported eagerly.

He smiled, and confirmed, "That'll work."

The woman with the wild hair smiled curiously as she sat Indian-style beside her fallen warrior.

Thatcher retrieved his duffel bag from the Chevy truck. He pulled out a pair of bollé sunglasses from his coat pocket, walked over to the *Wanderer*, and secured his bag onto the rear luggage rack. He stripped off his suit coat, reflected a moment, and silently apologized to Giorgio Armani as he tossed it to the ground and climbed on. He eased out the choke, and turned the key.

Pressing the start button, he brought the big V-Twin engine to life. For several seconds he immersed himself in the rumbling euphony before he rolled up his sleeves and peeled off his vest. Thatcher tapped the shift lever into first, then tapped it back to neutral. Pulling his tie free, he tossed it on top of the discarded Armani laying in the dirt. He eased out the clutch and slowly maneuvered the big cruiser to the narrow street.

Two

BENEATH THE HOT SHOWER, SHE STOOD MOTIONLESS AND stared at the tile floor as thin currents of water slipped around her feet and swirled into the drain. The water's soothing sensuality eased her mind. Again, she thought of the man at the airport. It had been such a long time since she had felt so strangely moved and aroused. The feeling renewed her strength, and momentarily erased the present.

It wasn't that long ago, she recalled coming off the beach after a strenuous workout with the single thought of rinsing off the sand, the sweat, and the sunblock. A quick cool shower, followed by a steaming hot one to soothe her aching muscles. Win or lose on the sandy courts, the hot shower was always her reward. But now she was no longer rinsing away the sand, and the sweat, and the UV 30. Nor was she soothing aching muscles. It was her soul, her spirit she attempted to console and comfort.

She turned off the water and pushed open the shower door. Reaching for her towel hanging nearby, she suddenly froze as the bathroom door opened.

"Wear the black dress tonight." He stepped into the bathroom tightening his tie. "The one I bought for you last week. And don't wear the pearls. Wear the diamonds." They were concise instructions.

Turning toward him, she avoided his eyes. "Aaron," she cooed, as she snatched the towel and wrapped it tightly about her.

Angered by the soft patronizing texture of her voice, he rushed toward her. Grabbing her wrists forcefully, he raised them above her head as he pushed her hard against the wall.

"You want it, don't you, Karlene?" he snarled. "You want it rough."

Then suddenly, he released her and stepped back. Karlene felt her body quiver as the towel fell to the tile floor. She accepted her vulnerability, and looked away.

Aaron assumed an insouciant stance in front of her as he coldly admired the wet, shimmering contours of her body. "I'll send Mr. Lane around for you at seven sharp."

Her eyes darted away; she could not cover the trembling in her voice. "I'm not sure I'm up to another..."

"I don't think I heard you." Through his menacing stare he made his message clear.

Picking the towel up from the floor, she clutched it in front of her. "Where are we going?" She delivered her line with interest as she assumed the role that was demanded of her.

"Just be ready when Mr. Lane arrives." Aaron's demeanor changed abruptly. "Karlie, I have to go. I'm meeting someone at the Yacht Club." He paused long enough for her to emit the expected smile. "I'll miss you." Winking, he added, "Tonight."

His sudden mood changes always startled her, like an unexpected plunge into icy water. It was eerie, frightening, and unnerving.

"Couldn't you have Mr. Stout drive?" Karlene adjured. "Mr. Lane..." She was cut short.

"Forget about it. My consigliere has more important responsibilities." He smugly misused the Mafia title. Aaron was no more than a "capo," or middle manager, and David Stout was merely a soldier under his jurisdiction. Karlene had been around long enough to know a consigliere was second only to the Don.

"I just want to be on time, Aaron."

"Mr. Lane will be driving you to the dinner party."

Against her better judgment, she added, "He was late picking me up at the airport." Immediately, she wished she had not brought it up.

"It's my understanding you were consorting with someone. Mr. Lane had to wait for you." His voice carried a gravity that demanded confession and repentance.

"I'm sorry. An old acquaintance."

"You'll introduce us some time." It was Aaron saying the opposite of what he meant. Translation: don't ever see him again.

"It's unlikely we'll ever run into each other again."

Smiling, he knew he had made his point. "Nevertheless, you know I'm interested in your..." he paused purposefully, "...old friends." He waited for her submission.

Karlene created the abdicating expression that was expected.

"Be ready when Mr. Lane arrives."

The gentleness in his voice did not disguise the edict. She watched him leave the bathroom and knew there would be severe penalties if not executed as prescribed.

The fierce lovemaking that had been the essence of their relationship in the beginning had insidiously evolved into domination and control. Desperately, she had wanted out.

After he left, Karlene stepped into the bedroom. Standing naked in front of the mirrored wall, she examined the fading bruises and contusions from a previous altercation with Aaron. She couldn't even remember the reason; reasons weren't required. It was simply the way it was.

Nearly thirty, Karlene could pass for twenty-two, yet she felt much older than her age. She walked to the large window overlooking Chicago Harbor and the Lake Michigan shoreline. She watched the traffic move swiftly along Lake Shore Drive, and imagined the day when she would escape from Lake Point Tower, or as she simply called it, The Tower.

As deliberately spaced as they were, and as strong as she was, the swift and unpredictable beatings were becoming more and more emotionally debilitating. The time when she would no longer tolerate Aaron Henderson's vicious cruelty was coming near. Karlene could sense her primitive instinct to survive steadily overtaking her civility. It frightened her, and at the same time, gave her hope.

The mid-morning sun was bright and warm against her skin. Stretching wearily in front of the large glass panel, she was unconcerned about telescopes aimed at the penthouse window from yachts in the harbor. Peeping was a regular pastime in the big city. It mattered little to her as she contemplated another sweltering day.

Karlene no longer cared for Chicago. The infamous wind blasted icy pellets in winter and humid viscosity in summer. A sudden shift to a southern wind brought northward the murky waters of Gary, Indiana, with its noxious mixture of discarded chemicals.

How she had become involved with Aaron Henderson seemed like a daytime melodrama, with an incredibly horrendous script.

As a youth Karlene had enjoyed growing up in the northern suburb of Skokie among the wealthy elite. It had been a difficult decision to leave when she was awarded a scholarship to play volleyball at UCLA. However, the lure of California prevailed.

In college she excelled in volleyball and good times. Eventually, her grades reflected her busy extracurricular schedule, and by the middle of her junior year she found herself ineligible to play.

Karlene had reached star status at the time her insolvent GPA caught up to her. Skilled and powerful at five foot nine, she possessed the competitive drive that intimidated opponents and brought Olympic coaches out to watch her play.

In the end, however, it was her statuesque and muscled physique that brought her the lucrative offer from a bathing suit company to play professionally on the beach volleyball circuit. With the NCAA and the Olympics fading from her future, she accepted the offer and left school. That was nearly a decade ago.

A year ago Karlene and her partner placed second in a tournament against the background of Bud Light banners and an ominous achromatic sky above the Chicago shoreline. They had been the favorites to take the tournament.

Her partner, a true Californian with exquisite volleyball skills and only modest complimentary looks, had been matched up with Karlene by their sponsor in an effective campaign for their product line. Karlene's blonde, blue-eyed, all-American beauty captured the admiring glances from potential sportswear customers.

She loved the attention. But it was always her unrelenting desire to win that motivated her. With an equally adept and competitive partner, Karlene nearly never failed to appear at the quarterfinals. The sponsor's product line consistently returned to center court.

Within minutes of their dismal fifteen to six loss in the final game of the championship match at the Bud Light tournament in Chicago, a company executive informed Karlene and her partner that their contract wouldn't be renewed at the end of the month. Procuring a new sponsor wouldn't be difficult, but cutting an equally profitable deal would be nearly impossible.

For Karlene, the bottom really fell out that evening at the downtown Hilton bar, when her partner, while sipping sparkling water with a twist, sheepishly confessed she was six weeks pregnant. With her sponsor gone, and her partner as well, Karlene suddenly found herself at a loss.

With her relatively comfortable and carefree lifestyle in great jeopardy, she was an easy mark for Aaron Henderson. He approached only seconds after her partner had left her at the bar. He was ruggedly handsome, charming, and rich with an "employment opportunity" she couldn't resist under the circumstances.

The *Wanderer* cruised effortlessly along the expressway bringing Thatcher back toward Chicago. The wind harmonized with the big V-Twin engine and created a primitive melody, capable of soothing and inciting, at the same time, a wayward soul.

His rambling thoughts, sifted randomly through his life, left Thatcher feeling oddly discontented. The million or so he had squirreled away in numerous accounts and holdings didn't seem to dissuade the advancing antipathy. It was as if the vibrating cadence of the big motorcycle and the warm summer wind against his face had begun to jar something loose.

Stopping for gas somewhere near Rolling Meadows, he bought a soda and called information for the number of a Harley-Davidson dealership in Chicago. He punched it in.

"Chicago Harley-Davidson." The voice was complacent.

"Where are you located?"

"6868 North Western Avenue."

"Near where?" Thatcher considered addresses useless in the city. "Give me a location." He waited through an unexpected silence. "Cross streets, or something," he added.

"South of Evanston, between Pratt and Touhy."

Being unfamiliar with that part of the city, he repeated the street names.

"Touhy with a T, not a P." She was curt. "Hey cowboy, just look for Flucky's."

Thatcher stood for several seconds with the receiver beside his ear. "I'm sorry. What..."

"Flucky's. F-L-U-C-K-Y-S, corner of Western and Morse. There's a McDonald's. M-C-D..."

"Yeah, got it." Thatcher smiled.

"Good. I don't give spelling lessons to everyone. So, whatdaya need besides learning to spell?"

"General maintenance on a Fat Boy. I'm heading west in a few days."

"Yahoo." She cleared her throat. "Can't do it today."

"What if I bring it in this afternoon and leave it over the rest of the weekend? Can it be done by Monday, early afternoon?" He wanted enough time to pick up a plate, and to call his insurance agent. Practical matters.

"Tomorrow's the Fourth." There was a momentary pause. "Yeah, bring it in. Monday we'll send you off into the sunset, or wherever it is you cowboys go."

"By early afternoon?"

"Yeah, right. I'll put in the word."

The line went dead. It occurred to him he was in no hurry to get anywhere. Places to be, he reminded himself, and Chicago over the Fourth was a good place to be.

Thatcher finished his soda and took off for the northwest side. He followed I-90 East, jogging north on I-94 North toward his destination. Other than almost being bitten in the tail end by a Mack truck bulldog, and hitting the shoulder at 75 miles per hour to elude a '74 Monte Carlo hell-bent on getting to Exit 205 B, he arrived in front of Flucky's Fried Chicken virtually unscathed. The dealership was across the street. He parked on the side of the building off Morse across from McDonald's. The aroma of fast food momentarily distracted him.

The service department counter was overseen by a young man with coal black eyes and dark hair cut into a precision trimmed flat top. He greeted Thatcher with the dismal expression of someone who had spent the entire day in grease, oil, and noise. Arrangements were made.

"Yeah, by the way," said Thatcher. "Where's a nearby motel?"

"Take a left on Touhy. Regency or Radisson or something like that. I think the corner of Lincoln maybe." For the first time, the young man looked directly at his customer.

Thatcher watched as a grin spread across his face.

"Dude," he lengthened the single syllable word into three. "The truth is out there." It was a matter-of-fact proclamation.

Thatcher straightened his collar. "I've been told."

"Hey." His head bobbed for a moment. "You need some jeans, dude."

Thatcher thanked him for his concise directions, and his fashion advice.

It was half past four as he went outside to bring the *Wanderer* over to the service entrance. It was a hot Friday afternoon in Chicago. While unstrapping the leather duffel bag from the rear luggage rack, he took a moment to retrieve his cap from the bag. As he adjusted the bill to provide maximum shade for his nose, he paused to admire his ride.

The young man from the service counter opened the garage door and stepped over to the bike. He swung his leg over the saddle, turned the ignition, and pressed the start button all in one motion. Thatcher was impressed. The engine rumbled to life.

The young man glanced back at Thatcher before disappearing into the garage, and shouted, “Nice ride, dude. Monday by noon. See what I can do.” He was out of sight.

Feeling abandoned, he turned to walk away when the side service door swung open and caught him on the right shoulder. A woman stepped out.

Startled, she exclaimed, “Christ, watch where I’m goin’.”

It was unmistakable. “Touhy with a T,” he said.

The woman stared at Thatcher. She was short and petite, dressed in fringed leather pants and a fringed leather vest that exposed her flat abdomen. Turquoise and silver was abundant. Her black hair was pulled tightly back into a single long braid. A small red rose was tattooed on a well-defined right shoulder. Her eyes were intense blue.

“Congratulations, you made it all the way here.” She scrutinized him carefully. “Nice riding duds. You on the lam from corporate America?” She flicked the bill of his cap with her index finger. “Or, you just here for the game?”

He shrugged insouciantly as he readjusted his cap. “Something like that.”

Nodding to his duffel bag, “Hope you got the right stuff in there.” She gave the briefest of smirks. “Hey, where’s your Fat Boy?”

He motioned toward the garage door. “Inside.”

Relinquishing her smile, she shifted her weight to the right, and placed her hands on her hips. “So, corporate cowboy, you gonna stand around here for the rest of the weekend? Or, what?”

“Reckon I’ll find a room.”

She cracked a broader smile. “A Texan from Toledo.”

Thatcher was amused. "Detroit," he replied.

"Not a rivet head, I can see that." Impressed by her own quick analysis, she continued, "Not a lawyer either."

He laughed. "Why not?"

"No way." Squinting, she continued unabashed, "Lawyers make me gag."

Thatcher laughed again. Attorneys had always been an annoyance.

"What's so damn funny?"

Thatcher examined her closely. Her slightly misplaced right canine tooth enhanced her unpolished beauty.

"What?"

"You're right," he said. "No way."

Scowling. "Yeah, like a said, I'd be gagging." She continued. "So, you don't have your ride, and you don't know what the hell you're gonna do."

Thatcher shrugged in agreement.

"You're all the same." It was a deliberate and well-rehearsed pause. "Just plain shithead stupid."

Thatcher howled with laughter.

Momentarily, the woman stared in disbelief. "What?"

It was contagious, and she sputtered into a restrained chortle. "Crazy." Laughing, she asked, "What's so goddamn funny?" as she stepped closer.

A sharp stiff arm to the chest knocked Thatcher off balance. As he staggered backward he said, "No ride. No where to go."

Standing a few feet apart in the late afternoon sun, they stared briefly at one another. Thatcher was intrigued.

Turning away, she said, "Come on." She walked toward an assembly of Harleys parked a few yards away. "What's your name?"

"Thatcher," he replied.

Following a couple steps behind her, he observed what could only be described as an exquisite primeval strut. She stopped alongside a black Springer Softail that was custom painted with red and yellow swirling flames the length of the front fenders, along the gas tank, and ending abruptly at the upturned rear fender. She swung her leg over and sat down.

"Call me Flame." She pushed down the passenger pegs on either side. "It's my Indian name." She glanced at Thatcher. "Hop on."

Holding onto his duffel bag with his right hand, he twisted his cap around catcher's style with his left and snugged it tightly over his head. He swung his leg over the seat and placed his left hand against her side.

Pulling his hand firmly around her waist, she said, "You'll want to hold on."

Her bare skin felt strangely cool against his fingers. He moved closer.

"So, corporate cowboy, which way from here?"

For the briefest of moments, that simple question baffled him. "Which way from here?" he repeated.

"Yeah, which way from here?"

For the moment, it defined his life, and even more aptly, his immediate predicament. He had only one answer, "Motel."

"You don't waste time," she shouted turning her head to the right so Thatcher would be sure to hear her over the rumbling engine. "Got a friend working at the Radisson over in Lincolnwood. Get you checked in, then maybe we'll all go out for some beers later."

She sped out of the parking lot and shot into traffic with the precision of a guided missile. Thatcher held on tightly.

Aaron Henderson listened closely to the voice on the other end of the phone.

"You can handle any arrangement?"

"Any." It was controlled arrogance. "Consider it done."

"Oh, I will after this evening. Count on that, Mr. Henderson. The Affiliation accepts no excuses."

Aaron set the receiver down and leaned back into the plush leather of the limousine. From a small bar he took a pill bottle and emptied the last two white tablets into his palm. He gulped the four milligrams of Diazepam, a.k.a. Valium, with a shot of Absolut, a.k.a. vodka. The pieces were in place. No excuses, he thought, none required.

Aaron Henderson was thick in the chest and slim in the waist. His body appeared ten years younger than his sun-weathered face, which reflected a man nearing fifty. He was a businessman and a bully.

He grew up on the streets of East Chicago. His father was an alcoholic and taught him to take beatings without a whimper. His spiritless mother taught him that a woman was without value until she was beaten by a man. It was a life lesson he learned well.

At age fourteen he beat and raped the girl next door. At age sixteen he popped a fellow gang member with a Saturday Night Special over the ownership of a fifth of Jim Beam. At age eighteen, reaching the menacing size of six-two, and two-twenty-five, he decided it was time to cut his family ties.

With vengeful pleasure, he battered his father with his bare hands to within an inch of death, while his mother watched with curious anticipation. Young Aaron Henderson left home with his father's Army-issued Colt .45 semi-automatic. He was off to seek his fortune.

With his size and strength, and his nasty disposition, Aaron was quickly recruited into the throngs of hoodlums, the non-made loyalists of organized crime, to do dirty little numbers on non-compliant clientele.

Aaron had made his first hit when he was nineteen: an elderly Chinese immigrant who refused to pay protection money. It was too simple. The little man walked up to the barrel of the .45 and repeated a brief phrase in his native language. Aaron, needing little provocation for violence, squeezed the trigger of his Colt semi-automatic, and earned five hundred bucks.

His ascension into the Mob had begun. The little man was buried without a face.

Thatcher's motel room was simple and complete. The air conditioner worked and HBO was included. It was around six o'clock when he lay down on the bed. It was around quarter to eight when a loud banging on the door rousted him.

"Hey! Thatcher! It's Flame!"

The room was nearly dark with the heavy drapes drawn. He turned on the light beside the bed.

"Hey! It's time to paaaarteee!"

He got up slowly. The late afternoon nap had hit him like a sledgehammer. He walked to the door, rubbing his temples. He pulled it open.

Running his fingers through his disheveled hair, he said, "Seraphs in black."

Faintly amused, Flame replied, "Whatever."

Looking past Flame, he saw a tall, broad-shouldered woman in a tight-fitting leather vest. Two elegantly illustrated tattoos of prickly vines encircled each of her large biceps. A tiny silver ring pierced a long angular nose. Her short-cropped, tragically bleached blonde hair suggested either a fanatical conspiracy against Miss Clairol, or a new look altogether: the Road Warrior meets Billy Idol.

Discerning her severe expression demanded clarity, he cleared his throat, and said, "Angels in black."

Stoically nodding with extraneous approval, she placed her hand on her partner's shoulder.

"Thatcher. This is Gretta." She glanced at her friend with a wide grin. "Like in Garbo."

"The resemblance is there." Glancing at Flame, he added, "The sunglasses."

"That's what everyone says." Flame looked back at her cohort.

The dominating figure slowly removed her black sunglasses and stared curiously at Thatcher. Gretta simply shrugged her muscled shoulders.

Thatcher pulled the door open the rest of the way and with a deliberate genteel swipe of his arm, said, "Please, come in."

Flame responded in kind. "Don't mind his attitude. He's just plain shithead stupid." She stepped closer and pinched his cheek hard. "But he's cute."

Gretta followed closely behind Flame, placed her hand on Thatcher's shoulder, and standing eye to eye, she spoke for the first time. "Nice pants. Red suspenders." She shook her head, and cuffed Thatcher gently alongside the head.

Smiling and snapping his suspenders, he noticed Flame was wearing a different leather outfit that looked the same as the one she had on earlier. Gretta, he observed, was wearing skin-tight leather pants that laced up the sides, exposing a long narrow strip of each muscular leg from the top of her silver studded boots all the way to her narrow waist. The top two buttons of her silver-studded vest were left undone revealing pectorals that imitated breasts.

"So, you gonna offer us a drink or what?" Flame asked.

Noticing the brown paper bag in Gretta's left hand, he said, "It looks like you brought your own." He slipped off his suspenders. "The wet bar is over there." He nodded in the direction of the small sink with the plastic glasses neatly wrapped in cellophane setting beside it and began to unbutton his shirt. "I'm taking a shower. Make yourselves at home."

"Good idea." She paused to watch her host unbutton six more inches of silk shirt. She smiled and added, "You look like crap."

Before turning toward the bathroom, he assured her, "I clean up real good."

Smirking to herself, she replied, "We'll just kick back, fix some drinks, and watch some TV."

As if on cue, Gretta pulled out a pint of JD from the paper bag. Crumpling the bag in one hand and holding aloft the sour mash in the other, she offered a brief soliloquy to the ghost of Jack Daniels. "Lead us into temptation, and deliver us from sobriety."

Her voice had a deep bawdy quality, with an intriguing tone that could excite, intimidate, and allow men bold expectations. With this thought, Thatcher stepped into the bathroom and closed the door.

Standing in front of the mirror, he stared at the image of a once-respected corporate big shot with a day's growth on his face dressed in Armani slacks, red suspenders, and a silk shirt. Thatcher turned on the shower and undressed as the room filled with steam.

Beneath the hot water his mind drifted away from crowded airports, away from oppressive boardrooms, away from absurd time schedules, and away from disreputable characters like JJ Burdick.

The bathroom door opened.

"Gotta piss." It was Gretta.

Thatcher said nothing and tried unsuccessfully not to envision her leather pants peeled down to her ankles. Closing his eyes, he waited. The toilet flush sent a sudden rush of hotter water, the sink faucet running momentarily equalized the rush from the flush. The bathroom door closed. Thatcher let out a sigh.

A minute later he turned off the water and swung back the shower curtain. Leaning against the doorjamb, their arms folded across their chests, their cups of Jack Daniels in their right hands, Flame and Gretta exchanged approving nods.

Saying nothing, Gretta smirked and turned away.

Smiling, Flame tossed Thatcher a towel. "Her idea."

Thatcher caught the towel and held it in front of him.

"Here." Flame handed him a drink. "Get dressed cowboy." And, as she began to turn, she added, "Ditch the fancy threads, and get on your riding duds."

Karlene was ready at seven o'clock, as Aaron had decreed. She dressed to his specifications, down to the diamond jewelry and exact shade of mascara. She didn't want to displease Aaron, not tonight. Unfortunately, Curtis Lane was late.

At the dinner party, Aaron, as Karlene assumed, found her at fault. "I told you not to be late. How am I going to teach you not to be late?" he whispered as they sat down at the dinner table encircled by his new business associates and their obedient wives and girlfriends. The stoic, expressionless women dressed by Versace, Gucci, and Givenchy frightened her as much as Aaron's cold, accusing tone. *The Stepford Wives* had never been so fashionable.

"Aaron, Curtis arrived late," she whispered back, not inclined to make reference to her lummox limo driver as Mr. Lane. She attempted to maintain her pleasant and adoring expression, all the time knowing any explanation would be unacceptable.

"Displacing the blame is another one of your shortcomings," was his quiet and forceful rebuttal.

Trembling, she said, "It's the truth."

Not wanting her fear to be exposed, but unable to disguise it, she felt vulnerable and weak. Karlene despised her own fragility.

"This will not happen again, Karlene," he said as he smiled and nodded in the direction of a new confrere across the table. "I'll see to that."

Karlene conceded and said nothing. She knew it would only worsen the real persecution that would come later.

At first, she denied it, but she held no doubt now. The abuse was coming more and more often. It wasn't the kind of abuse that would mar her beauty, which Aaron coveted and flaunted, but the kind that destroys from the inside, the kind that eats away at one's very spirit. It seemed this sudden acquisition of new business associates had totally consumed Aaron, and was releasing within him a fury that even she was unaware existed. The iceberg that was Aaron Henderson was beginning to upend itself, exposing its enormous and deadly dimensions.

Karlene desperately wanted to be free from his abuse, but running away had always failed. She was a possession. Aaron Henderson never gave up a possession without being well compensated.

As she sat quietly through dinner, and made small talk and smiled when required, Karlene felt a primitive rage well within, speaking silently to her in the language of survival.

Shortly after dinner Aaron accompanied her to his limousine. He had explained to his new associates that she was not feeling well and that he would have his driver take her home early.

"Take this worthless bitch back to the penthouse," he yelled to Curtis.

Looking back at Karlene he said, "I'll deal with this later. You've embarrassed me for the last time." He slapped her hard across the face and pushed her into the backseat of the limousine. "This is the last." With his fists clenched, his eyes narrowed into two points of darkness, he expounded, "Don't think you can run from me." As he backed away, just before shutting the limo door, he said, "I can find you anywhere."

Wincing in pain, her eyes teared, but she didn't cry. Instead, Karlene listened carefully to the silent conversation within her. She quelled her fear, guided her thoughts toward survival, and honed rage into retaliation.

Curtis, without saying anything, drove off in the direction of Lincoln Park. None of this had been part of his itinerary for the evening. First, the "parcel," now this? David Stout had not mentioned anything about a "parcel." He checked the time; it was going on ten o'clock. The electric whirl of the automatic window behind him caught his attention.

"Curtis." She took her finger off the button; the window stopped. "I want a drink!"

He didn't respond. Curtis Lane made a point of either hitting or ignoring demanding women. The latter was his only option.

"I'm not going back to The Tower." She leaned back into the seat. Speaking this time with forced cordiality, "I would like a drink."

Not knowing Karlene as a drinker, the request surprised Curtis. He glanced in the rearview mirror and saw her watching. Her cold, lucid stare startled him.

"You son-of-a-bitch," she said calmly. "You were late. The least you can do is take me somewhere for a drink." Her finger hovered over the button. She decided to keep the window open. If Curtis was to take a phone call, she wanted to hear.

Without saying a word, Curtis turned onto Lake Shore Drive and headed north. She wanted a drink. He knew a place.

Thatcher held securely onto Gretta's waist with both hands as they sped down the city avenues. For Gretta, speed limits were at best the suggested minimum velocity. She maneuvered and muscled her customized Softail between and around cars, taking corners at thirty-five miles per hour and curves without downshifting past fourth gear. Once on the expressway Gretta opened it up. Flame stayed beside her. With their nighttime goggles, Flame and Gretta reminded Thatcher of World War I flying aces.

The excursion ended at a windowless one-story brick warehouse turned roadside saloon. Mounted on the roof above the front door was purple neon script announcing Leather & Lace. Rows of Harleys were parked outside interspersed with an occasional rusted-out American-made pickup truck or two-door coupe with chrome wheels.

Flame was fifteen seconds behind. Pulling in alongside Gretta's bike, she turned off her ignition and slapped Thatcher hard on the back.

"Can that bitch ride or what?"

Thatcher wiped his sweaty hands against his jeans, tilted back his head, and howled. It was the same exhilaration he felt when he got word the IRS froze out JJ Burdick.

Looking at Gretta, Flame grinned. "That's a yes."

Dismounting upon Gretta's command, he held back the urge to beg her for more.

They were standing in front of the roadhouse, admiring the purple neon, when a rotund, bearded patron exited the heavy metal door. Blue haze billowed forth while Merle Haggard bellowed out, "Back to the barrooms again..."

"Gret-taa! Gret-taa! Shots and beer." Flame placed her arm firmly around her friend's shoulder. Turning to Thatcher, she reached out and snatched him by his black leather vest and pulled him close. "Come on. It's par-tee time."

Unequivocally abandoning his better judgment, Thatcher stayed in step with his new companions as they entered the Leather & Lace.

Three

By the time Aaron Henderson had returned to the party, he had taken only a brief moment to compose himself, the guests had been moved to the ballroom. He mingled for nearly an hour, and had yet to be introduced to the head of The Affiliation.

An attractive woman in her mid-forties, whom he hadn't noticed before, approached him. Dressed in a simple dark suit, she denuded glamour for ascendancy. She spoke with authority.

"Mr. Henderson, I am Mr. Revelle's assistant. He would like to speak with you. He's waiting upstairs, the second room on the right. Go right in."

Aaron was astonished to have been addressed in such a manner by a woman. He was not accustomed to accepting a woman in any type of authoritarian position, let alone the assistant to the head of The Affiliation. Nonetheless, he followed her instructions without question.

This was the opportunity that had eluded him for years: to be a respected member of The Affiliation. For Aaron Henderson this was to be a giant stride toward the summit. He needed only to carry out this one important assignment. And, in return, he would gain acceptance and be impressively awarded. The future was bright.

"Mr. Henderson." It was a cheerful greeting from the man at the other end of the room. "Please come in, and close the door."

Aaron stepped into the elaborately embellished library and closed the door. "I'm honored to have this opportunity. You will not be disappointed." Aaron was nearly groveling.

The man with snow-white hair smiled. "I'm certain of it. The parcel was delivered prior to dinner."

"I was expecting..."

"The Affiliation thought it better to deliver it in this manner. You'll find it secure in the trunk of your limousine. I assume your driver is not only loyal, but capable as well. He was not informed of the parcel's contents, only that you were expecting it and that it was of great importance."

"This parcel?" Aaron tried to conceal his confusion.

"Mr. Henderson, you need merely hold onto it until The Affiliation calls for it. Then half of its worth is yours. You are quite capable. That is why you were chosen."

Aaron said nothing. He nodded his acknowledgment, turned, and walked out of the library. Mr. Revelle's simple instructions daunted Aaron. Simplicity was one thing, but he wanted clarity. He wanted to know why. He wanted to know the location of his limousine. Whatever the reasons behind this esoteric task, its success began with procuring the parcel.

Curtis had not returned as of thirty minutes ago. If he had known The Affiliation was going to act in such a mysterious fashion, he would have had David Stout drive. Curtis Lane was tough. He was loyal. Curtis Lane was also an idiot. As Aaron Henderson descended the stairway into the ballroom, anger swept through him as he remembered Karlene's request for David Stout.

At center stage the Leather & Lace presented a chrome-plated pole: an exposition for the performing arts. As Thatcher and company passed through the doorway, a topless, dark-haired woman of generic proportions and imperfect symmetry danced tediously around the pole to the Haggard tune emanating from the jukebox. Lewd whistles, bawdy cheers, and an occasional bill tucked into the front of her black leather thong spurred on her apathetic performance.

Gretta walked straight to the bar. Flame took Thatcher's hand and led him toward the booth closest to the jukebox. Déjà vu crept over him: an eerie and nebulous visitation from the past.

"Whaddya think?" she asked as she pulled him into the booth beside her.

Watching a bearded, tattooed patron attempt to clamor onto the circular stage, he nodded with feigned approval. The topless dancer nonchalantly pushed her admirer to the floor with her bare foot. It evoked a standing ovation from the nearby tables.

"Entertainment, no cover," he said.

Flame laughed. "It ain't Vegas." Sliding close beside him, she nudged her shoulder against his.

Her incidental touch induced a rush of obscure memories to the nostalgia center of his brain.

"This is Gretta's booth." She spoke loudly over the debauched uproar and the guttural wrenching of Johnny Paycheck from the jukebox. "She likes to check out the prime stuff bending over the juke."

Thatcher, having noticed only the stuff of which plumber's cracks are made, wondered who might be the object of Gretta's voyeurism. A quick elbow to his ribs dissuaded further contemplation.

"Watch her work." Flame directed his attention toward the bar.

Twisting in his seat to get a better view, he sensed an emergence of memory, and like an old light bulb, it flickered and went out.

Gretta was sitting on one bar stool with her left foot propped against the one beside it, her right leg was thrown across the top of the bar. Interestingly, she was unlacing the side of her pant leg beginning at the bottom.

"She's working the first round from ol' Weezer." With an approving smile, she went on, "Gretta does this every time the ol' man's behind the bar."

Thatcher settled back into the booth and tried not to think about what he couldn't remember.

Flame cocked her head and looked at him with an inquiring expression. "So, you got a destination?"

He heard each word, but for some reason his mind failed to place them in any discernible order. Could it be, he considered, the one drink at the motel? He hadn't eaten much all day.

"Hey, you with me or what?" Hers was a playful scowl.

"I didn't catch it."

Placing the tips of her fingers under his chin, like a mother might do to her distracted child, she said very slowly. "So," she took a breath, "do you have a destination?"

"West."

She paused long enough to press her lips together. "That's a direction." She studied him for a moment. "Can't figure what's up with you, exactly." Taking a moment to smile, she asked directly, "What are you up to?"

Shrugging his shoulders, he indulged in another succinct reply. "Road trip."

To Thatcher's relief, Flame needed no further clarification.

"Gretta and I haven't been on the road since last summer. Rode out to Sturgis..." She frowned pensively. "It's not what it used to be."

Thatcher, not eager to show his ignorance, just nodded.

"Big rallies are turning into sideshows for Gold Wingers with trailers, and Harley neophytes with side cars." Flame shook her head with disgust. "These rich SOB's hit fifty, and they go out, buy a Harley, and come looking for adventure, or some bullshit."

This caught Thatcher's attention. He was certainly rich by her standards, and he had gone out and bought a Harley, at gunpoint no less. The adventure part, however, was not exactly correct. In fact, he was looking for a comfortable tedium, at least for awhile. He waited anxiously for her to continue.

"They sit around their campfire discussing the stock market, drinking beer out of green bottles, and hoping some biker babe with big bazoos offers to sit on their face."

Flame let out a big sigh as the final rupturing notes from Johnny Paycheck faded into the less-than-subtle roar of the biker bar.

Karlene stared out the window and allowed her mind to wander in and out of possible scenarios. They brought her no assurances. They were all frightening. Several minutes passed before she escaped her introspection. A storefront announced Waukegan Auto Body.

"Curtis, where the hell are we?"

"Sheridan Road." It was a glib response.

"We're in Waukegan."

Curtis flashed a contemptible glare in the rearview mirror. "You said you didn't want to go home."

Karlene sat upright. "You moron. I didn't say take me to Waukegan."

"You didn't say not to."

She placed her arms across her chest and feigned authority, "Curtis, turn around."

"I got business to take care of."

Karlene felt uneasy. She knew Curtis as a pathetic, moronic bully who would do whatever he was ordered to do by either Aaron or the second-in-command, David Stout. She didn't want to push him too far, yet she wanted nothing to do with his business in Waukegan.

With controlled complaisance, she admonished, "Just leave me out of it."

"Sweetheart, you just keep your pretty little ass in this nice, big limo and you'll be safe and sound," he said as he navigated the limousine into a crowded gravel parking lot.

Sinking into the backseat, she read out loud the neon sign perched atop the slanted roof. "Leather & Lace."

"Not your kind of place, Sweetheart?"

"This is a biker bar, and your idea of a joke."

Curtis Lane glanced toward her and grinned. "You could get yourself a lot of looks and a lot of free drinks in there, and who knows what else, Karlie baby."

She shuddered. It was the first time Curtis Lane had ever used any variation of her first name. It was always Ms. Ferrand in front of Aaron, or Sweetheart when they were alone. Her name had been violated.

He parked the limo and turned around. For the first time since leaving the dinner party, he looked at Karlene face-to-face. “You coming in?” he asked nonchalantly.

She stared through his contrived congeniality. “Take care of your business, then take me to a hotel.”

Smirking through his dark Stalinesque mustache, he inquired, “Steppin’ out on Mr. Henderson this evening?” He paused long enough to observe her response, then continued, “How ’bout that drink?”

Turning away, she saw a rotund, bearded patron urinating on the dumpster only a few yards from her window. “I don’t think so.” Before she could look away, the nefarious, hairy twin of the Pillsbury Doughboy glanced in her direction. With a swaggering step toward the limousine, he aimed it toward her and roared with a sepulchral cackle not far removed from a libidinous duck.

She heard herself whisper, “Oh, shit,” as she lowered her head. Without looking toward Curtis Lane, she said, “Lock the fucking doors when you leave.”

Curtis reached over and turned off the power to the car phone, then slid the receiver under the front seat. He didn’t want his passenger making any calls or taking any incoming calls that would encourage her to mention their location. Locking the doors, he got out.

She watched him enter under the purple neon sign.

Gretta set a tray of shots and beer on the table. “JD and Bud,” she announced as she tossed six feet of black leather lacing at Thatcher. “Do me up.”

As he gathered in the leather lace, he pivoted to face Gretta. In a bluesy twang he replied, “Do me up, but don’t do me wrong.”

Placing her hands on her hips, she said to Flame, "I like this one," then cuffed Thatcher alongside the head. "Do me up, and I'll do you right." Grinning down at him, she presented her long muscular leg by resting the heal of her boot against the edge of the bench, and nestling the toe of her boot against his groin. The split pant leg fell away and bared a resplendent profusion of orchids and vines. A tropical efflorescence, Thatcher thought, from a botanist turned tattoo artist and leg man.

Addressing Flame once again, Gretta said, "That ol' peckerhead wouldn't give up the third shot unless I let him pull out the lace with his teeth."

Flame howled in laughter. "I missed that!"

"You fucking missed his goddamn teeth falling out on the bar." Gretta was genuinely disgusted.

"No shit?" Flame took a quick swig of beer. "We gotta find a classier joint."

Precariously balancing on one foot, Gretta glanced down at Thatcher. "Hey, don't take all night."

Starting at the hip, he threaded and evened the lace. Once underway, he used the one-lace-at-a-time zigzag method, and worked swiftly. He was certain this moment would be one he would remember.

Gretta grabbed the chrome coat rack attached to the side of the booth as Thatcher reached the knee with the first lace. She snapped her fingers in Flame's direction. "Hand me a Bud. I'm dyin' of thirst here."

Reaching over the top of Thatcher, Flame delivered the beer to her partner, then nuzzled close to Thatcher's ear and whispered, "You don't get one 'til you're done."

Gretta burst out laughing. "He thinks you're talkin about a beer!"

Flamed nuzzled even closer. Caressing the side of his face, she whispered again, "I'm talking about a beer."

Thatcher glanced up at Gretta as he reached her ankle. "She's talking about..." pulling the lace through the bottom eyelet, he smirked, "a beer."

As Thatcher picked up the other half of the leather lace, Gretta took a long swig of Bud, and said, "Cowboy." Holding out her longneck to Thatcher, she winked.

He took a long swallow, and continued nimbly on with the opposite lace. Reaching the bottom, he tied the two ends together with a perfect square knot. At that moment, Gretta slammed the empty bottle down onto the table.

"Where is Mr. Daniels?" she shouted, as she moved to the other side of the booth and sat down.

"Gretta." Flame handed her partner a shot glass. "Show us the way!"

Thatcher watched Gretta create a perfect ethereal smile as she touched the shot glass to her lips.

He had little doubt that he was, in one way or another, going to regret this night. The avalanche was at hand. All he could do was stay out in front of it for as long as he could, and hope there would be a chance to jump out of the way.

Gretta threw her head back, and in one quick motion the Tennessee sour mash whiskey was gone.

He watched Flame dip her pinkie into her shot glass, and slowly lick the JD from her finger. Again, something seemed all too familiar. Why couldn't he remember?

She lifted the glass to her lips and took a small sip. "The smoothest sippin' whiskey ever made." Flame placed the glass to her lips once again and abruptly flung her head back. The whiskey was gone, her cheeks were flushed, and her grimace was fleeting. "But, who's got time for sippin'?"

Thatcher stared at the burnish amber liquid in his shot glass. His track record with Mr. Daniels was anything but exemplary. Intrepidly hoisting his glass, he saluted his two accomplices, and tossed it down in commendable cowboy tradition. Appropriately, Waylon Jennings belted out, "I've always been crazy..."

Gretta laughed, then turned leisurely toward the jukebox where a lean-muscled, clean-shaven, thirty-something Brad Pitt kind of guy in tight jeans and a black sleeveless t-shirt stood sliding quarters into the slot. She nodded with approval.

Flame placed her hand on Thatcher's shoulder, and looked

poignantly into his watery eyes. "You've got whiskey tears." Flame nudged in closer. "I'll help you through the night."

Sliding out of the booth, Gretta smirked. "I'll be back."

Thatcher noticed a large and unwieldy man standing at the bar. He was dressed in a pretentious three-piece suit, with a meretricious display of gold jewelry. Other than his attire, the man seemed to meld in with the coterie around him. Curiously, Thatcher thought he looked familiar.

He wasn't terribly surprised when Gretta changed course from the young man at the jukebox to attend to the gold-ladened, overdressed man at the bar. Possibly, he mused, her priority was profit before pleasure.

Gretta nudged against the wealthy customer at the bar and whispered in his ear. Thatcher saw him grab her wrist and force her onto the stool beside him. The man's jaw was taut, veins bulged from his massive neck.

With the Jack Daniels already buzzing in his head, he nudged Flame. "Hey, do you know that guy?"

Flame set her bottle down and leaned across Thatcher to get a better view. Without immediate concern, she replied, "He's been around before, but I don't know him." She picked up her beer. "Why?"

"Gretta whispered something, and he grabbed her."

Flame laughed as the opening drum beat of "Crumblin' Down" rumbled through the roadhouse. "She likes it rough."

"No, this didn't look friendly rough," he replied.

Flame took another look as John Mellencamp declared, "Some people ain't no damn good..."

"Oh, fuck!" she said as she shoved past Thatcher.

The force of Gretta's right jab snapped the big man's head back.

Instantly, the man's enormous fist whirled toward Gretta. She turned away taking a glancing blow to the side of her face. Falling to the floor, she watched as he came off his stool preparing for another, more accurate, strike. The big man did not see Flame's silver-toed boot, but he immediately folded in half upon its impact.

Thatcher thought this was all too early in the evening for Friday night at the fights. Evidently, so did all the other patrons. No one except ol' Weezer appeared concerned. Watching with interest, Thatcher slid from the booth as the old, wiry bartender attempted to evacuate the injured man from the premises. Thatcher was certain it wasn't going to happen.

Regaining his senses and shedding off the massive ache in his groin, the large man tossed the wiry bartender away as if discarding a stogie. Then turning toward Gretta and Flame sitting on the floor, he began his advance without suspecting another strike.

Thatcher's swift ankle high sweep easily upended the big man. He watched the ill-tempered thug collide head-on with the steel foot railing of the bar before going to his friends.

"Next time I go for the throat," Gretta was saying as she picked herself up off the floor, "I think I busted my fuckin' hand." She shook it furiously.

Flame looked toward Thatcher. "Thanks. That's a kick-ass move."

Gretta glanced over toward her fallen assailant, then back at Thatcher. "What the hell did ya do to him?"

"I caught him off balance."

The two large patrons, who moments ago had caught the bartender, approached. Thatcher stood up.

The largest one pointed his finger at Thatcher. "You, give us hand. We're gonna get rid of this garbage."

He was more than happy to take out the garbage. Thatcher and the two bikers hoisted Curtis Lane to his feet. The shorter one pounded the semi-conscious man twice in the face with his fist. Bleeding from the mouth, Curtis slumped back to the floor.

"We don't put up with this shit," announced the taller one. "This time he'll remember."

It seemed to Thatcher, as he helped pull the bleeding, semi-conscious man toward the door, that this particular misplaced patron had previously fallen into disfavor.

He overheard a scrawny waitress say to another, "The Stormies don't fuck around when they put the hurt on."

The second waitress replied, "They should've kicked his ass last time."

As Thatcher and the two bikers pulled Curtis Lane toward the door, Curtis Lane's head wobbled back and forth then dropped forward. The shorter one grabbed a handful of Curtis' hair and announced to the crowd, "Move the fuck out of the way!"

Thatcher struggled with his half of the two hundred and fifty pounds, and watched as a craggy faced patron standing near the door casually took out a six-inch folding hunting knife and began peeling an apple.

As they neared the door, the larger one called out, "Hey, Carl, save me part of that apple."

Just before reaching the door, the apple fell to the floor and Carl stepped into their path. The smaller biker stepped aside just seconds before the knife was jabbed into Curtis Lane's abdomen directly below the sternum. With a sharp twist the blade sliced across the aorta, and was withdrawn.

Thatcher backed away as the three others tossed Curtis Lane through the front door. Falling to the sidewalk with a thud, Curtis rolled to his side. Thatcher could see the blood permeating the woven material of his suit.

Curious patrons rushed to the door and pushed Thatcher out into the humid night air. Standing among others on the sidewalk, he watched as Curtis Lane struggled to pull himself to his feet using the split-rail fence that bordered the walkway. Staggering toward a black limousine a few feet away, he stumbled and fell across the hood.

At that moment a young woman exited through the limo's rear door. Thatcher expected an ensuing scream. She merely placed a hand to her mouth and stepped backward to the rear of the limousine.

Harley engines rumbled to life and a moment later three custom hawgs veered onto the highway as a festive crowd began to gather around the dying man slumped over the hood of the limo.

"A twenty says he's dead before..."

"Keep your twenty. The fucker's wasted, man."

"He's still breathin'."

"Hey, the fucker's dead. Gimme a light."

This was perplexing social behavior; Thatcher was at a loss. He had reveled with boorish company before, but no one ever died from epigrammatic jabs and execrable accusations.

Thatcher turned his attention to the young woman in the black strapless evening dress and the diamond necklace, who stood motionless with her arms crossed and her hands clutching her bare shoulders. She had not moved from the rear of the limousine. Sensing her silent panic, he felt compelled to help in some way. Ever since the Brewster hardware affair, he was becoming more and more sympathetic to those in distress.

A hand falling onto his shoulder startled him.

"You're being set up," said Flame.

He turned toward his companion. "What are you talking about?"

"They're going to set you up."

"They? Who?"

He thought he had vanquished the omnipotent "they" when he sent JJ Burdick scrambling to his accountants. Evidently, he concluded, "they" are everywhere.

Flame was upset. The woman, who had minutes ago dropkicked a man three times her size without flinching, was now noticeably alarmed.

"Flame, who are 'they'?"

"The Members." She drew in a gasp of air. "Most everyone here belongs to the Storm Riders." She noticed his uncertainty. "It's a biker club. This is their place."

With "they" identified, he said, "Go on."

"You're the stranger," she continued. "They're protecting their own." She paused as if taking time to select the right words, instead, she was blunt. "They're tagging you with stabbing that asshole."

His thoughts flashed back to the day before, when his greatest concern was in what direction to ride. Things change suddenly. "They" do it every time.

Gretta approached rapidly. Her eyes were clear, almost omniscient. "Man, you gotta get out of here." She pulled Thatcher close and kissed him on the mouth. "That's for luck."

The taste of whiskey was sweet, yet distressing on his lips. He wanted a little more explanation. He wanted a little more time to think. He wanted to go back inside and have another shot of Mr. Daniels.

"Thatcher," Flame's expression turned hesitant, "I'm sorry I got you in this mess." Her eyes darted away. "Gretta and I gotta split without you."

Gretta stepped over to Curtis Lane slumped over the hood of the limousine, and gingerly checked his pants pockets. His gold chain and Rolex were already missing.

"Fucking vultures," she mumbled as she spotted Dirk the Smirk admiring his new gold watch. Pulling out a set of keys, she walked back to her companions.

"See that silly-ass blonde over there with the diamonds?" she said to Thatcher. "Get her and this limousine out of here."

Thatcher took a long look at the woman in the evening dress. It was a direct and overwhelming collision with déjà vu, except this time his neuro-receptors left him momentarily dumbstruck. He knew it was entirely unrelated to the earlier one that he had already discerned as nothing more than Jack Daniels inciting his overactive imagination. Slowly, he turned toward Flame.

"She's right, Cowboy." Flame caressed the side of his face.

"Here." Gretta placed the keys in Thatcher's hand.

"This doesn't make any sense."

"There's no fuckin' time." Gretta stared grimly into his face. "This is the way it is."

Flame broke in. "They're gonna tag you for this whether you stay or whether you split."

"I suggest," began Gretta, "you take the fuckin' limo and get out of here. It ain't right, it's just the only thing you can do."

Having been in law enforcement, he understood any peripheral involvement in this homicide, as unintentional as it was, could cost him more than he wished to pay. He decided to, as Gretta had just put it, get out of here. Taking a deep breath, he turned toward Flame.

Flame reached up, pulled Thatcher's face near to hers, and kissed him long and hard. If he had known, he would have taken an even deeper breath. She broke away just in time for him to take a breath.

"I want you to remember me." Her smile was curiously demure. "I'll have your bike ready to go by tomorrow morning. Meet me at Wrigley Field at ten o'clock. I'll have it there."

He couldn't remember having had a good-night kiss that personified as much finality.

Maintaining a semblance of intelligence, Thatcher resisted the inane impulse to go to the young woman and tell her the truth. Still, he needed to tell her something.

Backing away as the stranger approached, the young woman studied Thatcher carefully. She wanted to run, yet she sensed she should hold her ground, at least for now.

Thatcher recognized her apprehension and decided that he had little time to convince her of any incidental noble intentions he might have. He grasped her by the wrist, and when she started to pull away, he said, "You need to trust me. I'm undercover." He had played a semblance of this role before: a long time ago.

Her arm went limp and he swiftly escorted her to the open passenger door. It always amazed him how effortlessly he could convincingly manipulate the truth.

Assuming a virtuous nature, he said, "I'll take you somewhere safe." He guided her into the backseat and closed the door.

Thatcher walked in front of the limousine and pulled the late Curtis Lane from the hood. The body fell to the gravel lot with a definitive thump. "Sorry." It was a bewildering apology to a dead man.

Not once had Thatcher thought he would ever drive a limousine; he didn't even like riding in them. Not surprising, the extended Fleetwood handled no worse than his Eldorado the time he hauled Geno's twenty-foot Baja up to Torch Lake.

Mesmerized by the night highway, Thatcher watched the center line ceaselessly rush toward him. He was trying not to think too much; bubble gum would help.

Glancing at the digital clock, he realized he had been driving for nearly fifteen minutes. It was eleven forty-five. The soft hum of the automatic window sliding open behind him reminded him he wasn't alone.

"Where are you taking me?" she inquired stoically.

Thatcher looked in the rearview mirror. Her soft, inquisitive voice brought him to the realization he was now responsible for another person: an attractive and apparently wealthy young woman he knew nothing about, a young woman who had, without much choice, placed her well-being in the hands of a dubious stranger who had led her to believe he was going to be her protector. He decided it was time to set things straight.

"I have a confession to make," he said as he watched her through the rearview mirror. "I'm not what you think I am." He tried to keep his voice light, his manner unthreatening.

"God, you work for him too," she hissed as she leaned back into the seat and crossed her legs and arms. With an inimical Bette Davis style, she went on. "You might as well kill me. I'm not going back to him." She glared at Thatcher's eyes reflected in the rearview mirror and raised her voice. "I won't give him the pleasure of laying his hands on me ever again."

Her words, precise and conclusive, sent a shiver through him. Thatcher was becoming increasingly concerned about whose limousine he was driving, and about the identity of this beautiful passenger. At the same time he was becoming increasingly concerned whether he had lost his mind, as he unsuccessfully tried to validate the decision to drive off in a limousine with an unknown stranger. In any case, it was time for clarification.

He pulled off the road just in front of a sign welcoming them to Lake Forest. He shut off the engine and the lights and he turned around. The outline of her face was barely visible.

"How are you going to do it?" she demanded boldly.

Thatcher rubbed his face with the palms of his hands. The shot of Jack Daniels had nearly dissipated, leaving behind a familiar ache around his temples.

"What's your name?" he asked.

She stared out the window into the darkness. "You don't even know my name. Aaron didn't even tell you my name. That bastard." Her words were embittered, yet matter-of-fact.

Again, he tried to keep his manner light. "I assume Aaron owns this limo."

The young woman, in a sudden swift movement, opened the door and began to run barefoot down the highway before Thatcher could disengage his seat belt. For just a moment, he considered letting her go. Then, without further thought, he got out and gave chase. He wanted some answers.

The sparse traffic from either direction appeared to give no indication that a woman in an evening dress being chased down a dark highway on a Friday night was eventful. Nonetheless, Thatcher sprinted as fast as he could. He wanted this scene over as quickly as possible.

Had she been wearing running shoes, he would not have come close to catching her. Thatcher was nearly out of breath as he grabbed her arm from behind. His fatigue made him an easy target for her right hook. It connected soundly.

Groaning and reeling backward, he stayed on his feet and maintained his grip on her arm. The left side of his face ached as he flung his arms around her.

Twisting and turning with all her strength she screamed. "Just do it! Just do it!"

Holding her tightly, he tasted the blood in his mouth. A semi-truck sped past them, blaring its horn. "Just do what?" he yelled.

The brief whirlwind from the eighteen-wheeler blew her hair about. "Just get it over with!" And, with one last great physical effort she broke free and faced him.

Thatcher stepped back, preparing for another right hook.

They stared at one another in the darkness.

Then, with an eerie calmness, she looked past him and said, "Just kill me."

Thatcher took another step back. Revealing the palms of his hands, he softened his voice, "I don't know who you think I might be, but I'm not." He paused only briefly. "I don't want to hurt you. If you want to go, take the limo."

"Who are you?" Shaken, her voice retained its querulousness.

Thatcher sensed her trembling. "Someone who's in a shit-load of trouble without quite knowing why."

"You didn't kill Curtis?" Her voice wavered. "And, you don't work for Aaron Henderson?" She ran her fingers through her windblown hair.

"Don't know the man," he said too casually. Then, a sudden chilling familiarity came over him: the pieces fell abruptly together. "Curtis, come get her, now," he said it as he had at O'Hare.

Covering her mouth, she murmured, "My God."

Eyeing one another suspiciously, a mutual thought, unspoken, collided with the moment. Unbelievable.

"You need to get out of here." Thatcher made a motion toward the limo. "I'm sure someone has called in this little escapade. And I have a strong inclination I need to avoid the police for the time being, at least until I can figure this out."

"What is your name."

"Thatcher."

"Mr. Thatcher," her voice turned listless, "the police are the least of your problems."

He watched as she turned and walked away in her bare feet and her strapless Vera Wang evening dress.

As her figure melded into the darkness, he turned and walked rapidly in the opposite direction. With a little luck, he thought, maybe he would find his way back to the motel without further incident.

When the black limousine sped past him he felt suddenly alone, and not particularly relieved.

Walking briskly, he considered his options, each one ending with his expedient exodus from Chicago. He was startled by the sudden flash of headlights from an abandoned gas station. He stopped dead in his tracks as the vehicle began creeping toward him. For lack of a better plan, he stood his ground.

As the outline of the limousine came into view, it seemed his options rapidly dwindled to one. He waited.

The crunching of gravel beneath its tires, and the low whirling whine of the automatic window sent a shiver through him. Her face remained obscured in the shadows, but her voice, soft and demure, was crystalline.

"Going my way?"

Saturday, July 4

FOUR

AARON CALLED DAVID STOUT WHEN HIS LIMOUSINE HAD NOT returned to the party. "Stout, where the hell is Curtis Lane?"

"He's with the limousine." David Stout showed no concern.

"He very well may be, but the limousine is not here!"

David Stout was for the moment without an explanation, other than Curtis Lane was sometimes prone to stupidity.

"Mr. Henderson, I'll come and get you." There was a brief pause. "Curtis will inevitably show up." Still, there was no concern.

"It's not that simple." Aaron was disturbed by Stout's equanimity. "There's something of great importance and value in the trunk." He paused and took a deep breath. "I ordered him to take Karlene back to the penthouse hours ago. He should be back by now!"

"He'll show up, Mr. Henderson." He hesitated. "Did you try the limo phone?"

"Forget about it! It's turned off. I want you to use the tracking system."

"I'll be there in ten minutes." Stout lowered his voice. "Then I'll take care of this."

Karlene couldn't get their chance meeting at O'Hare out of her mind. She wasn't one to make great significance out of random coincidence, yet an eerie feeling crept over her. It was as if he appeared at Gate 23 to launch her exodus from hell, and later to reappear at the moment hell might have reclaimed her. Taking a brief, yet searching, look at her passenger, she wanted to believe it was good karma.

Thatcher sensed staying with this woman was only going to bring him more trouble, yet the remembrance of the kiss at Gate 23 was roiling his sensibility and muddying up his judgment. The avalanche begun earlier was building momentum.

After passing through Lake Forest, Karlene turned south onto a road that was under construction. Without warning the road abruptly turned to washboard gravel, sending the limousine swerving from side to side. Thatcher grabbed the armrest to keep from sliding across the seat and colliding with the driver. He wondered why he hadn't buckled his seat belt.

Aptly regaining control of the vehicle, Karlene glanced toward Thatcher to see him fasten his seat belt. A fleeting smile crossed her lips. She turned away just in time to see several pallid eyes staring out from the darkness fifty yards in front of her.

Slamming on the brakes and gripping the steering wheel firmly, she readied herself for the countering maneuvers all over again. As the limousine went left, she pumped the brakes and turned right. As the momentum of the heavy vehicle forced her to turn sharply back to the left to avoid going off the road, she held her breath. The limousine spun around. An explosion erupted from beneath the vehicle, and the front end pulled hard to the right. Karlene muscled the wheel sharply to the left. Gravel pummeled the bottom of the limousine as it came to a grinding stop facing the opposite direction.

"That was exhilarating," she muttered, shifting into park.

"Right front tire." Opening the door, he said, "I'll check it out."

The tire was mangled. Walking in front of the limousine, he found Karlene waiting with the window down. Her expression was no more cheerful than his own.

"Flat?"

"Oh, yeah." Nodding toward the side of the road, he said, "Steer it to the shoulder. It won't take long to change it."

Pulling the steering wheel to the right, she eased the vehicle onto the shoulder. She turned off the ignition, popped the trunk, and retrieved a flashlight from the glove box. Karlene joined him at the rear of the vehicle. In the glow of the trunk's courtesy light, their eyes briefly acknowledged a simple solidarity.

Except for a heavy-duty aluminum case with large sturdy latches, the type that catches the eye and engages the overactive imagination, the trunk was empty. Pushing it aside, Thatcher pulled open the spare tire compartment, unfastened the tire and the jack. The tire iron lay beneath. He pulled the tire out and carried it to the front of the limousine. Karlene followed with the jack. Leaning the tire against the fender, he turned to Karlene. She handed him the jack.

"Shine the light down here, underneath," he said. "I need to see where the jack goes."

Kneeling quickly, she proved again she could move adeptly in formal wear. To Thatcher's surprise, he found the location quickly and nudged the jack into place. They rose to their feet at the same time.

"Tire iron," he said, and started back to the trunk.

Karlene aimed the flashlight toward the rear of the limousine to light the way.

As he reached for the tire iron, he noticed an object neatly wrapped in dark plastic tucked away beneath the spare. Thatcher curiously picked up the object. It was heavy for its size. Unwrapping the plastic, he stopped as soon as he recognized what it was, and quickly wrapped it back up. Placing it where he had found it, he noticed Karlene standing beside him.

"What is it?" she asked.

Thatcher looked at her, deciphering an element of dread in her voice. "Mr. Henderson isn't a respectable businessman, is he?"

"He's not respectable at all," she said with absolution.

He watched her eyes dart away. "That would explain the weaponry."

Walking nonchalantly away, she replied, "Mob."

Framed for murder by a biker club, and now theft of a Mafioso limousine, was not what he had planned for his impromptu holiday weekend in Chicago, reflected Thatcher.

Neither one spoke as they worked quickly to change the tire. Thatcher couldn't get the Uzi off his mind. From a past he wanted to forget, guns were very familiar and very inimical. Carrying the jack and tire iron back to the trunk, Thatcher wondered what could be next. Karlene's hand on his shoulder startled him.

Pointing the beam of light at the aluminum case, she said ominously, "I want to know what's in it." Karlene leaned into the trunk and pulled the aluminum case closer. "Hand me the tire iron."

"I don't think that'll be necessary," he said as he reached over and clicked opened each latch.

It was a sheepish expression. With a sigh she relented. "Let's just see what's in here." Slowly, lifting it open, she gasped. "Jesus."

Leaning against the upraised trunk lid, he announced wryly, "And, now that you've just won the grand lottery jackpot..."

"This isn't funny."

Neatly bound stacks of vintage one-thousand dollar bills added up to several million dollars and a small-caliber semi-automatic with a silencer set on top.

She looked up at Thatcher. "So." Her eyes zeroed in on his. "Are you a good guy or a bad guy?" There was a subtle lilt in her voice that made her question no less serious, and no less perusing.

Thatcher had always been amused how large sums of money could rapidly digress otherwise fine moral fiber into coarse binder twine. He knew little of the young woman's fiber, moral or otherwise. "Is this a query as to my intent?"

"It is."

His smirk amplified his apprehension. "Not interested." Reaching to close the case, it seemed the gallery of Grover Clevelands awaited an explanation.

Grasping his wrist with her right hand, she searched Thatcher's face for a genuineness she didn't expect to find.

"There's millions of dollars," her voice had taken on a high and unsteady pitch, "and, you're telling me you don't want any of it?"

"Easier the money, greater the risk." Lacking validity, he was nevertheless convinced that it was true. The Grover gallery remained stoic. "You go ahead, I can walk from here."

"You're serious." She let go of his wrist: veracity confirmed, idiocy suspected. "I don't believe it."

"I've got all the money I need."

Thatcher closed the case. He shrugged his shoulders and unintentionally spurred on the young woman's escalating impetuosity.

"You don't get it, do you?"

He said nothing as the crescendo began.

"You're already at risk!" Planting her hands on her hips, "You can't just walk away from this!" she exclaimed.

"I'll walk fast."

Taking a deep cleansing breath, an instinctual response to crunch time, Karlene attempted to become calm, to render a voice of reason. "All right, understand this." She looked into Thatcher's placid expression. "It doesn't really matter how..." Stopping in mid-sentence, she inquired with sensibility. "Are you listening to me?"

"Yes, I am." His tone was sincere.

"All right, then. Let me say this very concisely."

His eyes coaxed her on.

She began slowly, like a roller coaster approaching the summit. "It doesn't matter how or why you drove off with Aaron Henderson's limousine with millions of his dollars in the trunk." At the precipice her words, like a roller coaster, plummeted. "He's going to put a bullet between your eyes just the same. Bang!"

Thatcher remembered what one of his mentors had once told him early in his corporate career. "When someone wants to shoot you between the eyes," Thatcher recalled the deep gravel voice, "you've made it to the big time."

"Bang?"

Karlene nodded. "Bang."

In the languid glow of the courtesy light, her diamond necklace twinkled like a faraway constellation.

"Is that a Christian Dior?" Remembering the name from the pages of *Vogue* that the woman beside him on the United flight had been reading, he hoped to change the subject from bullets to anything else.

Bewilderment overcame her.

"The necklace," he said.

Touching it with her fingers, she realized she had forgotten she was wearing it. "I don't know." As she straightened the necklace, she looked up at Thatcher. "Can we get out of here?"

It was something between a shrug and nod.

"Good, I'm glad you're in agreement with that much." She reached into the trunk, closed the case, and pulled it out. "Think I'm going to hang onto this for awhile." She turned toward Thatcher. "If you don't mind?"

He tossed the tire iron into the trunk. It struck the courtesy light, and except for the narrow beam from the flashlight, the trunk went dark. He slammed the trunk closed. "I'm driving."

Thatcher shifted into drive and navigated the limousine carefully down the gravel road. Within a few hundred yards it turned to pavement once again. Two miles farther it converged with another highway.

"Which way from here?" He looked at the young woman sitting beside him.

"Where we going?"

"Lincolnwood."

"Turn right. It should bring us to highway forty-three. Drive to Deerfield, from there you can cut over to I-94."

Turning right, Thatcher said, "Did you know the last thousand-dollar bill was minted in 1934?"

"And that's relevant to anything?"

After several failed attempts to raise Curtis Lane on the limo phone, as well as coming up empty at Curtis' usual evening haunts, David Stout decided to contact Tony Poza, a non-made loyalist eager to make the status of mob soldier. He knew Poza was waiting for an opportunity to show his worth to Aaron Henderson. Anxious to climb the corporate ladder, Tony Poza certainly would go the extra mile. And, with Aaron Henderson becoming more irascible by the minute, Stout needed someone not only competent, but motivated to get the job done quickly. An eager Tony Poza was a good choice, even though Stout often hesitated using the lower ranks.

Tracking Aaron's limousine wasn't going to be a difficult task, presuming that it was somewhere in metro Chicago. As of a half hour ago, when Stout activated the device, there was no sign of it. If the limousine didn't show up soon, Stout recognized Aaron was angry enough to order a hit on Curtis Lane, without bothering to get it sanctioned.

Tony Poza was waiting at the designated lakeshore park at the end of Montrose Avenue when David Stout arrived a little after twelve-thirty. Poza promptly exited his Chevy and got into the backseat of Stout's Coupe de Ville. They exchanged pleasantries and got quickly to the business at hand.

David Stout spoke matter-of-factly. "I need not remind you that Mr. Henderson is not a patient man, and this assignment needs to be taken care of swiftly."

Using only the rearview mirror for eye contact, he waited for Poza to acknowledge the urgency with a nod.

"Curtis Lane has not returned with Mr. Henderson's limousine." Stout inserted the motivation. "At the moment Lane's job is on the fucking line. Tony, you do this quickly, and you do this right, you may be enjoying a higher lifestyle sometime soon."

With all his willpower, Tony Poza retained a stolid expression. Again, he simply nodded.

"Ms. Ferrand is in the limo, and was expected back at the penthouse over two hours ago. Like I said, Mr. Henderson is not a patient man. You need to find the limo, and if you have to, drive it back to the penthouse with Ms. Ferrand."

"Mr. Stout, consider it done."

Vainglory didn't impress David Stout, but it was a sign that Tony Poza was motivated. "I'll consider it done when the limousine and Ms. Ferrand are back at Lake Point Tower." He paused long enough for it all to set in. "One more thing, there's an aluminum case in the trunk. Make sure it's there. Under no circumstances should you open it."

"What's in it?"

"It's none of your concern." Stout lowered his voice. "Forget about it."

Tony Poza got the point. "Nobody's gonna touch Mr. Henderson's property. They can just fucking forget about it."

"You have someone with you?" Stout continued on.

"Yeah, just like you said over the phone."

Still using the rear view mirror, Stout added, "Work with him before?"

"Lots of times." Tony, confirming his leadership role, added, "Does what I tell 'em."

"What's his name?"

"Dean Adams."

David Stout wasn't impressed, and nearly considered ordering Poza to find another partner, but there was not enough time. "How's he doing now?"

"That metal plate in his head," Tony clarified, "fixed him up good as new. Didn't even need to take out that second .32 slug. He takes this medication for the herky jerkies."

Stout was not convinced Dean Adams was as good as new, but if Tony Poza could pull this job off smoothly with Dean Adams, he would have Curtis Lane's job tomorrow.

"I need to explain something to you." It was time for the technical training. "Get closer, you need to see this."

Poza responded immediately and leaned over the back of the front seat.

David Stout presented the tracking system. "It's like a fuckin' video game." David Stout communicated at whatever level he needed, to assure he was understood.

"ThinkPad 380."

And, at times, he underestimated his audience.

"Mr. Stout, who makes the software?"

Stout examined Tony Poza carefully. "Then, you can handle this?"

"I can handle it," Tony said confidently.

David Stout was still concerned. The thought of the .32 slug in Dean Adams' gray matter, and the metal plate holding his skull together gave him the willies.

"Who are you?" She turned toward Thatcher.

Without looking in her direction, he said, "You don't buy the undercover gig?"

She turned to look out her window. "I don't know what to buy." Crossing her legs and straightening her dress, she turned back toward Thatcher. "I don't know what to believe."

His was a brief and acknowledging glance.

Karlene went straight to the point. "Can I trust you?"

Thatcher stared ahead as the expressway rolled out in front of him. He said nothing.

"So. Can I trust you?"

Trust, Thatcher considered as his mind wandered back to an earlier decade. It was at the age of twenty-three that he had pledged his allegiance to the FBI. Four years later he had been hung out to dry in a grand jury investigation. He resigned and took his expertise to the corporate world. He found trust a liability.

"I don't know."

"Honesty." Her eyes turned away from his. "I appreciate that."

Wanting to give her something more than spur-of-the-moment candor, he added, "I'll do what I can."

"Fair enough, so what can you do?"

Running his fingers thoughtfully through his hair, he answered, "Offer you a place to sleep before planning your next move."

She frowned. "Then, I can trust you?"

His indistinct expression prompted her, after a prolonged silence, to continue. "Well?"

"I have a room at the Radisson in Lincolnwood. There's two beds."

"Offer accepted."

Five

The night had not gone the way Flame had hoped. Thatcher was gone. Gretta was gone. She found herself alone in her tiny apartment, sweating, and slouching in her only upholstered chair, watching her lava lamp as she listened to Janis Joplin screech out "Down on Me." In her right hand she held a glass with the fizzling remains of a Bromo Seltzer.

She didn't hear the key turn in the lock, or the door open. It was when the door slammed shut that she jumped from her chair. The hair on the back of her neck bristled, as the Bromo went airborne, spattering against the wall. Sporting only silk bikinis and a Bull's number ninety-one jersey she turned to confront the intruder.

"Hey, bitch!"

Flame stared at her friend. "Why do you always do that?"

Gretta grinned. "Because you always do that. Come on. It's a rush, isn't it?"

"Fuck you. It's a goddamn heart attack."

"Scored some prime dope from Brute." She pulled out a small bag from her vest pocket. "Care to partake?"

Flame placed her hands on her hips. "What'd it cost this time?"

"Hand job." Making a fist, she jerked it up and down several times. "That's my limit." Gretta tossed the bag to her partner. "Roll us a couple doobies while I strip down." She unbuttoned her vest. "You really need to get an air conditioner in this place."

Flame sat down at the dinette table and began rolling the first joint. "You're welcome to buy me one."

Gretta laughed as she threw her vest toward a chair. "You got some brewskis?"

Flame nodded toward the refrigerator. "Hey," her voice took on a serious note, "do you think we pimped Thatcher? I mean, maybe we should have stuck with him."

Gretta returned from the Frigidaire, set the longneck down on the kitchen counter, and began peeling off her leather pants. "We didn't have any fucking choice, did we? He was going to be fingered. There wasn't anything we could do about it." Gretta flung her pants over a dinette chair and snatched the beer from the counter. "Am I right?" Twisting off the cap, she waited for Flame's reply.

"You're probably right." Flame lit the joint and took a hit.

Gretta took a long slug of beer, then set the bottle back down on the counter. "You need a new fridge, this beer is almost warm."

"Buy me one." Standing up, she handed the joint to Gretta, who was leaning against the kitchen counter in a black satin "Eat Me" thong. She walked to the living room, and sat down in her only comfortable chair. She exhaled.

Gretta was holding in her first hit as she grabbed a dinette chair and swung it around into the living room. "You could use some more chairs too." She handed the joint back to Flame.

"Buy me one." She took her second toke.

Gretta swung her right leg over the seat and sat down, leaning forward against the back of the chair. Sitting spread-eagle in the small chair, she scooted it forward and tilted it onto its back legs to snatch the joint from Flame.

"I don't know," Flame sighed. "I feel like we cut out on him."

Janis sang out, "Get it while you can..."

Gretta exhaled. "We had to get him out of there." She handed the joint back to Flame. "Sorry you lost your date."

Flame pursed her lips just before taking her next hit.

Gretta smiled. "Dicks are really overrated."

Flame burst into laughter. "Christ!" Following a brief coughing spell, she blurted out, "I haven't had a chance to rate one in a long time!"

"It was a smart woman," Gretta remarked insightfully, "who discovered bi-sex-u-a-li-teeee."

"Tell me this." Karlene frowned. "What were you doing at a biker bar in Waukegan on a Friday night?"

Thatcher wondered what had taken her so long to ask. As he veered onto the Touhy exit, he replied, "It was an unusual sequence of events."

"Go on."

Thatcher told an abridged version of his ascension from the corporate world into bikerdom. Omitting the Phil and Stella incident, he simply stated the negotiations over the price of the motorcycle as going in his favor. He ended his account just prior to her chauffeur's demise.

"I'll buy that, even the part about getting the first round of drinks." Her smile rapidly digressed into a frown. "So, why did you drive away with me?"

Smoothing the creases across his forehead, he found himself speechless.

Karlene's eyes coaxed him on. "I do want to hear this."

His tone turned serious. "It seems," he began, "your chauffeur, for whatever reason, was killed by a member of a biker club called the Storm Riders. Flame and Gretta overheard that I was going to be set up for the murder."

Karlene brushed away a few loose strands of hair from her face. "I should believe this?" she quipped.

"Sure, why not?" Returning the gibe, "You bought the undercover gig," he reminded her.

"So, why you?"

"I was there. To quote Flame, 'The Storm Riders protect their own.'" Thatcher paused briefly to let it sink in, then continued. "Gretta took the keys from your driver, gave them to me, and told me to take the limo, and get you out of there."

"And that seemed like a good plan?"

"At the time." His eyes met hers in a disquieting stare. "So, what's your story?"

Karlene clenched her jaw, then simply shrugged her bare shoulders as she relocated another strand of hair. "Another time, maybe."

He understood.

"Another time."

"We got it." Dean Adams smirked. "We got the limo!"

"Where?"

"Right here." Dean pointed at the monitor. "Right, goddamn, here." Tapping his finger against the blue screen, he looked up at his corpulent partner.

Tony Poza flashed his partner a disconcerted look. "Where in the goddamn city?"

Dean Adams tilted his head back and forth. Eyeing the screen at different angles, he suddenly began pounding the left side of his head with his open hand.

Tony stared in astonishment. "What the fuck you doin'?"

Dean Adams shook his head violently. "It's the ringin'. It's nothin'." Holding his head in his hands, he repeated, "It's nothin'. Forget about it."

"Okay, forget about it. Now, where do we go?" Tony took out a cigarette and lit it. He regretted not letting Adams drive so that he could operate the tracking software. Then again, he had just watched his accomplice whack himself alongside the head. He didn't want his newly leased Lumina smacked up against a telephone pole.

Staring vacantly, Dean slowly removed his hands from his head.

"Adams," Poza spoke slowly. "Where the fuck do we go?"

Dean Adams glanced at the monitor. "North."

Tony Poza was valorously holding his patience. "Could you narrow it down a little?"

Dean's eyes darted back and forth between Tony and the monitor. "You know, north."

"How about a neighborhood, or cross streets." He took a long draft on his cigarette. "You know, some place I can drive to." Smoke swirled from his nostrils.

"Yeah, yeah, I'm working on it." He looked squarely at his partner. "Hey, this ain't fucking Mario Brothers, you know."

From Cagney to Brando to Johnny Depp as Donny Brasco, Thatcher had watched scores of cinematic gangster portrayals, to say nothing of his short tenure with the FBI. Mob surveillance was a popular venue.

He was convinced this beautiful young woman, without the assistance of an adept scriptwriter, had no chance of escaping with Mob millions.

There was no reason to pry into Karlene's life, yet there was one thing he wanted to confirm.

"Karlene," saying her name for the first time, "what do you know of the Mob?" he asked.

Catching her off guard, she turned toward Thatcher and succinctly replied, "There's no retirement plan."

Confirmation achieved.

"Leave the money, Karlene," he said with undeniable urgency.

"Leave it where?"

"I think we can walk away from this."

"You may be able to walk away. I can't, whether I leave the money or not. I've tried." Lowering her head, she turned away. "I'm a possession, Thatcher."

Watching her chest rise and fall with an unsettling sigh, he found nothing to say.

"Aaron doesn't give up a possession. He disposes of it when it's no longer of value." Turning quickly toward Thatcher, she said adamantly, "And, right now, I have no value, but I do have this money. It's my only chance of getting out."

He intercepted her truculent stare.

"Don't you understand that?" A tear slipped across her cheek.

Thatcher nodded as the Radisson appeared on his right.

"Let's not park in the lot." She rolled her eyes in Thatcher's direction. "For obvious reasons."

"For obvious reasons," he repeated.

He parked the limousine in an alley a couple blocks away. As they walked swiftly to the motel, he hoped no one would pay too much attention to their contrasting appearances, or the aluminum case that Karlene carried securely in her right hand.

He stopped abruptly in the parking lot. Thatcher stared toward the motel. "I didn't leave a light on," he whispered. It was almost a question.

"You're sure?"

Pressing his lips tightly together, he said nothing.

"Are you looking at the right room?"

"Yes," he replied as he nudged Karlene behind a parked Caravan.

As a blaring ambulance siren subsided, she looked at Thatcher and asked, "Now what?"

"I'll check it out," he whispered.

She grabbed his arm. "You don't have to."

"It's got to be Flame and Gretta," he said. "They're the only ones who know."

Raising her eyebrows, "You gave two strange women your room key?" she asked.

"Gretta's a housekeeper here."

"Convenient, she can loot rooms in her spare time."

Thatcher shrugged his shoulders. "She could do that."

He led the way to the side entrance. Switching the aluminum case to her other hand as she stepped through the door, Karlene continued to follow several feet behind as requested. The well-lighted hallway, the familiar motel smell did little to quell their uneasiness.

With the click of the lock he tried to shake off the apprehension as the door swung open. What he found was undeniably unexpected.

"Consider yourself fucked!"

After his meeting with Tony Poza, David Stout had returned to Lake Point Tower. His most serious concern was not locating the limousine, but rather setting the tone for the hunt.

With his back to Aaron, Stout mixed two drinks at the bar. He put little scotch into his own glass.

"Stout, it goes without saying, I'm holding you entirely accountable for this incident tonight."

Readily accepting responsibility, David Stout picked up both glasses and turned toward Aaron Henderson.

"Mr. Henderson, rest assured, I will handle this." He stepped toward his boss and handed him the glass. "I always do."

Aaron chose not to ignore the subtle jab. "Rest assured, your life depends upon it."

Nodding in acknowledgment, Stout knew it was the same terms that Aaron had accepted earlier from The Affiliation. They were simply being passed on. It was the way it was.

David Stout tipped his glass to Aaron Henderson. "To resolution."

Thatcher stepped into the room and faced his two adversaries. "Mr. Brogan, you brought your clown." He glanced at the other large man. "I'm sorry, did I say clown?" He shook his head feigning chagrin. "I meant clone." Sizing them up, he added, "Nice suits, fellas."

With the sound of the first thud, Karlene took a deep breath, walked through the doorway, and exhaled. "I've had a long, exhausting day, and I'm just a little keyed up at the moment. If it takes shooting someone to get some sleep, I can do that."

Thatcher looked up from the floor as the other two men froze in their tracks. "I could have handled this," he said.

"I can see that." Setting the aluminum case down on the floor, she grasped the small semi-automatic adeptly with both hands and took careful aim at the largest target. "Slowly stick your hands into your pants pockets."

The two large men wasted no time following the young woman's direction.

Thatcher casually stood up between them, and placed a hand on each one of their shoulders. "Gentlemen, I guess it's time for you to go." With a subtle nudge, he sent them toward the door.

Karlene lowered the handgun once they were both in the hallway. "They're not Aaron's thugs, otherwise you'd be dead. Who were they?"

"Where were you hiding that?"

"It was with the money, remember?"

Taking a deep breath, "Apparently not," he admitted.

"Apparently not," she mimicked as she shook her head.

Walking to her, Thatcher reached past her, and pushed the door closed. It stopped sort of latching. "The larger one, Mr. Brogan, we had a brief tête-à-tête this morning at O'Hare, just before we met the first time."

"You must have made quite an impression."

Suddenly, the door burst open, pushing Karlene into Thatcher. Before they could recover, Mr. Brogan, with eyes wide, was inside the room haphazardly waving a large chrome revolver in their direction. His associate stood nervously in the doorway.

"You wanna play fucking hardball?" he grunted. "I can play hardball." To his accomplice, he said, "Shut the fucking door."

To Mr. Brogan, the accomplice replied, "I'm outta here." And, closed the door.

Clutching Thatcher close to her, she concealed the gun in her right hand against the back of his thigh.

"Two against one, Mr. Brogan." Thatcher slowly inched his left hand toward the gun pressed against the back of his leg.

Mr. Brogan was taking his role much too seriously. Thatcher was certain JJ wanted him beat up and tossed into an alley somewhere. But as vehement as JJ could be when it came to eliminating his adversaries, he was not one to hire an assassin, particularly a bumbling one.

Mr. Brogan was acting on his own, and at the moment, acting crazy. Thatcher did not want to shoot him, especially in his motel room. Then, again, he didn't want to be shot in his motel room. Of the two, he would choose the first.

Mr. Brogan attempted to steady his gun as he leveled it at Thatcher's chest. His large meaty hand trembled. "Where's the fucking gun!?"

As Karlene placed the gun into Thatcher's hand, she made a slow deliberate nod toward the bed, "It's over there."

As the big man glanced in the direction of the bed, Thatcher pushed Karlene aside and swiftly raised the semi-automatic in his left hand. He assumed the stalwart, Sonny Crockett, two-hand stance to intimidate his already apprehensive opponent, and to disguise the fact that he didn't have the gun in his preferred shooting hand.

Karlene backed out of the way as the two men pointed guns at one another. It was becoming apparent that her new ally was a greater asset than she had first surmised. There was more to Thatcher than corporate counseling.

"Mine's bigger than yours." Mr. Brogan's sneer fell short of the mark.

"Mine's quieter. And, it appears that I have the steadier hand. .357 mags get heavy quickly. You ever notice that? The gun starts to shake." Nodding at his opponent's hand, he added, "Like now."

Mr. Brogan glanced at his trembling hand. He brought up his other hand to steady it. It shook even more.

"Strange how that happens." Thatcher paused long enough to allow the big man to think about his shaking hands.

"Shut up," he groaned.

"The damn thing just gets heavier."

Karlene watched silently.

"Shut up," Brogan whined.

"Could have put you down three different times, Mr. Brogan."

"Not without having your head blown off." It was a feeble attempt at bravado.

"Mr. Brogan," Karlene interjected, "the hammer's not back."

His eyes shot toward his revolver. "Shit."

"The moment that hammer moves, Mr. Thatcher is going to shoot you."

"Shit."

Mundanely, she offered, "Toss the gun on the bed and leave."

Turning in her direction, as if startled by her presence, he allowed the weapon to drop to his side: useless dead weight.

Providing a sympathetic shrug of the shoulders, Karlene nodded toward the bed.

Without looking he gingerly tossed the chrome revolver to the bed and stepped backward toward the door with his eyes downcast. A moment later he was out of the room.

"Any more surprises?" she asked, as she closed the door securely behind the down-and-out assailant.

"That's it for me. You?"

Straightening the strap on her Vera Wang, she replied, "No more surprises."

Simultaneously converging at the foot of the bed, they sat down.

"So, that undercover gig wasn't that far off after all?"

"I was more into the surveillance gig." He set the gun on the bed behind him.

"CIA?"

"FBI."

Karlene stood up and meticulously straightened her dress before glancing down at Thatcher. "I can't very well sleep in this, so here's the plan. After I come out of the bathroom, you go into the bathroom, then I get into bed."

He watched as Karlene stepped away, and replied, "Works for me."

Moments later she bolted from the bathroom, snatched the gun from the bed, aptly extracted the clip from the bottom of the hand grip, and inspected it. "Eight." she murmured.

"You mean, you just now checked the clip?"

Giving Thatcher no time to phrase the next question, she slapped the clip back into place with the palm of her hand and announced, "We need to get far away from here."

"You said no more surprises."

"So, I forgot one."

Thatcher waited for her to continue.

"The limo. It's electronically monitored."

It seemed reasonable to Thatcher, and he wondered why he had not considered it earlier.

"It's an absolute wonder we haven't been tracked down by now." Her voice faded. "Call a cab."

Thatcher didn't question her. If JJ's clowns had found him, certainly a mobster who was looking for his millions of dollars could do the same. He told the taxi dispatcher there would be an extra C-note if the cabbie hauled ass. She was there in six minutes.

"You answer it. I'm driving." Tony Poza pushed in the cigarette lighter as he turned onto Touhy Avenue. An unlit cigarette hung from his mouth.

"Fuck, man." Dean Adams stared at the cellular phone. "He's gonna be pissed." Wiping his nose on a Burger King napkin, he turned away from Tony Poza's dark piercing eyes.

"Pick it up! Tell him we're closing in." Losing his patience, Tony glared at his partner. "Tell him we're real close."

Clutching the phone, Dean asked irresolutely, "How close?"

"You got no fucking sense!" he bellowed. Lighting his Kool menthol, he regained his composure. "Tell him, real close."

Tony Poza imagined the .32 slug suspended in his partner's brain. "Hey. Forget about it." He lowered his voice. "I thought you said you understood that software."

"I got confused, all right. It ain't fucking Mario Brothers." Dean Adams answered on the fifth ring.

"Yes, sir."

"This is Aaron Henderson. You keep the fucking phone in the

trunk, or what?" Aaron's voice was low and raspy. "I expect it to be answered immediately!"

"Yes sir, Mr. Henderson."

Tony Poza moaned. Had he known it was Aaron Henderson, he would have picked it up at once.

"We took a wrong turn," he whined through his postnasal drip, "but we're real close. We're closing in."

Tony stared in disbelief at his associate as he reached for the ashtray. "Fucking idiot," he mumbled as he flicked the ashes.

Dean switched the phone to the other ear, farthest from his partner. "Real close." His jaw went lax. Nervously, he replied, "This is Dean Adams, sir." He was no longer anonymous. "We expect to be on top of them any minute."

"I want Ms. Ferrand unharmed, Mr. Adams." There was a definitive pause. "As for Curtis Lane, shoot him in the balls before you blow his fucking brains out!"

Dean Adams cringed. "Yes, sir."

"In the balls!" It was a maniacal whoop. "No one fucks with me."

Tony blew out a whirling cloud of smoke as Dean secured the phone to the console.

"Christ, you're a fucking idiot." Tony Poza glared at his partner. "That goddamn plate in your skull must be slippin'."

Fumbling with a cigarette, Dean replied hesitantly, "I told him exactly what you told me to."

"You told him we took a wrong turn. Did I say that?"

"I get the jitters. I get confused." Dean wiped his nose with the back of his hand before sticking the cigarette between his lips. "The doc says it's from the brain trauma."

Pulling a handkerchief from his coat pocket, Tony flung it in the direction of his partner. "All right, forget about it. How pissed off is he?"

"Real fuckin' pissed. He wants us to shoot Curtis in the balls." He wiped his nose on the handkerchief. "That ain't right, man!" Lighting his Lucky Strike, he looked toward Tony for affirmation.

Tony took the cigarette from his mouth. "Lane should have left that bitch alone." His tone was conclusive without sympathy.

"Screwin' around with Mr. Henderson's bitch." He shook his head emphatically. "Dumb fuck deserves whatever he gets. Just forget about it."

Tony Poza had no reservations popping a wayward colleague when the order was given. Especially when it would certainly bring about his ascension to the rank of Mob soldier.

"It still ain't right!" Dean looked toward the side window. "I seen the fuckin' cunt do her cock tease..."

"Fuck that!" Tony took a drag on his cigarette. "Curtis Lane would blow your jewels away without a second thought."

Staring into the whirl of passing lights, Dean Adams' cerebral cortex began misfiring; electrical impulses ricocheted uselessly inside his skull. He grabbed his head as if he meant to rip it from his shoulders. His chest heaved as he screamed.

Tony Poza looked at his associate in wild dismay as he coughed up a plume of smoke.

Suddenly, Adams thrust his hands against the dash. "It's her!"

"Where?" Tony slammed on the brakes.

"Over there." Shaking his head violently, he yelled, "Getting into a cab!" Fumbling with the seat harness, he whispered to the demons in his head, "Time to kill."

Poza turned the car abruptly into the opposing lanc avoiding an oncoming car by inches. "Are you fucking sure?" Displeased about placing his leased Chevy into harm's way, he turned and glared at Dean Adams.

"We're fuckin' sure! Right over there." Dean Adams pointed. "Right fuckin' there." Throwing himself back into the seat, he struggled to unsnap his holster. The oversized revolver tumbled into his lap. "Time to kill," he whispered as he pinned the gun against his thigh.

"I know this isn't a very dramatic getaway," he said as he opened the back door of the yellow taxi, "but, it's timely."

With the aluminum case clutched to her chest, Karlene got into the backseat and slid all the way over behind the driver. Thatcher tossed in his duffel bag.

"Sorry," he murmured as it tumbled against her. He slipped in quickly.

The cabbie watched from her rearview mirror and asked the question of the moment, "Where to?"

"Squealing tires," Thatcher said ominously as he pulled the door shut.

"Yeah," the cabbie drawled, "we get a lot of that in the city."

For the first time he looked at the large woman tucked snugly behind the wheel. He was taken aback by the Hawaiian shirt that was spread over her like a brilliant floral canopy. "You know, you look a little like..." He was cut short.

"Yeah, yeah. 'California Dreamin'' and all that crap. I don't sing, I don't even hum, and if you, in any way, refer to me as you know who, I'll smack you alongside the head." As she began to back out, she repeated her question, "Where to?"

At that moment, a dark-colored sedan sped into the far end of the parking lot from the Touhy Avenue entrance.

Thatcher announced, "It's time to go!"

As the sedan came to a halt, Thatcher saw a thin wraith-like figure fly out from the passenger's side brandishing a large handgun.

"Shiiiiiit!" Mama Cass shifted into reverse. "Duck Sweetie, I gotta see where I'm going." The yellow taxi sped backward towards the opposite exit.

Thatcher watched the gunman get back into the sedan. A big thump and the sound of the rear bumper scraping pavement announced Lincoln Avenue.

"North! First right!"

The large woman eyed the young woman in the strapless evening dress. "I hope you got a plan, Sweetie."

Karlene looked at Thatcher. "I do."

His curious expression was enough.

"In the limo trunk," she said.

Thatcher held the .32 semi-automatic in the palm of his hand. Mr. Brogan's unloaded revolver, wiped clean of prints, was in the trash canister in the motel hallway. He reconsidered briefly whether parting with the big revolver was a good idea. The fire power in his right hand was accurate, but it would do little to impede a pursuing car. Common sense told him the odds were not in his favor. He took a deep breath and exhaled. “Let’s do it.”

Thatcher felt for the limousine key in his pocket as the taxi swept around the first right. Karlene, still clutching the case, tumbled into him. Under different circumstances the collision, he thought, would have been one of those Grace Kelly, Cary Grant moments.

Pushing herself upright, Karlene moved back to her side of the taxi and gave the cabbie the rest of the directions. Thatcher kept watch for the dark sedan in the rear window. Mama Cass drove like a bat out of a flaming belfry. It seemed she was enjoying herself.

“Right here!” Karlene called out.

Slamming on the brakes, Mama Cass watched as her cab skidded past the alley. Calmly, she shifted into reverse and backed up.

“Two blocks.”

Flooring it, she asked cautiously, “What’s two blocks?”

“Black limo, you can’t miss it.”

Thatcher interjected, “Could you use an extra grand?”

“Sweetie,” she said as she cruised down the poorly lit alley, “I can always use an extra grand. You think these Hawaiian shirts come cheap?”

The back of stores lined the right side of the alley and a vacant warehouse rose three stories high on the left.

Reaching over the front seat, Thatcher laid down a hundred dollar bill. “I’ve got nine more.” Waving the bouquet of C-notes in his other hand, he asked, “Deal?”

“Oh, yeah. It’s a deal.”

“Drop us at the limo, and get the hell out. Circle back around and wait at a far distance.” He glanced at Karlene, then back at the cabbie. “When it’s over come get us.” Suddenly, his tone had become artificially optimistic. It escaped no one.

Mama Cass spotted the limo a hundred yards ahead. “I see it.” Her tone took on a nervous maternal edge. “I can lose these nimrods.”

"No! As planned," Karlene was absolute.

"We end it here."

The cab skidded to a stop behind the limousine. Karlene, case in hand, got out quickly. Thatcher followed. They reached the trunk as headlights appeared from the direction they had just come.

"Let's go." Karlene tapped excitedly on Thatcher's shoulder as she set the case down on the pavement.

Mama Cass, having been a victim of highway crime one too many times, decided during a split second of insanity to stand by her fares, to hold her ground, to take a bite out of crime. "This is fucking crazy," she murmured as she pushed in her favorite cassette. Watching her two passengers huddled at the rear of the limo, she began singing along with Johnny Mathis, "Chances are..." and parked the cab.

Thatcher inserted the key into the lock smoothly. Karlene watched the headlights approaching. He flung open the trunk and reached into the wheel well. His hand frantically searched in the dark trunk.

"It must have slid around."

"Keep looking." She was surprisingly calm.

"Keep looking," he repeated quietly to himself. "Got it!"

He struggled to unwrap it from the heavy plastic.

"Hurry."

Tossing the plastic into the trunk, he heard a thud on the trunk floor. Before he could recover the clip, Karlene snatched the submachine gun from his hand.

"Are you sure?" Quickly realizing there was no time to discuss the matter, he reached frantically for the clip.

"The clip?" She was cool.

Thatcher placed the clip in Karlene's outstretched hand. She slammed it into place as the headlights sped toward them. With amazing calmness, Karlene said, "Get down."

He moved to the passenger side of the cab and noticed Mama Cass wriggling herself as low into her seat as her ponderous body would allow. He pulled the small handgun from the back of his pants and leaned against the top of the yellow taxi. Taking aim on the dark sedan, he heard Johnny Mathis sing out something about the chances being very good. Thatcher hoped he was right.

Karlene stepped into the alley and backed up toward the front of the limousine. She stood her ground, holding the weapon out of sight in her right hand as the sedan approached.

Six

HIS CHEST POUNDING, DEAN THRUST THE .44 MAGNUM OUT the side window, waving the small cannon in gangster-style fashion. "She's mine!"

Tony stared straight ahead. "We ain't supposed to whack the bitch!" He was certain the metal plate had slipped for good.

The the ringing returned; flashes of light distorted his vision. Pulling the trigger, Dean Adams imagined the bullet exploding her chest wide open.

Tony watched in horror as Adams took aim once more. Pumping the brakes, he reached for his holstered .38. "Adams! You're a dead man!"

Dean pulled the trigger one more time. The explosion reverberated in the car as Poza pulled out his gun. Taking aim at the massive scar on Dean's temple, he hoped the .38 would penetrate the metal plate. The flash of the Uzi was the last thing he saw.

As the second bullet whistled past her head, she swung the small submachine gun around and held tightly with both hands. She carefully squeezed the trigger. The Uzi responded with the cyclic rate of 950 rounds per minute. With the Uzi jolting in her hands, she imagined rising above the net with a perfect spike.

The first few rounds went into the grill. A moment later she saw the windshield disintegrate. The sedan swerved toward her, out of control. Karlene leapt onto the hood of the limousine. Seconds later, as she slid off on the other side, the sedan sideswiped the limo and careened into a row of dumpsters across the alley several yards beyond. Match point.

Without taking her eyes from the wrecked sedan, she straightened her dress, and walked back to the cab. Clutching the weapon tightly with both hands, she called for Thatcher.

He hurried toward her.

Touching her arm, he asked, "You okay?"

Breathing deeply, she said, "I'm okay." Karlene glanced his way for the first time.

Thatcher looked toward the wrecked sedan. "Let's get out of here," he urged.

"I've got to know," her eyes flashed at him, "who they are."

"Does it matter?"

Steadfast, she said, "Yes, it matters."

Taking the safety off, Thatcher held the .32 firmly in his shooting hand and carried it straight-armed beside his right hip. Staying close beside Karlene, he moved quickly and cautiously toward the wrecked car. She held the Uzi with both hands aimed in the direction of the car. Thatcher noticed her hands trembling; he readied himself.

The driver was slumped forward, the right side of his head rested peacefully against the steering wheel. A dark, bloody divot was where his left eye had once been. The passenger wasn't in sight.

Anxiously, she whispered. "The other one?"

Thatcher sensed her panic.

She glanced quickly toward Thatcher. "Where is he?"

As they stood inches away from the left front fender, he whispered, "We're about to find out."

Stepping away to give himself more room to move, he realized he had never before felt so vulnerable, or so responsible for another person. He scanned the immediate area for any movement.

Swiftly Karlene leveled the Uzi toward the unmistakable sound of metal scraping metal.

"Get down," Thatcher directed.

Holding the Uzi firmly in her right hand, steadied by her left, Karlene stood her ground. "I'm going to finish it."

Unwavering, every muscle aching with anticipation, he waited, holding the gun motionless at his side. He had been in this situation only one other time in his life, but he was one of three, and he was not the lead. With his gun drawn Thatcher had felt certain that he would not have to pull the trigger. He had been correct: no shots were fired and the suspect was secured. It wouldn't be that way this time. Tonight he would have to pull the trigger.

More scraping and the banging of metal against the car gave way to a figure clumsily rising from behind the sedan. Staggering backward, a bleeding and dazed Dean Adams attempted to swing his large chrome revolver in their direction.

Karlene squeezed the trigger. The weapon clicked harmlessly.

"Empty?" A maniacal smile swept across Dean Adams' face. "It ain't fuckin' Mario Brothers!" he yelped as he tried to steady himself before pulling the trigger.

The Smith & Wesson resounded one more time. The .44 slug shattered the rear window of the Lumina and ripped through the front seat and the lifeless body of his one-time cohort before embedding itself somewhere in the engine compartment.

With the .32 still at his side, Thatcher watched as the injured man reeled backwards away from the sedan.

Karlene said coldly, "Shoot him."

Regaining his balance, and with the revolver dangling at his side, Dean Adams glared hideously at the young woman in the black evening dress. Shouting, "Die cunt!" he began raising the revolver one more time.

It sounded like a big balloon popping. Dean Adams dropped to his knees. His gun fell to the asphalt as he groped at the small hole in his chest.

Thatcher moved toward her, as the man folded in half and fell to the pavement. He placed his hand on her shoulder and he whispered, "It's over. We need to leave."

Karlene turned in his direction. Her expression was vacuous; she began to tremble only slightly.

"You should have called Eddie Greshem for this!" Aaron Henderson was irate. "I can't reach Poza! And, who the fuck is Adams?"

"Tony Poza is a good man." Stout switched the receiver to the other ear. "I'll look into this." David Stout wasn't pleased with the outcome so far. First Curtis Lane, and now he had lost contact with Tony Poza.

"I want you to get personally involved, and take care of this fucking mess!" Aaron took a few seconds to poise himself. "I want the limo, and its passenger, and its contents back here by sunrise. As for Curtis Lane, he'll be retired, if he isn't already."

David Stout knew he was being purposely upstaged in front of The Affiliation with the contract on his soldier, Curtis Lane. "I understand, Mr. Henderson."

"I'm glad that you do."

The line went dead. David Stout set the receiver down. He would have no part in an unsanctioned hit on Curtis Lane; there were higher bosses to answer to than Aaron Henderson.

Sirens rose above the distant traffic noises as Thatcher nudged Karlene toward the taxi. Mama Cass rolled down her window and rested her bulbous arm on the door.

"So. Bonnie and Clyde, shall we get the hell out of here?"

As if snapping out of a trance, Karlene suddenly rushed to the rear of the limo. Thatcher kept his stride. She picked up the case, turned to her accomplice and stated the obvious. “It’s time to go.”

As her passengers clamored into the backseat, Mama Cass twisted around cumbersomely and asked, “Which way from here?”

“Evanston,” Karlene said softly. Turning toward Thatcher, she clarified, “I have a place to go: a place from my other life, a long time ago.”

“Got an address, Sweetie?” Turning back around, she ejected Johnny Mathis from the tape deck.

“No, just a street. Get us to Evanston, Oakton Avenue.”

“I’ll get you there.” Just before shifting into drive, she asked, “By the way, are we done playing with guns?”

“For now,” she replied succinctly.

Thatcher looked toward Karlene as he set the .32 on the seat between them. Her expression, stolid and fierce, expressed an emerging rage. As she set the Uzi on the floor between her feet, Thatcher sensed she was no longer trying to escape, but rather was declaring war.

Karlene turned to Thatcher, “It’ll be safe there. She’s an old friend from before I became entangled with Aaron Henderson.” Pausing for a moment, she considered her next words carefully. “Tomorrow, what are you going to do?”

He remembered what he had said only hours before, about getting the hell out of here, however, now he was unsure. It didn’t seem as simple as that anymore.

Karlene turned away. Without divulging her motive, she needed to persuade Thatcher to stay with her to the end. He had demonstrated admirable skills that could help save her life, and make her very rich. She knew she shouldn’t have any expectations. However, at this point, it seemed to her they weren’t quite even. She had provided him an avenue of escape from the biker bar, and then rescued him from Mr. Brogan. He had merely put down one of two gangsters from Aaron’s first barrage. Nonetheless, asking more of him was asking him to lay his life on the line again. Tomorrow she would have to think of a way to persuade him.

"My bike will be at Wrigley Field tomorrow morning." Despite his display of confidence, he was far from certain that was true.

Sensing an opportunity to instill a reasonable doubt, she asked soberly, "Do you know that for sure?"

With both hands, he rubbed his face and abruptly turned toward Karlene. "At ten-thirty Flame and Gretta will be there."

"Will they?" She continued her ploy.

Catching Karlene's less than subtle dubiety, he assured her they would be there. Yet, he couldn't help considering the possibilities. What if Flame and Gretta were questioned by the Storm Riders? It was obvious they had been with him. What if they were detained? What if they simply lied?

He rubbed the bridge of his nose. "They'll be there."

"Don't take the chance." Karlene forced a smile as her confidence increased. Why couldn't he see it as simply as she did? Why shouldn't he stay with her, at least for awhile longer? It made all the sense in the world. "I'll buy you a new motorcycle."

His timid smile was fleeting. "I like the one I have."

"If you still have it," she retorted, with more coercion than she had planned.

Attempting to repeal her previous statement, she added with an air of pensiveness, "I mean, you never know."

The taxi traveled north on Western Avenue, which changed into Asbury upon entering Evanston. Shortly after, Mama Cass turned west onto Oakton. Passing over the North Shore Channel bridge, she pulled off to the side of the street. From the rearview mirror she saw the young woman's vacant stare.

"Sweetie, we're on Oakton. North Channel Bridge."

Karlene quickly snapped to. "North Channel, we're in Skokie."

"Could be, I don't get up this way much."

"We need to turn around." As the taxi began to move, she said, "Wait."

Thatcher, having been lost in his own thoughts, turned toward her. "What is it?"

Reaching to the floor, she picked up the Uzi and placed it on the seat beside the pistol. "Throw 'em in the channel."

Thatcher released his seat belt, picked up the weapons, and before getting out of the car, he stated for the record, "I hate guns."

Gretta slept soundly on her stomach as Flame lay awake and stared at the ceiling. She wondered where Thatcher was; there had been no answer at his motel room an hour earlier. She expected as much. He probably stopped there just long enough to pick up his gear.

The sound of early morning traffic, along with the oscillating fan in front of the opened window, kept her awake. She rolled off the bed to turn it off, but instead walked into the living room and sat down in her comfortable chair. Watching her lava lamp in the darkness, she recited an Indian prayer that her great-grandmother had taught her as a child. It was a prayer for bountiful harvest. Broadly translated, Flame used it to wish someone good luck.

Fifteen minutes and several turns later Mama Cass pulled her yellow taxi into an alley off a side street that was named after a dead president. She stopped behind an old two-story Victorian house.

"It's been so long," Karlene said as the cab pulled slowly into the short driveway.

Turning off the engine, the cabbie glanced over to Thatcher. "I'll stay until you give me the high sign."

He nodded, and wondered what a high sign was in this circumstance. He'd make one up.

Karlene slowly opened the door. Before getting out of the taxi she said nervously to Thatcher, "Wait here." She held her eyes on him momentarily. "I came here to get away." It was a wistful thought spoken out loud.

As he watched the svelte woman in the black evening dress walk toward the house, Thatcher recalled the incredible scene an hour earlier, when she stood undaunted in a dark alley facing down a mobster's henchmen with a submachine gun. He was now certain that fear, when pushed to its limits, could retrieve courage from the antediluvian depths of the human spirit. Or, on the other hand, it can leave one totally screwed.

Thatcher watched as Karlene waited on the back steps. When a yellow porch light flashed on, he jumped. He continued watching as the door cracked open. A round dark face appeared. Thatcher moved quickly from the car as two heavy arms reached out and pulled Karlene inside. Uncertain of what to do, he ran up the walkway, then stopped short when he heard boisterous laughter.

"Karlie, look at you! Dressed to kill."

"I am, aren't I?"

"You are indeed, girlie."

Thatcher walked to the foot of the steps. He shoved his hands into his jeans pockets, and felt himself smile.

As Karlene embraced her old friend, she once again felt the kindred spirit that she had truly shared with no other. For a brief moment all was right with the world.

"What brings you to my door in the middle of the night?" The old woman's expression confessed concern as she released her embrace.

"Lilly, I'm in a little trouble. I need a place to stay until morning."

"Karlie, you have a place right here." The voice, discerning and gentle, gave Karlene comfort.

Thatcher listened.

"I have a friend with me." She didn't have to wait for Lilly's acceptance.

Without hesitation, the old woman said, "You bring 'em right in, Karlie girl."

Karlene wasn't surprised to see Thatcher waiting just outside. "It's okay. Come in," she said.

Thatcher pulled open the screen door and stepped inside. A regal black face greeted him without disguising any misgivings. With a thoughtful motion, Lilly Robinson swiped a hand over her steel gray hair that was pulled tight against her head.

Karlene pulled him closer. "Lilly, this is Thatcher."

Her dark eyes became two tiny slits as she examined him. "Karlie, he's got the looks of a hoodlum."

Karlene smirked. "It's just a costume. We were at a party as *Lady and the Tramp.*"

With less suspicion, she said, "I can see that." Turning back to Karlene, she said, "You go ahead and send that cabbie away."

Karlene glanced at Thatcher and gasped. "Oh, the case."

"I'll get it," he said.

"Mr. Thatcher."

Karlene touched Lilly's arm. "It's just Thatcher."

Lilly readjusted her housecoat and snugged the belt around her copious middle. "Just Thatcher," contriving a fleeting scowl, "you go pay that cabbie."

Lilly paused for a moment as she waited for Thatcher to leave. "Now, Karlie," she began as the door banged behind him, "what's this trouble?"

Karlene returned a sheepish grin.

"Karlie girl. When you going to learn? You always had too many young men after you."

Karlene gave an innocent grimace.

With a worrisome expression, the old woman advised, "Karlie. You need to listen to Lil now and again." Placing her hands on her hips, she squinted omnisciently. "She's been around."

Karlene was thankful that her old friend didn't consider the absence of nearly ten years as a fault, but rather as an unintentional hiatus.

Thatcher walked back to the taxi where Mama Cass was waiting for the high sign. He reached into his pocket and pulled out the remaining hundred dollar bills he had promised.

This was, no doubt, the high sign she wanted to see.

Karlene and Lilly were talking at the kitchen table when Thatcher returned. Thatcher carried the aluminum case under one arm and his duffel bag in the other.

Lilly turned in his direction. "Take it upstairs and find a room. Any one, none of them are used much anymore."

"Lilly, you're a sweetheart." Karlene moved closer and kissed her on the cheek. Lilly smiled briefly and slowly rose from her chair.

"Now, you all go on, and find yourselves a place to sleep."

Karlene guided Thatcher up the open stairway: the banister displayed decades of wear from generations of weary hands. The walls, papered so many times, presented the texture of crinkled aluminum. The upstairs hallway was narrow, two abreast would rub shoulders against the pale lilac walls.

Karlene opened the door to the second bedroom. "I've slept here often." She turned on the light, stepped inside, and looked toward the ceiling. Several seconds passed before she said, "Above the bed," she pointed toward the ceiling, "you can see the constellation Pegasus in the cracks." Recognizing Thatcher's amusement, she smiled. "I was into constellations when I was a kid. I used to go to the planetarium whenever I could." Karlene took another step. "I used to dream of..." Embarrassed, she fell silent as she walked to the bed. "I always slept well here," she said quietly.

"Dream of what?" Moving farther into the room, he set down his duffel bag; the aluminum case remained in his other hand.

Looking past him, she said, "It's just a dream I used to have when I slept here. This was my safe place." Her eyes met his. "I came here when things weren't going so well."

His expression coaxed her on.

"Pegasus," she began, "would swoop into my dreams and carry me away from whatever it was that might hurt me."

Thatcher smiled. "Maybe you should sleep here tonight."

"The bed in the other room is really small; you wouldn't fit." Karlene moved closer, and in a silky tone whispered, "And this one isn't big enough for two."

Purposefully, he said nothing.

Karlene stepped back. "I'm going to go with you in the morning." She searched his eyes for permission and moved her hand to touch him, then stopped. "I need to see that you get off okay."

"It's too risky." He considered reaching for her hand, to hold it for just a moment as he explained that there was no reason for her to come with him.

"I'm going." Her tone was resolute. "Then I'll charter a private flight out of here."

Choosing not to argue, Thatcher simply held the case out to her. Karlene took it to the closet and slid it into the narrow cubicle.

"Sleep tight," she said as she slipped out of the room.

Karlene was right, there was no room for two in the small single bed. There was barely room for one.

Within a half hour, Thatcher fell off into a restless sleep. His conscious thought, colliding with a turbulent dream state, propelled him into a vortex of indistinguishable images. A predominating helpless sense of immobility swept through him like a whirling and chilling wind.

Flame lay awake, staring at the ceiling and listening to the fan humming and Gretta snoring. She couldn't stop thinking about hooking up with Thatcher, maybe traveling to the west coast, maybe spending some time in Mexico. She hadn't been to southern California since 1989. It had been the first road trip with Gretta. They both rode Harley Low Riders: hers, an oil spouting '77, and Gretta's, a silky smooth '88. She smiled as she recalled their misadventures traveling down Highway 1 from San Francisco to San Diego. The most exhilarating calamity occurred in LA, and it only cost them ninety bucks and three days in jail.

Rolling toward Gretta, she caressed her partner's bare backside and traced the outline of the green and gold sea serpent acquired at a beachside parlor just north of Big Sur. It was Flame's favorite.

The thought of tripping out to California without Gretta was unthinkable. The three of them, she thought, would simply have to go together. It became too inspiring to think about. She turned her thoughts to getting Thatcher's bike ready and to Wrigley Field on time.

Seven

He awoke at first sunlight soaked in sweat and craving bubble gum. He lay there for many minutes and stared at the ceiling. Creating abstract images from the cracks, he couldn't find the winged horse. A soft knock on the door startled him. Turning toward the side of the bed where he had dropped his jeans just a few hours before, he snatched them off the floor as the door opened slowly.

"Thatcher," Karlene whispered.

Leaning in the doorway with her arms across her chest, Karlene appeared strangely demure. She wore only a diamond necklace and an extra-large white dress shirt with the sleeves rolled up to her elbows. Thatcher's image of her flying away on the back of Pegasus didn't include the tattered white shirt, yet it seemed suitable.

She smiled. "This is all I could find." Tugging at the long shirttails, her smile digressed into a coquettish smirk. "Lilly's husbands seem only obliged to leave their clothes behind." She looked away as Thatcher got out of bed.

Standing with his back to her, he pulled on his jeans.

Karlene stepped into the room, leaving the door slightly ajar. She came to the foot of the bed and sat down. Folding her hands and placing them in her lap, she waited for him to fasten his jeans.

Sufficiently attired, Thatcher turned to Karlene. "Van Heusen never looked so good."

"Who?"

Thatcher grinned.

"Oh, the shirt," she said as she fastened the button just below her sternum.

She appeared very young to Thatcher, and impulsively he asked.

"Twenty-nine," she answered, "but I feel much older." Standing up, she walked past Thatcher to the window. As she moved the curtain aside to look out, she softly repeated, "Much older."

The morning sunshine exposed the sensual outline of her body beneath the thin cotton fabric. He admired her seemingly guileless sensuality.

Karlene turned and faced him. As she crossed her arms against her chest the motion pulled upwards on the Van Heusen. A shift of her right hip widened the crease between the shirttails. A voyeur's good fortune was Thatcher's cue to look away.

The unveiling of her blonde integrity, Thatcher discerned, was an exposition of her intentions as well.

"After this morning," her voice was soft and yielding, "I guess we go our own way." She began to frown, then forced it away with a timorous smile. "Well, who knows? Maybe we'll run into each other again under better circumstances."

Thatcher decided to end the pretense and walked over to her and took her into his arms. He kissed her soundly on the mouth, encouraging her to kiss him back. After she did, he broke away. "Karlie girl... There just isn't any time."

Karlene smiled sheepishly, and momentarily glanced away. "I overdid it, didn't I?"

Standing inches apart, Thatcher waited for her to look in his direction. "It was pleasant nonetheless."

Unabashed, she ran her fingers through his hair and asked affectionately, "Join me in the shower anyway? There's only enough hot water for one."

"I need a cold shower."

Karlene laughed. "And that, you'll get." Her right hand caressed his left cheek as she walked away.

He heard the sound of the shower through the thin walls of the old house. He resisted. It would only make things more difficult, more complicated, more dangerous. Reason told him he didn't need to get more involved with the young woman in the black, strapless evening dress, even though at that moment she wasn't wearing it. He lay on the bed and thought of the girl who had found solace in the cracks on the ceiling.

Minutes later, Karlene came to his room wrapped in a faded pink towel. Her hair was still tangled, and her feet were wet. She stepped just inside the room. Thatcher sat up on the bed.

Willfully, her eyes held his stare as she took a half step closer.

He remained anchored to the bed, despite the beckoning current pulling at him. Was hers a sincere chagrin, or a continuation of the charade? He didn't want to think about it.

She wrapped her arms about herself, as if there was a sudden draft. "There's towels in the linen closet across from the bathroom."

"Karlene."

Her eyes seemed to looked through him.

"I'm glad you're seeing me off."

Smiling, she stayed a moment longer, then left without a word.

As Karlene had predicted, Thatcher ended up with a cold shower. Shivering, he reminded himself, it was all for the best. He dressed quickly and went down to the kitchen where Karlene, appearing out of place with an apron over her Vera Wang evening dress, was helping Lilly scramble eggs and fry bacon.

He overheard Lilly say, "It doesn't matter what kind of trouble you're in Karlie, a good breakfast isn't going to make it any worse."

"Smells good," said Thatcher, announcing his presence. He stepped toward the neatly set table with the red gingham tablecloth. The entire kitchen embodied the warmth of a Norman Rockwell illustration. It had been decades since he had heard coffee percolating.

"Sit yourself down, Just Thatcher." It was direct, unadorned hospitality. "There's plenty to eat." Glancing toward Karlene, she said, "Karlie dear, flip those hot cakes."

Karlene picked up the metal spatula from the counter and carefully flipped over each pancake on the blackened cast iron griddle, precisely trimming the edges of excess batter.

"How's your appetite?" Lilly asked Thatcher, again without turning from the stove.

Eagerly sitting down at a place setting, Thatcher replied, "Never better."

"I'm glad of that," she replied.

Thatcher was very hungry. He was surprised how his hunger, for the moment, superseded all other senses.

Lilly served him a large helping of eggs and a half dozen strips of bacon. He resisted thinking about the sizzling cholesterol in front of him. Karlene set a plate beside him that was stacked with four large hot cakes heavy with syrup and butter.

Lilly was pleased with his ravenous response.

Karlene joined him, but ate sparingly. She seemed sullen and pensive. He was nearly certain it had nothing to do with his cold shower.

Thatcher ate a second helping of eggs, and two more hot cakes before pushing himself away from the table.

"Lilly," he said, "I haven't had a breakfast like this for longer than I can remember."

"By the way you ate," breaking into a broad grin, she paused briefly, "I believe that to be true."

Back in his room Thatcher rearranged the contents of his duffel bag. He tried to concentrate on getting back on the road again, of riding west, of seeing mountains on the horizon. His thoughts were interrupted when Karlene came into the room. She said nothing and went straight to the closet. He watched as she pulled out the case and opened it. Uncertain of what to say, he said nothing, and returned to packing until he felt a tap on his shoulder.

Karlene held out a stack of thousand dollar bills. "I know, you said that you didn't want anything to do with the money, and I believe that." She paused long enough to study his cool blue eyes and added, "I respect that." She moved the money closer to his hand. "Still, you may need this."

Thatcher felt sincerity in her proposal, as spontaneous and irrational as it may be. "I really have no need for it."

She dropped it into his duffel on top of the blue cap. "Things change." She turned and began walking toward the door. "Are you ready to leave?"

Before zipping his duffel bag closed, he snatched his cap from beneath the small fortune Karlene had just bestowed to him. As he put it on, he said, "Ready."

Aaron Henderson stood motionless in front of the tinted glass panels of his bedroom and stared out over Lake Michigan. His expression was intense. His temples throbbed.

The police report that Stout had faxed to him earlier confirmed that Poza and Adams were dead. Tony Poza had been taken out by a 9mm submachine gun as he sat behind the wheel of his Lumina, and Dean Adams was killed by a single shot to the chest as he stood at the rear of the car. Undoubtedly, it was the Uzi from the trunk. The weapon wasn't found. The entire scenario troubled him.

There was no indication the parcel was confiscated. Of course, that didn't mean a few of Chicago's finest weren't planning an early retirement. He attempted to pacify himself by reasoning that it was better to have the parcel at large, even in the hands of a few rouge cops, rather than locked up somewhere within the Chicago Police Department.

The phone rang. He walked over to the bed and sat down. Lifting the handset to his ear, he snarled, "Yeah."

"Mr. Henderson, it wasn't Curtis." David Stout's voice was clear and direct. "Lane was knifed at some biker joint in Waukegan last night."

"What the fuck was he doing in Waukegan?"

Silence.

"Maybe she asked him to take her there. Maybe she knew about the money. Maybe she's more clever than either one of us thought."

"Maybe she planned this?" Aaron's head throbbed. "Who mentioned anything about money?" Aaron paused. "How do you know it's money?" His voice faded slightly. "I don't even know." He swiped his tongue over his dry lips. "Mr. Revelle only told me half its value would be mine. It could be a fucking salami for all I know."

Hesitating, David Stout wished he had not so eagerly attempted to implicate Karlene. "Curtis called me last night while you were at dinner. He said a parcel was placed in the trunk of the limo." David Stout explained. "I just assumed it was a payment of money."

Aaron rubbed his temples vigorously. "Why didn't he tell me about the parcel!?" He exhaled loudly. "Last night, when I told him to take her back to the penthouse."

"Curtis probably assumed you knew about it."

"Assumed! Fuck!"

"Well, it seems," David Stout cleared his throat, "for what it's worth, she drove off in the limo with the guy who stuck Curtis."

"And the goddamn parcel, whatever it is."

"It was taken from the trunk before the police arrived. That's why I believe she knew about it, and that it is a large sum of money." David Stout sighed heavily.

"Of course, she wouldn't have need for a salami would she?"

Stout heard the line go abruptly dead.

Aaron threw the cordless phone against the wall and walked into the bathroom. He opened the medicine cabinet and reached for the prescription bottle labeled Valium. He emptied three tablets into the palm of his hand and gulped the six milligrams of Diazepam.

Sliding aside the heavy wooden door, he took a moment to inhale the cool, musty scent of the garage. It reminded him of his grandfather's cellar in northern Michigan. The morning sunlight sliced into the garage and revealed a well-used 1978 Bonneville surrounded by a collection of gardening tools hanging on rusted nails against the old, unpainted walls.

Scanning the old Pontiac, he offered, "We could take a cab."

With authority, Karlene said, "This is safer." She touched Thatcher's shoulder from behind. "I don't want any more people involved." As Thatcher turned, she added, "Not this time."

Karlene walked to the driver's side of the Bonneville. As she opened the door she shot a curious look toward her intended passenger, who was still standing where she had left him. "Are you coming?"

Thatcher looked down at the right rear tire. "These tires are cracked and bald."

Pursing her lips, she broke into a subtle fleeting smirk. "Are they flat?"

He shook his head.

"Good." A benevolent scowl urged Thatcher to get in the car.

Lifting his duffel bag a little above his head, he squeezed along the passenger side of the car and slipped precariously past hanging shovels and rakes. Karlene was amused.

"Guess I could've backed out first."

He grimaced as he ducked out of the way of a garden spade, the edge of it caught the bill of his cap. Setting his bag down on the roof, he straightened his cap and assured her, "I'm doing just fine." Then he eased open the creaking door.

She smirked, "Meet you inside."

He watched her slip easily into the front seat. He opened the door as far as it would go. Grabbing his bag from the roof, he stuffed it through the narrow opening and over the top of the front seat into the back.

Finally, sliding in beside her, he said, "See, no problem." He pulled the door shut, and the garden spade fell against the side of the car.

Karlene laughed and turned the ignition. The radio blared a bluesy tune as the engine cranked itself into a rumbling state of congestion.

Thatcher turned toward her and grimaced.

Karlene frowned as she shifted into reverse. The engine stalled. "Don't say it," she warned.

He bit his lower lip.

Shifting back into park, she turned the ignition. The engine started and quickly assumed a steady rumble. "It needs to warm up a bit," she said affectionately while patting the cracked, sunbaked dash.

Sharing a little humor made them both feel more relaxed. Thatcher leaned back into the seat.

"Lilly is more than just an old friend."

"What do you mean?" she asked.

Thatcher fastened his seat belt. "I mean, there must be some kind of a story."

Thatcher had always made it a point to know the people whom he worked with, whom he negotiated for, and whom he was to do battle against. He always looked for an edge. Information was an edge. This time he was simply curious.

Karlene shifted the car into reverse. "It just happened." Backing out into the alley, she studied his expression.

He gently insisted. "How?"

Sensing his sincerity, she gave in. "I wasn't any better at choosing boyfriends when I was seventeen than I am now choosing men." She continued to study Thatcher's expression to see if he was truly intent on listening to her story. She shifted into drive, and went on. "One afternoon I was leaving a shopping mall with this older collegiate all-American kind of guy I was dating at the time. We were arguing." She paused for a moment to check traffic, then pulled out onto the street. "We argued a lot. I finally said something he really didn't like, and he hit me in the face."

"And, Lilly was there."

"And, Lilly was there," Karlene repeated solemnly. "She was walking toward us. I'd started to cry, and my nose was bleeding. He was shouting at me."

She sighed thinking of the moment she first saw Lilly. "She pulled me away, and held onto me real tight. She didn't say a thing." A smile came to her. "She just stared him down, and he backed away like a scared little kid. I remember thinking how odd it must've appeared to other people." Her voice quivered. "But, I didn't care. And, she didn't care that I got blood all over her dress."

Several minutes passed in silence, each left to their own thoughts, each left to plan the day ahead of them, and each to consider being on their own.

Thatcher suggested she drop him off a couple blocks from the stadium. "It'll be safer that way," he assured her.

Turning onto Clark Street, she countered, "What if your friends don't show?"

"They will."

"What if they don't?" she said persistently.

Without a legitimate answer, he turned away.

"Forget it, Thatcher," she said sternly. "Like I said, I'm going to make sure you get on your way safely. I owe you that. And, if they don't show?"

Forcing a smile, he said, "Then, we're together for a while longer."

"Don't look so excited." She imitated a pout. "Hasn't it been incredible?"

His smile came easier.

The home of the Chicago Cubs rose unobtrusively from a quiet neighborhood of stoic two-story brick dwellings. Sports bars with neon signs along Addison Avenue swore their allegiance to beer, baseball, and the Chicago Cubs. It became obvious to Thatcher why the Cubbies had such a devout following of fans — and this year there was Sammy Sosa. It was the humble and unsophisticated origin of the team, and its simple unadorned stadium. It seemed to emulate the virtuous lucidity of the all-American game, even in the era of walkouts, closeouts, and contract disputes.

Turning left onto Addison, they drove alongside the historic ivy-shrouded stadium. Thatcher was impelled to remove his cap, and as an act of tribute, place it across his chest. Karlene laughed.

"What?" he asked, in a mock defensive tone as he reverently placed his cap back on his head.

"Nothing." She laughed harder as he stared quizzically at her. "It was cute," she said through her laughter.

Looking away he searched for his bike along both sides of the street. Thatcher couldn't see it among the parked cars.

Karlene turned left onto Sheffield. Her laughter subsided as she peered hopefully at Thatcher. Halfway down the block he spotted Gretta leaning against her Fat Boy with her arms across her chest. Just beyond her was Flame sitting sidesaddle on the *Wanderer*. He felt his chest pounding.

"They're over there."

"I was under the impression," she began insouciantly, "they were both women."

He grinned and said nothing.

Waiting for Thatcher to say something, she finally turned in his direction. She had an anxious and disheartened smile. "So, this is it?" It was more a declaration than a question.

A sudden, unexpected reticence fell over them as she pulled over to the curb. Too much had happened within a modicum of time. No farewell seemed adequate enough, or seemed complete enough to justify words.

Thatcher unfastened his seat belt and began to open the door. Turning back toward her, he said, "Be careful, Karlie."

She gave him a fleeting smile.

Reaching over the back of the seat, he grabbed his duffel bag. Karlene looked the other way as he got out of the car.

EIGHT

"WHERE'S THE LIMO?" FLAME SLID OFF THE SEAT OF the Fat Boy. "Or, did it turn into that piece of shit at the stroke of midnight?" Peering over the tops of her amber sunglasses, she nodded toward the Bonneville sedan as it pulled away from the curb. "I see the princess is still wearing her jewels, and you still have that raggedy cap."

Thatcher began strapping his duffel bag onto the luggage rack. He had expected a kinder greeting. "It's been a long night," he said without looking up.

"Hey, you ain't pissed that we had to leave you last night, are you?" Her voice took on the tone of the one he had heard over the telephone the afternoon before. "I mean, Gretta did supply you with a nifty set of wheels and a real nice date."

"Yeah, and I thank you for both." He returned the sarcasm. He was suddenly in the mood for sarcasm. He unstrapped the left saddle bag and took out his pair of sunglasses.

"Everything's there. But, there's the matter of payment." Flame stood in front of him with her hands on her hips. Her onerous expression broke into a smile. "Shit, Thatcher, I'm just raggin' on you. Lighten up." She dropped her hands to her sides. "It's on me. We only had time to change the oil and check the fluid levels."

"The carburetor needs tweaking," Gretta added as she walked up beside Flame. She stood with her hands in the back pockets of her tight leather pants. Her lips parted into a sly grin.

Flame nudged her friend with her elbow. "It was Gretta's idea to give you a hard time."

Thatcher put on his sunglasses, then leaning over his duffel bag, he unzipped it and pulled out two portraits of Grover Cleveland from the stack of bills that Karlene had put there. He handed one to each of them.

"I appreciate what you did for me." It was a genuine and generous requital.

"Christ." Flame held it up to the sunlight with both hands. "Is this real?"

Gretta tucked hers into her front pants pocket. "Of course it is." She yanked on Flame's long single braid. "Let's roll."

Suddenly, a dark blue Taurus sedan appeared at the corner and accelerated toward them. Stunned, Thatcher sensed every muscle in his body tighten. It felt as though he could leap over Wrigley Field, and he was willing to give it a try at the first sound of gunfire.

The sedan squealed to a stop several yards away and blocked the street in front of them. The driver quickly swung open his door. In one hand he held a semi-automatic, in the other a detective's shield.

"Chicago PD! Hands where I can see them. Please, biker folks, no quick moves." Sarcasm was at a premium this morning.

Pushing her wraparound shades to the top of her head, Gretta was the last to raise her hands. "Well, if it isn't Joe Fucking Friday."

The other detective positioned himself on the passenger side of the car leaning against the roof with a shotgun aimed at Thatcher.

"Everyone stay very still," said the driver of the car. "Smits, call this in. I have control here."

Smits followed his partner's order and pulled away the shotgun and slid back into the car.

Thatcher was relieved to have the large stainless steel barrel no longer pointed in his direction.

"Blondie, you and your friend move closer together and keep your hands up." Detective Pasco lived for these rare moments of controlled confrontation when the only gun was his own. He was going to have some fun.

Flame moved closer to Gretta. "Shit, what is this?"

"We've been set up by the Stormies," Gretta said with disgust.

Flame glanced at her articulate accomplice. "What did you tell Brute last night while you were whacking him off?"

Gretta slid her shades back in place as the detective began to approach them. The 9mm was pointed in Thatcher's direction.

"Mister, you just stay very still." Pasco's indolent drawl was becoming irritating. "Ladies, don't be whispering. I might think you're planning an escape," he cocked his head to one side. "Of course, you don't have much of a chance."

Gretta, ignoring the detective's drivel, spoke from the corner of her mouth. "I didn't tell him shit." She kept looking at the approaching cop. Then suddenly she stomped her boot on the pavement. "Fuck, I did say something about catching an early gig at Wrigley."

Flame, clenching her jaw, looked up at Gretta.

Gretta glanced down. "What?" She could feel Flame's glare.

Within moments the detective stood only a few feet away. "Ladies, ladies, you're much too talkative."

He was really beginning to irritate Gretta.

Pasco continued. "Have you been caballing?"

Gretta shifted her weight to one side and placed her hands on her hips. She looked quizzically into the craggy, acne-scared face of Detective Pasco. She looked over to Flame. "Have we caballed lately?"

"I've kept my pants on." With her hands still raised, Flame watched the detective closely as she spoke. "You're the one caballing and blabbing." Flame was still angry.

Ignoring her partner, Gretta looked at the detective. "Since when," she directed the question to Detective Pasco, "is a fuckin' hand job caballing?"

Grinning broadly, Pasco slowly shook his head. "That, I wouldn't know, but the two of you will have plenty of time to discuss it downtown."

The annoying cockiness of the city cop prompted a familiar melody in Thatcher's head.

The cop turned to his male suspect. "What's with you?"

With his hands well above his head, Thatcher shrugged his shoulders and heard Mellencamp's lament in his head. "They like to get you in a compromising position. They like to get you there and smile in your face..." He had nothing to add except the chorus. "I fight authority. Authority always wins."

Pasco looked peculiarly at his captive before sneering, "You're right." Smiling slyly, he proclaimed, "I win."

Flame modified her acerbic tone. "What are you taking us in on?"

He terminated his grin immediately. "Questioning in regards to a homicide last night in Waukegan."

"This is a fuckin'..." Gretta felt a sudden jab to her ribs.

"We don't have anything to say," Flame glanced at Gretta. "Do we?"

Gretta glared at Flame. "A fuckin' joke, I was gonna say."

Thatcher noticed the neighbors were beginning to take an interest, and traffic was slowing down at either end of the block. From the corner of his eye he saw a car turn onto the street from the direction that the blue Taurus had come. It moved slowly, to within twenty yards of the police car, then accelerated, squealing its cracked, treadless tires.

As Detective Pasco turned his head in the direction of the speeding car, Flame caught him in the groin with her pointed boot. It was a familiar sight. Gretta swiftly disarmed him and caught him across the jaw with a right hook as the old Bonneville crashed into the squad car. Officer Smits was knocked cold after his head slammed against the dash and bounced into the windshield.

Gretta dropped the clip to the pavement and tossed the gun several yards behind her. Flame had the Fat Boy revving as Gretta jumped on the back.

"Remember whose bike this is!" shouted Gretta.

"Just fucking hang on!" Flame leaned the big bike to the right and made a U-turn in front of the detective's car.

As the Fat Boy sped past Thatcher, Gretta yelled out, "You're on your own for now!" She was grinning with her fist in the air.

The detective lying in the street was beginning to stir. Thatcher stepped past him toward the old Pontiac hissing and spewing coolant from its radiator. Karlene pushed opened the door, and emerged quickly to join Thatcher. He grasped her hand firmly and pulled her swiftly toward the *Wanderer* parked a few yards away.

"I hope you can really ride that thing," she said dubiously.

"I'm getting better every day."

"How long have you been riding?" Her eyes darted back and forth between him and the custom Harley cruiser.

"Couple days." Thatcher heard her sigh.

The Fat Boy started without hesitation. Pushing down the passenger foot pegs, he watched as a large bystander wearing an XXL Cubs t-shirt began rushing toward them.

"We have company." Thatcher threw his leg over the seat. "Can you manage in that dress?"

"No problem," she said as she hoisted the dress to near her waist.

He felt Karlene's hand on his shoulder, then her body nudged against his. "Hold on," he said as he twisted the bill of the cap to the back, catcher's style.

For no apparent reason the large Cubbies fan stopped cold a few feet away. His expression, curiously enough, was pleasant astonishment.

Thatcher leaned the bike into a U-turn. Unexpectedly, a dozen or more male baseball fans standing along the curb began cheering and waving their caps.

After straightening the bike, he yelled back to Karlene. "What the hell was that all about?"

She leaned forward and whispered above the rumble of the engine. "I guess they noticed I'm not wearing any panties."

"She's not wearing any panties," he said to himself as he shifted into third gear. Imagining her pouty smile, he called back to her, "Let's not try to attract too much more attention."

Thatcher turned right onto Addison, then right again onto Clark. While stopped at the Irving Park Road intersection, Karlene leaned forward and said, “It’s a little chilly back here.”

Glancing back, he saw her bare thighs snuggled up against his hips.

“There’s some stores along Montrose, thought I might go shopping.” She paused for a moment. “You do have something smaller than a grand?”

He nodded.

“Take a left just past the cemetery.”

He nodded once more, thinking it would be wise to have a less conspicuous passenger.

Thatcher pulled into a shopping center on Montrose Avenue and parked alongside a delivery truck to conceal the bike from the street. Karlene waved to a well-dressed elderly gentleman standing a few yards away as she dismounted. Thatcher watched as the gentleman’s slack jaw quivered into a disconcerted smile.

Thatcher turned the front wheel to the left, he kicked out the stand, and leaned the bike into it. Surveying the parking lot, he said, “Don’t take too long. And buy a pair of sunglasses.”

Karlene tipped her head forward, shook it from side to side, then tossed her head back before running her fingers through her hair. “I need to braid my hair.” Looking toward Thatcher, she asked, “Money?”

Thatcher took several fifty dollar bills from his wallet. Playfully, she snatched the bills out of his hand.

“Be back soon,” she said as she turned away.

Watching her walk lithely away, Thatcher found it hard to imagine she had, only hours before, stood stalwart in a back alley facing down Henderson’s hitmen.

Karlene returned twenty minutes later dressed in tight Calvin Klein jeans, and a matching denim jacket with a simple white cotton blouse beneath. Her hair was pulled back into a French braid. Her black leather boots were adorned with silver studs. A pair of sleek reflective sunglasses and the diamond necklace finished the look.

As she reached Thatcher, she pirouetted with her arms above her head. She came to a graceful stop. "What do you think?" Placing both hands on her hips, she added, "And, I have panties."

Thatcher tried to conceal his enjoyment. "What took you so long?"

"I'll let you know," she scowled, "I bought this complete outfit from head to toe in one single shop in less time than I usually take ordering dinner at Ambria." She took a breath. "And," cocking her head to one side, "I braided my hair. What do you think?"

Smiling, he suddenly felt less like a fugitive and more like a teenager on a date.

"He likes it," she whispered.

The sensation of frivolous normality was a welcome reprieve, if only for a moment. Thatcher stepped over to the bike and swung his right leg over the seat. Sitting down, he nudged the kickstand upward, and began backing the bike out of the parking space.

Karlene watched with interest. "Put it in reverse."

Straining, he slowly moved the custom Harley backward. Had he noticed the slight downward slope to the parking space, he would have backed in. Unfortunately, his attention had been on numerous other details.

"No reverse?" It was serious inquiry.

"Not on real motorcycles," he grunted. "Give me a push!"

Straddling the front fender and leaning against the handlebars, she began pushing. "We have to do this every time?"

"Hopefully not," he groaned.

"Why didn't you back in!" It was a genuine revelation.

"Next time."

As the bike came free of the parking space, she stepped away. Thatcher turned the ignition and pressed the starter. The engine rumbled to life.

Karlene effortlessly settled onto the passenger's seat. Snuggling close to Thatcher, she whispered, "We have some cash to pick up."

They rode west on Montrose and then north on Western Avenue. Just the day before he had taken the same route to the Harley-Davidson dealership: a brief layover before riding west. Things change, he thought.

The one thing that didn't seem to change, however, was Karlene's ability to leave and to reappear: twice at O'Hare, once on the dark highway, and now this morning at Wrigley. It was becoming a pattern, one Thatcher was certain would continue until this matter with Henderson was ended. With her arms tightly embracing him, the wind in his face, and most of his faculties intact, he conceded he was in for the duration. She would be happy to know that, then again, perhaps, she had known that from the beginning.

A couple blocks from Lilly's house, Thatcher pulled into a 7-Eleven and stopped beside a public phone. Shutting off the engine, he said, "It's polite to call first."

Leaning against him, she asked why.

"The police must have traced the license plate of the Pontiac by now."

Karlene's face turned pale. "God, I never thought of that."

The young and beautiful assassin from the night before was now simply young and beautiful. Thatcher wondered if she truly comprehended what she had done. He wondered what she might do when that realization eventually found her.

She dismounted. Thatcher leaned the bike into the kickstand. Struggling to reach into his pocket, he eventually pulled out some change. Karlene plucked two quarters from his open palm, and walked slowly over to the phone. She inserted the coins and pushed the numbers; all those years and still she remembered the number. It rang five times.

"Come on Lilly." She whispered to herself. It rang twice more. Karlene glanced anxiously at Thatcher.

"Hell-o." Lilly's voice was buoyant.

"It's Karlie."

"Are you all right?"

"Yes, I'm fine." She turned toward Thatcher. His eyes were fixed upon hers. "I got into a little accident, sort of." She rolled her eyes at Thatcher.

"Karlie, you smacked into a police car the way I hear it."

"I didn't know that at the time." She paused. "The police were there?" Karlene looked for Thatcher's reaction.

He shoved his hands into his jeans pockets and leaned against the side of the building beside the phone. To Karlene, he appeared indifferent.

"I just scooted them out the door when the phone started ringing. Thought it might be you."

"Lilly."

"Oh. I told them my car must have been stolen by some hoodlums. Told them I keep it in the garage, but the door doesn't lock, and sometimes I'm forgetful and leave the keys in it."

"Did they believe you."

"Got a lot of practice talking to the police with my second husband. That man couldn't stay out of trouble to save his soul." Lilly paused only briefly. "Now Karlie, I'm not one to be asking questions, but I know if you're in trouble it isn't all your doing, and I know you wouldn't be smacking into a police car unless you had a damn good reason."

"Lilly, it's a long story."

"Child, I know that it is!" There was another pause. "You can tell it to me later."

"I will." She lowered her voice to a whisper as if someone were trying to listen. "Lilly, I need to pick up some things."

"Karlie, I have a feeling maybe you should stay away for awhile. I have a feeling they'll be watching."

"Lilly?"

"Your things will be safe with me."

Karlene hung up and looked at Thatcher. "Lilly thinks we should stay away for awhile." Her eyes had lost their exuberance.

Thatcher recognized her uneasiness. Pulling off his sunglasses, he said, "She's right."

NINE

DAVID STOUT WAITED PATIENTLY FOR HIS EMPLOYER TO arrive. He sat at a corner table in the main dining room of the Ritz-Carlton. He had just returned from his sister's house in Skokie with something that he knew Aaron would be pleased to see.

Upon Aaron's entrance to the dining room, David Stout began straightening his tie. He smoothed the edges of his mustache as self-assurance spread over him. His previous investigation of Karlene Ferrand had now proven to be of immense value.

Aaron seated himself. "What do you have?"

"The police have no ID on the guy who stuck Curtis. They think he's a transient."

Aaron loosened his tie. "I could care less about who whacked Curtis. I want to find Karlene Ferrand."

"I think she's with the guy who stuck Curtis. I think it's someone she's known for a long time. I think they planned this together."

He pressed his hands against his face, and slowly pulled them downward, eventually resting his chin on his fingertips as if in prayer. "The old friend at the airport," he mumbled.

David Stout fed the fire. "Curtis mentioned that scene to me. It sounded like they were really close old friends." He watched Aaron's face contort into rage.

The concept that a woman, a woman he held dominion over, would attempt to destroy him, infuriated Aaron. He had not had this kind of anger since he severed his family ties decades ago. "I want some background on Karlene." His eyes narrowed. "What do you have?"

David Stout dabbed the sweat from his brow with his handkerchief. "She's from Skokie."

"I want to know about her family. I want some leverage. I want to know where she might be going."

"Her parents are dead."

Aaron was irate. "Well, they won't prove to be much help, will they?"

A young waiter approached. Aaron ordered a scotch and water before the young man had a chance to speak. David Stout ordered the same.

Without looking up, Aaron said to the waiter, "Leave us." The young man nodded and left quickly.

Looking directly at Stout, he snarled, "Tell me something I can use."

David Stout was saving his best information for last. "Her name isn't Ferrand." Pausing long enough to pull Aaron to the edge of his chair, Stout continued, "It's Swanson. And, she has a twin sister."

Growling abjectly, "I don't have time to waste." Aaron stared at his associate. "Confirmation! Do you have it?"

David Stout reached into his inside jacket pocket and brought out a folded page from a book. Sensing Aaron's anticipation, he said in a low voice, "My niece is about Karlene's age."

He pressed his lips together tightly."Get to the goddamn point."

"They went to the same fucking high school in Skokie." Stout handed Aaron the folded page. With eagerness, he said, "Look for yourself."

Aaron unfolded the page that had been torn out of a high school yearbook.

David Stout pointed toward the bottom of the page. "Karlene and Theresa Swanson."

An almost imperceptible smile swept across Aaron's face. "That's interesting."

"They're identical."

"Find her!"

Karlene stood beside the pay phone looking at Thatcher. "You look rather calm." A fragment of a smile attempted to cloak her uneasiness. "That means you know what we're supposed to do next."

Thatcher stepped away from the building, his hands still stuck into his jeans pockets. "Get out of town." The cliche was delivered with more triteness than he had intended.

"No!" Her abrupt conviction settled rapidly into a lament. "I'm not leaving without the money."

Pulling his hands from his pockets, Thatcher sensed any eloquent rhetoric would be wasted cerebral energy. "The bad guys," he began, "are trying to shoot us, and the good guys want to lock us up." He stepped over to his bike, leaned against it, and reiterated. "We need to get out of town."

Karlene removed her sunglasses and moved to within inches of Thatcher. "No." Her stare was defiant, and her voice was fierce. Unblinking, her eyes studied Thatcher's resolve. "Thatcher, I'm not leaving without it."

As inflexible as she portrayed, he was certain she understood the implausibility of retrieving the money, at least at this time. "The money can wait."

"I stay with the money."

Despite last night's poignant explanation about why she had to take the money, Thatcher still considered the money the sole reason mobsters were trying to kill them. It had not entered his mind that she could possibly keep it. The mere forty-eight grand of mobster loot in his duffel bag made him extremely nervous.

Pulling his bollés to the tip of his nose, he leveled his eyes. Without hesitation, he said, "You stay alone."

Dealing with large figures was certainly nothing new, but it had always been on paper, or computer monitors, never in neatly stacked bills minted in the era of Al Capone.

Outside of the need to operate an occasional vending machine or buy a newspaper, Thatcher found cash relatively obsolete. And now, it was extremely dangerous.

"I stay alone."

Standing face-to-face on the side of the 7-Eleven, they contemplated one another's resolve. As an Evanston City Police cruiser turned into the parking lot, Thatcher calmly removed his sunglasses. Pulling her close, he whispered, "Police," then kissed her hard on the mouth as he watched the robust officer emerge from the vehicle. Evanston's finest glanced once in their direction, then quickly walked to the front door.

Thatcher eased away. "Donut stop."

"I thought we were trying to avoid attention," she replied softly.

"A passionate kiss," feigning actual statistical facts, he explained, "deters intrusion from others."

"Is that true?"

Manufacturing a stolid expression, he answered, "It is."

"I think..." Pressing against him, she delicately removed his cap, and whispered, "I think then, we should be extra careful." And, with an unexpected desire, Karlene kissed him back.

He continued to hold her as he watched the rotund officer roll out of the store with two coffees in hand and a box of Little Debbie's under his chin. Evanston was in good hands.

Breaking away from his embrace, Karlene placed the cap back on his head. "You would leave me?" she cooed. "Alone?"

Thatcher watched the Little Debbie's fall to the asphalt as the patrolman attempted to open the car door. He held his silence.

"You would." It was a practical realization.

Thatcher slid his sunglasses into place and twisted his cap into riding position. "It's time to go, Karlie girl."

It was the toe of her left Reebok cross-trainer catching the edge of the molded plastic Reebok Step that sent her tumbling forward to the floor. The image of the nineteen-year-old, know-it-all, sales clerk reassuring her that, "Cross-trainers are the way to go," flashed before her. Gingerly rolling to her side, Eve Jensen sat up and wiped the sweat from her forehead.

At that moment the telephone rang. Reaching for her stereo remote, she pressed stop, and derailed Tom Scott and the LA Express in the middle of "Midtown Rush."

By the seventh ring she found the cordless phone beneath the *Tribune* comics. "Jensen," she answered.

"Wonderful day." The voice on the other end was dangerously jocose. "The kind of day one should share with a friend." And verbose.

Restraining her smile, she replied, "I have plans to do just that. Sam and I are going on a picnic." She glanced over to the fat Siamese cat spread over the back of the couch.

"My apologies to Sam."

"Kenyon," she moaned. "I was taking this Saturday off; you know, like real people."

The gentle baritone turned serious. "Something is stirring in the Aaron Henderson case."

"Give me an hour."

"Forty-five minutes."

Riding west on Dempster Avenue, they passed the city limits of Morton Grove. With each mile placed between them and the Windy City, Thatcher felt just a little more at ease, even without an exact destination. Distance, for now, was good enough.

Karlene vigorously tapped Thatcher's shoulder. He downshifted, turned onto a residential street, and pulled over to the curb.

"I need to know." She subdued her distress. "Do you have any idea where you're going?"

"West. Out of town."

Karlene dismounted. Thatcher killed the engine.

She stood on the sidewalk with her hands on her hips. "We need a destination." She sauntered back and forth beside the motorcycle.

Thatcher took the opportunity to remove the hardened remains of a bumblebee from his sunglasses. He had just spit on the lens of his bollés when Karlene asked, "What are you doing?"

"Cleaning my eyewear."

She watched with curiosity as he wiped the lens with a portion of his t-shirt. "Looks like you're going to need more spit."

Pausing, Thatcher inspected the smeared lens. "You're right."

Karlene looked the other way as he dribbled more spittle onto the lens. She waited for him to finish the procedure before continuing.

"I know where to go," she reported.

Thatcher slipped on his sunglasses and leaned against the handlebars. He waited several seconds before asking where.

She looked at him and removed her sunglasses.

"You want those cleaned?" he asked.

"No." Karlene nearly concealed her smile.

"So, where we going?"

"Michigan."

"The U.P.?"

Karlene nodded. "My sister lives in Crystal Falls."

Thatcher pushed off from the handlebars. "We have a destination." Crystal Falls made as much sense as any other location, and for the moment, it was far away from Chicago.

Traveling toward a destination, Thatcher had to admit, made much more sense than traveling in a direction. Leaning forward and shouting, Karlene directed him toward Route 21. The traffic was surprisingly light, and Thatcher needed to remind himself to stay within the speed limit. It would be a disconsolate end to their adventure to be picked up because of a traffic violation.

Outside of Libertyville they stopped at Auntie May's for lunch.

Before going inside, Thatcher tucked his cap into his duffel bag concealing the stack of bills.

Auntie May's was bustling with the brunchtime crowd of blue-collar patrons and senior citizens. Karlene was lucky to grab the corner booth from where both the front door and the rear exit were visible. The front and side parking lots were in view from the large adjacent tinted windows. Once again, she was thinking like a person on the run.

The *Wanderer* was backed conveniently into the first space in the side lot just outside their window. It was also in plain sight of every vehicle turning in off the highway.

After ordering sandwiches and coffee, the two fugitives stared incredulously at one another. Karlene rested her chin in her right palm.

"You know," she began, "it wasn't that long ago, I was just another strand denizen." Laughing quietly, Karlene rolled her eyes. "It was a game my sister and I played. We'd go to the dictionary and come up with weird names for things, places, people, each other. After flunking out of UCLA, she came up with strand denizen."

"Beach dweller."

Karlene's eyes widened. "You're good, but actually Theresa's version was more like beach bum." She took a sip of water. "I played volleyball."

"Pro circuit after college."

"You're real good."

"I'm good at puzzles."

Karlene smiled, "I had to make a living somehow. You going to tell me how you figured all that out?"

Thatcher waited for the waitress in pink to set down the coffee. "I was trained in the art of intelligent guessing."

"Something else. You always appear to be telling the truth."

"That's another artistic ability."

"Manipulation of the truth," she whispered slowly.

Thatcher smiled. "Lying."

Karlene stirred two packets of sugar into her coffee. "Thatcher." Glancing toward the entrance, she murmured, "You worried?"

"Cautious." He lifted his coffee cup and paused, "It's good to be cautious."

Eating greasy BLTs, they kept an eye on the front door. Neither touched the watery coleslaw. Thatcher looked toward his bike and the duffel bag strapped on the back. Forty-eight thousand dollars sat beneath his Cubbies cap. He grinned with a curious blend of chagrin and amusement.

"What is it?" Restraining alarm, she glanced about the restaurant. "What is it?"

"Fifty grand." He directed her with a quick nod toward his bike. "It's just sitting out there on the back of the bike."

"Real cautious, you are." Karlene smirked.

Thatcher shrugged, took a drink of coffee, and said, "About some things."

Flippantly raising her eyebrows, she inquired, "Not money?"

"Earned income only."

Karlene picked up her coffee. Leaving it suspended halfway, her eyes abruptly darted to the side. "Thatcher."

His peripheral vision picked up the patrolman standing a head taller than the elderly couple at the cash register.

She drew her eyes back to Thatcher and set down her cup. "What do you think?"

"Time to leave," he said as he observed another patrolman strolling along the sidewalk toward the *Wanderer*. "His partner." He motioned in the direction of the officer walking past the window behind her.

Karlene didn't bother to look.

"Think you can distract them," he whispered. "I'll head out the back."

She leaned forward. "Is this necessary?"

Watching the patrolman stop to look at his bike, "Yes it is," he said.

Karlene glanced out the window at the officer standing near the motorcycle. "I just remembered," sliding from the booth, she said coyly, "my car wouldn't start. Perhaps that officer over there could help."

"Didn't you park it way over there?" He nodded toward the farthest end of the lot.

Picking up her glass of water, she said, "I think I did." She took a sip and set the glass down. "I'll meet you in back," she said decisively.

Reaching for his wallet, he concurred, "In back."

Thatcher laid a fifty on the table as he watched Karlene approach the officer. Casually getting out of the booth, he glanced one more time at the patrolman on the sidewalk, hoping it was admiration and not an APB that lured the patrolman to the customized Harley-Davidson.

Once outside, he stepped quickly to the corner of the building and took a deep breath. He slowly peered around the corner.

He saw the patrolman standing a few feet away from the *Wanderer* looking downward and facing the other direction. It appeared he had just finished writing down the plate number.

That, of course, would only lead the police to Phillip's rusted-out double-wide. He smirked, imagining Phil's expression as he opened his door to a couple of uniforms. He moved back out of sight. The next move depended upon Karlene. Thatcher held his position.

With the tall officer following close behind, she walked hastily along the sidewalk, searching for a likely vehicle to substantiate her story. Crossing to the far end of the parking lot, she stopped beside a late model Firebird with a crushed right fender. She tried to open the driver's side door.

"Oh, it's locked." She turned toward the officer behind her. "I hope I didn't leave the keys in the car."

The officer stepped closer and peered into the car window. "No, they're not in the ignition."

Portraying a frantic young woman checking her pockets for her car keys, she lamented, "I'm so stupid." Her arms dropping to her sides, she looked up at the patrolman. "I must've left them in the restaurant. I'll be right back." Hurrying toward the front entrance, she glanced back to determine the patrolman was staying with the car.

The other officer intercepted her as she reached the door. "Is there something wrong?" he asked.

"I couldn't get my car to start," she said, "and your partner was going to help me, but I left my keys inside." Karlene took a long exasperated sigh, and pulled open the door. "Oh, sir." Turning back around, she said, "I think your partner wanted to talk with you." She pointed in the direction of the Firebird.

As the young patrolman turned in the direction of his colleague, Karlene entered Auntie May's and rushed through the crowded restaurant toward the back door, dodging a youthful busboy and a runaway two-year-old.

Grasping her forearm as she emerged from the back entrance, Thatcher asked, "You okay?"

"I'm okay."

He let go.

Nervously brushing aside wayward strands of hair, she reported, "They're over on the other side."

Thatcher smiled approvingly. "Let's roll."

Rushing along the side of the restaurant toward the bike, Karlene stumbled and fell against Thatcher.

"Sorry," she murmured as she grabbed onto his arm. "I move better in my bare feet."

They mounted the Harley with precise synchronization. The engine rumbled to life. A moment later the *Wanderer* shot from the parking space and quickly onto the highway heading north. Checking the rearview mirrors, Thatcher saw no patrol car in pursuit. Just the same, he accelerated quickly. Traveling no more than a mile, he turned right, then left, then angled off to the right at a "Y" intersection. Now, surrounded by suburbia, he eased over to the curb beneath the overhanging branches of a maple. Thatcher shut off the engine.

"Now what?" she asked. It was an honest inquiry.

He took a deep breath and exhaled loudly.

Karlene leaned into him. "I was hoping for something a little more definitive." She dismounted, and stood on someone's crab grass.

Thatcher, wishing he had a pack of bubble gum, leaned the bike into the stand and got off.

"Got any gum?"

"No. Got any ideas?"

"We have to assume the plate number has been taken." Thatcher didn't want to take any chances.

If they did pay a visit to Phil and Stella, it was likely they would come across his leather planner left in the pocket of his Armani jacket, and if they happened to run prints, he would be identified via his FBI past.

She pulled off her sunglasses. "Got any ideas?"

"Yeah, I do."

Ten

Eve Jensen met John Kenyon in front of her Hyde Park apartment building in just less than the prescribed forty-five minutes. Her short, dark, curly hair, still wet from the shower, glistened in the afternoon sun. She wore jeans and a pale blue blouse. She carried a small purse with a long narrow strap slung over her shoulder. It held a coin purse, a compact .32 automatic, and her detective's shield.

John Kenyon reached across the front seat of the Crown Victoria and swung open the passenger's side door. "Eve, you look ravishing."

"Flattery won't get you Auntie Gezelda's fruitcake today." Getting into the car and slamming the door, she avoided the robust grin and impish green eyes of her six-foot-three, strawberry blonde, twenty-years-her-senior, partner. "Sam's really pissed at you."

"Tell 'em I'll bring 'em some sockeye salmon next time. He'll get over it."

Leaning forward, she massaged her left knee.

"Exercising again?"

"You should try it sometime. Dropping twenty pounds would do you some good."

Kenyon pulled away from the curb. "Men over fifty should avoid injuries. I read that somewhere."

"Men over fifty should avoid a lot of things." She pulled the seat belt across and fastened it. Turning toward her partner she noticed a Bugs Bunny Band-Aid stuck to his cheek. She pressed her lips tightly together to restrain a smirk. "So. What's up, Doc?"

Running his fingers through his thinning hair, he faced his partner. "Three of Henderson's soldiers ended up dead last night."

"That really breaks me up." Her terseness suited the news. "Any clues?"

"Ballistics have a match." He saw anticipation in his partner's eyes.

"A match." Eve held in her excitement.

"We have enough evidence to bring him in."

Her eyes widened. "Who?"

John Kenyon pulled out his ever-present notepad from his breast pocket. Flipping it open with one hand, he appeared to be scanning his scribbles. "Here it is. Last name Sam. One, Yosemite Sam. Personally, I was disturbed."

"Animated murder." Eve had, over the course of her five-year tenure with her partner, acquired an adroitness for Kenyonesque humor.

"Self-defense!"

Eve pulled down the visor and checked her right contact. "Damn, these new lens are bothering me." Blinking several times, she flipped the visor back in place. "Tell me more, John."

"Henderson lost three. Actually, two. A Dean Adams was just tagging along with Tony Poza."

"I don't know Adams. Small time?"

"Very small, but with big aspirations." John scanned his notes once more. "Curtis Lane was stabbed in a biker bar in Waukegan, and Poza and Adams were shot in a back alley on the north side."

"Do you think they were related?"

Pulling pensively at his chin, he announced, "Absolutely."

"Go on," she said eagerly.

He paused as he turned a corner. "Lane was knifed during a barroom brawl in Waukegan."

"Sounds like a typical Friday night," she added.

"And, you're going to get a kick out of this." He waited for Eve's eyes to light up. "Apparently, the suspect fled in Henderson's limo with Henderson's girlfriend, Karlene Ferrand."

"Kidnapping?" It was a dubious response. "Or outrageous stupidity?"

"Probably the latter, but I'm sure Aaron would like us to believe that he too can be victimized."

"He'd never pay a ransom." She twisted the rearview mirror to check her lens once more. "Not for his own mother." She twisted it back. "Do you think the suspect and the Ferrand woman are connected?"

"I don't have any reason to believe either way right now." Kenyon stopped the car at a red light, readjusted the rearview mirror, and pushed in the lighter.

"Why do you still do that?"

"What?"

"Push in the lighter?"

"Reflex, I guess."

"Kenyon, you haven't smoked for years."

"Twelve years, ten months, and thirteen days."

Eve began laughing. "You're describing a love affair."

"I am?"

"So why do you think the killings on the north side are related?"

"The limo was found across the alley from where Poza and Adams were found dead." He readjusted the rearview mirror one more time. "Poza was shot with a 9mm. Probably an Uzi by the number of holes he was sporting. He was still behind the wheel. Adams was stretched out in the alley. He caught a single .32 in the chest."

The cigarette lighter popped.

"I still can't figure why Henderson would enlist Dean Adams." John Kenyon gingerly ran his fingers through his hair. "Am I still losing hair?" Glancing at his partner, he enlisted his "don't tell me the truth" expression.

"Not a bit, John. That Rogaine was a good investment."

The light turned green; he accelerated through the intersection. "In any case," he looked disheartened at the several strands of hair in his hand, "chasing down Henderson's limo turned out to be more than Poza and Adams bargained for."

Thatcher steered into the Harley-Davidson dealership on Belvidere Road. He parked alongside a blue Electra Glide.

"I know there must be a reason why we're here."

"We need helmets if we're going to leave the state."

Karlene stepped to the ground with her left foot and held onto Thatcher's shoulder while she pulled her other leg high across the strapped down duffel bag.

"I don't need a helmet."

"In most states it's the law."

She shrugged her shoulders. "All right."

Inside, no one eagerly greeted them. Two men in their early fifties leaned against the parts and accessories counter in the back, munching pastries and drinking coffee from stained and chipped mugs. They sported black t-shirts proclaiming allegiance to Harley-Davidson and social expatriation. Their suspenders strained to keep the waists of their Wrangler jeans nestled beneath their prized rotundity. They appeared to be in the midst of an abstruse conversation concerning parts and accessories, and didn't immediately notice the potential customers.

Thatcher and Karlene walked the narrow aisle between two rows of late-model Harleys. Thatcher stopped abruptly as he came upon a displaced Triumph Bonneville, circa 1969, immaculately restored, parked at the end of one row.

Karlene pulled on his arm. "The helmets are over there." Pointing exuberantly in the direction of the apparel department, she glanced down at the purple and white two-tone Triumph. "That's cute."

Thatcher knelt beside it and rested his hand on the seat as he inspected its svelte simplicity more closely.

"The lady says it's cute." A booming voice resounded across the showroom. "It's hers for eight grand."

Looking up, he saw the two aging motorcycle afficionados eyeing Karlene appreciatively as she wandered toward the helmets.

"The lady doesn't ride up front," Thatcher said as he rose to his feet. "Likes it in the rear." Immediately, he wished he had chosen his words more carefully.

Exchanging approving nods, the two bikers grinned as they glanced over at Karlene.

"It's a classic," he said in an attempt to draw their attention back to motorcycles.

"British," said the taller one with the ponytail. It bordered on disdain. "All original."

Thatcher nodded in agreement as he turned to join Karlene, who was diligently examining the headgear.

"This one doesn't look too uncomfortable," she said to Thatcher as he approached. Karlene picked up a small half-helmet and carefully eased it over her French braid. "Does it fit?"

"Strap it on." Thatcher watched as Karlene fumbled with the chin strap. "Here." He pulled the end through and snugged it tight. "Shake your head a little."

She followed his directions.

"How does it feel?"

"Okay, I guess."

"Too tight, too loose?"

She pursed her lips and placed her hands on her hips. "It's a little hard to tell."

"Let's see."

Interrupted by the deep raspy voice, she turned around.

The taller one with the silver ponytail approached. He placed his large hands on either side of the helmet. "Turn your head."

Not having anything else to do, she obliged.

"It's a good fit." He stepped back and examined her attire. "You need leather."

Karlene glanced at Thatcher. He nodded in agreement. Unstrapping the helmet, she said, "I like the jacket with the fringe."

"Who owns the Electra Glide out front?" Thatcher interjected.

The large man with the silver ponytail nodded toward his compadre leaning against the counter. "Earl, there."

Thatcher squinted one eye toward Karlene. "Fringe?"

Smirking, she carefully removed her new helmet.

The large man standing beside her grinned. "I'll fix you up." He smelled a big sale evolving.

Thatcher walked over to Earl. Had he been a foot shorter and a foot thinner he might have passed for Danny DeVito's brother. Thatcher decided on a colloquial greeting. "How ya doin'?"

Earl nodded as he shoved the remainder of his glazed apple fritter into his mouth. He then folded his arms across his chest. Thatcher couldn't help reading Earl's XXXL t-shirt, "Where legends roam" it explained. Earl appeared to roam mostly in the direction of Dunkin' Donuts.

"Your friend mentioned you own the Electra Glide out front."

"Yeah, I heard you askin'."

"What year?"

"Ninety-three." Earl stepped away from the counter. "Where you from?"

"Detroit."

"Used to work at the Ford plant in Ypsilanti back in the seventies." Earl stated it with utmost importance, as he smoothed the sugary glaze into his graying beard.

Thatcher folded his arms across his chest and leaned against the counter. He sensed that it was a standard pose for conversation in the establishment. "I've been thinkin' about tradin' my Fat Boy in on an Electra Glide."

Earl smirked. "Tired of a sore ass?" Earl turned to look out the window. "What fucking color is that?"

Thatcher just shrugged his shoulders. Then he nodded in Karlene's direction. "She's wantin' a better ride." He watched Earl's eyes shift in Karlene's direction. "Consider tradin'?" Thatcher had lowered his voice.

Earl's eyes slowly shifted back toward Thatcher. "For the right price."

Thatcher said, "Of course."

"Make me an offer," Earl responded arrogantly.

"Even trade." It was more than a generous offer.

"Fat Boy's a nice machine, but if I wanted one, I wouldn't be ridin' what I got."

"How much?" Thatcher asked in a lower voice.

"I just did some customizing last month..."

Thatcher had noticed a few tawdry accessories implying Earl's civil discontent. "We've been through a lot together." He spoke as if the motorcycle was a faithful palomino, "I'm fucking attached," he asserted.

Thatcher, resigned to getting the raw end, asked, "How much?"

"The Fat Boy and another two grand."

"Fifteen hundred." Thatcher countered. "And a trial period. Say, a week. We meet back here next Monday." If he was still alive a week from now, he would like the opportunity to retrieve his bike.

"After riding that Softail for a week," Earl glanced one more time at the Fat Boy, "I might want my Glide back."

It wasn't difficult to discern that Earl was bullshitting. Thatcher knew he had just given Earl a deal that would provide barroom bragging rights for quite some time.

"And, I might want my Fat Boy," Thatcher added.

Earl was silent, then broke into a broad tawny grin. "That fifteen hundred is nonrefundable."

The telephone rang. Thatcher glanced at Earl, expecting him to pick it up.

"Nonrefundable," Earl repeated as the telephone rang again.

Thatcher smiled to himself. Earl was being an opportunist. "Half now; the other half later."

Another ring and Thatcher watched as Earl scratched himself.

"Deal, seven-fifty secured: nonrefundable," Earl confirmed.

With the fourth ring of the phone, Earl turned toward the back room. "Jolene! Answer the damn phone!"

From the back room in a low, raspy voice, "Kiss my ass!"

Thatcher smiled as Earl glared in the direction of Jolene's voice. The phone was silent.

Earl stuck out his hand. "What the fuck. I'll enjoy ridin' a Softail for awhile."

He shook Earl Hoeskema's hand. "Let's do it."

"I want cash, no checks." Earl was assuring Thatcher that he was no fool.

"No problem, Earl."

Karlene met Thatcher outside. She was wearing a fringed jacket abundant with chrome snaps, conchos, and studs. Her aviator's glasses were pulled down to the tip of her nose. With her hands on her hips she threw back her head and gave Thatcher a sassy pout before asking, "What do you think?"

Had the executive editors of *Cosmopolitan* and *Easyriders* coupled in the boardroom, Karlene would have been the consummated cover girl.

"It's you, Karlie."

Karlene presented Thatcher with a new leatherbound half-helmet with the Harley-Davidson winged shield on the front. "Got you a present. It matches mine. What do you think?"

"I like it," he lied.

She watched as he began switching his belongings from the saddlebags to the trunk of the Electra Glide. "What are you doing? Or, should I ask, why?"

He continued his task. "A different bike. A less conspicuous bike."

"You traded that guy in there?"

"Yes, I did," he confessed as he closed the trunk lid.

"I like your's better."

"Me too."

Thatcher unstrapped the duffel bag from the *Wanderer* and placed it on the luggage rack atop the Electra Glide's trunk. After securing it in place, he stepped back from the bike, surveyed it critically, and lamented, "Only for a week."

She walked to the other side of the bike, and commented, "Backseat."

✦

After leaving the Ritz-Carlton, Aaron Henderson returned home. He was exhilarated from the information David Stout had given him. It was just a matter of time, he thought, before he would have the pleasure of meeting Karlene's sister. And, of course, the money would then be recovered in short order.

Walking over to the bar, he poured himself a scotch and water. The phone rang as he turned from the bar.

David Stout's voice was loud and clear. "Crystal Falls! Theresa Swanson teaches school in Crystal Falls, Michigan."

He took a sip from his drink. "Where is it?" he said calmly.

"Not far from the Wisconsin border."

Aaron set his glass down on the bar. "Get Duran to fly Simon and Greshem up there, and bring her back."

"Why Greshem? He's not reliable. Personally, I think he's crazy." David Stout was not fond of Eddie Greshem for the simple reason that killing was Eddie's favorite pastime, which made David Stout nervous.

"Oh, I'm sure he is. And if there's trouble, I want him there." Aaron, although his assassin days were essentially over, still found pleasure in the kill, and found a remote kinship with Eddie Greshem.

Stout recognized the resolution in Aaron's voice and decided not to argue. "Do you think there might be trouble? I mean, all they have to do is pick up a schoolteacher."

"Lane, Poza, and that other moron are dead. I'm not taking any chances." Aaron Henderson maintained his matter-of-fact tone. "The Affiliation will not look kindly upon one who gets ripped off by one of his own, and a pathetic two-bit biker."

"The biker's name is Thatcher," David Stout said. He had picked that up from his police informant just minutes ago.

Picking up his glass, Aaron made a supercilious salute. "It's my hope that Mr. Thatcher remains in Miss Swanson's company long enough so that I can thank him for whacking Mr. Lane, just before I blow his pathetic brains out."

David Stout smoothed the edges of his mustache and made a silent wish that the biker, Thatcher, would disappear. He didn't want unknown elements in the formula, particularly one who had been an FBI agent. That information he would keep to himself.

John Kenyon placed the receiver down and looked across his desk toward his partner. "We have an ID on the suspect who fled in Henderson's limo."

Jensen pulled her chair closer.

"It's an interesting report." He took his half-glasses from his shirt pocket and slipped them on. "One of the northern precincts was given an anonymous tip early this morning that the suspect, the guy who drove off in the limo from the Leather & Lace, was going to show at Wrigley Field this morning."

"Wait a minute. The what?" Jensen leaned forward and placed her elbows on the desk.

"The what, what?"

"Leather and what?"

"Lace. Leather & Lace," he said, as if it was an exposition at Disney World. "It's a biker bar in Waukegan."

"Guess I don't get out much." She settled her chin into her cupped hands.

"Well, I'm sure it isn't your kind of place."

"I'm sure it isn't."

He picked up a copy of the report, scanned it for a moment, and continued as he drummed a pencil against a notepad. "The caller stated the suspect was going to be at Wrigley Field around ten o'clock this morning to get his ride back."

"Ride back where?"

Peering over the top of his reading glasses, he said nothing.

"Motorcycle," she paused thoughtfully, "is a ride."

"Yeah." He tore off a piece of paper from the bottom of his notepad, scribbled something on it, and handed it to her.

"What's this?"

"It's Bubba's number."

She looked dubiously at her partner.

"He's a friend of mine, owns a Harley. Call him up for a ride on his ride. You need some diversity."

She crumpled the paper and playfully tossed it back. He shrugged his shoulders.

"John, will you just tell me the rest?"

"You keep interrupting me."

Eve frowned.

"All right, all right. Two women on Harleys show up at Wrigley Field, on Sheffield Avenue." He glanced at his report and he continued, "That was a few minutes before ten. A little while later an old green Pontiac pulls up to them. A guy dressed in jeans and a t-shirt gets out. He says good-bye to the driver, a young woman matching the description of Henderson's girlfriend, and then he walks over to the two women on the motorcycles. The young woman in the car drives off."

"I sense you're building toward something, something you think is funny."

Ignoring his partner's interjection, Kenyon continued.

"The suspect talks to the biker ladies. He passes them each a single bill. Then Pasco and Smits decide to break up the little party..."

Raising her head from her cupped hands, Jensen said dryly, "You mean Starsky and Hutch?"

Kenyon slid his glasses to the tip of his nose. "Starsky and Hutch." It was a reflective pause. "Now that was a team."

Eve broke into laughter. "Go on. The funny part is coming. Go on."

With a straight face he pushed his glasses back to the bridge of his nose and glanced at his notes. "Pasco confronts the suspect, and his would-be accomplices while Smits backs him up with the shotgun."

Holding back her grin, she settles her chin back to her cupped hands.

"The young woman in the old Pontiac returns." A reticent smile betrayed his feigned formality. "Rams their car and knocks Smits unconscious."

Jensen swiped her fingers across her lips to suppress her widening smile.

"He's fine by the way. A minor concussion."

Anticipation overwhelmed her. "And Pasco?" she said briskly.

With a broad smile, John Kenyon replied, "He gets drop-kicked in the family jewels by one of the women."

Unable to restrain her laughter, she glanced around to see most everyone looking at her. With her attention returned to Kenyon, she completed the report. "And everyone gets away?"

Kenyon nodded.

Attempting to become serious, Jensen inquired, "They were able to ID the suspect?"

Kenyon pushed his chair away from his desk and stretched his arms over his head. "Not exactly." Cracking his knuckles, he brought his arms back down. "They did take down the description of the bike that the suspect and the young woman, who, by the way, was wearing a black evening dress, rode away on."

"Not tremendously helpful without plate numbers."

"Did I mention," John Kenyon's eyes peered exuberantly above his glasses, "that the young woman was wearing nothing underneath her formal wear?"

"No, you didn't." She strived for a disapproving glance. "Shall I ask how you know that? And what possible relevancy that might have?"

"According to eyewitness accounts..."

"You sound like an anchor for *Hard Copy.*"

Kenyon grinned and continued. "When the young woman lifted her dress to get onto the motorcycle, a would-be citizen hero who apparently had intended to thwart their escape, was momentarily distracted."

"How do you get these vivid accounts?"

"Did you know *Vivid* is an adult movie label?"

"I did not know that." She went on quickly. "As I was saying, without plate numbers it's not tremendously helpful."

Kenyon pulled himself nearer the desk. "Well, that may be true." Taking off his glasses, he laid them beside his stapler. "However, a while later the same bike was seen at Auntie May's, a restaurant outside of Libertyville."

"And the suspects?" She momentarily lifted her chin from the cradle of her hands.

"A woman matching the earlier description, now dressed in jeans and a blouse, and presumably undergarments, was observed close up."

Grinning, she inquired, "How did they get away this time?" Settling her chin once more into her hands and leaning forward on the desk, Eve couldn't let go of the image of Pasco catching it in the jewels. Jimmy Pasco had come onto her more than once. She considered him a jerk of prodigious proportions.

"It seems she put on the helpless female routine, and the two patrolmen bought it. While they were conferring about the young woman's situation, she slipped away with her associate."

Frowning, Eve Jensen emitted a low frequency, "Hmmmmm."

"We have a plate number." Kenyon watched his partner's frown lift. "The motorcycle belonged to Phillip Morris of East Dundee. He sold it for cash to someone he didn't know."

"And that leads us where?" She knew her partner had more; he was just playing it for all he could get.

"Well, we got lucky."

Kenyon's smiling Irish eyes evoked from Jensen a semblance of a smirk. "Tell me, John. How lucky?"

"It seems the buyer of Phillip's chromed-out Hog..." He paused just long enough to encourage a response.

"By deductive reasoning," she slipped her hands away from her face and sat back into the chair, "I'm making the wild assumption that 'hog' is a pseudonym for a motorcycle."

"For a Harley-Davidson."

Folding her arms across her chest, "Please, delay this conversation one more time," she said solemnly, "to tell me the story behind this particular name anomaly."

"Another time, maybe."

Jensen rolled her eyes.

"The buyer, as I was saying, left behind a rather expensive jacket and vest, evidently deciding it was nonessential for riding a Harley."

"Go on," Jensen encouraged.

"The inside jacket pocket held a daily planner."

"With ID."

"Not exactly."

"Where are you going with this?"

"They lifted prints from the planner, and from the seller's truck where the suspect had ridden." Kenyon held his pause long enough to make his partner grimace impatiently.

"John, you do this just to irritate me. Do we have a match?"

"The prints belong to a Thatcher of Birmingham, Michigan."

Furling her forehead, she quipped, "This guy has no more to his name?"

A jaunty grin came over him. "The Biker Formally Known as..."

"Why do I ask?" she groaned. "Anything else?"

"Actually, something quite interesting. He's an ex-FBI agent. That's why his prints were on file."

"An ex-Fed. What do you make of that?"

"Nothing at the moment, other than it's interesting, and he's not a typical fugitive."

"How about the car that rammed Smits?"

"What you really want to know," Kenyon grimaced, "is the name of the woman who drop-kicked Pasco."

Smiling, she replied, "I think a commendation is in order."

"Oooh, that's cold." Then, referring back to the report, he added, "Green Pontiac belongs to a Lilly Robinson of Evanston. Seems it was stolen."

ELEVEN

THATCHER AND KARLENE HAD RIDDEN NORTH ON I-94 TO Milwaukee. The Electra Glide plowed smoothly along the highway, like a cast iron bathtub on two wheels. With fringe rustling in the wind, Karlene had allowed her mind to wander generously, mile after mile, as she resided comfortably in the "backseat."

Connecting with I-43 just north of Milwaukee, they rode through to Sheboygan, where they stopped for gas.

"I need to walk around and stretch my legs." Karlene maneuvered off the rear seat and removed her new helmet. "What time do you think it is?"

"Quarter to five," he said, noticing the clock inside the service station. "Are you hungry?"

"Are you?"

"A little." He took off his helmet.

Karlene looked over toward the vending machines on the side of the building. "How about a Coke and a Snickers?"

"Chips."

"Afraid of sugar?"

"In mega doses," he replied.

Thatcher filled the tank and paid the attendant. He steered the bike over to the vending area and parked it.

Karlene approached with a Snickers and a couple of Cokes.

"No chips," she said as she handed him the Coke.

"Thanks."

She offered him her Snickers Bar. "A bite?"

"Maybe later." He popped open the Coke and took a drink. "Do you think you should call your sister?"

She took a big bite from her candy bar. She held her hand in front of her mouth as she attempted to mumble through the peanuts and caramel.

He was amused. Karlene ate candy like a ravenous eight-year-old.

"I don't think so." Her eyes darted purposefully away from him. "Theresa and I haven't gotten along too well for some time. It might be better to just surprise her." She unzipped her jacket. "I mean, then she won't barricade the doors and windows."

Thatcher slipped his sunglasses into his vest pocket and sat down on a nearby picnic table. "How come you didn't mention this before?" There was a trace of concern and interest in his voice.

"It's no big deal. We just haven't been that close for awhile."

"How long a while?"

"Since high school."

"That's a long awhile."

"Her boyfriends liked me better." Karlene tried to make it sound matter-of-fact.

Obviously there was more to it. Thatcher couldn't help exploring the subject a little further. "You haven't gotten along with your sister since high school because you fought over boys?"

Karlene sat down next to him and smiled sheepishly.

His eagerness to listen prompted Karlene to continue willingly. "There were no fights." She shrugged her shoulders. "They were always attracted to me. My personality, I guess. We're identical. Did I mention that?"

"No, you didn't." Thatcher thought before speaking, however not too carefully. "You couldn't find your own boyfriends?" As soon as his words slipped out he regretted it.

Glaring, she said nothing.

"It was a joke." Failing to recognize that the conversation was over, he went on talking. "After all this time." He was cut off abruptly.

"I'm not." Her voice rose defensively. "She's the one who won't let it go."

Precariously, he had treaded upon sibling rivalry better left alone. Thatcher moved from the picnic table. "It's none of my business," he said with more emphasis than required.

"You're right," she chided. "It's none of your business."

After a quick slug of Coke, he briskly walked over to the Electra Glide. Staring at the air filter cover medallion proclaiming, "Live to ride. Ride to live," he sighed deeply and yearned for the *Wanderer*.

A moment later, Karlene approached. "We should get going if we're going to get there before dark," she said.

Since Sunday was Gretta's last day off from her housekeeping duties at the Radisson for the next six days, she wanted to get an early start on Saturday evening. She sat in a corner booth in an already smoke-filled bar in Lincolnwood. Upon finishing her first beer she lit a Marlboro and inhaled the first draft of smoke with the tenacity of an Electrolux.

Flame was already fifteen minutes late. Gretta ordered her second Bud. She was not known for her patience, nor for her subtlety. As Flame entered the bar Gretta slid out of the booth and yelled. "Where the fuck have you been? I'm on my second piss!" It was only her first, but she wasn't known for her honesty either.

She sauntered toward the restrooms as Flame made her way to the booth. There was a line for the ladies' room. Gretta hated waiting, particularly in a line. She stepped over to the men's room and went in; she was greeted by two regulars.

"Hey, Blondie," the one at the urinal called out as she entered the only stall, "Remember to leave the fucking seat up."

"Remember to zip up your fucking pants," she said as she unbuckled her belt. "We wouldn't want that pathetic peckerhead to expose its shortcomings."

The one at the sink roared with laughter as he wiped his hands on his pant legs. The towel dispenser had not been filled since the Bears won the Super Bowl. In fact, it hung cockeyed on the wall with only one toggle bolt keeping it from crashing to the floor.

Flame was sipping her first beer and slipping a dollar's worth of quarters into the juke when Gretta returned from the men's room. She punched in four Springsteen tunes.

"What's goin' on?" Flame called out as Bruce recalled Mary dancing across the porch as the radio played.

Gretta picked up her Bud longneck, took a long drink, and slid into the booth. "What's goin' on?"

Flame sang along. "Darling you know just what I'm here for..."

Gretta rolled her eyes.

She shrugged her shoulders. "I had to go into the dealership for a few hours this afternoon. Nancy's on a wicked PMS trip this week. Brett doesn't want her behind the counter on a hormonal high."

Gretta nodded in acknowledgment of bad PMS trips. "Hey. I'm sorry about this mornin'." It was a sincere atonement. "I had no idea that fucking idiot would say anything."

"Quit fucking around with idiots." Flame barely held back her grin as she slid in across from her cohort. "Hey, you know how much I like kicking lawmen in the balls."

"How many is that now?" Gretta inquired with sincere interest.

"Do rent-a-cops count?"

Gretta shook her head. "No guns, no points." Taking another long drink from her longneck, she added. "I wonder where Thatcher is."

Her response was quick. "Wisconsin."

Gretta waited for no more than three seconds. "Well."

"He and his date," Flame continued, "dropped in at the dealership in Waukegan. Bought some riding gear and helmets."

"I'm no fucking genius," Gretta had a propensity for unwittingly professing the truth, "but last I heard Waukegan was still in Illinois."

"May I continue?"

Gretta flipped another Marlboro between her lips. “By all fucking means.” The cigarette bobbed up and down.

Flame was constantly amused by her companion’s relentless pursuit of boorish commentary. “They bought helmets.”

“So.”

“So, they’re leaving the state.

“So, they’re leaving the state.” Gretta was getting bored with the conversation.

“And, after Waukegan, what state is a piss stop away?”

“Depends which way we’re goin. And how many beers.”

“North! We’re going fucking north.” Her impatience was emerging.

Gretta swept her fingers thoughtfully through her short bristly hair. “A six-pack might last ’til Racine.”

“And what state would that put you in?”

“A state of piss alert.” Gretta lit her cigarette.

“Jesus Christ, it puts you in Wisconsin.” Taking a quick swig of her beer, she stared at her incredibly obtuse associate.

Gretta exhaled a plume of smoke over her friend’s head. Flame gathered her composure. “He traded his Fat Boy for an Electra Glide.”

For Gretta, that was pertinent information. “No fucking shit!” She snatched the Marlboro from her lips. “That was a real nice ride. Jesus, what was he thinking? A fucking Electra Glide.” She squinted hard, as if a thought would evolve. “How do you hear all this shit?”

“I had to call Waukegan about some parts. I got on the line with Jolene. She started telling me about this guy riding a kick-ass Fat Boy who had this leggy blonde fashion princess tagging along. It wasn’t hard to guess who that might be. I asked if she caught a name, and she said it was some English royalty name. Well anyway, she was referring to Margaret Thatcher.”

Gretta interrupted. “So, that’s the Queenie’s name.” Smoke oozing from her nostrils suggested a moment’s doubt. “Queen Margaret.”

Flame considered explaining, but decided to just let it go. “She was sure the name was Thatcher after I asked.”

Gretta plucked the Marlboro from her lips. "Queen Margaret," she whispered to herself. Leaning forward, resting her elbows on the table, she set her chin into the palm of her hand. Smoke curled upward past her right eye.

"She also picked up our little escapade at Wrigley on the police scanner." Flame shifted in her seat. "Give me a cig."

"I thought you were quitting?" Gretta slid the pack of Marlboros across the table.

Flame leaned over the table as Gretta held out her Zippo. Flame inhaled quickly and blew the smoke directly into Gretta's face. "I am."

"How did she know it was us?" Gretta was intrigued.

Flame began grinning as she inhaled. She held the smoke in her lungs for a few extra seconds before exhaling. "The description."

Gretta smiled broadly.

Flame continued. "Would you be the tattooed Amazon?"

Gretta was pleased.

Eve Jensen was home for less than an hour before the phone rang. She continued stroking Sam under his chin while he sat like a feline Buddha in the living room chair. By the twelfth ring she knew it was Kenyon; only he would allow the phone to ring and ring and ring. She picked it up.

"Jensen."

She cut him off sharply. "It's Saturday evening, the Fourth of July to be exact. I would like to spend it with Sam and an exciting rerun of *Dr. Quinn, Medicine Woman*, if you don't mind." Being direct wasn't going to dissuade John Kenyon in the least.

"Oh, I don't mind at all. It sounds like an exciting evening, just you and Sam and who?" John Kenyon commanded his own remote as he talked, flipping from NASCAR to Bassmaster to *Xena, Warrior Princess.*

"Good, then you don't mind."

It was a nondefinitive retort acknowledging the inevitable; her evening was about to be disrupted. Switching the receiver to the other ear, she waited.

"I mean, I don't mind going to Michigan all by myself." He paused to watch the princess knock the crap out of a well-deserving scoundrel. "You know how I love the north country: the trees, the rivers, the lakes, the wildlife."

Jensen was not about to interrupt. He was on a roll. Instead, she covered the mouthpiece and confided in Sam. "You know, this job really stinks sometimes." She watched her fat Buddha cat roll onto his back and close his eyes.

"Did I mention the fresh air? Eve, have you ever seen a starry, starry night? The aurora borealis? Magnificent. I can't begin to describe the emotional uplift."

Eve knew that he would just keep going. It was time. "Okay!" Glancing down at her fat cat, she said, "John Kenyon, this better be good. Real good."

"Oh, it is." He clicked off the princess just as she slung her metal Frisbee at an evil, lightning-brandishing princess from Hades.

"By all means continue," Eve said with restrained interest.

"There's some more movement in Henderson's camp. His private helicopter took off not too long ago with an unusual destination. Crystal Falls, Michigan."

"What's in Crystal Falls?"

"More aptly, who's in Crystal Falls?"

Jensen raised her voice an extra octave. "Who's in Crystal Falls?"

"I had Lucille in records check into Karlene Ferrand a little further. Real name is Swanson. She has a sister in this quaint little U.P. town just across the Wisconsin border." He paused a moment. "I'm afraid she's going to have some uninvited guests this evening. I want to be there."

Eve Jensen was silent.

"Henderson will do whatever he needs to get his assets and his respect back."

"Assets?"

"Didn't I mention that, Eve?"

"Must have slipped your mind, John. How much assets?"

"The word is millions."

"Cash?"

"Most likely. I don't consider Henderson sophisticated enough to deal in any other commodity. Anyway, he scored big somewhere, and absentmindedly left the goods in the trunk of the limo. At least that's the word on the street."

"How many millions?" Eve Jensen felt her heart racing as a smile swept across her face. She knew that Aaron Henderson was a careful man, but with millions at stake careful men can become careless. Her smile vanished. It can also make them extremely dangerous, she thought.

"After the first couple what's it matter?" Kenyon's enthusiasm was apparent.

"This woman is in real danger."

North of Green Bay, Route 141 ascended into the north woods as the sun descended into the west and cast a soft amber hue across the horizon. It provided a peacefulness to the end of their otherwise tumultuous day.

Karlene leaned comfortably against the cushioned backrest of the Electra Glide. She reflected about the past two days and found it nearly impossible to comprehend what had transpired in such a short period of time. Her thoughts progressively led to her sister. She'd had little contact with Theresa since becoming involved with Aaron Henderson.

Not wanting her sister to know that the carefree indulgence of beach volleyball had transgressed into the depravity of organized crime, she believed it had been wise to maintain a distance from her sister.

A mind-numbing revelation jolted Karlene upright. Frantically, she pounded on Thatcher's back. Downshifting rapidly, he eased the Electra Glide onto the shoulder of the highway.

She sprang from the seat of the big bike and shouted, "Oh my God. Thatcher!"

He had all he could handle to keep the big Harley upright. "What is it?" He turned to the right, then to the left, before locating his passenger. The dread in her eyes startled him.

"She's in real danger! He's found out about her. I know it. God, how could I be so stupid?" Karlene began kicking at the gravel and swinging her arms in a frenzy. "He knows about her." She let go with a high-pitched scream. "I'll kill him! I'll kill him!"

Thatcher quickly leaned the bike into its stand and dismounted. He left the engine running in neutral. Knowing well the capabilities of men like Aaron Henderson, and the extremes they would go, he was astounded he had not considered this long before Karlene's revelation.

"You've never told him about her?"

"No, never!" She grabbed him by both shoulders and pulled him closer. "But he has ways of finding out anything about anybody." She stared through Thatcher. "We have to get to her first." Her eyelids fluttered as she closed her eyes tightly.

He pulled Karlene close and felt, for a brief moment, her body go limp. Then, in a sudden burst of strength, she pushed him away.

"How fast does this thing go?"

Twelve

THE BELL 206 JETRANGER HELICOPTER SPED AT NEARLY A hundred and twenty miles per hour above the woodlands of northern Wisconsin. Wearing faded Levi's, an equally worn Steel Wheels Tour t-shirt, and a pair of Nike cross-trainers with a missing Velcro strap, the pilot resembled more a Rolling Stones roadie than an aviator of a sophisticated helicopter. The two passengers were dressed like cheap lawyers in light gray suits. Their polyester ties were loosened.

"How much longer?" asked Grant Simon.

Michael Duran, without looking in Simon's direction answered. "Thirty minutes."

Duran didn't care for this particular assignment. Until now he had been merely Aaron Henderson's taxi or delivery service. Never had he been a direct accomplice to any malicious felony. And, to make it even worse, this particular affair was kidnapping, which he was certain would lead to murder. It gave him the creeps. Grappling with the idea of sabotaging their mission, was nothing less than grappling with the idea of being executed.

"We'd fffffucking be there by now if yooooou wouldn't have

taken so gggoddamn looong to get to the tamarack." Eddie Greshem spoke with a high-pitched stutter only when he flew.

"Tarmac." Grant Simon made no big deal about correcting Eddie's perpetual abuse of thc English language.

"Thhhaaaat's what I said." And Eddie made no big deal about denying his desecration.

Michael Duran had all he could do to not smile, despite his disparaging predicament. Smiling at Eddie Greshem, particularly at Eddie's expense, could cost one serious physical damage. That was why Duran situated Eddie directly behind the pilot's seat. This seating arrangement had been easily accomplished many flights ago by telling Eddie that more passengers survive helicopter crashes when sitting directly behind the pilot.

Soaring to near ninety, Eddie's IQ was wired into a nasty disposition and a quick temper. It created a dangerously stupid and unpredictable lout, with large fists connected to a large body.

"I was busy, Mr. Greshem." It was a soft-spoken declaration.

Simon spoke with feigned defense. "Michael was busy. Just forget about it, Eddie."

"Forget about it." Eddie, without a stutter, stretched the phrase out with the finesse of pulling off a condom. "He was busy playing with hissss ffffucking self!"

Coughing to cover any possible chortle, Michael Duran covered his mouth as he imagined Eddie Greshem and Porky Pig having a debate over jerking off.

Grant Simon had learned to tolerate Eddie's simplemindedness, along with his in-flight speech impediment that seemed to confirm Eddie's intellectual insufficiency, which was second only to his emotional deficiency.

However, Simon would not forget the time when Eddie rescued him from certain jail time. It had been in the early years of the Henderson "loan company," during a simple leg-breaking transaction. Grant Simon had been interrupted by two Chicago PD patrolmen. Eddie emerged from the alley and eagerly pounced on the two cops from behind, slamming their heads together like a comic strip villain. Grant Simon did not mind working with Eddie Greshem.

"Are you going to be able to find a place to set this thing down?" Grant Simon paused. "Eddie, where we going?" He made a point to confer with Eddie, to make him feel consequential and to momentarily distract him from the flight.

"Crystal River."

"Falls," Duran whispered.

"Crystal Falls." Eddie was able to put the two words together quickly without having to acknowledge an error.

Simon continued, "Are you going to be able to set this thing down close enough to this woman's house?"

Duran glanced down at Simon's alligator shoes. "Didn't wear your hiking boots?"

"We didn't cccccome here to go hiking, fffffunny man."

Greshem's acidic tone, as well as the spray on the back of Duran's neck, indicated that any humorous commentary should be contained, and that sitting in front of Eddie in close quarters had its drawbacks. Michael Duran, pretending to massage the back of his neck, assured Simon that the walk to Theresa Swanson's house would be short.

Police helicopters were not easy to come by. As Kenyon and Jensen stood outside a hangar at Ravenswood, it was evident that they were particularly scarce on the Fourth of July.

"You know how I hate waiting."

Jensen watched as Kenyon started his pacing once more.

"Do you have to?"

He stopped abruptly. "What?"

"Pace. You keep pacing." She placed her hands on her hips and she scowled. "I hate waiting too, but I really hate waiting when you pace."

John Kenyon acknowledged his partner with a brief nod, and continued his moving vigil. Closing her eyes, she bowed her head.

A moment later, a distinctive whirling resonance announced the approach of the helicopter.

"Christ, it's about time." John Kenyon looked toward his partner for her affirmation.

"Christ, John, it's about time." Stepping closer to Kenyon as the helicopter began its descent, she asked, "How far is this place from here?"

"Hour and a half, maybe."

Eve Jensen tried to block the blast of wind as the helicopter settled onto the nearby tarmac. "Do you think," she shouted, "Thatcher and Karlene Swanson are headed there too?"

Kenyon appeared oblivious to the whirling wind. "That's a good wager."

"She touched her partner's arm and announced, "This is quite a race."

"And we're way behind," John Kenyon said solemnly.

Ducking beneath the rotating blades, they began their approach to the helicopter,

"By the way, Eve," he shouted, "did I mention that this Thatcher turns out to be a recently retired corporate counsel, as well as being an ex-fed?"

"You didn't mention that," she yelled back as she stepped past Kenyon and into the police helicopter.

Kenyon climbed in after her. "It seems Thatcher left the FBI twenty years ago after getting shafted in front of a grand jury: apparently the Bureau sacrificed one of its own. He took his talents to the business world, and did quite well."

"You've kept Lucille pretty busy."

"She mentioned that herself." He sat down beside Eve. "He retired prematurely after snitching to the IRS on one of his corporate clients. It seems he thwarted a hostile takeover of a small hardware chain for a noble cause."

"How noble?"

"Noble enough. He gave up a pretty lucrative lifestyle."

She snatched her seat belt and added, "He did allegedly stab Curtis Lane." Eve smirked as she fiddled with the seat belt. "I suppose that could be considered socially conscientious, if not noble."

"Possibly."

"So, how does Thatcher fit into all of this?"

"Maybe he came into some big money and could afford to be socially-minded."

"He and the Swanson woman premeditated the theft of Henderson's assets?" Eve glanced skeptically at her partner.

John Kenyon shrugged his shoulders. "It's a theory. Although, there is nothing to suggest they knew each other prior to Friday night, or that either one has suicidal tendencies."

"Your theories. How do you do it?"

"Graduated come loudly from the University of Columbo."

Jensen laughed. "Why do I laugh at that?"

"Hmmm." Furling his brow, he said, "Don't have a clue."

"It could be an interesting reunion in Crystal Falls." Her eyes turned serious.

"Yeah, it could." He bit his lower lip and fastened his seat belt. "I contacted the Michigan State Police Post in Iron Mountain to meet us there."

Thatcher was more than a little nervous about reaching speeds of nearly ninety miles per hour on a highway he didn't know, riding on a bike he didn't know. But, it was apparent that it was a risk he had to take.

The Electra Glide crossed into Michigan at 8:04 P.M. As they closed in on Crystal Falls, Thatcher attempted to establish scenarios that produced positive conclusions. Not so long ago it was one of his functions as "Counsel for Hire" in Corporate America. He was good at it. The scenarios came to him, racing through his mind like picnic ants over cheesecake. He was almost optimistic.

Chilling out in her favorite bib-jeans and an oversized t-shirt, Theresa Swanson relaxed on her front porch glider. Pushing off every few seconds with her left foot, she encouraged the old glider to squeak melodiously with the early evening sounds that emerged from the cedar grove surrounding her small cottage-style house. A large golden retriever snoozed beneath her, enjoying the occasional nudge from her bare foot. It was a pleasant summer evening in Crystal Falls. She paid little attention to the helicopter passing overhead.

"How ddddooo you know thaaaattt's Crystal River?"

Duran hesitated to correct Eddie one more time. "I just know these things." Navigation, he knew, beyond following a sidewalk to a deli or a strip joint, was way over Eddie Greshem's head.

Eddie strained to scan the landscape below. "I haven't seen any waterfalls, just a river."

Duran thought a moment, then said it anyway. "Edward, perhaps you were right. Maybe this is Crystal River."

Grant Simon glared at the pilot. He knew Duran's proclivity for fooling around with Eddie's simple mind. He didn't like it, and he didn't like what it might cause Eddie to do. Simon wanted the pilot in one piece to fly them back to Chicago. He had tickets for a twilight doubleheader at Comiskey Park; he wanted to catch the second game.

"Hey," Eddie implored, "I don't think this is the place."

"Eddie," Grant Simon's voice was reassuring. "This is the right place."

"Grant, I haven't sssseen any waterfalls." Eddie was obviously worried. "Where's the fffffuckin' fffffalls?"

Duran spoke up. Even he was getting tired of Eddie's brainless twitter.

"Edward, there are no falls. And, there is a story behind it. Just trust me. There are no falls in Crystal Falls." Michael Duran knew this from a previous trip a couple years ago.

Eddie appeared perplexed. "Grant?"

"Duran's probably right." Turning toward the pilot, he spoke with a touch more emphasis. "The smartass is probably right." His voice returned to its normal nasal character. "Eddie, forget about it. Don't worry about the falls."

"Yeah. Just forget about it." Leaning forward in his seat, Eddie wanted to make sure the pilot heard him. "The smartass is pretty smart."

Michael Duran coughed.

"Luke." Theresa nudged the big golden retriever with her bare foot. "Luke, you lazy old man, let's go for a walk."

The dog rolled over on his back and waited for the ceremonious belly rub. His mistress obliged with the bottom of her foot. Luke closed his eyes once again, enjoying the moment. Pressing her foot against his broad yellow chest, she proclaimed, "I'm done!"

His large brown eyes fluttered open and pleaded for more.

"No. I'm done. It's time for a walk."

As she removed her foot, he agilely flipped over and was dancing on his hind legs before Theresa was able to get up from the squeaky glider.

"You do have some life in you."

Running her fingers through her chin-length blonde hair and glancing about the front porch, she said, "Give me a minute to find my shoes." Theresa returned her attention to the jumping and twirling retriever in front of her. "Luke! Stop it!"

Abruptly, to her surprise, he sat obediently at her feet. "Luke, where are my shoes?"

He cocked his head to one side and looked up at his mistress for no more than five seconds before becoming an ecstatic whirling yellow dervish. Shaking her head, she pulled open the screen door and went inside.

By the time she reached the porch steps with fanny pack secured, shoes tied, and leash in hand, Luke was poised and impatiently waiting for her at the entrance of his favorite path into the cedar grove.

"Okay! Okay! I'm coming."

As Theresa Swanson walked leisurely along the path, Luke, with his nose to the ground, sniffed and snorted in frenzied exuberance. Then, the ritual began; every few yards he lifted his leg with male canine authority and left his signature on selected tree trunks. Theresa, as always, slowed her pace.

The early evening was very warm and still. A brilliant sunset was at hand, as were the swarming hoards of mosquitoes. Walking slowly, she retrieved a small can of Deep Woods Off from her fanny pack and sprayed herself down. Theresa headed west toward a little rise where she and Luke could watch the final moments of the sun before it melted into the horizon.

"Come, Luke! I don't want to miss it." He dropped his hind leg and cocked his head in her direction, measuring her sincerity.

"Come!"

The yellow dog made a great leap and bounded off ahead of her. He had decided to meet her at the spot and maybe flush some grouse on the way.

"Luke!" Theresa ran her fingers through her hair once more as she watched him disappear into a thicket. "You big jerk," she whispered.

Knowing that he would eventually rendezvous with her in time for the sunset, she set off at a brisk pace.

Karlene had held on tightly, leaning securely against Thatcher during the last twenty miles. She tried to rest her mind, as well as her body. Her fears left her unsteady and uncertain. Memories of her childhood flourished. Scenes that she had not played back for years came to her in perfect clarity. Karlene didn't notice that she had begun to cry.

As they passed a small billboard announcing the "finest motel in Crystal Falls," Thatcher leaned back slightly to get Karlene's attention.

"We're getting close," he shouted.

She straightened her back, then slowly arched backwards to stretch the muscles that had grown stiff from being in one position for so long. Karlene looked around to get her bearings. She had only been in Crystal Falls three other times, the last time being shortly after beginning her so-called employment with Aaron Henderson.

However, the time she tried to remember was during a two-week period between tournaments; her partner was nursing a sprained ankle. Karlene took the opportunity to visit her sister. It was an obligatory gesture; a reunion of sorts to remember their parents who had been killed several months earlier in a car accident. Karlene could recall little of that visit, except that her appearance completely baffled Theresa's three-month old puppy.

"Over the next hill," Karlene again leaned against Thatcher. "Start to slow down." She spoke loudly. "There will be a narrow road that goes to the right. She lives a mile or so down, in a small brown house."

Thatcher nodded.

Michael Duran was enjoying the scenery below. He didn't often get a chance to venture very far from Chicago. As he surveyed the countryside, from an eagle's eye view, he made a mental note to get away more often.

Like Karlene, who he knew only casually, Michael had been offered an employment opportunity from Aaron Henderson that he couldn't refuse, but in recent months he wished that he had. Frequently, he played with the idea of ripping off Aaron Henderson's JetRanger and starting a tourist guide enterprise in the Caribbean. Of course, he realized his venture would last only as long as he could elude the likes of Simon and Greshem, who he knew would be sent to locate Henderson's stolen property.

It was not hard to imagine Eddie's immense pleasure the moment he could place the eight-inch barrel of his cherished Smith & Wesson Model 586 .357 Magnum against Michael Duran's temple, and pull the trigger.

Duran knew the weapon well. He had often watched with peculiar interest while Greshem fondled it, describing it in minute detail to himself. Eddie had given it life. Michael swore if ever he began caressing and chatting with the JetRanger, he would ask Eddie to take the precious Smith & Wesson and shoot him.

"Duran!" Grant Simon, among other character deficits, had little forbearance, particularly during a high priority job. "Set this thing down over there!" He pointed toward a clearing that he believed was about a half-mile from Theresa's house. He double-checked the county map. The directions he had been given over the phone by an overly helpful local storeowner appeared to substantiate the circled area on the map.

Simon had found amusement in the trusting nature of small-town people. Not only had he received the directions to Theresa's house, he was given her post office box, her telephone number, and the description of her 1994 teal green Subaru wagon, right down to the plastic branch of yellow forsythia hanging from the rearview mirror.

"Duran! Let's go! Get us down there!"

Michael Duran took the JetRanger into a sharp turn and headed in the direction of Simon's clearing. Greshem moaned from the backseat. Duran suspected that Eddie had been quietly anguishing over a bout of air sickness since passing over the forty-fifth parallel.

"Fuck you, Duran!" was barely audible. There was no stutter.

Michael Duran smirked briefly as he leveled off the aircraft and began the descent. A couple minutes later the helicopter touched ground. The three men emerged, bowing underneath the rotating blades. At a safe distance Duran stretched his arms in the air, Simon checked his map, and Eddie tossed his cookies on a nearby cedar sapling.

Eve Jensen watched out the window. "Sunsets have an entirely different feel up here." Adjusting her headset, she complained, "These are annoying."

John Kenyon acknowledged with a brief nod. He was looking east, watching Green Bay disappear into the distance. Had there been more time he would have instructed the pilot to circle Lambeau Field. To Kenyon, Lambeau was Mecca.

Worried about time, he hoped the state troopers out of Iron Mountain were making his request for a safety check a top priority. He knew his polite insistence with the post captain was no guarantee.

Sensing her partner's concern, Eve grasped his forearm. "John, I think we're doing all right with the time."

"I wish we were there, and Greshem was cuffed."

John Kenyon had arrested Greshem three years earlier for felonious assault on a young woman who was trying to keep herself off the street by turning tricks. The judge had to dismiss the case when the victim failed to show at trial time. She failed to show anywhere. He knew sooner or later Greshem would be locked up, but also he knew there would be more victims until that time came. He wanted that time to be now.

Luke lay beside his owner on his back with his eyes lolled back into his head as her fingers slowly scratched his chest. He had arrived just after her, as she knew he would, at their sunset place.

"Luke, you are one spoiled dog." She looked down at his hopelessly sanguine expression. "Do you know how good you have it?"

Writhing with pleasure, he opened one large brown eye and gazed toward his companionable human.

Theresa busied herself by composing a mental to-do list for Monday morning, things that needed to be done before visiting a friend in Escanaba. She never ventured far from home on the weekends. She left the weekend madness to tourists and those unfortunate ones who had to work during the summer months. She loved her summers off, perhaps as much as she loved teaching fifth graders the rest of the year.

Luke suddenly flipped over onto his feet and began barking. Theresa expected to see a troop of raccoons emerging from the underbrush on a mission to desecrate someone's garden. She hoped it wouldn't be hers again.

"Luke. Quiet. You're disturbing the sunset."

She grabbed him by the nape of his neck and pulled him down

onto her lap. Immediately he sprang back to his feet. As she reached to snap his leash onto his collar, he bolted.

"Damn you!" Sighing, she promised. "If you get sprayed again, you'll spend the rest of the summer sleeping on the porch."

She took one last look at the sunset and slowly got up. "Please, not porcupine quills," she mumbled to herself. "I don't want to go through that again either."

Theresa looked off into the direction where her wayward companion had disappeared. "Luke!" She reached into her jeans pocket for her whistle, but only found a wad of lint and a stale dog biscuit. "Damn."

Theresa continued walking, calling, and occasionally cursing under her breath as Luke's bark grew fainter. She had never known him to run deer, but it certainly seemed that something was luring him away at a good speed. Deer harassment was not an acceptable activity for dogs. Then her worst fear echoed through the cedar grove: a gun shot.

"Oh God!" Hearing herself cry out, she began running toward the ghastly sound as the echo faded into the forest.

"What the fuck are you doing?" Grant Simon's disagreeable temper flared like a flamethrower in Greshem's face. "You fucking moron!"

Michael Duran wanted to concur, but his previous wisecrack regarding the decimation of the local fauna with the remains of the burrito supreme Eddie ate for lunch had not gone over well.

"It was a fucking wolf!"

Simon watched as Duran rolled his eyes, but said nothing.

"It was a fucking wolf!" Eddie, flailing away at a swarm of mosquitoes, was so desperate for confirmation he turned toward Duran. "You saw it."

Michael Duran, against his better judgment, said it anyway. "Yeah, these parts are famous for blonde wolves. What's the genus-species? Lupus Madonnis?"

Grant Simon quickly glanced at Eddie, hoping that his witless partner was not taking aim on the pilot. The statement had obviously skimmed over Greshem's gray matter without impact, and Grant Simon decided to let it go without even a fleeting glare at Duran.

"Eddie," Simon's voice took on a forced fatherly tone, "we are not here to shoot anyone." He glanced over to Duran and added, "Or to shoot rare fucking species of wildlife." He returned his eyes to Eddie. "Put your gun away, and forget about it."

Thatcher turned onto a narrow road paved with the residual crushed rock of nearby iron ore mines. It gave the surface a reddish tinge. Meandering deliberately along the contour of the wooded landscape, Thatcher realized this was a road he had envisioned somewhere along his travels. He hoped this one would lead to an amicable end.

As the evening shadows enshrouded the winding road, Thatcher reminded himself that he still had no definitive plan once the sisters were reunited. And although shooting from the hip was often his preferred modus operandi, it had recently resulted in real bullets whizzing past his head.

As he leaned into a sharp curve the pavement abruptly disappeared, diminishing into soft reddish sand and gravel. Downshifting rapidly, he straightened the handlebars as much as possible, and hung on. The front wheel shimmied as it hit the soft roadbed.

Thatcher heard Karlene's gasp just as the eight-hundred-and-fifty pound machine tipped over. He watched as Karlene somersaulted away. He admired her athleticism and hoped she was equally as strong. Lifting an Electra Glide out of a sand pit was not a one-person task.

"You all right?" he asked as he came to his feet.

Sitting in the middle of the road, she produced a ingenuous smile. "Did I mention the road turns to sand?"

"You didn't mention that." He brushed himself off as he stepped over to her. Reaching out his hand, he nodded toward the fallen motorcycle and inquired, "How strong are you?"

As he pulled her to her feet, she said, "I might need some help."

Theresa collapsed and slowly fell to her knees in a patch of tall ferns. "Luke!" Her voice faltered. "Luke! Come boy." Her words faded away in favor of a gasp of air.

She wanted to cry, but before the impulse was transported from her brain to her already swollen eyes, yellow fur bolted through the ferns, and a wet lapping tongue smothered her with kisses. She held on tightly and began to cry. Wrestling him to the ground, she snapped the leash onto his collar.

"Bad dog," she murmured. "Bad dog."

Gently stroking his head with one hand, she wiped her tears with the other. Luke eased over onto his back, and the tummy routine began again.

Before the big bike came to a complete stop beside the Subaru station wagon in Theresa's driveway, Karlene leapt off and sprinted to the front door, calling her sister's name. Once inside she pulled off her helmet and tossed it on the couch.

Frantically whirling around in the small living room, she called out, "Trese! Trese!" Not having used her sister's nickname since they were teenagers, it sounded strange to her.

Thatcher, hoping to see two of a kind, entered through the screen door, only to find Karlene throwing punches like a shadow boxer out of control. Abruptly she stopped and stared at Thatcher.

"He has her!" she screamed. "God, I swear It. I'll kill him. I'll kill every one of them!"

He walked to her, pulled her close and held her tightly. He knew very well she had the capacity to kill them all. He had hoped the killing was over.

There was something about the surroundings that suggested to him they were the first to arrive. Theresa Swanson was safe, at least for now. He was sure of it.

He nudged Karlene gently away, without letting go. "She's just out. She's probably in town, or visiting a friend."

Karlene's dubious stare demanded an explanation.

"It's too peaceful. Nothing seems disturbed or out of place."

His eyes asserted an omniscience Karlene desperately needed. Breathing heavily, she fell against him. "We have to find her," she murmured.

He held her close. "Let's go look in town."

"Her car is out front," she whispered.

"Maybe she walked somewhere. It's that kind of evening."

Her transient smile thanked him. "You're right."

Stepping away from his embrace, she added, "You ride through town and see if you can find her." She allowed another brief smile. "I think you'll recognize her; she wears her hair short." Sighing timorously, "I'll stay here and wait."

Before turning to leave, he said, "Lock the door, and stay alert."

She wiped her eyes with her fingertips, "I will," she whispered.

Karlene watched from the porch as Thatcher maneuvered the Electra Glide out to the narrow road. Walking slowly back into the house, she locked the door behind her. Karlene stood in the middle of the living room. Closing her eyes, she breathed deeply and pushed her thoughts aside. The scent of fresh-cut flowers startled her. Slowly opening her eyes, she wanted to see Theresa holding daylilies from her garden. Karlene found herself alone, the lilies setting in a simple vase on the table nearby. She went to the couch and fell onto it, her left hand striking the helmet. Without thinking, she placed it on the floor, then slipped off her leather jacket and laid it across the back of the couch. She leaned back and closed her eyes once more.

THIRTEEN

AS DAYLIGHT BEGAN TO FADE OVER NORTHERN WISCONSIN, John Kenyon turned to his partner. He slid the headset off momentarily. Jensen did the same.

"Whatever is going to happen in Crystal Falls," he announced, "is beginning."

Jensen hated the sullenness in his voice. It usually meant something was going down badly. She never mentioned it to him, but his somber moods, as infrequent as they were, carried a high percentage rate for predicting unfavorable results.

Aspiring to evoke a smile, she said, "Hey, Eddie Greshem could be cuffed and stuffed into the back of a state police cruiser."

"I hope you're right." His tone didn't changed.

Grant Simon led Eddie and his pilot through a cedar grove to a dirt road. Checking his county map, he announced, "This is the road," with an air of satisfaction, if not certainty.

"That's great, Mr. Simon. I guess I'll just get back to the helicopter and wait for you all."

"I'd rather have Eddie here shoot you. In fact," Simon turned toward his frequently less-than-competent associate, "Eddie, you have my permission to shoot this little smartass pilot if he tries to split without us."

Duran watched both men stare at him with sublime malice. "Well." He shrugged his shoulders with as much carefree composure as he could pull together under the circumstances and began walking toward his esteemed passengers. As he passed them, he said, "I don't know about you guys, but your pilot, let me emphasize, your only pilot, loves the great outdoors. I wouldn't want to miss a single step of this hike through the woods." He tucked his hands in his jeans pockets and began thinking about the bright blue Caribbean.

Thatcher returned from cruising through downtown Crystal Falls for the second time. He came across no one resembling Karlene's sister. As he reached the top of the hill where the two main streets intersected, he noticed a wooded park area beside the courthouse and post office. It seemed a likely place to rest after an early evening walk to town.

He parked in the end space farthest from the courthouse and stood beside the Electra Glide feeling disheartened as he surveyed the park and the picturesque view of the small rural town. Envisioning the panoramic view flushed with autumn colors, he made a mental note to return the first week of October. His thoughts returned to Karlene. He mounted the Electra Glide as an eerie feeling crept over him.

Simon gave out orders to his accomplices. He repeated them three times to Eddie Greshem, carefully choosing words that would not confuse him. Duran was given the acting role. He seemed perfect to play the part of the lost tourist.

Michael was to go to the front door to ask directions. The rest, as Simon had said to Eddie, was a piece of cake: a metaphor he was certain Eddie would understand.

As Michael Duran stepped onto the front porch he made, if not the biggest decision of his life, the most dangerous. And the only one he could ever live with.

The sound of footsteps on the front porch propelled her off the couch. Calling out, "Thank God, you're here," as she raced toward the front door, Karlene felt her words crash into oblivion with the sight of Michael Duran on the other side of the screen door. Why had she been so careless to allow Aaron's thugs to sneak up on her? A split second before she was going to turn and run, she heard the back door creak open. She was trapped. It was then that it came to her. Karlene composed herself and walked to the door and unlocked it.

"Hi," Michael produced a toothy Tom Cruise grin. "I'm kind of lost."

Karlene smiled. "Did you come in from the highway?"

"I was hiking through the cedars. Could I bother you for a glass of water, and directions?"

"No bother." Pushing open the screen door, she asked, "Would you like to come in?"

Michael quickly slipped inside, knowing his time alone with Theresa Ferrand was going to be very limited.

"Theresa," he whispered. "You're in danger."

"No shit, Duran," she said soberly. "Whose side are you on?"

Duran did a double take. "Christ. Karlene? What are doing here?"

"Protecting my sister." Her eyes narrowed. "Who's side?"

"Yours. There's no time. You need to follow my lead."

"Who's out there?"

"Simon and Greshem."

Closing her eyes, she whispered, "God."

Michael Duran understood.

A moment later Greshem burst through the screen door with his .357 drawn. Simon adroitly stepped into the room after entering from the back door. He scowled at Eddie. "Put that goddamn thing away. Who do you think we got here? Bonnie Parker?"

Eddie thought a moment. "I don't think so."

Duran stepped closer to Karlene. "Let me introduce the sister." He glanced back and forth between his unsavory cohorts, and added. "Damn, they look alike. Don't you think?"

Karlene prayed Michael Duran had more to his plan than a simple switch in identity; she had already decided that much for herself.

Although the sight of Eddie Greshem made her skin crawl, the knowledge her sister was safe gave her strength. She would do whatever was needed.

Months ago, shortly after meeting Michael Duran for the first time, Karlene had concluded he was trapped by Aaron much like herself. Although that alone didn't elicit her trust, the circumstances at hand gave her little choice.

"Piece of cake," said Eddie Greshem as he smiled at his partner.

"Let's get out of here." Grant Simon was pleased. Everything was working out just fine. As Eddie had just said, a piece of cake. Neither one noticed the leather jacket slung over the back of the couch or the helmet setting on the floor.

Luke had led Theresa a considerable distance from the path. In an effort to backtrack she became momentarily lost.

"If I thought you knew how to get home, I'd let you lead."

Turning his head without missing a stride, Luke directed his big brown eyes toward his human as if to proclaim, "Follow me!"

Theresa stopped abruptly and gave a little yank on the leash. "Sit." She had to repeat it as usual.

Luke sat.

She glanced back and forth and pointed indecisively. “Let’s go this way. Everything looks different when it starts to get dark.”

Luke, eagerly keeping in step, was unconcerned.

Karlene and Michael Duran walked a few steps ahead of Simon and Greshem. She was patiently waiting to follow Duran’s lead, but so far he had only led her farther down the dirt road. Knowing Aaron’s helicopter was nearby, her anxiety escalated.

Michael Duran knew he needed to think of something very soon. If Karlene got on the helicopter, she would be dead within forty-eight hours. Slowing his pace, he questioned why he was sticking his neck out for someone he hardly knew. A quick glance into Eddie Greshem’s baneful expression made the answer unequivocally clear. He was not one of them.

As Duran purposely stumbled over a Louisville slugger-sized beech limb in the waning daylight, he envisioned the thirty-eight ounces of hardwood cracking the back of Eddie Greshem’s head. Stooping down quickly, he pulled loose his shoelace, then started to tie it. Everyone stopped.

Karlene knew this must be the moment, but what was she supposed to do? She then noticed the sturdy tree limb. Let’s not be too obvious, she thought. In amazement she watched Michael Duran sit down in the middle of the road and begin taking off his shoe. Expecting the worst, Karlene held her breath as Eddie Greshem stepped toward Duran. She knew Eddie Greshem could readily shoot the pilot, and then stupidly wonder who would fly the helicopter. She readied herself. Karlene felt an adrenaline rush building: a match point hanging in the balance.

Greshem bent over Duran as far as his rotund middle would allow and bellowed. “What the fuck you doin’?”

Duran concentrated on his shoelace as Eddie’s projectile spittle subsided. He imagined a two-hundred-and-seventy-five pound semblance of Daffy Duck standing over him with a .357 Smith & Wesson.

Looking up woefully at Daffy and Grant, their faces blending into the shadows, he held up his shoe. "Stone in my shoe." To his own astonishment his voice sounded sincere. "You guys go ahead, I'll catch up."

It seemed to Michael Duran an eternity before Grant Simon relinquished his dubious stare and stepped past him with Eddie a half-stride behind.

This was it, Karlene thought, as she was forced to turn away by Eddie's less-than-gentle nudge. Seconds later a loud crack resounded.

"Christ," she muttered, "he did it."

Whirling around, she saw Simon falling to the ground and Greshem reaching for his gun. Before the stainless steel barrel cleared the holster a second crack resounded; the beech branch broke in half over Eddie's useless skull. The .357 Magnum fell to the ground.

"Jesus!" He swallowed hard. "I knew there were rocks in there."

He snatched Karlene's arm as she reached for the shiny revolver laying on the dirt road. "We don't have much time!"

Simon began stirring.

"The gun!" she exclaimed.

Duran pulled her away in the direction of the helicopter. "What are you going to do?" He gasped for air. "Shoot 'em?"

Her reply was succinct. "Yes."

They were running at top speed, with Duran still pulling her along as they entered the cedar thicket. "Remind me," Michael Duran said as he pushed aside bough after bough of cedar, "not to ever piss you off."

Karlene was breathing heavily. "Michael, I can't go with you!" She broke free from his grasp. Breathing hard, she stood facing her rescuer. "I can't leave my sister."

"I don't see that you have much choice." He panted. "Those two assholes won't be far behind and they're really unhappy with me."

Karlene glared. "You should have let me shoot 'em!"

There was no doubt in Duran's mind that she was serious. "Maybe you're right... I hope you're not."

"My sister." She was regaining her breath. "I can't leave my sister!"

"They think you are your sister!" He returned a glare of his own. "Let's get the hell out of here!"

Locked in silent combat, their eyes held steadfast. Michael released his stare. "Okay, you stay," he said almost casually.

As Karlene turned, he grabbed her wrist and pulled her forcefully along for several feet before she anchored herself to a cedar branch with her free hand.

"Let the fuck go, Duran!"

He jerked his arm away. "It's right there." He pointed toward the JetRanger in the clearing.

One thunderous shot echoed through the cedar grove. They shared a brief disquieting stare.

"Get yourself killed." Michael dropped his hands to his sides. "Where does that put your sister?"

Her eyes moved slowly away from his. She knew that he was right. She looked toward the helicopter.

Duran wiped the sweat from his brow. "We'll figure it out once we're in the air."

Grant Simon had chased after them for nearly a hundred feet, but his short legs couldn't carry his ponderous body any farther. He stood, staring into the cedar trees and rubbing the back of his skull. He was huffing like a locomotive. His .38 Special dangled uselessly at his side as he turned around. Gingerly, he slipped it back into its shoulder holster as he began his march back toward his partner.

Eddie had not moved from where he had been fallen by Duran's beech limb.

"If the son-of-a-bitch can't walk," he said to himself, "and, if I don't have a stroke by the time I get to him," he took a deep breath, "I might just have to shoot him." Grant Simon was a poor loser, and when he lost, he always felt better after shooting something. "Fuck," he mumbled. "I might shoot him anyway."

By the time Simon had reached his partner, Eddie had brought himself to all fours. Still dazed, Eddie groped for his precious Smith

& Wesson Model 586 laying in the road. He carefully lifted the revolver from the reddish sand. It appeared he was going to administer first aid.

"Get your ass out of the dirt!"

Eddie raised up one knee, and then with one mighty effort came to his feet. "Man we are fucked! Just plain fucked! When I find that smartass son-of-a-bitch, I'm gonna," Eddie said it correctly, but had not enough breath to finish his sentence.

Simon allowed him to finish.

Inhaling deeply, Eddie started again. "I'm gonna shoot his fuckin' balls off." Eddie held his .357 Magnum upward in a poignant and punctilious gesture. "Just before I shove this up his goddamn ass." He pulled the trigger.

Unmoved by his partner's spirited, nonsensical soliloquy, Grant Simon grabbed Eddie's arm. "Put it away," he ordered. He pulled him in the direction of the wood-framed house. He noticed a trickle of blood coming from Eddie's ear. Simon hoped it wouldn't create a big problem.

Within a half-mile of leaving the village limits of Crystal Falls, the flashing lights of a State Police cruiser came rushing up from the rear. Twisting down the throttle, and glancing at the speedometer were two contiguous and futile movements beyond Thatcher's control. He veered toward the shoulder as he checked his left mirror to see nothing behind him except open highway. At that moment, the cruiser sped past him.

Before he could recover from the adrenaline rush, he saw the cruiser's brake lights flash. Thatcher heard himself groan as the cruiser turned onto Theresa's road.

Certainly it was no coincidence. Aaron Henderson was after Karlene and Theresa, and the authorities were after Henderson. It was like a food chain, and he saw himself as an appetizer on both menus.

Downshifting to third, Thatcher made the decision to follow at a safe distance. He needed to know what was happening, and he needed to get Karlene out of there, if he could.

As if it hadn't just become convoluted enough, the appearance of a helicopter swerving southward just above the treetops added to the complexity of the situation. The unmarked aircraft could only belong to one person.

Bombarded by the unknown, he lightly tapped the rear brake. Who was in the helicopter? Was it Theresa? Was it Karlene? In the pit of his stomach something cold and harsh struck maliciously. Did Aaron Henderson have them both? He needed answers. Being arrested became inconsequential. He downshifted into second and turned onto Theresa's road.

The evening shadows along the narrow bending road were converging into darkness. He immediately pushed his sunglasses to the tip of his nose so he could peer over them. As he approached the end of the pavement he eased the Electra Glide into first. Without warning, a large golden retriever, with a young woman in tow, burst through the underbrush, directly into his path. Leaning to the right and clamping tightly onto the front brake, Thatcher found himself sprawled across the gas tank by the time the tour bike came to a stop. This time he managed to keep the big V-Twin out of the sand.

The startled young woman yanked vigorously on the leash. The big yellow dog, uninhibited and eager to make friends, dragged the young woman toward him.

He shifted the Electra Glide into neutral and stared at Theresa Swanson. It was remarkable. Without the Meg Ryan haircut and the Osh Kosh overalls he would have believed he was looking at Karlene.

"Luke! Stop it! Luke!" Having enough of golden retriever antics, Theresa used both arms as she put all her might into a final yank. "Luke!"

To Luke's amazement, he found himself momentarily airborne, then flat on his back in the middle of the road.

Thatcher pulled his eyes away from the twin sister to watch Luke gingerly rise to his paws and shake off the red road dust. He took off his sunglasses and slipped them into his vest pocket. He returned his attention to Theresa Swanson.

"I'm sorry." Theresa brushed her hair back. "I'd like to say he never acts this way," she rolled her eyes just a little, "but, he always acts this way." She allowed an apprehensive smile.

Luke sat obediently with his head cocked and studied the noisy vibrating object beneath the new human.

Thatcher needed to be calm, precise, and expedient. Delicate communication would be required to convince the young woman that the bizarre story he was about to tell was the truth. He reminded himself that he didn't exactly exemplify respectability.

He needed to begin by letting her know her sister was here, and that he had brought her. He needed to say it without alarming her.

"You must be Theresa." His manner was easy.

"Should I recognize you." Her demeanor was calm, although she was obviously taken aback.

"I'm a friend of Karlene's." Here goes everything he thought. "I dropped her off at your house not too long ago." Thatcher could not help thinking that Karlene was flying toward Chicago in the custody of Henderson's men. That thought made his blood run cold.

"Karlene's here?"

She was surprised, yet Thatcher, as he reached for the red kill button, could not discern if she was pleased. The engine fell silent.

"Well, yes. She is."

"You don't sound so sure." She cocked her head. With a dubious look, she asked, "Who are you?"

He didn't have much time. The state troopers could be coming back this way at anytime. Being arrested now would do nothing to help Karlene, and could possibly place Theresa in great jeopardy. It kept getting more complicated.

A gunshot shattered the tranquillity of the summer evening. It echoed eerily through the woodlands.

"Damn them!" she said immediately as she turned in the direction of the sound. "That's close to my house."

Thatcher found Theresa's reaction perplexing.

"They were shooting at Luke earlier," she said. "God, I wish I knew who they were."

Luke was on all fours with his ears perked, looking toward his home.

Thatcher spoke carefully. “Who do you think they are?”

“Oh, some stupid hunters.”

Another shot, apparently from the same gun, resounded. Luke whined and sat down.

Thatcher decided there was no point informing her that hunting season was more than two months away. More importantly, he was trying to speculate who was firing on the troopers. He was certain the helicopter that passed overhead moments before belonged to Henderson. He wondered if they purposely left someone behind. And, why?

A chill went through him as he concluded he was the intended target.

Luke was in the process of twisting his leash around Theresa’s legs. “Luke, sit.” Luke sat as she untangled herself. “You haven’t said who you are.”

“A friend of Karlene’s.”

Her brow furled and she examined him more closely. “That, by the way, doesn’t impress me very much.” She glanced down at Luke, then back at Thatcher. “My sister has a habit of choosing poor friends.”

Thatcher could not argue the point. “I know, I’ve run into a few.”

“So, you’re insinuating you’re different?”

“I’m different.”

“Who are you?”

“Thatcher.” He extended his hand.

Theresa continued to examine him carefully. Believing she should be apprehensive, perhaps even intimidated, she was surprised that she felt neither.

She reached out and took his hand. His grasp was firm and gentle at the same time. There was a quality about him that evoked a sense of trust; it was unquestionably not his appearance. She studied his face, his eyes. Both seemed familiar.

Releasing her hand, he decided to continue before she began asking more questions. "Fate put us together at the wrong place at the wrong time."

Frowning, she interrupted him, "Then you're not one of her friends?"

It was her doubt that urged him to move swiftly on with the story. He said brusquely, "We met two days ago under very unusual circumstances."

"Maybe you should leave until I talk with Karlene." Her voice was clear and unfaltering. "I'm not really comfortable."

"Theresa," he said with respectful familiarity. "You need to hear this."

Leaning over to pet Luke, she looked up at Thatcher. "I don't know."

Thatcher didn't hesitate. Time was running short. "Listen, please." His tone purported an urgency that Theresa couldn't rebuff.

"Okay," her eyes narrowed with skepticism. "I'll listen."

"Keep in mind Karlene doesn't have a knack for choosing good friends."

"Does that include you?" she said calmly.

"I wasn't chosen."

His point was made.

"Go on."

"Karlene and I, one might say, accidentally took some money." Shrugging his shoulders he hoped to suggest an absence of malice, without confirming outright stupidity.

Theresa was direct. "Or, one might say, it wasn't an accident?"

"Someone might certainly say that."

"Who might that be?" She was not sure that he would answer her questions, but she did sense that he would tell her the truth.

Thatcher found himself stumbling into a conversation he had hoped to avoid. He held his silence long enough to watch Theresa place her hands on her hips. "That's not relevant at the moment," he finally answered.

Leaning lazily against Theresa's leg, Luke appeared to be losing interest in the entire affair. She glanced down at Luke and patted him on the head. "Good boy."

She returned her attention to Thatcher. "How much money?"

"A million or so."

"A million dollars?" It was neither skepticism nor amazement. It was merely clarification.

Thatcher added his own insouciance. "I'm sure it's probably more than a million."

"It's here?" Her voice rose an octave. "The money?"

"It's back in Chicago."

Three more shots resounded. He was certain they had all come from the same gun. Luke emitted a small whine as more shots followed. Theresa bent down and hugged her dog. Thatcher saw that she was shaken.

Thatcher continued. "I think we should go somewhere else, and I'll attempt to explain."

Two more shots, this time it was from a different gun.

"Who's shooting?" She didn't wait for an answer. "It's not hunters. It's about the money." Her eyes widened as some of the pieces began to fall into place. "My god, where's Karlie?"

"We should leave." His voice was urgent.

"Where's Karlie?!"

"I'm not sure." He decide to say no more for the moment. "Theresa, we need to leave."

"Together? Without Karlie?" Theresa's voice was almost a whisper.

"Yeah, together." He paused, then lowered his voice. "We'll find her."

"You expect me to trust you?" Her voice wavered. Her eyes swept over him quickly. Although she had already made up her mind, she needed to hear him say it.

He was candid. "You need to trust me."

Another two rapid shots came from the original gun. Thatcher was certain it was a .357, or possibly a .44. Then, another shot from a smaller caliber, probably a 9mm from the troopers, he deduced.

Thatcher's previous training in small arms provided him with some expertise, yet made him no less daunted. He wanted to get far away from the gunfire. He became even more candid. "You need to trust me now."

"What's going on?"

Thatcher could see her hands trembling. And, when a single blast from a large-gauge shotgun was heard, he watched her crouch beside her big yellow dog. She hugged him tightly as one more shot resounded. Thatcher discerned it was, indeed, a .357.

Through a tremulous whisper, she asked, "What about Luke?" It was her concession.

"A neighbor?"

Theresa nodded as she knelt down and gave Luke another hug. "Come on boy. You're going to visit your old buddy Jake for awhile."

Bouncing up and down like a kangaroo, Luke appeared to accept the idea with extreme enthusiasm. He was off, pulling his human in the direction of a narrow two-track a few yards up the road.

Thatcher watched as Theresa and Luke disappeared around the sharp bend in Jake's narrow driveway. Daylight had all but slipped away as he retrieved his night goggles from one saddlebag. Beneath the canopy of beech and maple the night sounds emerged from the stillness in a complacent harmony: nature's unyielding rebuttal to human intrusion.

Exhausted, out of breath, beleaguered, and dazed, Grant Simon and Eddie Greshem had just sat down on the steps of Theresa Swanson's front porch when the Michigan State Police cruiser, with lights flashing, pulled into the sandy drive.

Troopers Cozart and Williams had anticipated talking a few minutes with a young woman by the name of Theresa Swanson, and then catching a late bite to eat just outside of Crystal Falls, before heading back to Iron Mountain. Instead they were greeted by a windshield-shattering slug from a .357 Magnum. They were not pleased with how their evening was unfolding.

"Holy fuck!" was Cozart's initial commentary as he slammed on the brakes and jammed the transmission into reverse. A second slug embedded itself into the radiator as the police cruiser sped backward down the driveway. Williams shouted into the radio for assistance.

Simon and Greshem, like two frantic cartoon villains, scrambled into the cottage. They found themselves on the floor leaning against the wall beside two adjacent windows in the living room: a celluloid scene from a late-night Cagney movie. Grant Simon hadn't pulled his gun. He was staring at his partner in disbelief.

"Eddie. You're a dumb fuck. Did you know that?"

Eddie Greshem was a dumb fuck, and now he was also dumbfounded. "Whaddya mean?"

"I mean, you're a dumb fuck." He wiped the sweat from his brow. "The troopers are calling in for more troopers."

Eddie's confusion remained. "So, we kill 'em, and get the hell out of here before the others come. We'll steal their fuckin' cruiser." He beamed with the notion of pulling out in a state police cruiser, not considering the simple fact its distinct appearance made it a lousy getaway car, and that it had a hole in its radiator.

Simon took a deep breath and exhaled. He was not yet recovered from their recent bout of physical activity. "In a few minutes, we're going to be just like Butch and Sundance."

Eddie was grinning broadly.

"That's not a good thing."

"Grant, which one am I?"

Grant Simon groaned as he began adding up the charges in his head. They easily added up to a good share of the rest of his life in the pen. "This is not good," he mumbled to himself.

Eddie smashed the window and fired three times in the direction of the cruiser. Simon said nothing. This time shots were returned. One came through Simon's window. He was mentally going through a list of the best criminal lawyers in Chicago.

Cozart and Williams were crouching behind their cruiser with their Colts drawn. Beside Williams was their Ithaca Mag-10 Roadblocker; the scatter gun offered insurance for any potential attack. Williams was hoping he would not have to use it. The shoulder-bruising recoil, and the gory mess it made of anything it hit made it his last weapon of choice. A moderate amount of blood was tolerable, but the Mag-10 created carnage. The kind of carnage he was trying to escape when he transferred from Detroit to Iron Mountain.

Gleefully dramatic, like a ten-year-old playing cops and robbers, Eddie said, "Cover me," as he crawled to the front door. Glancing at Grant Simon, he grinned as he filled the empty chambers of his Smith & Wesson. "I'll be back."

Grant Simon shrugged his shoulders. Prison wouldn't be so bad. He had connections. Early retirement, he figured. He smiled at Eddie Greshem and thought it was just like him to have his last words be, "I'll be back." He never did know what the fuck he was talking about, the dumb fuck.

Within moments of Eddie's exit Grant Simon heard Eddie's deranged scream followed by blasts from the .357. He was attacking. Simon waited. He didn't bother to provide Eddie cover. He wanted to show the police that he had not fired his gun. Any little thing would help his defense. Besides, Eddie was dead either way.

Cozart fired once then nodded toward the Mag-10. Officer Cozart had been under fire once before and had taken one in the arm, which in his opinion was responsible for his ever-increasing golf handicap. He wasn't willing to take another bullet, and it appeared obvious that they were under siege by someone without all his neuro-transmitters working. The loosely wired were the most dangerous.

Williams snatched the scatter gun and took aim on the ponderous zigzagging target. It reminded him of sighting in an enormous woodchuck. It's just a big woodchuck, Williams told himself. The blast blew the top off of a small cedar tree.

The near miss caused Eddie to stumble, while firing with reckless abandon. The final shot came as he tumbled to the ground.

Williams lowered the Mag-10. There was no need for a second blast.

The report had come over the radio as the police helicopter approached Crystal Falls. "Unit 94 has engaged in gunfire. Two more units are on their way."

"Civilians?" asked Kenyon.

"It appears to be two armed men. No hostages." The voice crackled. "Hold on."

Kenyon and Jensen exchanged hopeful glances. Several seconds passed.

"One Grant Simon is in custody." There was a pause. "One Edward Greshem provoked return fire."

Kenyon, with the mention of Eddie's name, went rigid. "What about Greshem?" He tried to keep his voice calm.

"It appears he inadvertently shot himself."

Kenyon let out a burst of air. "Dead?"

"Blew a big hole in his chest with his own gun."

John Kenyon slid off the headset

"The Swanson woman?" Jensen asked.

"No signs of anyone else," announced the crackling voice.

FOURTEEN

As the blades began to whirl above them, Karlene stared vacuously out the side window of the JetRanger barely noticing the sensation of rising. Thinking only of her sister, Karlene prayed Thatcher had found her in town and had been able to avoid Simon and Greshem. Too many questions crowded her thoughts. Would Thatcher be able to tell Theresa the events of the previous two days? Would she believe him? How would she react? Would she trust him? Her sister was always so sensible.

As her mind filled with more and more doubts, she realized that all she really needed to know, for now, was that Theresa and Thatcher were together and were safe.

After ten minutes in the air, Karlene turned to Michael Duran. "We have to find my sister, and my friend, Thatcher." Her expression was solem, her eyes fierce and steadfast with conviction.

Trying not to look in her direction, Duran looked out his side window at the blackness. He knew it would be easier to let her down if he didn't look at her. However, he made the mistake of glancing sideways. He couldn't help himself.

"You said you'd think of something once we were in the air."

Nearly a demand, she stared austerely. "Well, we're in the air. What did you think of?"

Michael Duran swallowed hard and began whistling "Rain Drops Keep Falling on my Head." He avoided her eyes.

"You don't have the slightest fucking idea what to do, do you?" It was criticism of the highest order: an angry and despairing accusation from someone who had recently proven she possessed the capacity for shooting people.

Being careful not to sound defensive, he looked toward her and said, "I got us away." He felt a twitch beside his left eye. "Getting us away should count for something."

She leaned back into the seat and looked upwards. She sighed, "Of course it does, Michael." There was no use, she thought, in getting the pilot miffed at her.

Karlene didn't know Michael Duran very well. She always thought he was quite pretentious and deceptive, despite the favor he did for her following her parents' death. He was not unlike herself, she considered. It had not been her intention to become what she had become, and likely it was the same for the young pilot sitting beside her.

The situation was so far out of hand that a case full of money in Evanston seemed insignificant at the moment, but perhaps Duran would be more inclined to help her if there was a payoff at the end.

"Michael, I need you more than you need me."

Michael wanted to agree wholeheartedly, but decided a simple shrug of the shoulders would be prudent.

"As you may have heard," she confided sheepishly, "I accidentally took a few million dollars from Aaron when I left town."

Michael Duran's eyes widened. "No shit?"

This time, without forethought, Karlene smiled and nodded. "No shit."

"And all I have," he replied, "is his fucking helicopter."

They laughed, almost hysterically.

Aaron Henderson was well into his fourth scotch and water. Mendelssohn's Concerto for Violin and Orchestra, Op. 64. on CD had just begun. The violin carried him off into a deeper state of self-gratification. He visualized Karlene's expression upon hearing that her twin sister was staying with him for awhile. Feeling exulted in the inevitable return of his money, he imagined the pleasure he would have in destroying, and then eliminating, Karlene Swanson. He would do it personally. That would only be right.

Karlene would watch in horror as he pried the barrel of his 9mm Beretta between her sister's teeth. He would hold it there long enough for absolute fear to engulf both of them. The 9mm would explode the back of her skull. Henderson visualized the soft gray matter, the blood, and Karlene's terror-stricken eyes. It excited him. Karlene would not die so quickly.

As the Mendelssohn concerto entered andante, the telephone rang. He knew it would be David Stout. Theresa Swanson would be in Chicago very soon.

"Mr. Henderson," David Stout's voice was flat and despondent. "Greshem is dead." He knew that news in itself would mean little to Aaron Henderson. Greshem was expendable.

"The Swanson woman?" Aaron's voice was direct.

"She got away."

"What do you mean, she got away?" Rage swept through him. "How can a schoolteacher get away?!"

"From what I can determine, it seems that Duran somehow subdued both Simon and Greshem long enough for him and the Swanson woman to get to the helicopter and escape."

"Duran? What the fuck do you mean, Duran?"

Aaron Henderson had always delighted in Duran's indiscriminate raillery directed toward the likes of Curtis Lane and Eddie Greshem. Being duped and double-crossed by Michael Duran enraged him even more. Michael Duran would be executed a little bit at a time.

"Michael Duran and Theresa Swanson flew off somewhere in the JetRanger. Grant Simon is in custody. Greshem was shot. I don't know anything more."

"I want details. I want that son-of-a-bitch, Duran!"

The evening was warm, yet Thatcher knew his new passenger would become chilled after several minutes without a jacket. He hoped to find a place for the night soon. They traveled southbound toward Wisconsin on Route 2.

Thatcher couldn't get the image of the helicopter out of his mind. Nothing he could think of convinced him that Karlene wasn't aboard. He did not want to believe that it was over. He did not want to believe that Karlene would soon be killed.

Another thought occurred to him. Something a bit outrageous, but something Karlene would do, and something she could very well pull off. Downshifting and pumping the rear and front brake in unison, he pulled off onto the shoulder of the road.

"What is it?" Theresa's voice was yielding and apprehensive.

Thatcher kept the bike running in neutral. Pulling off his helmet, he turned his head to one side so Theresa could hear clearly. "When I first saw you, I would have sworn you were Karlene." Biting his lower lip, he confidently announced, "She's being you."

Theresa understood very little of what was happening. "What do you mean?"

"She's pretending to be you."

Theresa provided only a quizzical look.

"There was a helicopter. It flew overhead the same time we started out."

She quickly put it together. "My God, you're saying Karlene was on the helicopter? Abducted?"

"I believe so." He watched dread spread over the young woman. Trying to be encouraging, he continued, "I believe she can pull it off for as long as she needs to."

"What are we going to do?"

"For now, we need a place to stay for the night."

Theresa sighed deeply as the pieces began to fall together. "I was to be kidnapped?" Her voice fell to a whisper. "Because of the money?"

Thatcher nodded.

Taking a deep breath, her response was direct. “Mr. Thatcher, or whomever you are, it’s time to tell me exactly what’s going on.”

Thatcher turned off the ignition. “Yes, it is.”

As they stood beside the silent motorcycle in the summer twilight, he described the events and players that had brought Karlene and himself together.

Theresa listened intently, occasionally running her fingers through her hair. She stopped him only once.

“And you believe she’ll be safe as long as she can convince them she is me.” Another sigh. “Do you think she can do that?”

“I do. It gives us time.”

“To find her.”

“To find her,” he replied.

The dissertation took less than ten minutes. Thatcher believed it unnecessary to tell of Karlene’s relationship with Aaron Henderson.

“As weird as this sounds, I believe you.” Pausing briefly, she ran her fingers through her hair one more time. “You look surprised.”

“I am; a little.”

Theresa pressed her lips tightly together. “Me too.”

They smiled at each other accepting a common bond.

Pensively Theresa looked past Thatcher. “She’s played this part before...”

Thatcher didn’t consider asking, and instead replied, “She’ll be all right.”

Theresa nodded.

He slipped his helmet back on and pulled the strap tight. Thatcher threw his right leg over the seat of the Electra Glide, and asked, “Where can we get rooms for the night?”

“There’s a little town up ahead.” Theresa slipped in behind Thatcher. “Tomorrow?”

“We go to Chicago.” Thatcher started the engine. Speaking loudly to be heard above the rumble of the V-Twin, he declared, “We find Karlene.”

Theresa leaned close to Thatcher. “How?”

“I’ve got a plan!” he called back as he eased the Harley back onto the highway.

"Care to share it with me?" she shouted.

As soon as I think of it, he thought. "Later!"

Kenyon sat down on Theresa Swanson's couch. He leaned back and crossed his legs. Jensen stepped away from the broken window where Eddie Greshem had begun his last stand. Both ignored the commotion of the evidence gatherers sent by the county sheriff. They watched with humorous interest as a local constable eagerly followed a pair of state troopers. The balding, past-middle age constable appeared ecstatic as he was enlisted to assist stringing the yellow tape across the outside of the small porch.

Jensen walked closer to her partner sitting on the couch. "Other than the broken window and a couple of bullet holes in the wall, there doesn't seem to be much to look at."

Leaning over the side of the couch, Kenyon picked up a black helmet. "What's this tell you?"

Eve Jensen stepped over to the couch and picked up the leather jacket with two fingers at the back of the collar. "Theresa Swanson is a biker?" She set it back down.

Kenyon smiled. "Maybe." He put the helmet back down on the floor beside the couch. "I think it's more likely that she had an unexpected visit from her sister and Mr. Thatcher." Interlacing his fingers, he cracked his knuckles.

Jensen cringed as she sat down beside her partner. "You do that to annoy me."

"Yes, I do." Pressing his hands against his thighs, he continued. "Eve, Karlene Swanson and Thatcher were here."

Nodding in agreement, she asked, "Where do you think they are now?" She knew a theory was evolving.

He shrugged his shoulders. "I don't know, but I don't think the three of them are together. Motorcycles, as you know, carry only two."

"Sidecar." Eve was pleased with her snippet of motorcycle knowledge.

"Sidecar." Kenyon pulled on his chin. "Sidecar. I hadn't considered that."

"You're smiling, John. Are you making fun of me?"

"Of course not," he said looking into her startling blue eyes. "Weren't they brown yesterday?"

Shaking her head, she asked, "Brown what?"

"Your eyes?"

"Contact lenses, John." It was never obvious whether he was having fun or being serious. "Could the three of them be together?" Waiting patiently, she finally asked, "Well, what do you think?"

"You know," he tugged at Bugs Bunny on his cheek. "I just have the feeling that there is a fourth player."

Jensen raised her eyebrows. "What are you thinking?"

"Henderson's pilot."

"Michael Duran."

Kenyon nodded.

Dubiously she replied, "That could fit." Eve Jensen stroked the side of her cheek and went on. "Or Duran just bailed on them. Maybe slipped out the back when the troopers arrived."

"Bailed," he said thoughtfully.

"Bailed, you know, cut out, skipped the scene, split."

"Yeah, yeah. But, what if he didn't?" Pausing, he grinned before he said, "Bail."

"So, where is he and the helicopter?" Eve challenged. She expected an answer that would lead her to yet another question.

"Duran's gone for sure."

Eve had assumed correctly. She went along with it, but refused to phrase it as a question. Shrugging her shoulders, she said, "He bailed."

John Kenyon let out a short laugh. "Okay, okay. They bailed. But they had planned to bail."

"They?" Jensen stood up and looked down at her partner. "This has been a lead-in to one of your theories." Placing her hands on her hips, "Continue," she said.

"Karlene and Duran are both about the same age. Both have been with Henderson for about the same length of time, and they're both egocentric. Neither one fits a stereotypical criminal profile."

Running her fingers through her hair, she stared into Kenyon's smiling Irish eyes. "And they've decided to retire from Aaron's employ, probably with a substantial cash dividend."

John Kenyon uncrossed his legs and placed his large hands on his knees. "Duran flies Simon and Greshem up here to pick up Theresa Swanson. Instead of Theresa they are greeted by Karlene."

"Karlene, as her twin sister." Eve sat back down.

Kenyon went on. "And then at the right moment, Karlene and Duran take Simon and Greshem by surprise. They have just enough time for their escape in the helicopter, leaving Simon and Greshem behind."

"But what does Thatcher have to do with all this?" Jensen sat down beside Kenyon.

"I'm leaving that part up to you."

"So," she began, "Theresa could now be with Thatcher on the bike."

"That could fit," he mimicked his partner's earlier dubiety. "Or Theresa was not at home, maybe was never going to be at home, and Thatcher just bailed, after dropping Karlene off."

Eve glanced toward the leather jacket. "That might explain why the helmet and jacket were left behind?"

"It could." He pulled at Bugs one more time. "Or it might suggest a fast getaway."

"Then Thatcher and Theresa could be together?"

"Could be."

Eve Jensen let out a long sigh. "In either case, do you think they can pull it off?"

"With a lot of luck." He shrugged his shoulders and stood up. "It's going to be interesting."

Walking over to the kitchen, Kenyon took a can of soda from the refrigerator. One of the official evidence gatherers provided a derisive glance which Kenyon ignored.

"You want one?" he asked the young detective.

The local detective looked away without comment. He didn't care for the intrusion by the big city cop.

"Jensen?" He held up the bright red can.

"Too much sugar."

Kenyon laughed as he popped the top and took a sip. He walked back to the couch and projected to Eve, "Aaron Henderson is really pissed off by now, and his ranks are somewhat depleted." John Kenyon thought a moment. "This may just work to our advantage."

Eve Jensen listened intently.

"Henderson may be forced to do some of his own dirty work." John Kenyon lowered his voice, as if talking to himself. "He just may be irate enough to do something really stupid."

"Michael, I think we should go back to Chicago."

Duran stared at Karlene incredulously.

"I'm not crazy," she added. "Well, not any crazier than you."

Duran couldn't argue that point, but Chicago didn't sound like the place to go. He was thinking northwest, somewhere in northern Minnesota. Actually, he was simply thinking of getting as far away from Henderson as he could. He wanted to live to be thirty.

"Well, say something." Karlene was staring at him, waiting for his response.

"I turn thirty this November. I'd like to celebrate that landmark."

Contemplating his remark, she asked, "Who's going to be dumb enough to think we would go back to Chicago? I mean, think about that." Karlene turned away from Duran and sank back into her seat. "I have to do it." She hesitated, then slowly turned toward Michael. "If I don't kill Aaron Henderson, you, my sister, and I will spend our lives looking over our shoulders, waiting for a bullet in the back of our heads." Breathing deeply, she closed her eyes and said, "He will never forget." Her eyes flashed opened. "And I won't live that way."

Michael Duran's moot expression was expected.

"Believe me, Michael," she continued, "I didn't plan any of this. It just happened."

It was Michael's turn to take a deep breath and to sigh. "You're going to kill Aaron Henderson?"

"I have no choice." Karlene said it stoically. "It's him, or it's us. It's that simple."

Duran stared out the side window at the blackness. Northern Minnesota seemed like a good idea; the Cayman Islands even better. "We'll go back to Chicago," he relented, as the sunny Caribbean vanished into the black hole of his abandoned thoughts.

"How will you do it?" His voice was soft and listless. He was certain the woman beside him would actually try to kill Aaron Henderson.

"I'll probably shoot him." She leaned her head back and stared upwards. "I've just recently acquired a knack for shooting people."

There was only one room available in all of Florence, Wisconsin. It had a double bed and a plastic-coated chair. Air conditioning consisted of an open window and a fan manufactured circa 1950.

"This is quaint," she said.

He tossed his duffel bag onto the bed. The springs creaked.

"Thatcher, may I be direct?" She walked over to the television.

Thatcher nodded as he unzipped his duffel bag.

Theresa turned on the set. "You and Karlene?" The television showed no interest in producing a discernible image; she switched it off.

Thatcher had anticipated the inevitable inquiry, yet until that moment he had no idea how he would respond. He was succinct.

"There was no time." He pulled out toothpaste and a toothbrush. "Excuse me. I really have to brush my teeth." As he entered the bathroom he said, "I'll sleep on the floor."

Thatcher's objective, other than brushing his teeth and staying alive, was to bring the twins together. And, after that was done, he would be on his way.

Flame pulled into the parking lot of the Leather & Lace a few minutes past eleven. She found Gretta's Fat Boy in its usual space. She eased her Springer beside it. She ran to the side entrance ducking under the massive hairy arm of Dirk the Smirk, Bouncer Extraordinaire.

"Hey, Flame!" Dirk smirked. "Respectable women use the front door."

Twirling around gracefully, she countered, "You wouldn't know a respectable woman if she sat on your face."

Dirk smirked even more as he lit his Lucky Strike with a wooden match. Respectability had never been a requirement for Dirk the Smirk.

Gretta was in her usual booth. She was arm wrestling for shots. Flame slid in beside Leo, a lean, wiry, and poignantly unattractive young man no taller than herself, and no match for Gretta. She glanced at the three full shots of Yukon Jack on Gretta's side of the table. She grinned at her friend.

Leo was rubbing his left biceps. Flame leaned into him and whispered, "You know damn well you're not going to beat her left arm."

Leo continued rubbing his sore arm and stared at his opponent. "This woman ain't real," he manufactured a deep raspy voice that was several octaves lower than his own.

Gretta picked up the nearest shot and slung it down. "Leo," she was staring at his arm, "what is that?"

He glanced at the tattoo across his aching biceps, then looked up at Gretta with a contemptible glare. "One toss. Kill 'em all," he proclaimed.

Gretta set the glass down on his side of the table. "Yeah, I can read. But what is it?"

Flame leaned away from Leo and cocked her head from side to side as she examined the drab, unskilled sketch on his left biceps. Turning toward her companion, she said, "I don't know. What do you think it is?"

"Hmmmm." Gretta looked wide-eyed at Flame, then aimed her exaggerated expression toward Leo. "Pomegranate."

"It's a fuckin' grenade!" he shouted. "One toss, kill 'em all!" Scabrously glancing between the two women, he pushed past Flame and slid out of the booth. "Kill 'em all!"

"He's a bit malevolent tonight," Flame said as she watched the diminutive Storm Rider strut away.

Raising her narrow eyebrows, Gretta repeated the word, "Malevolent," as she pushed a shot of Yukon Jack toward Flame.

Picking up the shot glass, Flame watched a broad appreciative grin come across her partner's face. They quickly toasted one another and slammed down the liquor.

Shrewdly, Gretta inquired, "Malevolent is what?"

Flame set down the empty shot glass on the table. Leaning conspicuously toward her companion, she whispered, "It means he's got a bad, fucking attitude."

Gretta set down her glass and pulled a Marlboro from the pack in front of her. "I gotta remember that." She snatched her Zippo from the table and lit her cigarette. "He's a fuckin' malevolent." She flipped her Zippo shut, and set it on the table.

Flame sat back into the booth. "I think Thatcher is in deep shit."

Gretta exhaled a plume of smoke and slid to the corner. She leaned against the wall and crossed her arms on her chest. "I could've told you that last night." She moved her legs onto the bench, and crossed her ankles. The smoldering Marlboro hung from the corner of her mouth.

Ignoring her partner's omniscient demeanor, Flame went on. "Jolene called me at home. She said she picked up on the scanner bits and pieces of a shootout in the U.P. She thought she heard the name Thatcher come over one of the blurbs."

"The U.P.?" Gretta furled her brow. "What the fuck?"

"I'm just repeating what Jolene heard."

Gretta smirked. "You got a thing for this guy." She took the cigarette from her mouth; smoke seeped from her nostrils.

"Hey, maybe I do." Flame shrugged it off.

Gretta nodded with approval. "What else she hear?"

"Not much. Something about the woman."

"You got some competition."

"Not his type," Flame said with assurance.

"Not interested in the tall, leggy blondes?" Gretta laughed. "He's more the short squaw type?"

Flame scowled at her tall, leggy, blonde associate. "A descendent of an Ottawa Princess."

Gretta raised her narrow eyebrows, as if it was the first time she had heard about the princess connection. "Indian royalty."

"Are you up to a road trip?" It was a challenge as well as a change of subject.

Gretta inhaled deeply and stared at her friend. She exhaled slowly, "So Pocahontas, you want to rescue your Joe Smith?"

Ignoring the unessential error, Flame gave her a wide-eyed glance and said, "I didn't know you had any interest in American history."

Gretta ignored the sarcasm. "I go to the movies."

Flame continued matter-of-factly. "I want to help him out, if I can."

"You wanna get laid."

"Objections?"

Gretta flicked her ash into an empty shot glass. "You got a plan, Princess?"

Michael Duran plotted a course to Antioch Airport northwest of Waukegan near the Wisconsin border. He didn't want to get too close to Chicago. Plus, there was a place to stay in nearby Channel Lake. However, there was the delicate matter of explaining Karlene to Olivia.

Duran had, on many occasions, told many implausible prevarications with astonishing success. However, Karlene's suggestion of telling the truth seemed implausible. He had to draw the line somewhere.

Earnestly, he said, "This is not a good time for the truth."

Upon arriving at Olivia's house, Michael introduced "cousin" Karlene from California, and asked if they could spend the night. Cheerfully, Olivia invited them in and promptly introduced Michael and Karlene to "cousin" Jim from Vermont, who coincidentally was visiting for the weekend.

Eve Jensen was exhausted as she let herself into her apartment. The light above the electric range illuminated the kitchen in a fluorescent glow. Sam leapt, with some difficulty, onto the counter nearest the refrigerator and bellowed in his guttural, "Where have you been? Feed me," howl.

"Sam, my fat cat. I bet you're hungry." Eve stepped toward him and realized that it was a silly thing to say to the cat whose quintessential purpose in life was to eat.

Sam bellowed again and proceeded to go into his usual starved cat antics. He nudged her arm relentlessly as she attempted to clamp the opener onto the twelve-ounce can of Friskie's liver and beef.

"Sam, just wait."

She scratched him between the ears as she pushed him away. With the first grinding whir of the can opener, he went into a frenzy, knocking her hand against the slowly twirling can. The can disengaged and spilled an ample amount of its gelatinous contents onto the countertop. Sam wasted no time and began to lap up the goo before locating the first slimy chunk.

"I hope you're happy, you little twit." Eve walked away defeated. "I'm too tired for this. Serve yourself."

Immersed in liver and beef chunks, he didn't bother to look up.

She slipped off her shoes and sat on the end of her bed. She began going over the facts of the Henderson case, attempting to piece together her own hypothesis. In what manner Thatcher was involved with Aaron Henderson's affairs bothered her. Then it began to dawn on Eve that Thatcher had, perhaps, only by chance become a catalyst setting in motion the beginning of Aaron Henderson's ruin. It excited her, and frightened her. Henderson, she knew, would not go down without vengeance, without bringing others with him. Eve Jensen was certain events were going to occur within the next forty-eight hours that might permanently close the Henderson file.

Before crawling into bed she wished Thatcher, the ex-FBI agent, and ex-corporate counsel, well.

Sunday, July 5

FIFTEEN

AWAKING A LITTLE AFTER SUNRISE, FOLLOWING A RESTLESS night rolled up in a polyester blanket on the matted shag carpet, Thatcher's first image was of Theresa. She lay close to the edge of the bed, her face turned toward him. Like her sister, she was simply beautiful. Yet, there was a distinct difference, he believed, that would always separate them. Theresa possessed the look of someone at ease with herself and with her life (the last few hours being exempt).

Startled from her sleep, her eyes met Thatcher's. She gasped and pulled back. After a long sigh her lips parted, but she said nothing.

"I know," he said quietly as he propped himself up on one elbow. "I was hoping it was a dream, too." He sensed an imperceptible smile behind her troubled expression.

"Karlene will be all right." Her voice held the fuzzy essence of one who had just awoken from another, more peaceful place.

"Yes, she'll be all right." Aaron Henderson, he thought, doesn't realize the trouble he's in. And that certainly was an ace in the hole.

Theresa swung her feet over the edge of the bed and sat up. Her Osh Kosh's and t-shirt were no worse for wear after a restless night of sleep. Thatcher slowly came to his feet. His body ached from the hard floor. Sitting down beside her, he pressed both hands against the small of his back and arched backwards.

"Rough night," she said.

"Rough night."

"What's the plan, Mr. Thatcher?"

"We ride to Chicago."

"I know that part." Theresa produced a subtle smile. "You don't have a plan, do you?"

"Not exactly."

"I didn't think so." Her voice was light and airy, almost perky. "I appreciate your honesty." Looking intensely at Thatcher, she announced, "We'll have a plan by the time we get there, and whatever it is, we'll pull it off."

Her contrived optimism didn't make her resolution less genuine. However, he sensed they would need a little genuine luck as well. "I think Karlene would say it's getting close to crunch time."

"Yes, she would say that." Moving from the bed, she faced Thatcher, "And, Karlie really hates to lose." She brushed her hair back with both hands and asked, "Could I borrow your toothbrush?"

Aaron Henderson looked down from his penthouse upon the Chicago Yacht Club and the Windy City shoreline. He became mesmerized by the unending motion of early morning traffic that moved along Lake Shore Drive.

Everyone with a destination, Aaron brooded. How many would never arrive? How many would end up somewhere they never intended to go?

How could he, in a matter of forty-eight hours, be misguided into such disaster? His empire had been so close to its summit, its zenith. His acceptance into The Affiliation had been all but sealed, and then within hours, he could only watch as it careened dangerously off course.

Who was the engineer, he mused, behind this catastrophe? Chance could not produce such precise destruction. It took brilliant and intricate planning. Karlene possessed the desire, he knew, but not the capacity for designing his demise.

It was a man by the name of Thatcher, disguised as a biker thug, who had done this to him. Who was he? Who did he work for?

Suddenly, Aaron Henderson felt an old, familiar spasm in the pit of his stomach. The ache he would feel just moments before the callused fists of his father would strike him.

This was the ultimate test provided by The Affiliation, and he was failing miserably. He knew that no one walked away from The Affiliation. Failure was death.

He turned away from the window. The vengeance that he felt so vehemently the night before now slipped into an anguishing fear. He walked into the bathroom and vomited: the spectral figure of his father hovering above him.

Flame had convinced Gretta to quit early the night before. Walking out the side door of Leather & Lace a few minutes before one, Gretta agreed to be at Flame's apartment in Lincolnwood at seven the next morning.

Gretta arrived at seven thirty-three, according to the digital clock on the Tappan range. In full road regalia, she came bursting through the door to be met by Flame's onerous expression.

"You're late." Flame stood a few feet from the door with one hand on her hip and the other clasped around her Garfield "I don't do mornings" coffee mug.

Gretta, without acknowledging her friend's nasty tone, walked toward the coffeemaker on the kitchen counter. On the way she snatched a stained coffee mug from beside the sink, and within seconds was eagerly pouring her coffee.

"There are clean ones in the cupboard." Flame's inflection became less daunting.

"I like this one. Why don't you ever wash it?"

"I keep my dish sponge in it."

"And I thought your fucking coffee was just bad." Gretta took a sip. "Actually," she tilted her head slightly and peered into the coffee mug, "it's not too bad this morning."

"I haven't been able to find my dish sponge for awhile."

Gretta glanced at the pile of dirty dishes in and around the sink, then took another sip. "So, what's your fucking plan?"

"I'll buy a new one."

"You're a dumb bitch sometimes."

Flame walked past Gretta and poured more coffee into her cup. "You're the one drinking out of my dish sponge cup." She didn't bother to hold back her grin. "Besides, I knew what you meant." She took a sip of coffee. "I don't have a plan."

Gretta walked over to the small kitchenette table and sat down. "Of course you don't. I have the brains... you have the braids." She was immensely amused. "Brains, braids."

Ignoring her friend's last remark, Flame sat down across the table from her. "I want to help Thatcher." She flashed a worried expression toward Gretta. "I just don't know how."

"We ride up to Waukegan. We talk to Jolene." Gretta grinned at the prospect of dropping in on her old mentor. "We ask around, see what we find. Maybe we come up with a plan." She watched Flame's eyes. "There's something you're not tellin' me."

Flame looked up from her coffee. The sudden softness of Gretta's words startled her.

"You know, I feel like I got him into this mess." She sighed. "I don't want anything to happen to him."

"You wanna take up with him," Gretta said with approval.

"I like this guy." Flame pensively bit her lower lip. "What do you think?"

Gretta shrugged her shoulders and grinned. "He's got a nice ass." Withstanding her friend's glare, she leaned back into her chair.

"I just want to help him out if I can." She shrugged it off and took a sip from her cup.

Gretta rose suddenly. "You ready to ride, you crazy Indian?" Her moment of sentimentality had ended.

John Kenyon arrived at the precinct a little after seven thirty on Sunday morning. He had not slept well, and was not in his usual jovial mood, which was evident when he turned down a jelly Bismarck from Lucille in Records, and when he did not compliment Stan for having the coffee ready.

Stan made lousy coffee, but it was always hot. Lousy coffee needed to be hot, or even iron-gut thirty-year veterans like John Kenyon wouldn't drink it. Stan's coffee was always hot.

Kenyon sat at his desk drumming his pencil and sipping hot, lousy coffee. He didn't expect Jensen to be in until later. In fact, he wouldn't blame her for not coming in at all after their last minute crusade to the U.P. the evening before.

John Kenyon never felt good after a shooting, even when it was the likes of Eddie Greshem blowing a hole in his own chest. Even though Eddie's poetic demise would assure that he would never destroy another life, there would always be someone to take his place. John Kenyon was feeling ineffective.

His phone rang. It was Jensen.

"John, I've been thinking. Remember your theory about the collaboration between Karlene and Michael, and possibly Thatcher?"

"It's just a theory." His demeanor was flat.

"I don't know." Eve Jensen paused. "Maybe none of this was planned. Maybe the players just happened to come together. And the events just began to happen: the domino effect. Perhaps all this was just contingent upon one player who is the catalyst. An outsider, someone who had not been involved at all."

John Kenyon smiled a little. Jensen, he mused, was thinking more and more like him. He continued listening.

"I call it," pausing for melodramatic effect, "the Thatcher Contingency." She waited for her partner's retort; none came. "Well? How do you like it?"

John Kenyon laughed. He suddenly felt much better. Eve had a way of doing that. "Sounds like a Ludlum novel."

There was silence on Eve's end of the line. Kenyon imagined her pout. "Eve, I like it! By the way, weren't you coming in this morning?"

Michael and Jim, "cousins" to Karlene and Olivia respectively, had slept on the floor and couch respectively in Olivia's cramped living room. It was not what either had anticipated. Karlene slept comfortably in the spare bedroom.

Michael Duran had awakened a little after sunrise to a chorus of crackling grackles. His back ached from the hard floor and his head ached from a disquieting sleep. He appreciated being alive, and suspected he would appreciate it even more each day.

As he had lain staring at Olivia's living room ceiling listening to the avian melody, he wondered what Karlene would ask of him today.

Michael was questioning whether he had chosen wisely when he had pointed the nose of the JetRanger in the direction of Chicagoland. He couldn't help believing that he would be feeling much more at ease at a Motel 6 outside of Duluth.

Karlene slept through the chorus of grackles at dawn, and the racket from the neighbor's dogs plundering the garbage cans two hours later. Nevertheless, it was her dreams, not the indigenous sounds, that disallowed her a restful night.

There was a series of dreams with her and Theresa, or rather, distorted flashbacks that had been extremely distressing and abstruse. An opprobrious icon of Aaron Henderson appeared ominously in each, taking on different roles: as a chaperone at their first junior high dance, as a referee at their first varsity volleyball match, and as the principal at their high school graduation.

The most confusing and alarming was his appearance as himself at their parents' funeral. Karlene, at the time, had been wary about telling Aaron about their deaths, and eventually had decided against it. Nor had she wanted to allow him any knowledge of her sister. It seemed the right decision then, even though she had not known why. In recent days it had become painfully apparent that her intuition had been correct, as well as ineffectual. She awoke in a start at a quarter to nine. Her first thoughts were of finding Trese, and of getting her hands on a gun.

The early morning sun was subdued by a low ceiling of clouds that kept the temperature hovering in the upper sixties. Thatcher assumed it was only a matter of time before the haze would abate and the temperatures would soar into the mid-eighties. He spent much time considering the weather as they rode southeast on US 2. It would be a five-hundred mile ride to Chicago; inclement weather would make it seem even farther. A long day was ahead of them.

It was not until they passed over the Menominee River and back into Michigan heading toward Iron Mountain that Thatcher remembered Theresa wasn't wearing a helmet. This could present a serious problem in daylight. Helmets were optional in Wisconsin and Illinois, but in Michigan they would be pulled over for not wearing one. Damn, why hadn't he taken Karlene's helmet with him when he had gone to look for Theresa?

Not knowing an alternate route that would keep them in Wisconsin, he decided to risk it. They would be in Michigan for only a short time. Recklessly he concluded that he may have to outrun a patrol car, which wasn't likely on an Electra Glide.

Thatcher anticipated stopping in Green Bay to eat lunch and to buy Theresa some riding gear and other essentials. He could feel her hanging on tightly, more for warmth than for security. She had willingly accepted one of his denim shirts, but at the moment it wasn't enough to keep out the briskness of the morning.

Thatcher wondered what was going through Theresa's mind. Twenty-four hours ago her life had been hers to live as she wished. And abruptly, it was turned into a series of inexplicable events. He was amazed that she was taking it in stride. Theresa and Karlene, despite their differences, apparently possessed similar intrepidity directed by the same perseverance.

There was an urgent tap on Thatcher's shoulder.

"I have to talk to you!" she shouted.

Thatcher nodded and began downshifting. They had just passed the city limits of Iron Mountain. Pulling off into the parking lot of a closed ice cream stand, he caught the glimpse of a royal blue state police cruiser a couple blocks ahead coming their way. Ecstatic about the fortuitous timing, he parked the Electra Glide in the shade of a large Norway maple.

As if prompted, Theresa dismounted immediately. Thatcher did not hesitate to do the same, and to avoid any helmet controversy he stood close to Theresa, shielding her from the passing patrol car. She was unaware of his deliberate maneuver.

Her hair was askew. She brushed it back and asked, "Who do you think has my sister?"

Thatcher was puzzled by the question. Theresa anticipated his quizzical expression, and continued, "I mean, maybe she wasn't in the helicopter." She waited for an encouraging reply.

"We don't know for sure." His voice did not carry the optimism that Theresa had hoped to hear.

"Maybe she's still in Crystal Falls. Let me call the state police. The post is here in Iron Mountain." She could see Thatcher's apprehension. "I'll say I'm a concerned neighbor. I'll dig for information. People around here are noted for their endless quest for information about each other. I've got to find out whatever I can. Please." Hers was not a plea, but a cordial demand.

Thatcher could not come up with a concrete argument, nor had he the right to prevent Theresa from doing what she felt was important. Digging into his jeans pocket, he extracted several dimes and a quarter. He held them out to her. The Cold Spot Dairy Castle offered a pay phone.

Moments later, he watched as her left index finger pinned the state police number against the page of the directory while her right hand slipped the change into the slot. He stepped closer to listen.

"Hi. How ya doin' this morning? Wonderful day." She had easily transformed her voice into a buoyant cascade of friendly colloquial platitudes. "I'm not one for nosin' around in somebody else's business, but I am a concerned neighbor. Theresa Swanson, over here in

Crystal Falls... Well, there was a real ruckus there last night 'round sunset."

Thatcher was amused, particularly the word "ruckus." It seemed to fit.

"Connie Rucker. I live just a little ways from the Swanson girl."

Thatcher smiled as he folded his arms and leaned against the small white building. He wondered if there was an actual Connie Rucker.

"Is she okay?" Her voice took an edge of excitement. "I know I heard shots. At first I thought it was just the Carter brothers shootin' off their damn guns again. Is that legal, I mean so close to town and all?" She watched Thatcher for his response.

He provided an approving nod. Returning a brief smile; she was unable to disguise her apprehension.

"Well, I will call the local police about that." Her fleeting scowl expressed her frustration and the fear that she was not going to get the information she wanted. "Is the Swanson girl okay?" She listened intently.

"Oh, they haven't found her yet. Well, maybe she's visiting friends. She does like to gallivant around." There was a brief pause. "You know, I think she was expecting a visit from her sister?" Theresa phrased it as a question.

"No, I've never met her. I understand they're twins." Again, another pause. "I hope they arrested whoever was shooting."

Her eyes motioned for Thatcher's attention. He moved closer and waited.

"Well, I'm glad to hear that." She nodded in agreement. "So, there were two of them. What on earth were they doin'?"

Thatcher sensed the conversation was about to end.

"Of course, I get the paper. I will do that." She lowered her voice into disappointment. "You're not authorized to give out that information?" She pursed her lips and ended the conversation with the most infamous riposte given to all public servants. "Well, you know, my taxes pay your salary!"

Theresa hung up the phone. "Always wanted to say that." Shrugging her shoulders, she continued, "Well, we still don't know much." She let out a sigh. "God... at least she wasn't shot, but we still don't know where she is, or if she's all right."

"There were two?"

"That's what she said."

"Arrested?"

"Officer Tilden led me to believe that." She allowed a subtle smirk. "I'm sure she didn't want a nosy, law abiding taxpayer to think the crooks got away when they didn't." She gave Thatcher a quizzical look. "You thought there was only one left behind?"

Thatcher nodded. "To kill me."

"Why two?"

"Maybe they thought I was a Stallone kind of guy." He smiled.

"You don't really believe that do you?" Her question feigned sincerity.

"Probably not."

"So, why two?"

He shrugged his shoulders. Sensing an emerging theory from Theresa, he waited.

Her eyes widened with excitement. "It was a mistake! Something went wrong."

He was very interested. "What do you mean?"

Theresa shuddered. "What if no one was meant to be left behind? What would be the purpose? Really."

Thatcher began to speak.

Quickly she said, "Let me finish."

Nodding obligingly, he leaned back against the building.

"Sorry, I don't believe this guy, Henderson, thought you were important enough to kill, that he would want someone left behind. How would his thug get back to Chicago? Steal my Subaru?"

Thatcher was amazed something that simple hadn't occurred to him. Perhaps he was not that important after all. Not being important was something new to him.

Theresa's face lit up. She gasped just a little before she said, "I don't know why it took me so long to remember this."

Thatcher's expression pressed her on.

She breathed deeply, more to gather her thoughts than to catch her breath. "The last time," she began, "Karlene came to visit me was sometime after our parents' funeral. I picked her up here, in Iron Mountain, the park over there." Theresa pointed eastward. "She was playing hoops." She smiled recalling the scene. "She was holding her own against some unruly ten-year-olds."

Thatcher watched her eyes light up.

"I know ten-year-olds real well." Theresa looked toward the park, as if to recapture the moment. Returning her eyes to Thatcher, she began to explain. "It was her boss's pilot, Karlene said, who had secretly flown her in." Theresa's voice took on an eagerness. "She used the word 'secret.' I didn't think too much about it at the time, but it makes sense now."

Thatcher felt her enthusiasm as she took a replenishing breath.

"Anyway, he had flown her to Iron Mountain in a helicopter. I didn't ask any questions, but I do remember thinking that this guy was a friend." Theresa glanced away.

"Actually," she continued, "and I'm not proud of it, but I thought it was just another one of her... conquests."

Thatcher's thoughts raced to the morning before. He succinctly understood.

"I guess I've had some low opinions of Karlene for quite some time."

Blinking her eyes to avoid wiping the tears, she continued. "Anyway, what if yesterday this was the same pilot, and they are at least acquaintances. What if, for some reason, he helped her get away?"

Thatcher said nothing.

"What if?" Her voice quavered.

Thatcher stepped closer and Theresa slowly and carefully placed her arms around him and lay her head against his shoulder. He embraced her gently.

"What if I believe you could be right?" He felt Theresa's embrace become tighter. He felt himself become optimistic.

Sixteen

Arriving at Aaron's penthouse just after nine Sunday morning, David Stout was not prepared for what he found. He had never seen his employer in such absolute despondency. It was extremely uncharacteristic, unimaginable for Aaron Henderson to have lost control over his dominion. He commanded, until now, with indisputable and absolute authority. Others around him had always carried out his will without failure, and always without question. David Stout mused, was that time over?

Aaron, dressed in his silk pajama bottoms, swung the door open, turned away, and walked back to the chair he had been sitting in for the last hour.

David Stout promptly seated himself in an opposing chair and said nothing. They had often sat in these same positions, discussing business strategies over coffee and pastries; strategies that frequently included extortion, abduction, and homicide.

This morning was very different. Sitting silently for nearly fifteen minutes, he waited for Aaron to speak. David Stout was a patient man.

"David?" It was unlike Aaron Henderson to call any man by his first name. He often used no name at all. Aaron did not want anyone too close to him.

Stout was taken by surprise. It was only the second time his employer had called him by his first name. The previous time had been during a rare uncontrolled drinking bout many years earlier, following a disheartening decision to have a close associate taken out.

Aaron Henderson had said to Stout. "Business is war, David. To win the war people must die."

Stout had chosen the winning side that time. He would choose the winning side again.

David Stout answered calmly. "Yes, sir."

"You know of The Affiliation, but you don't know about them." Aaron remained looking toward his reflection in the long, tinted windows. "It is the new order. It is the future. It will own everything in the next century, and what it cannot own it will destroy." He paused and swallowed hard.

David Stout said nothing.

"The payment from The Affiliation was not a gratuity or a reward. It was a test. A test to see if I was capable."

David Stout understood what his employer was saying perfectly. It soon may be time for him to choose once again.

Michael Duran had suggested to "cousin" Jim to rent a car on his VISA Gold for he and Karlene. "Cousin" Jim, being extremely eager to get the unexpected guests on their way, agreed. The rental was made over the phone. "Cousin" Jim was so pleased about their departure that he drove Karlene and Duran to the car rental place over in Antioch.

Standing on the driver's side of the purple sub-compact, Michael watched as Karlene glided into the passenger's seat. "I don't know why you want me to drive," he said, as he began his descent into the tiny car. "This is a Geo, not a Bell 222."

"Is that a telephone or some kind of helicopter?"

Duran produced a sarcastic grimace toward his passenger. "It's a very fast helicopter."

"Could you find us one for later?"

He ran his fingers through his hair. It was a motion of frustration. "No problemo." More sarcasm. "You got a few hundred thousand to spare?"

Karlene smirked.

"Yeah, right. I forgot you've come into some money." Hesitating, he continued. "That just might get us killed."

Karlene's expression became suddenly compassionate. "Michael. Calm down." Her voice was gentle. "We'll get through this."

He sighed. "Shit, I don't even know where the hell I'm going. In fact, I don't have the slightest idea why I'm not somewhere in northern Manitoba by now."

Karlene buckled herself in.

"Are you listening, Ms. Ferrand?"

"It's Swanson," she said with renewed self-regard. "Yes, I'm listening. You want to be somewhere in northern Manitoba. Although, its seems you would be more of an Aruba kind of guy." Her voice remained calm, almost stoic.

"And that's where Henderson would look first." He provided Karlene with a woeful expression. "And, you? Where do you want to be?"

"For now, just drive to Elmhurst."

"Why there?"

"Why not?"

Michael Duran shrugged. "Why not." He started the car and shifted it into drive.

After several minutes of silence, Karlene spoke softly. "I want you to call Aaron."

Michael Duran glanced wearily at Karlene. "Say what?"

"I want you to call Aaron."

"Is this something you've been thinking about for some time now, or did it just come to you?"

Karlene looked sternly at Duran.

"It's no whim." Her voice assured Michael Duran that it was no vagary of any sort.

"I'm sorry, I can't think of a single thing to say to Mr. Henderson." It was his best sarcastic retort.

"I'll tell you what to say."

His sigh produced a weary and fearful sound. "Why doesn't that surprise me?" He glanced quickly in her direction. "And why don't you just talk to him yourself?"

"Because I can't hold myself for ransom, can I?"

Duran abruptly pulled off the side of the street into a deserted gas station. The Geo squealed to a stop. He shifted it into park and turned off the ignition. "What exactly are you suggesting?"

Karlene glanced toward the huge "Out of Business" signs plastered against the boarded up windows of the station. "I hope we don't need any gas."

Michael Duran produced a glare that momentarily took her aback. He said nothing.

"All right, already." Karlene softened her expression, and lightened her voice. "Michael, just hear me out, okay?"

He looked away briefly, then returned with a more obliging expression.

"Say things went badly in Crystal Falls." Her voice yielded a sense of understanding, yet held its firmness. "Tell him Eddie Greshem started to go ballistic on Simon, and you thought it best to take off without them. He knows Eddie's an idiot. Tell him you have Theresa Swanson, and that you're sorry, but you've got to submit your resignation." She hoped his misgivings were beginning to diminish, however slightly, with the concept that he could, in fact, resign.

"This is your plan?"

"And, this will really kill him." She smiled like a Mouseketeer on cue. "Let him know you're collecting your retirement a little early. In return, you hand over Ms. Swanson."

Michael Duran looked closely at his accomplice. "He'll fucking blow my brains out without a second thought."

Misgivings completely intact, she thought as she went on. "You're absolutely right." Recognizing she wasn't going to seduce him into enthusiastic acceptance, she returned to the abrupt sarcastic approach. "He would, but we're not going to let him do that. Are we?"

Duran was quiet. He simply stared at Karlene in amazement.

"Whether you've figured it out or not, we have a dangerous little war on our hands," she said with remarkable repose.

"As in," he murmured, "take no prisoners." It was a subdued, nearly despairing declaration.

Karlene clenched her lips tightly together. "I'm afraid so. Like I said last night, it's him, or it's us."

"And, I suppose, you're just going to shoot him?"

"Yes."

Riding with Gretta was hazardous. Riding with Gretta on a mission was bordering on suicidal. Flame regarded it as a challenge. I-94 North, the Eden Expressway, skirting the edge of Skokie, brought in the weekday commuters from the northern communities. On Sunday mornings, however, traffic was relatively light.

Gretta and Flame blasted north toward Waukegan. The duo arrived at the Waukegan dealership about the same time that Jolene was having her first legitimate coffee break. Her cup was rarely empty before noon, at which time she changed over to any diet soda offering sufficient caffeine.

As they entered the showroom Gretta said to Flame, "I'm over here," nodding toward the leather goods.

"I'll roust Jolene." Flame headed toward the back counter.

Gretta, standing in front of a full-length mirror, was slipping into a jacket when she glanced up and recognized an unwelcome figure looming behind her.

"Don't think you can toss us another VISA."

"Fuck you, Fat Bob. It's Citibank. It's got my picture on it!" Gretta had not yet made eye contact with Fat Bob.

"I don't care whose picture's on it. It's no good here."

Gretta shrugged as she zipped up the jacket. She turned her back to the mirror, to get a rear view of the chrome-studded jacket with the large embossed H-D. "Hey, Fat Bob." Still she did not look directly at him.

He was reluctant to answer, expecting reference to some ludicrous line of credit that he had no intention of allowing. And he was in no mood to get into a tedious and cryptic conversation with Gretta.

"No credit, Gretta." It rolled off his tongue effortlessly. He wished he had said it long before now.

She made eye contact for the first time. "Fat Bob, I paid that bill off." She pulled off the jacket and handed it to him. He immediately hung it back on the rack, as if saving it from certain abduction.

Fat Bob faced Gretta once more. He sucked in his rounded cheeks and stroked his beard. "Yeah, you paid that bill off. I remember how difficult that was. I don't want you to go through that emotional trauma again." He rolled his eyes a little too much; his sarcasm was a little too blatant.

Gretta slowly slipped her long fingers into the pocket of her leather pants. She pulled out a single bill. It was the thousand that Thatcher had given to her the morning before.

"I have cash today." She watched Fat Bob's eyes widen as she quickly inserted it back into her pocket. "Hey," changing the subject, she continued, "I think a friend of mine stopped in here yesterday. He has a real kick-ass Fat Boy. He was hangin' with one of those dizzy model-type babes. Name's Thatcher. You seen him?"

Fat Bob smiled. "Real dumb fuck, your friend."

Gretta scowled.

"Well, hell." Suddenly it occurred to him that his defamatory declaration had probably cost him any chance of claiming any portion of Gretta's inexplicable wealth.

"Nice guy," he continued in a much less maligning tone, "just doesn't know Harleys, or how to deal 'em. He made a deal to trade that chromed-out Fat Boy along with some cash for Earl's Electra Glide. Your friend should have been putting extra cash in his pocket, not Earl's. He even gave Earl another five hundred or so just to try it out for the week." He was rambling. "Even if your friend changes his mind, Earl has the five hundred."

Gretta squinted her left eye. "Earl got a last name?"

"Hoeskema."

"He been around since?" she asked.

"Earl?"

"No, you dumb fuck. My friend." Gretta started to feel a little protective over Thatcher. If anyone was going to call Thatcher a dumb fuck, it was going to be her.

Fat Bob shook his head and turned away. Any bill over a twenty that Gretta had in her possession was of suspicious origin and best left alone. It suddenly occurred to him that he had never seen a thousand dollar bill before. Curiously, he wondered why.

Gretta headed for the back room, where she knew Flame and Jolene would be. The young man behind the counter, having been on the job for less than a month, thought twice before inquiring as to where the tall, square-shouldered, tattooed blonde might be going. As she passed him on her way to the back room, she smiled curtly, exposing the gap between her front teeth. He said nothing, and immediately felt the relief of choosing wisely.

"Hey, bitch!" Gretta was addressing her old mentor.

Jolene was a formidable woman. She was considerably shorter than Gretta, thick around the middle, but just as broad across the shoulders. Her long auburn hair was streaked with gray. It was pulled tightly into a braid, identical to Flame's. Jolene's panoply of tattoos and her dark, rugged complexion from decades in the wind and the sun gave her a toughness that Gretta respected and emulated.

"The Amazon Bitch from Chicagoland." Too many filterless cigarettes over too many years gave a raspy texture to Jolene's voice. The voice demanded attention. "What the fuck brings you up here?"

Gretta instantly grabbed Jolene from the front and lifted her off her feet, and then abruptly dropped her, in what Flame recognized as a typical greeting between the two friends. Jolene promptly slugged Gretta in the left shoulder and reared back for another.

"This is all very touching," Flame interjected.

"Yeah," Gretta was respectfully rubbing her left shoulder. "Flame here is lookin' for a date." There was emphasis placed on both the "d" and the "t," giving the two consonants equal dominion over the four-letter word.

Gretta noticed Flame's jaw tightening. "We're trying to track down this Thatcher who was in here yesterday. Dumb fuck traded his custom Fat Boy for a goddamn Electra Glide."

Flame glared at her friend.

Gretta shrugged her shoulders. "It was a dumb fuck thing to do."

"Let's say," pausing long enough to get the attention of both women, "you've got this bitchin' ride. It's chromed-out. It's custom painted. Let's say it's bright red with *Wanderer* written in black along the tank.

"Would you trade that bitchin' ride... for a fuckin' Electra Glide?" Gretta grinned at her impromptu rhyme.

Flame removed her sunglasses and looked straight at Gretta. "Let's say you got a whole lot of trouble on your ass." She paused. "That bitchin' ride would be pretty hard to hide."

Gretta got the point and the rhyme.

Kenyon called Eve back on her car phone and suggested they meet at his favorite pizza pub for lunch. In stride, he accepted her lecture about fat and cholesterol, and as anticipated, he conceded the sausage and pepperoni in favor of peppers and broccoli.

As always, they kept cellular contacts brief and void of important information, on the chance that one of the new order of "techno-criminals" or "phone phreaks" were listening in.

Selling official police information was a booming business among the swarthy criminal underground. And with the new technologically advanced electronics becoming more and more friendly to the average criminal intellect, the informational airways were becoming even more seriously compromised. Kenyon read about it in *Time* magazine.

Eve arrived first at Vinnie's Pizza Pub. As Kenyon surmised, the pizza was ordered by the time he walked through the door.

Sitting down across the table from his partner, he inquired, "I don't suppose you ordered double cheese?"

She smirked. "A little low-fat Mozzarella provides protein and calcium."

"I'm a big guy I need double cheese."

Eve took a sip from her flavored sparkling water. "I'm sure you'll eat twice what you need."

Kenyon looked toward the counter where Vinnie was actively giving instructions to a young apprentice about the fine art of hand tossing dough. The tutelage came in English; the emphatic rifts came in Italian. The young man wore flour and scraps of dough on his apron as evidence of his shortcomings in dough tossing.

"Vinnie, Vinnie. Give the kid a break!"

"Yeah, I give him a break every day at 2:30. What do ya want, Kenyon?"

"Large cola." He glanced at Eve. "Extra sugar."

"Sugar's on the table." Vinnie returned his attention to his young apprentice.

Eve slid the sugar dispenser out of her partner's reach.

Ignoring her maneuver, he began, "You know Eve, The Thatcher Contingency has validity." Glancing at the sugar dispenser, he interjected, "You can let go of that now."

Eve pulled it a couple more inches toward her and let go.

"This guy, Thatcher, may have just fallen in the middle of this. But I can't help thinking that Karlene Swanson and Michael Duran may have had some kind of conspiracy that got out of hand, and now they're just shooting from the hip, as they say."

"And by the body count," Jensen eagerly injected, "someone has been shooting pretty damn well."

"Someone has."

Eve leaned on her elbows, her chin cupped in her hands. "Henderson's going to do something really stupid, and we're going to get him." Her anxiety betrayed her smile.

Kenyon felt her anticipation. His eyes became serious. "Henderson's really worried. He's lost control, he's being backed into a corner."

He paused as the youthful pizza maker set down two plates and a large soda in front of him. Kenyon pulled out the straw and took a sip. "And he's recently lost some of his soldiers." He handed his partner a plate.

Weighing her words cautiously, she waited several seconds before replying. "Alone and cornered, Henderson will be very dangerous." Enthusiasm slipped into dread. "He could do something very ugly."

Not wanting to eat in somberness, John Kenyon needed to lighten the mood. "Like putting broccoli on pizza."

Eve smiled in appreciation of his effort. "Like broccoli on pizza," she murmured.

From there, the conversation purposely slipped into friendly drivel: Kenyon's bowling team's miscues, Jensen's dissatisfaction with cross-trainers, and Sam's gluttonous affection toward albacore.

Approaching quickly with the medium pizza, Vinnie set down the stainless steel pedestal and slipped the pizza onto it in one smooth motion. Kenyon eyed the small pizza and inquired as to when his would be ready.

"You order, I make. You don't order, I don't make." Vinnie squinted at Kenyon. "What part of that don't you understand?"

Jensen began to laugh. "He doesn't understand anything but a large double cheese with pepperoni and sausage."

Kenyon glanced at his partner. "And bacon."

Vinnie stared soberly at his dear old patron of many years. "That what you want?" He winked at Jensen.

"Not today. I'm eating light this noon."

"Have it your way." Vinnie turned abruptly and walked toward his counter.

"John Kenyon," Eve began, "you've done a good thing for your body." Nodding with approval, she added, "You've made me proud."

He lifted his glass toward Eve in a brief appreciative salute. Then he took a long drink from his cola. "Did you know that Vinnie's Pizza Pub delivers after five?"

Jensen slid a slice of pizza onto her plate. "We'll take it one meal at a time."

They pulled into the Harley-Davidson dealership off US 41 outside of Green Bay. Parking the Electra Glide away from the front entrance, he turned off the ignition.

"You need to get some riding gear. There are miles to go yet."

Theresa dismounted and asked complaisantly, "What do I need?"

"Helmet, jacket," he glanced down at her worn canvas shoes, "boots, sunglasses." Finding the pastoral fashion of Osh Kosh bibs charming and demure, he hesitated before suggesting, "Jeans, leather if you like."

Smiling through a contrasting reticence, she asked, "Don't like the farmer's daughter look I have going?"

As stunning as she would appear in a strapless evening dress, as epicurean as she would appear in tight leather jeans, at that moment Thatcher couldn't imagine her in anything except her baggy overalls. He broke into a smile. "Don't change a thing."

Taking his advice, she chose an unobtrusive gray sweat shirt to fit beneath her Osh Kosh's in favor of a leather jacket. The boots were logger style, with laces and rounded toes, as much at home on the farm as on the road. Thatcher fitted her with a black three-quarters helmet.

Standing in front of a full-length mirror, she slipped on reflective aviator's glasses. "The farmer's daughter is ready to ride." Her words, insisting on an exuberance, lacked resolve. Nonetheless, it was enough to coax Thatcher to come and stand behind her. He gave the encouraging smile she had hoped he would provide.

Theresa slid the glasses down to the tip of her nose and looked upward toward Thatcher's reflection. Her smile was fleeting: nearly obscure.

"What do you think?" she asked softly.

"It's you," he said enthusiastically trying to tempt another smile.

"I know what you're thinking," she said matter-of- factly. Her eyes had locked onto his.

Her benign allegation took him by surprise. He had been thinking of a Reuben sandwich.

His silence was unexpected. "You know, you're right. It is me."

Slipping off her helmet, she added, "I'm not sure what I meant by that remark."

Absolutely certain he was no more enlightened then she, he simply said, "It's you, Karlie." And with that, both understood.

It was the first time he had attempted to call her by name. Subliminally, he had failed. Being too much to process in mere milliseconds, his mind willfully flashed back to the Reuben garnished with a deli dill.

His unequivocally dumbfounded expression reflected in the mirror affirmed his repentance. Pulling off her glasses from the tip of her nose, Theresa aimed her blue eyes toward Thatcher.

"We're going to find her," she said quietly.

He took a deep breath. "We will."

Nervously biting her lower lip, she turned toward him. Standing inches away, they studied one another. He chose to say nothing. She said, "I'm ready."

Seventeen

Karlene told him exactly what to say. She told him exactly how his voice should sound. He rehearsed it for over an hour, first while driving the rented Geo south along Sheridan Road, and later while sitting on a bench under a beech tree overlooking Lake Michigan on the Northwestern campus.

Staring out across the water, Michael Duran considered how different it looked from ground level. He preferred to be above it, cruising at 120 miles per hour. He preferred to be above it all... cruising.

"You're ready. I want you to call." Karlene's voice was cheerful, encouraging, and too eager.

He looked intrepidly into her elated blue eyes. "You're excited about this, aren't you? You can hardly wait." Accusingly, he said, "You can't wait to pull the trigger."

"Calm down."

He turned his head away from her soothing voice and said nothing.

"Michael, I do need you. I can't do it alone." Offering a tranquil overture, she promised, "You won't have to shoot anyone."

Michael Duran couldn't imagine firing a gun, let alone aiming it at another human being and pulling the trigger.

Karlene placed her hand on his shoulder. "Michael?"

Turning toward her, he whispered. "Yeah, I'll call the son-of-a-bitch."

"Hey, slide the sugar over here."

The truck driver three stools down from Gretta didn't look up from his sizzle steak sandwich. His large, fleshy hand flicked the sugar dispenser in her general direction. Gretta snatched it just before it careened off the edge of the Formica counter.

"And they say chivalry is fuckin' dead." She poured two tablespoons worth of sugar into Flame's coffee. "Do you want me to stir it too?"

"Would you mind?" Flame returned the sarcasm in equal measure.

Gretta plopped the spoon into her friend's cup and stirred, clanging out a familiar diner melody. She pulled the spoon out and dropped it on the counter. "Shall I kiss your pretty ass as well?"

Flame pursed her lips and lifted her cup slowly to her mouth.

"That fat ass really pissed me off," Gretta announced.

The trucker looked up as he pushed in the final scrap of his sizzle steak sandwich, and glared at Gretta.

"Another fat ass." Gretta squinted inquisitively at the three-hundred pound trucker. "By the way, do you want that there?" Pointing to her right cheek, she said, "The Heinz 57."

He ignored the remark and picked up his coffee.

"That's okay," she added. "Leave it there. It's a good look for you."

Flame nudged her friend in the side.

Gretta twisted around. "What?"

"I'm in no mood to get into it with that guy. So lay off."

"Hey, I'm cool." Shrugging her shoulders back and forth, Gretta glanced around in time to see the trucker wipe off the sauce with a napkin. "Got some change?"

"Don't I always leave the tip?"

Gretta cocked her head. "I need to make a phone call."

Sliding off her stool, Flame struggled to pull out several quarters from her tight leather jeans.

Gretta took them all. "I'll be right back. I just need to crank Fat Bob's ass one more time today."

Flame watched as Gretta strutted toward the pay phone on the wall. Turning back around to the counter she leaned forward against her elbows and sipped her super-sweetened coffee. Flame wondered where Thatcher might be, and smiled to herself as she recalled the stunned expression on his face when he had pulled the shower curtain aside. Playing back in her mind the events of Friday night, she wondered how it might have turned out differently. She was abruptly snatched from her thoughts by Gretta's ungentle nudge, and by hot coffee spilling over the rim of her cup.

"Jesus!" Flame set down her coffee and grabbed a napkin. As she wiped off her hands, she asked, "What the hell you doin'?"

"That crazy son-of-a-bitch. He's heading back."

Flame whirled toward her friend. "What do you mean?"

"I'm speaking English. Am I not?"

With her hands firmly grasping Gretta's shoulders, Flame had no need to repeat her question.

"Hey, all right." Noticing a pickle slice on the counter left over from a prior meal, she reached past Flame, and flicked it onto the floor. "Fat Bob was out stuffin' his face, so I talked to Jolene for a moment."

"What?!"

"Christ, you haven't been laid lately have you?" Quickly translating Flame's expression, she went on. "All right, all right. Jolene called Green Bay for a part, an Evo-Knucklehead conversion."

"I don't care what she called for!"

Gretta rolled her eyes. "She asked about your beau."

"And?" Flame's eyes widened.

"And?" She mimicked. "He was there with Blondie, said they headed south. So where do you think they might be going?"

Flame stood up in a rush. "Let's go!"

Gretta grabbed her arm. "Sit down." She said each word with emphasis on the final consonant.

Flame scowled and sat down.

"I'm not going anywhere until I eat my..." As if on cue, the burrito was placed in front of her. "Burrito." Gretta watched as a plate was slid in front of Flame. "Your taco salad."

Still glaring at her friend, Flame picked up a tomato wedge and bit it in half.

Gretta tapped the corner of her mouth and said, "Tomato seed."

Flame turned away from Gretta and delicately removed the seed with her pinkie. "I have a plan," she said quietly.

David Stout was gone. Aaron Henderson had given him no instructions, no orders. Stout had simply left, as if he had things to do. Aaron's people never simply left. They were directed. He was the puppet master. The strings were his to pull, to control. It was always about control. Control was gone.

Having showered and dressed in a casual yacht club fashion, he sat quietly, awaiting the inevitable: contact from The Affiliation. Contact that would undoubtedly lead to his termination.

Expecting it to be The Affiliation, he allowed the phone to ring more than a dozen times before finally picking it up. "Yes."

The voice was shallow and wispy, as if the caller was nervously out of breath. "Mr. Henderson... I have something you want, or should I say somebody?"

"Who is this?" His heart began racing. He could not be sure whether it was fear or exhilaration. He waited several seconds. "Who is this?"

"Duran."

Recognizing this may be his way out, Aaron quickly composed himself. His mind raced. "Tell me. What do I want? What could you possibly have that I want?" Redemption was at hand.

"A helicopter?" He was ad-libbing.

"I'll buy a new one." Confidence returned.

"It's amazing how much alike they look. You'd be astonished, Mr. Henderson." Duran was returning to his script. He cleared his voice and resumed with an air of cockiness that had always been his trademark. "I'm putting in my resignation. The JetRanger is, of course, more than I expected at retirement, but you've always been very generous." He glanced over toward Karlene.

Smiling, she encouraged him with a confident nod.

"Mr. Henderson, I was thinking."

"You were thinking, Mr. Duran. That is a surprise." Aaron's confidence began to soar.

"Yes, it is, sir." He couldn't help but counter Aaron's arrogance. It was his style. Henderson would expect it.

Karlene squinted at Michael. Her expression told him to keep to the script.

"Mr. Henderson, as you know, it takes substantial bucks to maintain a JetRanger in tip-top shape. I'm sure you would want it taken care of in the manner which it is accustomed."

"Of course, Mr. Duran. And do you believe I would cover that initial cost?"

"Like I said, it's amazing how much alike they look. You might say," he glanced at Karlene as he veered once more from the script, "they're one and the same." He looked away quickly to avoid any censure.

"Mr. Duran, I have underestimated your creativity. How much would you want in exchange for this commodity?"

Of all things, he and Karlene had overlooked the actual amount he would demand. He covered the mouthpiece. Karlene cocked her head.

"What?" she whispered.

"How much?"

"How much what?" she scowled.

Michael Duran rolled his eyes. "How much money? Ransom?"

"Two hundred grand."

"Quarter mill," Duran said quickly.

Without hesitation Henderson told him where to be and when to be there. He hung up and walked over to the large window overlooking the breakwater and Chicago Harbor.

His destination was suddenly clear once again. He would have a drink and consider the fortuitous change of events before paging David Stout.

Michael Duran stared past Karlene, with the receiver in his hand.

"Duran. What?"

"He hung up." It was an honest surprise. "I'm not done with my lines."

She said nothing.

"We're supposed to go to Adler Planetarium at four o'clock. That's not in our plans."

"It is now." She exhaled slowly, remembering all the times she had looked out over the Lake Michigan shoreline from Aaron's penthouse. The rest of the city shoreline could escape her attention, but the dome structure setting upon the narrow peninsula jetting out into Lake Michigan always conjured childhood memories, always reminded her Pegasus would come. So often she had thought of returning to the planetarium. Today she would.

"The place and time make no difference." She turned away from him as he hung up the phone. "Let's go. I have to buy a gun." Karlene said it as if she was off to the delicatessen for a pound of provolone.

Duran walked quickly to catch up to her. "Where?"

"For chrissakes, this is the big city. This is Chicago! Guns are a very big deal here."

Jensen sat behind her desk shuffling through unfinished reports: endless loose ends to cases that were still unsolved. She hated that part of detective work: the loose ends, pending resolutions, many of which never came.

She sipped a sparkling water while reading one more time the report about a young schizophrenic who had been shot through the chest when he challenged two youthful thugs during a holdup in a small neighborhood grocery store. He had been dressed in a costume of his own design, a bright yellow Spandex body suit and a lime green satin cape.

Howard Stilson, the elderly owner of the store, had reported that he knew him only by the name Banana Man. Mr. Stilson, within the report, explained that the young man believed that a single banana every day gave him the super powers he needed to "uphold the righteousness of the universe," and the bananas at Stilson's Grocery were proclaimed the most powerful of the "earthly galaxy." Howard Stilson said he began giving the young man a banana whenever he came in.

"No charge," Howard Stilson would tell him. "This neighborhood needs someone with super powers."

During the police interview, Howard Stilson said, "There was always a twinkle in his eyes. It made you want to believe him."

In exchange for the powerful Stilson banana, Banana Man swore his allegiance to Stilson's Grocery. And on a sunny Wednesday afternoon in May, Banana Man was killed as he collided headlong into reality.

Eve Jensen remembered the gentle brown eyes staring into space. She had seen the death stare before: an eerie emptiness. Banana Man, except for the hole in his chest, appeared to be daydreaming, perhaps of the "earthly galaxy."

Jensen set the Banana Man report aside, took another sip of her sparkling water and sighed. The sight of the blood-soaked Spandex suit remained with her. There had been several weeks when she couldn't get herself to buy bananas at the store. Now, there was never a time that peeling a banana didn't remind her of Banana Man.

Jensen watched as John Kenyon approached, his gait unhurried. When Stan called to him from across the office, he simply raised one arm and smiled. Jensen recognized his "don't bother me now" signal. He leaned against her desk, his large weathered hands pressed against its chipped and scratched veneer surface.

"Nothing," he said. "I've had Douglas positioned in front of his high rise since daybreak. Stout entered a few minutes before eight and left before nine. Nothing since."

"We keep waiting then." She didn't know what else to say.

"I told Douglas you and I would relieve him around three." He glanced at his watch.

"Which means we're late."

John Kenyon shrugged his bulky shoulders and slowly pushed off from the desk. "Yeah."

The piquant zing of sauerkraut and corn beef stayed with Thatcher all the way from Green Bay to Milwaukee. He wished he had ordered a cheeseburger instead of the Rowdy Reuben Deluxe. It was going on three-thirty when they pulled into a Shell station on the south side of the Beer Capital of the Universe.

Standing beside him as he filled the tank, Theresa slipped off her helmet and held it wedged between her arm and her side.

"You have a plan?" she inquired.

Thatcher eased in the last quarter gallon with precision. "Sure," he replied as he hung the nozzle back in place.

"Do you mind sharing?"

He kept it simple and direct. "We go to the money."

A revelation. Theresa closed her eyes solemnly. "Then it is about the money, isn't it?" Her voice was almost a whisper.

Thatcher immediately recognized her misunderstanding, and her disappointment. He would explain.

"Theresa."

He was cut off sharply. "It's always been about the money," she said stepping back. "Why am I here? So I wouldn't go to the police? So you could keep an eye on me until you got what you wanted?"

Thatcher took a deep breath. He thought he had made it clear to everyone; he didn't want the money. Sensing it was the tension, he knew he needed to remain calm. "Believe it or not," he said unabashed. "I have all the money I need."

Theresa momentarily looked away. He waited to catch her eye.

"We go where the money is because that's where Karlene will go."

Theresa said nothing for several seconds. She was embarrassed by her brusqueness. Her eyes glanced downward and then toward Thatcher. "You're right, if Karlene is able, she will return to the money." She stepped close enough to touch his shoulder. "I'm sorry."

"It's the tension."

The sounds of traffic intermingled with nearby voices melded together and seemed to mute their thoughts momentarily.

"And you know where the money is?" she asked quietly.

"I know where it is."

Her eyes pressed him on.

"It's at a friend's house."

The tenseness was lifting.

Theresa ran her fingers through her hair. "Millions of dollars are just setting at a friend's house?" Her smile emerged.

"Actually, it's setting in a bedroom closet," he said as he began walking toward the service station.

Theresa was leaning against the Electra Glide when he returned. Her helmet was still snugly wedged between her arm and her side. Her aviator glasses were pulled down to the tip of her nose, a pose Thatcher recognized.

"You don't remember where this friend's house is, do you?"

He put on his sunglasses and swung his leg over the seat. "I know where it is. Approximately."

"Whoa, partner." She walked around to the front of the bike to look Thatcher straight on.

"Evanston," he said. "It's in Evanston."

Theresa pushed her sunglasses into place and began putting on her helmet. "But you don't know where in Evanston."

Flame and Gretta had cruised north on I-94 to Dundee Road at Glencoe. The afternoon was sultry and well above eighty degrees. As they leaned against their bikes parked on the overpass watching the traffic pass beneath them, Gretta complained.

"We could be sitting in some air-conditioned dive getting down on some brewskis." Gretta had stripped down to her bare leather essentials. "He's not going to be through here for hours," lowering her voice, she added, "if at all."

"I'm not taking any chances."

Gretta rolled her eyes. “I’ve never seen anyone work this hard to get a date.” She threw her arms into the air. “I’m going for drinks.”

Flame continued staring toward the southbound traffic.

“He might not be coming down 94,” Gretta added.

“It’s the fastest, most direct way into Chicago.”

“Why not 294, or 43?” Gretta slipped on her vest.

“He’s coming in on 94. I know it.”

Shaking her head, she asked, “Princess, you want an Arizona?”

“Raspberry. Don’t take too long.”

Gretta grinned. “No problem.”

Aaron Henderson spent much of the mid-afternoon preparing his gold-plated Beretta 92 for another business transaction. The 9mm weapon had been chambered for subsonic ammunition and its muzzle velocity had been modified to just under 1,000 feet per second. With its sound suppressor, it was Aaron’s silent partner. The Italian-made sidearm had been his most loyal business confrere over the years.

He cradled it in his left hand and admired its smooth lines. He caressed its cool metal, reacquainting himself with its weight and its feel.

“We have business to attend to, my friend.” He spoke to it as he passed it quickly to his right hand. Aiming it at the brass lamp setting on his desk, he squeezed the trigger. At the sound of the click, he grinned. “You’re dead.”

The excitement of the confrontation ascended Aaron Henderson into a near-euphoric state. Despite the five milligrams of Valium he had taken with a shot of Dewar’s thirty minutes earlier, he felt his pulse quicken.

He would measure the expectancy in Duran’s eyes. He would force him to stare into the small black hole while holding the Beretta just inches away from his head. Watching Duran’s final moments slip into absolute horror, he would squeeze the trigger. Transaction closed.

For Karlene, Henderson mused, a single bullet penetrating the skull and ripping through the cerebral cortex would be insufficient. She had taken him to the brink of self-destruction. For that, she would pay dearly. A simple closure was out of the question.

The sound of the telephone interrupted his thoughts. He set the gold-plated handgun down gently into its red-velvet-lined case and picked up the receiver.

"Yes."

"It's Stout."

"I paged you over an hour ago." Aaron walked over to the large window overlooking the Chicago Yacht Club far below. "The Swanson twin is in town."

"How?" David Stout was surprised.

"Duran."

David Stout said nothing.

"He apparently left the other two behind with extortion on his mind. He brought back the sister, and he wants to cut a deal."

"What do you want me to do?" Stout asked without hesitation.

"Adler Planetarium. Be there at four o'clock. I'm going to handle this personally. I want you there to help with the Swanson woman after I've permanently closed the deal with Mr. Duran."

"Yes, sir."

Karlene directed Duran to a small business establishment off South Boulevard in downtown Evanston. Its bright yellow sign announced: instant cash for your jewelry, electronics, and guns. Duran pulled the egg-shaped Geo into the small, eroded asphalt parking lot and parked to the far right of the gray cement block building. The steel bars across the windows and the front door seemed to emanate urban paranoia.

"You coming in?" she asked as she opened her door.

"I'll guard the car."

Karlene shook her head in mock agreement. "Someone should do that, Michael."

Michael Duran watched her enter the front door as if she was an everyday customer. He imagined a short, rotund middle-aged man with hereditary baldness sitting on a stool behind a glass counter chewing on the butt end of a stogie. Michael was prone to watching too many late night movies.

The slender energetic young woman behind the knotty pine counter greeted Karlene cheerfully. Her faded and torn sleeveless denim shirt tucked into her Calvin Klein jeans declared a style of her own. Her mocha skin and dark curly hair suggested a delicate ethnic blending.

"Hi." Glancing around, Karlene concluded she was the lone customer. "How you doin'?"

The young woman shrugged her shoulders. "Doin' the nine to five thing, you know. Except Sundays, it's noon to five." Her dialect was a sweet fusion of rhythm and blues and gangsta rap. Karlene guessed she was in her mid-twenties.

"Not too busy today."

"You and me."

Karlene was direct. "Lookin' for a .32 caliber." At close range it would be lethal.

The young woman leaned closer. "You bein' stalked, girl?" She whispered as if someone else might be listening.

"Not anymore."

Grinning with approval, she sensed this tall blonde knew bad times, and was ready to deliver herself. She reached her hand across the counter. "Name's Regina."

Karlene grasped her hand. "Karlie."

Regina led her to a counter at the rear of the store. In a locked glass display case were several handguns of various calibers.

Regina walked behind the counter. "There's a waiting period, and papers to fill out. You know, the standard stuff."

Karlene hesitated, and glanced away momentarily. "What if I really can't wait?" Her voice conveyed her urgency. Her eyes conveyed her exigency.

Regina put aside her cheery demeanor. "Comin' down soon?" She crossed her arms over her chest.

Karlene nodded. She needed to leave the pawn shop with a gun, or she would have to go elsewhere, and she did not have a lot of time. Feeling Regina would come through, Karlene pressed her hands against the glass countertop and leaned closer.

"Four o'clock."

Uncrossing her arms, Regina's expression became apologetic as she said, "It's gonna cost."

Karlene pulled out five wrinkled one hundred dollar bills from her jeans pocket and laid them on the counter. It was the rest of the money that Thatcher had given to her the day before.

"I'll be right back." Disappearing into the back room, she was gone for less than a minute. She returned with a small nickel-plated semi-automatic.

"It's a .22 long rifle. Unregistered. Safety's on, the clip's full, eight shots." Regina handed it carefully to Karlene.

Karlene read the name "Taurus" stamped into its barrel.

Regina glanced down at the five bills. "Four of those will do it. That's what it'll take to replace it."

Karlene nodded toward the bills. "That's all I have. It's worth all I have."

It was the appreciative expression. Regina stuffed the bills into her pocket. "I don't have any more bullets."

Karlene released the clip and inspected the cartridges. Karlene's voice took on a sullenness. "I won't need any more." She replaced the clip.

Impressed with Karlene's handling of the firearm, she said, "Girl, someone's gonna pay for messin' with you." It was a compliment.

She noticed Regina was wearing a small, black, nylon pack over her right hip. Nodding toward it, Karlene asked, "Could you part with that?"

"It's yours." Regina released the plastic buckle.

Karlene set the handgun onto the counter as she watched Regina dump a collection of inexpensive cosmetics, a change purse, and a ring of keys onto the counter.

She presented the nylon pack to Karlene. "Here."

Karlene smiled briefly as she picked it up. Placing the handgun into it, she zipped it shut, and fastened it around her waist.

Regina extended her hand. "Girl, you be careful."

"I intend to."

Both women held firmly to each other's hand.

Karlene had been gone for less than fifteen minutes, yet by Michael Duran's expression, it appeared she had been gone hours.

Anxiously he asked, "Well?"

"All set." She patted the nylon pack on her hip.

"Now what?"

"What time is it?"

He glanced at his watch. "Almost three."

"I'm craving a milkshake and fries." She fastened her seat belt. "Head toward Adler and stop at the first Burger King you see."

Duran turned the key. The small engine rattled to life. "You're off to shoot someone and you want to stop and eat first?"

Eve Jensen eased the black Crown Victoria onto Lake Shore Drive. The drive south along Lake Michigan reminded her of summer afternoons from her youth. Allowing her mind to wander away from the Henderson case, she looked over at her partner.

"John, what was it like back in the fifties and sixties?" Her question caught him off guard. "You know what I mean," she was grinning, "back when you were a kid."

John Kenyon glanced quizzically at his partner.

"Tell me about the first time you went cruisin' down Lake Shore." She restrained herself from smiling too much. "What was on the radio?"

John Kenyon was too slow with an answer.

"Let me guess, John." She bit her lower lip to suppress her grin. "Elvis. And, wait. I saw this movie preview just the other night on WGN about Buddy Holiday."

"Buddy or Billie?" He imagined a duet and smiled.

Jensen thought a moment. "I know Billie."

Her emphasis on "know," suggested to Kenyon that she probably had the entire 1945–1959 Verve collection.

"It's Buddy Holly and the Crickets," he said informatively.

Eve Jensen moved into the passing lane and accelerated past a delivery truck. "Crickets? You're kidding?"

Shaking his head, Kenyon asked, "Where have you been?"

She frowned. "John, I was born in 1966."

"Then you missed the best of rock and roll."

Eve frowned even more. "I've got all the Beatle's Anthologies, and I've had the White Album since high school."

Kenyon nodded with approval. "And, who do you think the Fab Four listened to back in Liverpool?"

Eve didn't need to consider the answer long. She knew how Kenyon's mind worked. "Buddy Holly and the Crickets," she beamed.

"Your deduction is superb, as always."

"Thank you."

Their sanguine conversation faded into a pensive silence. Several minutes passed.

Kenyon leaned back; his eyes were closed. "Eve."

"Yeah?" She glanced quickly at her partner.

"This is the day."

The austerity in his voice surprised her. She knew exactly what he meant.

"He's going down." Eve spoke with a vivacity that disturbed Kenyon.

"Eve," he said soberly.

"What is it, John?"

He took a deep breath. "I want you to be very careful."

"By the book," she said.

"Yeah, by the book." Kenyon, for a brief moment, studied the young detective.

Eve acknowledged him with a glance and a quick smile as Lake Point Tower loomed ahead. "I know."

EIGHTEEN

THE OMNIPRESENCE OF HARLEYS ON THE HIGHWAYS CONverging on Milwaukee was of no surprise to those residing in southern Wisconsin. The pilgrimage of American riders to the birthplace of their beloved iron steeds had become an annual summer event. The sapphire blue Electra Glide Thatcher and Theresa rode south was merely one of more than a hundred Harleys that might cruise along I-94 on any given day.

Thatcher was confident that they would go unnoticed by whomever may be looking for them. He still had not entirely accepted the idea that he was a refugee of the law, and of the gangster from whom he had inadvertently taken several million dollars. He continued to become increasingly apprehensive as they closed in on greater Chicagoland.

Crossing over into Illinois a little before four, Thatcher collided with the rush of traffic advancing upon one of the main arteries feeding Chicago its commuters, tourists, and fugitives.

The gentle pounding on Thatcher's right shoulder got his attention. He leaned back and cocked his head to listen.

"I've got to go!" Theresa's right arm sprang out with a forceful thrust pointing to the side of the highway.

"What?!" Thatcher shook his head.

She pulled herself closer. With her mouth close to the proximity of Thatcher's ear, she yelled one more time. "Rest stop!"

With successful communication completed, Thatcher accelerated past a Mack tanker and veered to the right, across the path of the big truck. He hit the exit ramp to the rest stop with near precision. Two downshifts later the Electra Glide eased into third gear, and if not for a renegade Boston Terrier fleeing from the dog run area, the descent into the parking lot would have been flawless.

As the little dog sprinted in front of him, he locked up the rear brakes. The big bike began to slide to the right. Thatcher's right foot released the brake, his left foot downshifted to second, while his right hand tugged gently on the front brake. The Electra Glide straightened out, and a few moments later he pulled into a parking space. Shifting into neutral he turned off the ignition and steadied the bike as Theresa climbed off.

She undid her chin strap and pulled off her helmet. "It's an absolute wonder I didn't wet my pants!" She handed Thatcher her headgear and ran her fingers through her hair.

Setting her helmet over the top of one mirror, he watched as she pulled the bulky sweatshirt over her head, and tied it around her waist. As she walked away from him, he admired the strong graceful gait, the long brisk strides, and the subtle, purposeful sway of the hips. It was Theresa, yet for a millisecond his mind told him that it was Karlene.

Thatcher took off his helmet and set it atop the other mirror. Dismounting gingerly, he slowly stretched his arms above his head, and arched his back. Road weary and sore, he walked onto the grass and lay on his back. Allowing his eyes to close, he was certain he could drift off to sleep.

Moments later, a light kick to the bottom of his boot slowly brought him to. When he opened his eyes he found Theresa sitting Indian-style beside him on the grass.

"I want to apologize again for what I said before. I don't know why."

Propping himself up, he waited for her to continue.

Theresa rested her elbows on her knees. "So, why are you doing this?" Placing her chin in her cupped hands, she continued. "Risking your life for Karlene? For me?"

"It's what I do."

Frowning, she lowered her eyes. "It's what you do?"

"Today, it's what I do."

"And, tomorrow?"

"I do something else." It seemed clear enough.

"And, something else would be?"

Thatcher began to get to his feet. "I'll know tomorrow." He offered her his hand. "Time to go."

Parked beside the motor home of the "Meanderin' McMillans" of Sunrise Beach, Missouri, the purple Geo was hidden from the rest of the Burger King parking lot. Karlene hastily licked her fingers after popping the last french fry into her mouth. The chocolate shake cradled between her thighs was only half gone. She picked it up and held it out to Duran.

He shook his head.

"Here, I can't finish it."

"Not hungry."

Karlene brought the straw to her mouth and took a long drink. "You don't have to be hungry to slurp a shake. Why do you think they sell so many?"

Duran shrugged his shoulders.

She studied him for a moment. "You think you're going to die, don't you?"

Imposing more brusque forthrightness than her accomplice could endure at that moment, she watched as he slumped over the steering wheel of the cramped car and released a sigh emulating a man's last breath.

"It's crossed my mind." Without raising his head, he turned toward Karlene in time to see her roll her eyes. Michael Duran, baffled by her equanimity, asked, "It hasn't crossed your mind that just maybe Aaron is going to survive this assassination attempt? And we end up in the *Sun Times* obit."

Casually. "No. It hasn't." Karlene took another long drink.

"The delusional power of revenge," he murmured.

Ignoring the remark, Karlene glanced at the digital clock on the radio and said, "Time to get going."

Shaking his head, he whispered, "You're going to get us killed."

Karlene needed to set it straight with her reluctant ally. "You saved my ass up north." Her tone had turned earnest. "I owe you. Count on it."

Perhaps it was the way she said it, or the resolution in her eyes, or perhaps it was simply that she knew. Whatever it was, it was, for the moment, enough for Michael Duran. He began thinking about the bright azure skies above the Caribbean.

He spoke softly. "You owe me."

Karlene handed him the chocolate shake, then wiped the moisture from her hands onto her jeans.

"You owe me," he said again as he brought the straw toward his mouth.

"Christ, I gotta pee." Flame's proclamation was not unexpected.

"Of course you do." Gretta was leaning against the steel railing watching the southbound traffic. "You emptied two tall ones." Turning toward her partner, "I'd say that makes a piss and a half."

Flame stood statuesque; her arms across her chest. She stared stoically out over the oncoming parade of rush hour commuters. "This is really not a good time."

"There's a gas station down thata way." Gretta provided a rendition of a Texas twang on her three final words, then waited momentarily for Flame's predictable scowl before motioning westward with a nod of her head.

"I know where it is," Flame replied.

"Or you can squat right here."

Flame ignored the remark and walked over to her Springer. Throwing her leg over her steed, she pulled out the choke, then nudged it in a quarter-inch and turned the ignition. Punching the start button brought on the rumble of the V-Twin. She yelled to Gretta. "Keep watching! It's about the right time!"

Gretta turned her attention toward the oncoming traffic as she shrugged her shoulders.

Glaring over the top of her shades, Flame shouted once again. "Keep watching!"

"What else am I gonna do?" Gretta's words dissolved instantaneously into the dissension of sounds booming from the expressway below.

Flame had been gone for less than a minute when Gretta decided to have a smoke. As she moved toward her Fat Boy to retrieve a Marlboro from the inside pocket of her vest she caught a glimpse of a big V-Twin moments before it disappeared beneath the overpass.

"Holy fuck!"

For a brief moment she hesitated. She was not absolutely sure it had been an Electra Glide, or even if it was blue.

The plan had been that one of them would intercept any southbound blue Electra Glide, and the other would continue the vigil until the other returned with or without Thatcher.

Flame had decreed the plan simple and effective. Gretta had considered it almost useless, yet she considered the overall situation amusing, and if on the outside chance they could catch up with Thatcher, it could turn out to be quite entertaining. With that final aspect she had accepted the scheme.

"Christ." Gretta mumbled to herself as she flung on her leather vest. "It's about the right time." Sarcastically mimicking her friend, she added, "Jesus, if she knew this was about the right time why didn't she piss a half-hour ago?" Gretta fastened the bottom button of her vest and threw her right leg over the seat. "Shit a brick, if that's not Thatcher."

A moment later the Fat Boy careened into the traffic heading towards the entrance ramp to southbound I-94.

To anyone else summer holiday traffic was an agonizing plague that swept across the suburban and metro thoroughfares three times a season. To Gretta it was an excuse to ride the centerline, the shoulder, and the meridian at madcap speeds. It allowed her a means to exhibit her superiority over vehicles possessing more than two wheels.

Merging headlong into the unrelenting tide of traffic, Gretta took the centerline at 75 miles per hour as if it were a tightrope. Gliding effortlessly past startled and disgruntled motorists, she was abetted by hostile horn blasts.

Before the lapse of the second mile she caught sight of a blue Electra Glide. There was a passenger. Gretta twisted what was left of the throttle and pulled closer. The passenger appeared to be a woman.

It was going to be good to see Thatcher again, she thought.

David Stout was dressed in khakis and a polo shirt with a light summer sports jacket that concealed a holstered .38 Special. A camera hung around his neck. He appeared as much a tourist as anyone standing in front of one of the large Oceanarium viewing windows. A family with twin boys about the age of ten, and a younger girl swarmed around him. He stepped back and to the side.

The young girl pointed toward a quizzical face staring back at her. "Look, Mommy! A beaver!"

Both brothers broke into hysterical laughter, and shouted in unison. "A beaver!"

The mother frowned in their direction, and then whispered something to her daughter. The little girl nodded in acknowledgment, then stuck out her tongue at her notorious brothers.

The sea otter drifted by the window carefully, observing the faces staring out from the other side of the glass. He seemed particularly interested in the little girl who was playfully contorting her face. He pressed his broad black nose against the glass. Slipping under the railing, she giggled as she did the same. The otter slowly drifted upwards and away.

"Mommy, he likes me."

The mother gently guided her daughter back beneath the railing. "I think he does."

The mammal seemed contented to gradually drift away from the glass. However, when its eyes eventually met the dark narrow stare of David Stout, it swirled around with a quick flip of its powerful tail and was out of sight.

"Mommy, I don't think he liked that man." She turned and pointed at David Stout.

The little girl's mother ushered her away from the large man standing near them. "He just needed to get a breath of air. You know, sea otters breath, just like we do."

David Stout moved into the vacated spot in front of the viewing window. He checked his watch. It was nearly four o'clock. He would visit the penguins and then leave.

Aaron Henderson pulled out from the harborage of Lake Point Tower in his black Mercedes 450 SL. The top was down and he was an easy mark for Kenyon and Jensen, who had positioned themselves near the entrance of the elite lakefront high-rise.

"Bingo!" Kenyon turned toward his partner. "He's all yours."

Jensen accelerated into the traffic two cars behind the black SL. "I love this part." She smacked her lips. "It's exhilarating."

Kenyon got on the radio to begin his narration of Jensen's pursuit. "Keep the patrol cars out of the way. Henderson's driving could earn him numerous violations by the time he gets to wherever he's going. I don't want him stopped." Pausing, he glanced toward his partner and added. "I have little doubt he'd shoot any poor son-of-a-bitch trying to pull him over." He paused as Jensen swerved into the left lane. "And if he didn't, I might consider it." Kenyon ended the call.

Jensen swung quickly back into the other lane, and Kenyon slid against thc door.

"Sorry." She glanced over at John Kenyon. "I'm sure he didn't spot us; he's just driving like an asshole."

At that moment another car cut in front of Jensen and braked suddenly. Jensen slammed on the brakes as the car in front of her careened into the next lane. Both of them lurched forward. As Jensen accelerated once again their eyes met briefly.

"Asshole," they said.

Aaron slid Beethoven's Symphononie No. 3 into the CD player and cranked up the volume. The first crashing notes of Allegro con brio penetrated the thick Chicago air and were quickly whisked away, swirling into the humid afternoon as the 450 SL convertible moved out against the pressure of Aaron Henderson's right foot.

Bathed in a cool current from the air conditioner, he swayed theatrically as if he, and not Herbert Von Karajan, was conducting the Berliner Philharmoniker.

Reaching into his jacket pocket he pulled out a small silver pillbox. He opened it and, with a single quick movement, deposited the two small tablets into his mouth and swallowed.

Flame had returned to the Dundee Road overpass to find Gretta gone. At first she was furious, thinking her partner had skipped out on her. Staring westward at the Sheridan Hotel a quarter mile away, she knew it wasn't a likely place for Gretta to be chilling out, but it was the closest beer stop.

While she sat on her Springer, absorbing the soothing vibration from the V-Twin and contemplating what she might do to her mutinous compadre, it suddenly occurred to her that Gretta might not have zipped over to the Sheridan after all. Instead she may have spotted Thatcher, or at least a blue Electra Glide cruising south, and she was now in pursuit.

She turned off the ignition; the Springer fell silent. Flame sat for several seconds and stared at the intersection of the northbound off-ramp. It felt like several minutes. What if Gretta was bringing Thatcher back right now, she thought. They could be here anytime. Flame felt her hands trembling.

"Christ." She held her hands in front of her and watched her fingers shake ever so slightly. "What the hell is this?" she said softly. "It's gotta be the caffeine." She felt her chest pounding as well.

Five minutes seemed like thirty as she paced back and forth along the rampart, keeping one eye on the southbound traffic and the other on the northbound exit. Then came the blast from Gretta's horn above the monotonous drone of the traffic below; it sent shivers through her. At the exit ramp intersection appeared Gretta's Fat Boy, and a few yards behind it, a blue Electra Glide. Gretta's fist flashed into the air. Thatcher was back.

Karlene and Michael walked rapidly from the parking area south of Soldier Field all the way to Solidarity Drive. She suggested that holding hands would make them appear as a couple spending a Sunday afternoon together. Duran could hardly resist expressing his opinion that walking hand-in-hand with a vengeful woman packing a loaded gun in her fanny pack was far from his idea of an afternoon walk in the park. Particularly since they were on their way to meet a gangster, for the sole purpose of shooting him before he shot them. It was the middle of the afternoon with a hundred potential witnesses milling around. It was absurd.

He stopped suddenly and pulled Karlene directly in front of him. Standing face to face, he asked, "Why are we doing this?"

She looked at him and said nothing.

He nervously scratched the side of his head and looked around, briefly noticing out of the throngs of people two boys romping around on the grass near the walkway coming from Shedd Aquarium. He was certain they were twins, which brought his thoughts back to Karlene and her sister.

"Okay, I know why we're doing this." His voice was deadpan. "It's him, or it's us." Glancing around, he added, "But, here?"

Karlene leaned momentarily against him. Michael Duran expected to hear a sigh: evidence of apprehension, of uncertainty, or of fear. There was only the busy sound of the summer afternoon along Lake Shore Drive.

He looked over at the two brothers now whirling one another around on the grass; a younger girl stood nearby and watched with a comical expression of dismay.

"We'll take care of this," he said, "then we'll go find her." His gallant declaration was as much for him as it was for Karlene. Heroism was not second nature for Michael Duran.

As they followed the black SL south on Lake Shore Drive, Kenyon paid little attention to the traffic as he stared off into Grant Park bordering Chicago Harbor. Aaron Henderson's driving had dramatically improved over the short distance and Jensen had no problems staying close, yet out of sight.

"Where do you think he's going?" Jensen asked.

"The museum?"

"A cultural outing."

Kenyon smiled. "He's one cultural SOB."

The Field Museum, with its classic Roman architecture lay straight ahead and Soldier Field beyond. Shedd Aquarium and Adler Planetarium were directly to the east on the Lake Michigan shoreline.

Lake Shore Drive collided with summer construction just before it divided at the museum, the southbound traffic that once veered to the west now veered to the east. The cultural campus was a major tourist attraction; the sudden traffic jam verified its popularity.

"I wish they'd get this road work done," Kenyon scowled.

Jensen recognized the potential for another dissertation on the city highway system. She was not interested. A distraction was required.

"You like spiders?"

Kenyon couldn't help but smile as he stared straight ahead at the large colorful banners hanging between each column of the museum. The banners composed a giant mural of a less-than-menacing spider.

"If they don't bother me, I don't squash them."

"Arachniphobia?"

"I know that word. No, I'm not afraid of spiders."

Jensen smirked. "Well, let's go to the exhibit during lunch sometime next week."

"Just because I said I'm not afraid of them, doesn't mean I want to have lunch with them."

"Come on, John."

"You're not going to let this go are you?"

"Probably not."

Kenyon begrudgingly nodded. "Why not?"

Watching as the black SL move to the left lane, "He's turning," he said.

"I see." Jensen maneuvered quickly to the left. "The aquarium?"

"The planetarium?"

"Maybe it is a cultural outing after all," she added.

Turning to each other, their eyes reflected cognate concern.

"Do you think something's going down here, with all these tourists?" Jensen began the turn onto Solidarity Drive.

"Maybe he's made us."

Jensen scowled. "Never."

"Just turning back north," Kenyon offered.

"Don't think so, John."

Kenyon called in their location.

She abhorred situations where large numbers of civilians could be used as cover, or easily used as shields, or worse, hostages. Jensen had never been directly involved with a situation where a hostage had been taken, but she had seen the aftermath.

A young boy had been killed in view of his parents. The sight of the hysterical woman laying atop her son as onlookers stared in disbelief still haunted her. It was the only time she had actually considered resigning from the force. A half-dozen sessions with the staff psychiatrist had pulled her back from an abysmal depression. She couldn't help remembering. It sent a chill through her.

"Eve, you're right. It doesn't appear he's going to turn around." Pointing toward the black convertible as it turned into the planetarium parking area, he added, "I think we have a stargazer."

Adler Planetarium was straight ahead.

"I think so," Eve whispered.

Leaning against her fringed and chrome-studded saddle, Flame watched the fat gangsta whitewall of the Electra Glide as it crept up alongside her Springer. As the big tour bike came to a stop beside her, she slowly began shaking her head.

When their eyes met, she said, "Just plain, shithead stupid."

Thatcher smiled. As unexpected as it was, it was good to see Flame and Gretta. It was good to have two more allies, at least for the moment.

Gretta's Fat Boy pulled up on the other side as Flame leaned over and kissed Thatcher firmly on the mouth. Their eyes held, fixed upon the other. Lightly biting his lower lip, she slowly moved away. To Thatcher, it seemed as natural as it seemed unnatural, as clear as it seemed unclear.

Gretta, sitting on her Fat Boy, her arms folded across her chest, was amused. "This is so fucking sweet, I can hardly stand it." Looking squarely at Theresa, she asked, "What do you think, Blondie?"

Theresa dismounted and removed her helmet. She stood on the other side of the bike from Flame, and only a couple feet away from Gretta. She turned toward the tall, muscular woman who straddled the large motorcycle with ease. In an agreeable tone Theresa replied, "Sweet."

"Not the jealous type?" Gretta studied her partner's apparent rival.

"I know," she lowered her voice, "it pisses me right off when some bitch comes onto my stuff." Slowly unfolding her arms, she placed her hands on her hips. "Pisses me right off."

Theresa could not avoid taking a long look at Gretta's broad tattooed shoulders and her large muscled arms. Stepping beside the tall woman, Theresa surprised herself when she casually placed a hand on one broad shoulder. "Not my stuff," she said.

Gretta eyed her closely, then reached out with her right hand, palm up, offering it to Theresa. Theresa grasped it firmly.

"I'm Gretta," she said with direct affirmation.

"Theresa."

With a deliberate nod in the direction of her partner, Gretta announced, "That's Flame." Lowering her voice and returning her eyes to Theresa, she added succinctly, "She's horny as hell."

The two newly acquainted women smiled as they turned their attention to Flame and Thatcher.

"Christ, what've you been up to?" Flame inadvertently placed her hands on her hips, then immediately dropped them to her side.

Gretta interjected. "What kind of shit did you fall into now? We send you off in style, after kicking some dumb cop's ass, and here you are again." She turned her attention to Theresa. "Where's the diamonds?"

Theresa smirked. "You mean this guy is a jewel thief too?"

Looking toward Theresa, Thatcher sighed deeply as he took off his helmet. "Things have gotten a little complicated," he began. "This isn't who you think it is."

Theresa shook her head in acknowledgment. "It's a sad, but familiar story. I've once again been mistaken for my evil twin."

Flame and Gretta stared at one another, then simultaneously they looked from Thatcher to Theresa, then back toward one another.

"It's true," Theresa confirmed with a somewhat droll conviction. "I am the intelligent and judicious one."

"Judicious." Gretta repeated the word slowly. Suddenly catching the gist of Theresa's proclamation, she grinned.

Theresa laughed. "Well, until now."

Nineteen

As Jensen waited for a Windstar to back out of a parking space, Kenyon called in their position and situation. He was adamant about keeping all uniforms out of the immediate area.

"I don't want anything resembling a law enforcement vehicle within a half-mile of Adler." Kenyon's voice was calm and direct. "That includes meter patrol." He was remembering an incident that occurred a month ago in Oak Lawn.

A member of the parking meter patrol was shot as she placed a citation on the windshield of a car parked directly behind a getaway moped. A pellet-pistol-packing twelve-year-old who had just lifted a prized NBA rookie card from a nearby hobby shop panicked at the sight of a uniform. The grandmother of five took the small piece of lead in the right shoulder. She was treated at the local emergency room and released. The perpetrator was apprehended later that afternoon as he practiced his fadeaway jumper at a nearby playground.

The incident made statewide news, but fell short of catching Oprah's attention. Nonetheless, it reminded the public of the inflated worth of sport heroes, and the hazards of wearing uniforms depicting authority.

Kenyon turned to his partner. "You've been here before." It wasn't a question, but rather a confirmation.

"You haven't?" Jensen countered with wide-eyed amazement.

"Well, it's been a few years."

"You need to get out of the bowling allies more often, John." Jensen gave him a tenuous smile, then glanced toward Adler Planetarium. Its carved stone architecture had always given her a sense of tranquil civility, as antiquity seemed to embrace contemporary science. She came here often to soothe her curious spirit, and to chill out after a harrowing day of criminal investigation.

"What now?" she asked.

"I assume you know this place well?" This time it was a question.

"I do."

"How about a tour? Who knows, perhaps we'll run across something of interest." His tone turned serious. "We need to find out what the hell he's doing here."

Jensen broke into a subtle grin. "We're visitors to the Museum Campus."

"That's right."

"I'll be the intellectual one, and you'll be..."

"Homer Simpson."

Eve Jensen laughed, even though she had little knowledge of Kenyon's favorite cartoon character. Hers had always been Wilma Flintstone.

Browsing in the planetarium gift shop, Aaron was aware of the neatly dressed young woman watching him from the lobby. Her discreet signal to the gray-haired man at the entrance of the shop didn't escape his notice. If they were to pose a problem, he thought, they could be eliminated. For that matter, whoever was to get in his way could be eliminated. His mind staggered between supposition and reason.

The Valium and the scotch had begun his irreversible descent into delirium. As his mind erupted into vivid flashes of paranoia, he placed his hand quickly inside his jacket. The touch of his Beretta excited him. As his fingers closed around it, a hand fell lightly onto his shoulder.

"Mr. Henderson," Stout's voice calmed him instantly. "They're here."

Karlene and Michael ascended the escalator from the Universe Theater into the domed Sky Theater just as the lights began to dim for the scheduled presentation of "Skies of Africa." They kept to the back wall near the top of the escalator.

"How do you know he's going to be here?" Duran asked, as his eyes turned upward toward the dome ceiling. There was complete blackness.

Karlene felt Michael Duran's arm against hers. "He said four o'clock at Adler," she said with assurance. "It's four o'clock. This is Adler."

He glanced toward Karlene, even though he could not see her. "I mean, in here?" He tried not to sound anxious. "He'll find us. Watch the show." Her voice was extraordinarily calm.

Suddenly, he heard her gasp and felt her body shudder beside him. He held his breath.

It was a light touch on her shoulder that caused Karlene to heave. A deep baritone whisper followed.

"Sorry, miss." The voice was familiar. "Let me guide you to a seat." He aimed his pinpoint-beamed flashlight a few feet ahead.

The handsome middle-aged man that had provided the introduction to the planetarium a few minutes earlier in the Universe Theater led Karlene and Michael to nearby seats.

There was a chorus of "Ooooohs" as they sat down. Their attention was drawn upward, where the summer skies above the Sahara were duplicated with more than a thousand points of light across the domed ceiling. A soft classical melody enveloped the theater.

Karlene whispered. “I haven’t been here since I was a kid.” At that moment she noticed the shadowy figures of two boys three rows down and across the narrow aisle from her. She could see well enough in the darkness to discern their nudging and poking with elbows and fingers. Without a doubt, she knew they were twins, and that the younger girl beside them was the displeased little sister. Leaning against her mother, it was obvious she was attempting to escape her brothers’ annoying antics.

“I’m not sure that I want him to find us.” Michael began as he leaned against Karlene. “I’d rather find him first, and then, if I suddenly change my mind, I can get the hell out of here.”

Karlene nuzzled against Michael in the dark. “We have to let him think we are here on his terms. We have to let him think he has control, or...”

“Or what?” Michael tried to whisper calmly. “He’ll leave without killing us?”

“Remember, he wants the money first. He wants to kill us second. I’ve got the money, and I want to kill him first. Get it? We have control. He’s here on our terms.”

Within his disconcerted mind, Duran mulled over Karlene’s logic. “Okay.” He didn’t know what else to say.

“It’s a sundial, right?”

“Very good!

John Kenyon smirked as he walked toward the large metal sculpture in the center of the small concrete courtyard that separated the original domed structure from the newer entrance to Adler Planetarium. He walked slowly around the sundial with his hands clasped behind his back.

Eve Jensen recognized the purposeful gait. John Kenyon was thinking. She watched intently, waiting. Within a minute Kenyon was standing beside her once again.

“I’ve been giving it some thought.” He glanced at Jensen. “But, you already know that.”

She smiled. After a moment's silence, she shrugged her shoulders and she replied, "And?"

"I don't know." Sticking his hands into his pockets, he said, "A meeting?"

Her eyes widened, her voice interposed too much intrigue. "An exchange?"

Furling his brow, Kenyon uttered one name. "Ludlum."

"That's twice in two days." It was an amiable warning.

Wisely changing the subject, he pointed toward the dome. "I remember going in through those doors."

"It has been awhile, hasn't it John?" Jensen pulled him toward the glass front entrance. "We go in here. I don't believe you. It's been that long?" she said as she opened the door for him.

"It's been a few years." Smiling at the greeter standing just inside the door, Kenyon asked, "How do we get over there?" He pointed at the dome.

Before the young woman could answer, Eve nodded to her and said, "I know the way." She took John's arm. "It's down this way."

"Underground." It was a revelation.

"They're in the Sky Theater." Stout nodded in the direction they needed to go.

Aaron Henderson glanced around excitedly. "This place is infiltrated; the locals called in the Feds." His eyes darted about. "Over there!"

Aaron pointed toward the gray-haired man in the light summer jacket who was now talking with a young Asian man. "I don't mind adversity." He winked at David Stout.

Henderson's right-hand man nodded toward the exit as he casually put his hands into his pants pockets. He had anticipated correctly. His boss had popped too many milligrams of Valium with too many shots of scotch, and the resulting delusional paranoia would need to be channeled carefully. Aaron had become very predictable over the years.

With a touch of his hand, David Stout led his boss from the gift shop.

"It was simple deduction," Flame said as she ended her explanation on how she had known where to intercept Thatcher upon getting word that he was heading back to Chicago.

"It was fucking luck."

Flame glared at her partner for the third time since beginning her story. "You're an intrusive bitch."

Gretta crossed her bare arms and leaned back into the booth. "Whatever."

Excusing herself, Theresa slid from behind the table and headed intrepidly toward the door marked "FEMALE."

"Let me get this shit straight." Gretta lit her Marlboro and flipped the top down on her Zippo with a snap of her wrist. "You took off Saturday morning with Blondie on the back of your scooter, which you later traded for that tour hawg out there." She nodded in the direction of the smoke film-covered window of Ernie's Good Time Bar & Grill and the gravel parking lot beyond. She couldn't help shake her head in exaggerated anguish.

Flame interjected with a less-than-friendly derisive smile, "I thought I explained that to you?"

Gretta turned toward her friend. "You fucking well did." She returned her attention toward Thatcher. "So. You ride all the way to some podunk town in Michigan to get to Blondie's sister before this badass Henderson gets to her?" Smoke swirled from her nostrils as she stared at Thatcher, who sat across the table from her.

"Didn't he just get done telling us all of this?"

She glared at Flame. "I'm just trying to get this straight, all right with you?"

Flame took a sip of her ice water and shrugged her shoulders. "Sure. Continue by all fucking means."

Gretta momentarily studied Thatcher as she inhaled long and hard on her Marlboro.

"So, you're one of these biker-hero types?" The cigarette bobbed up and down between her lips.

"No, he's just plain shithead stupid," added Flame.

Thatcher acknowledged Flame with an agreeable nod.

"All right. You get there, and Blondie's sister ain't home." Gretta went on. "She's out walking her dog, but you think that maybe these gangster types already have her. Blondie waits at her place while you ride off looking for what's-her-name. You find her, but before you get back to her place, the bad guys show up."

"Something like that," he replied somewhat reluctantly.

"And now you think Blondie is pretending to be her sister." Gretta glanced up as Theresa approached. "Or, you're sayin' maybe she escaped with the helicopter pilot who had this thing for her."

"Something like that," he replied.

Theresa slid into the booth beside Thatcher.

"How's the crapper?" Gretta exhaled a huge plume of smoke as she got up.

"Invidious."

"Invidious." Gretta repeated the word slowly. "Fucking good word. You can tell me what it means when I get back."

Flame smirked at Theresa. "It means, piss behind the dumpster in the alley."

A moment later, they all watched as Gretta strutted purposefully out the back door.

"This place is bigger than it looks." Kenyon looked across the expanse of the first floor with its numerous exhibits. "Is that a restaurant?"

"Cafe. I don't think they have tacos."

"That's a shame."

Shaking her head, she added, "It's not Wildwood Lanes and Pool Pavilion."

"Show me around."

"After you." She kept in step with her partner.

"This is the bottom floor?"

"It is. The second floor is actually under the Sky Theater."

John Kenyon presented a questionable glance.

"There's two levels in the other building. The Sky Theater is the dome."

"Yeah, got it." He walked over to the exhibit area depicting historical events of the American space program. "We should come back another time."

Nudging him away from the Apollo 13 display, she said, "Yes, we should."

Gretta's words slipped forth effortlessly. "Holy craparoni." Her eyes widened and shifted from Thatcher to Theresa, and then back to Thatcher. She then looked about the seedy tavern to confirm they had not been overheard.

Flame remained calm. "This is for real, isn't it?" she said to Thatcher.

He nodded.

Gretta reached across the table and grasped Thatcher's forearm. Her stare was intense. "Let's go get it," she said like a ten-year-old adventurer.

Flame poked at the ice cubes in her ice tea. "We're not going to go get it." She licked her finger.

Glaring confoundedly at her friend as she released Thatcher's arm, she imitated Flame's derisive tone.

"We're not going to go get it."

Flame took a sip of her water.

"What the fuck do you mean?" Gretta wasn't finished. "You heard how much money there is. I'm not saying we take it all. We take a few hundred thousand each." She stared into her friend's sober expression. "Hey, I'm not greedy."

Flame's voice turned to a deep whisper. "Do you know who this money belongs to?" She didn't allow Gretta time to answer. "Someone who will find you, and will kill you."

Gretta glanced at Thatcher. He acknowledged with a reluctant grimace and a nod.

"And you're sure Blondie is going to show up where this money is?" Flame asked Thatcher.

"I fucking would!" Gretta crushed out her cigarette in the chipped glass ashtray. "I don't fucking believe it. There's millions just sitting around in some old closet in some old house in Evanston, and here we sit."

"Gretta." The softness of Theresa's voice curiously captured Gretta's attention. "I know that what happens to my sister doesn't really concern you." She glanced at Flame. "Either of you. But, I'd like you to come with us."

"Now I'm supposed to be..." Gretta acknowledged her friend's impatient expression. "What? Am I a goddamn girl scout?"

Flame turned her attention to Theresa. "I'm in. Holy hell fires, just being near all that money will be a trip."

Gretta rolled her eyes. "Just being near all that money is going to make me crazy!" Then, looking toward Theresa, she said, "Let's go find Blondie."

The lights came on gradually, slowly illuminating the Sky Theater. Voices rose from whispers into conversations. Duran looked around quickly as he stood up.

Karlene pulled him closer and whispered. "He's not going to be in here." Her expression denoted expectancy.

It gave Michael Duran an eerie feeling, as if she was withholding a small, yet priceless, piece of information from him. Then it hit him, chilling needles piercing his spine.

Karlene nudged him toward the aisle, nodding in the direction of the exit. He moved slowly.

"Michael."

"Make way." He turned toward her. "Dead man walking."

"Duran." She stopped, tugged on his arm, and said, "You've got about thirty seconds to pull this together, or..."

"Or?"

Leaning into him, she whispered tenderly in his ear, "Or we will be in the deepest shit you could ever imagine."

Into her ear, he whispered, "Deep shit rising."

Karlene stepped back. "Michael." Positioning the fanny pack onto her right hip, she continued, "You are the abductor. I am the abducted." She pulled back the nylon zipper a half inch. "Play your part. I'll play mine."

Stepping into the aisle leading to the outer hallway, Duran lurched forward from a sudden shove in the lower back. He heard a young child's scream followed by...

"Derrick! Darin!"

The two young boys darted around Michael and Karlene in a mad rush toward the exit. A slender, dark-haired woman approached quickly with her young daughter in tow.

"I'm very sorry," her hand touched Karlene on the shoulder. "They can get so out of control."

It occurred to Karlene that it was a common event. "Oh, don't worry. They're twins?"

The young woman smiled. "Yes."

Karlene returned the smile. "I understand. I'm a twin too."

Suddenly, Karlene felt her smile wane as she watched the little girl look toward her mother and state matter-of-factly for the record, "I hate 'em."

Her mother caressed the top of her head. The little girl saw her mother put her finger to her lips. It had been anticipated, and she quickly looked away.

"Daddy, get 'em!" she called after him as he passed by, beginning his casual pursuit.

The mother proceeded toward the exit with her young daughter still in tow.

"Daddy's gonna get 'em this time." The little girl quickly glanced back at Karlene, as if searching for confirmation.

✦

David Stout had directed Aaron to the museum on the second floor directly below the Sky Theater. He was careful to affirm Aaron's belief that he was there to take orders and to carry them out. It was not a difficult ruse with the swirling chemicals in Aaron's brain.

Being eminently aware that a flash of paranoia could send his boss into a lethal frenzy, David Stout kept very close. Side by side they meandered through the museum waiting for the Sky Show to conclude. Soon, the right time would present itself.

TWENTY

THE RIDE TO EVANSTON WOULD HAVE BEEN UNEVENTFUL except for the fact that Gretta went a little crazy. Twice Flame had to coerce Gretta with a series of expressive hand gestures to pull over to wait for Thatcher. Flame even lost sight of her partner after one of Gretta's infamous maneuvers that included darting between two semis side-by-side. Flame had done that only once, then concluded it was a sure way to become roadkill.

While Flame and Gretta sat on the shoulder of Eden's Expressway, waiting for Thatcher to catch up for the second time, Flame indelicately explained to Gretta why it was imperative to slow down.

"Ease up, bitch! You're going to get us all fucking killed!"

Gretta responded by simply pulling down her wraparound shades to the tip of her nose and glaring.

The encounter began without drama, without the heartstopping lump in the throat that Michael Duran had anticipated. There were no threatening gestures, no paralyzing glares, no weapons drawn.

There was only David Stout, appearing like a roly-poly tourist from Toledo, and Aaron Henderson, a middle-aged refugee from J. Crew, standing in the hallway as Michael exited the Sky Theater with Karlene pulled securely against his right side.

Karlene was encouraged to see Aaron's glazed-over eyes, indicating too many pills with too many shots. Convinced his chemical intoxication gave her the edge, she needed only to be concerned with Stout's role.

Duran moved cautiously, edging his captive forward. He was the abductor, but he saw no evidence of the ransom. His mind began racing.

"Michael," Aaron addressed his pilot affably. "You've done well for yourself. I must say, though, you've surprised me."

Duran shrugged insouciantly. "And you, Mr. Henderson, have surprised me. I see no medium of exchange."

Aaron Henderson slipped his right hand into his pants pocket, pulled out a single key and held it firmly between two fingers. "The key to your future, Mr. Duran," he said before slipping it quickly back into his pocket.

David Stout presented a subtle nod to the abducted. Without thinking, Karlene allowed a vaguely discernible raise of the eyebrows. Looking away, she felt dread spread over her. She had been so concerned with Aaron, and with Michael's performance, she had not remembered her own part.

In an effort to re-establish her role, she jerked her arm away as she contrived an expression of dread. Michael, trying hard to swallow his own apprehension and play his part, did not anticipate Karlene's ploy. Her arm came free from his grip. For a long second each froze, as actors struck with stage fright. Their wide eyes met as Michael grabbed her arm ferociously and pulled her back to his side.

Aaron snickered. "Kidnapping is a skill, Mr. Duran, and I'm afraid you have a lot more to learn." His grin was demonic.

Glancing down toward her right hip, she reminded herself it had to be the right time, the right place. She would have to be patient, be cool, and most of all, be swift.

"Come with us, Mr. Duran."

David Stout glanced toward Karlene. "Miss Swanson. Is it?"

Karlene suddenly no longer needed to feign alarm; it was real. She was certain Aaron's right-hand man knew of their ruse. And why wouldn't he? It was becoming obvious Michael Duran wasn't capable of this criminal act. Why had she ever thought this plan would succeed?

Karlene nodded and softly said, "Theresa," as she attempted to decipher David Stout's motive. Why didn't he simply tell Aaron and end the masquerade?

David Stout led them to a heavy wooden door with a sign declaring this section as "Private." Pulling the door open for Duran and his abductee, he said with serene cordiality, "After you."

The dimly lit stairwell, Duran thought, created a befitting scene for his murder. Why hadn't he fled earlier? There had been no gun to his head. Why was he now standing in a secluded stairwell? The notion that this could be the final moments of his life was numbing. He couldn't help but stare at the nylon pack on Karlene's hip.

Reaching into his pants pocket, Aaron addressed Duran, "I want to thank you for delivering this young woman to me." He pulled out the same golden key. Grinning with all the comical malice of the Grinch, he lowered his voice to a near whisper. "I'm so sorry to say, this key..." His grin digressed into a maniacal sneer as he held the key in front of his pilot. "This key belongs to my gun case."

Michael Duran swallowed hard. "I was hoping for tens and twenties."

"Always the jokester, Michael." And with feigned benevolence, he continued, "I'm going to miss you."

"I'll send you a postcard."

Aaron turned his attention to the abducted. "Miss Swanson." He looked closely at Karlene. "I'm sorry, I don't think we've been properly introduced."

She glanced toward David Stout. He kept his stoic pose, offering no suggestion of what he was going to do.

"My name is Aaron Henderson. This gentleman behind me is my associate, Mr. Stout." Still, David Stout made no indication that he was going to identify her.

"I hope you have not become too fond of young Michael here." His eyes shifted to Duran. "He will be leaving us very soon."

As he smiled and released Karlene's arm, Michael's mind stumbled onto a plan.

He would extend his right hand in a gesture of a farewell handshake. Aaron would of course be amused, and accept it. He would then pull Aaron off balance, and quickly push him back into Stout. Roly-poly Stout would then tumble backwards down the stairway. That's good. That'll work. Then what?

Karlene would take it from there. She's been waiting for this moment. She would retrieve her gun and blast away. Blam! Blam! Blam!

He would then pull her through the door as Henderson dropped dead to the floor. They would be out of there before he would have to see any blood.

Unlike his brain which was working in milliseconds to devise the entire escape, his right hand moved not at all. It hung uselessly at the end of his arm. Then, with one last willful burst of energy, he felt his fingers twitch. As his right hand slowly began to move, the door suddenly burst open, pushing Duran into Karlene.

A young boy nearly fell to the floor between Henderson and Stout. Aaron clumsily, yet swiftly, grabbed the boy by the hair as the door closed. Before the boy could utter a noise Aaron's other hand went over his mouth.

"Now this is an inconvenience," Aaron said to Stout.

Michael Duran stared in amazement at his right hand extended toward the mobster.

As the young boy began to struggle, Aaron tightened his grip. Within moments the boy became still. Glaring at his mutinous pilot, he said to Stout, "I've got my hands full, and Mr. Duran seems to be waiting for something."

Michael quickly withdrew his hand.

Karlene sensed Aaron was moments away from snapping the slender neck, and discarding the child like litter down the stairwell, with Michael soon to follow.

As if there was a silent communication from one captive to another, Karlene reared back her clenched fist just as the boy's heel came down on the end of Aaron's Italian loafer. It was timed perfectly. Her fist connected with a powerful right hook to Aaron's chin. Rage from months of cruelty and domination sent the mobster reeling against the wall. The young boy broke free. Scrambling past David Stout, the youngster pulled open the door and was gone. At that instant, Stout threw his weight against Henderson. It was no contest.

Like a chicken's neck, the vertebrae snapped, crackled, and popped in David Stout's massive arms. Aaron Henderson's lifeless gaze appeared abject and astonished as he slumped to the floor. Standing emotionless above his fallen employer, David Stout turned toward Karlene and Michael.

"It was his time." Stout spoke dispassionately. "Mr. Henderson has been retired." His dark eyes, lacking malice, turned to Michael Duran.

Taken aback, Michael, without thinking, placed a hand to his neck.

It provoked a fleeting comical expression as David Stout spoke. "I believe you have somewhere to go?" With subtlety Stout nodded toward the door. "Mr. Duran?"

Michael stood dumbfounded as he stared at Karlene.

"Oh, don't be concerned. I have no intention of harming her." He was amused with young Michael's confusion, and his loyalty. "Your release is a gesture of good faith to Ms. Swanson." Looking toward Karlene, he inquired thoughtfully, "Or, may I call you Karlene?"

She nodded.

"And, would you please take that off?" He gestured toward the nylon pack on her waist. "Slowly. And hand it to me." Answering her silent question, he said, "Yes, I have one too, and it's very accessible."

David Stout manufactured a sly grin, as if to play the role of villain. "Truly, I have no intention of harming you," he said as he accepted the pack from Karlene. "You simply possess something that I must have."

Glancing at Aaron's body slumped on the floor, he said to Karlene, "I do apologize." His eyes suggested sincere remorse. "I know you were planning to kill Aaron yourself." He pulled the small gun from the pack and examined it. "Up close and personal."

"That was my plan."

David Stout slipped the gun back into the pack, took a step backward, and dropped it into a covered waste receptacle. "It was my contract; I was obligated." He shrugged his shoulders. "As you know," it seemed almost a despairing tone, "Aaron and I had been associates for quite some time. It was merely time to dissolve the association. It's the way it is."

There was a moment of silence before he looked back to Michael Duran. "I know you have a fondness for sunny weather and an ocean breeze. Take a nice long vacation. The JetRanger, I believe, is still at your disposal."

David Stout took no pleasure in killing, and saw no need to take out Michael Duran. With the offer he had just made to young Mr. Duran, he knew the pilot would pose no further interference.

Taking one last look at Karlene, Michael began to speak, "I..."

"Aruba." She tried to smile.

"Come visit me." His voice was shaken with excitement, and with regret.

"I will," she said.

Karlene watched as the door closed soundly behind him. "So, it's just you and me." She turned her attention to David Stout.

"We have some money to retrieve." There was only a brief pause. "Oh, and my new employer is a bit more insistent than my previous one. I would never want to disappoint him. It's a matter of honor, you understand."

"A matter of life or death." Karlene posed it as an addendum.

David Stout returned an approving nod, "You do understand," he said as he gestured toward the unlit stairway. "We'll go this way."

Once on Oakton Avenue Thatcher took the lead. After a couple times back and forth over a three-mile stretch, he pulled into a gas station minimart.

Hitting the kill button was cue for Theresa to dismount. Thatcher leaned the bike into the kickstand.

Flame and Gretta pulled up on either side of him. Simultaneously, the two V-Twins fell silent. Gretta stood up. Balancing her Fat Boy between her legs as if it was no more than a Schwinn, she crossed her arms over her chest and scowled. "You don't know where the fuck you're going, do you?"

Glancing in the opposite direction, Flame made no effort to come to his defense. Theresa walked a few steps away.

Faced by the challenge of returning Gretta an acceptable repartee, Thatcher took a deep breath and said, "Sort of."

Gretta, once again, pushed her wraparound shades to the tip of her nose. Slowly unclenching her jaw, she sighed. "So. Do I sort of have time for a smoke?"

Security at Adler Planetarium consisted of large, neatly groomed young men dressed in fashionable uniforms. These were security officers that were respected.

The officer in charge of the day shift was Ellis Petry; he had played defensive end for the Bears two pre-seasons ago, but never made the final cut. He had been told he was a step too slow.

On this particular day he again had been a step too slow, which in this case was very fortuitous. His youth and strength would have been no match against David Stout.

Ellis Petry, accompanied by two other youthful officers, approached the door from which the ten-year-old boy had escaped just minutes before.

"Security," he announced. "You are in an unauthorized area." Ellis Petry's voice demanded acknowledgment.

Had Aaron Henderson's spinal cord not been severed between the fourth and fifth vertebrae, acknowledgment would have been lethal for young Petry. Slowly pushing open the door, Ellis prepared himself for a physical confrontation. He could feel his muscles flexing with anticipation. His first day of practice as a pre-season Bear had evoked a similar response.

It was the leather sole of a woven Italian loafer that Ellis Petry saw first. It was the astonished expression of a man lying prone on the hard tile floor that made him jump back, just before a hand fell against his shoulder.

"Chicago PD." The voice presented a confident tone.

Ellis turned and looked into John Kenyon's clear green eyes, then at the badge in the large freckled hand. Taking a deep breath, he murmured, "Jesus."

Kenyon nodded solemnly. "Okay, son. I've got it from here." He allowed the young man to gather himself. "I want you to keep everything looking like nothing has happened. And, I want to talk to the young boy."

"No problem, detective." The quaver in Ellis Petry's words betrayed his composure. Swallowing to regain his baritone voice, he asked, "Have you seen anything like that before?"

"Not even on league night."

Looking peculiarly at the large red-headed detective, he glanced one more time at the body on the floor. "Damn."

Ellis nodded respectfully to the woman detective standing in the doorway as he backed out. He quickly gave instructions to his security officers, as he walked toward the two young boys standing close to their mother. Addressing the father, who held tightly onto the young daughter, Ellis Petry requested they all come with him to the security office.

John Kenyon knelt beside his fallen adversary and studied the lifeless body. Aaron Henderson's body appeared pathetic and impotent in its morosely distorted posture in the dusky stairwell. Death had come ignominiously. Eddie Greshem had faired better in his final clumsy act of imbecility.

Kenyon looked up at his partner. "How do you suppose this happened?"

Eve stepped into the small corridor. "Nasty fall?" It was a sullen reply.

"Very nasty."

Stooping beside her partner, "A hit," she suggested.

"From an old friend."

Eve Jensen looked curiously at her partner. "David Stout."

"Who else could get this close?" Rising slowly to his feet, "Christ, my knees can't take this," he muttered as he rubbed his right knee. "I'm sure we'll get a description from the boy that resembles Aaron's longtime associate."

As Michael Duran pulled onto Lake Shore Drive with the intention of navigating the purple Geo northward in the direction of the Antioch Airport, there was a curious smile across his face. He had survived, and with any luck, he planned to be sipping a concoction of rum and tropical punch under a swaying palm tree by tomorrow evening. How quickly, he thought, fortunes can change.

Michael, with his smooth, amiable personality, had made enough unscrupulous acquaintances over his tenure as Aaron Henderson's pilot, that unloading the JetRanger at a handsome price, with or without the title of ownership, would be relatively easy once he was out of the states. Perhaps he could acquire, through one of his less-than-virtuous contacts, a reputable counterfeit title of ownership in exchange for his piloting services.

Remembering the lyrics of a Tom Petty song, Duran broke into a snappy rendition of, "Into the great wide open..."

David Stout insisted Karlene drive the black Coup de Ville. He did not trust that her cooperation would continue if he could not convince her that he had the advantage. Driving through city traffic would keep her mind and body occupied. That was to his advantage. Having no doubt she knew exactly where the money was located, he was confident she would drive him there without incident. With Henderson dead she had no other purpose except to survive.

Karlene drove north on Lake Shore Drive. She decided to take her time. Perhaps she could think of something, perhaps something would present itself. She hadn't entirely given up the idea that the money was hers, at least part of it. Reparation.

"So, Mr. Stout, what are you going to do with all that money?"

David Stout wasn't one for unnecessary dialogue, however his imminent success was making him feel relaxed, and at the moment, willing to talk.

"Return it to its rightful owner."

"Aaron's dead. I presume," Karlene glanced in his direction, "you killed him for the money?"

He regretted making reference to a rightful owner. He decided to change the subject. "Again, I apologize for taking that from you." He paused. "You did intend to kill him?"

"You're correct, Mr. Stout." She kept her tone formal and respectful. "And now that Aaron is dead, who might the rightful owner be?"

There was a long pause. "I am sorry to say that it is not you, Miss Swanson." His tone was stern.

Karlene was silent.

"Ah, you are still under the impression that you deserve a handsome atonement?"

Karlene moved into the left lane. "I'm the only one who knows," she stumbled over her words briefly, "where the money is. That should be worth something."

"It is." His dark eyes measured her poise. "It is worth your life. So, I suggest you get up to the speed limit and take us there without delay." Stout smoothed the edges of his thick mustache. "Mr. Thatcher may, himself, have plans for that money."

Karlene stiffened as she pressed the accelerator. David Stout knew more than she expected. Suddenly, she was no longer certain of her safety. What if the money was gone? She had not considered that possibility. She was not home free by any means.

"Karlene," his voice was almost paternal, "a speeding ticket will only put off our quest."

As he turned slowly onto the same narrow street for the third time his tired brain kept wandering. It kept thinking about Karlene. The chance of finding her at Lilly's began to seem more and more remote, but first he needed to find the house. Glimpsing Gretta's reflection in his mirror, he noted her shades were pulled down to the tip of her nose. Her tempestuous glare appeared more diverting than threatening. Nonetheless, he hoped that something would look familiar real soon.

He felt Theresa's hands pulling against his shoulders. Cocking his head to the right, he listened.

"Monroe," she shouted. "It's on Monroe Street."

It came to her as a vague recollection. She had driven Karlene to this neighborhood ten years earlier. It had been the afternoon Karlene had testified against a boyfriend in circuit court on assault charges. The fragments of memory slowly fell together.

"ESP?" he shouted.

"Yeah! ESP. Or do you want to rely on your memory?"

He glanced into his mirror. Gretta was less than a bike length behind; her expression had not changed. "We're on Dewey," he said. "There must be a president nearby."

Moments later Theresa pointed toward a corner street sign. "Madison!"

Thatcher traveled one more block and turned onto Monroe Street. Within a few minutes he found the gray two-story house. He led his small caravan to the alley. Pulling onto the cracked concrete carport beside the garage, a peculiar sense of well-being swept over him.

"It's about fucking time!" were Gretta's first words as she slid her glasses to the top of her head.

Flame caught Thatcher's attention with a roll of her eyes. "Ignore her," glancing toward Gretta, she added, "or she'll drive you nuts."

Dismounting the Electra Glide, Theresa asked apprehensively, "Do you think she'll be here?"

"Somehow," he returned an assuring look, "she'll come."

Thatcher knew from her expression he was convincing, yet for him a rush of questions bombarded his mind. Had Karlene already been here? Was she enroute? How long could they wait for her? Was there someone else waiting for them? Had he led his companions into danger? How could he convince Lilly that Gretta was not a hoodlum? Within moments his questions would begin to be answered. His sense of well-being quickly digressed.

Twenty-One

THE YOUNG BOY HAD GIVEN A DESCRIPTION IN THE ENDEARing style of a ten-year-old overexposed to cable TV and *People Magazine*.

"He was big and tough, like the guys on Wrestlemania." He concluded with, "The *Baywatch* babe helped me escape."

Even though the description was, for legal purposes, vague and inexact, it was enough for John Kenyon to substantiate his hunch. As they walked hurriedly from Adler Planetarium they passed three emergency medical technicians trudging up the steps toward the large wooden doors of the Sky Theater, where Ellis Petry waited. They both overheard the youngest EMT morosely inquire about whether it was appropriate to place the body supine, or prone, or whether in this case, it mattered at all.

Eve Jensen sighed deeply knowing that however the body was arranged in the bag, the Henderson case would soon be zipped shut for good.

The immediate question now was how to locate Karlene Swanson. Eve had recently taken a special interest in the young woman after having an old police report turn up that indicated the Swanson woman had had an assault charge placed against a boyfriend when she was still a teenager. Patterns, she had thought, are hard to break.

"Now what, John?" Eve asked over the roof of the car as she unlocked the driver's side door.

Kenyon took a deep sigh. "Unlock my door."

Once in the overheated car they lowered their respective windows and looked at one another. Jensen started the car and turned on the air conditioner. As the blast of warm air gradually turned cool, Eve Jensen's eyes grew wide.

"Fuck!" Her uncharacteristic expletive captured his full attention. "I don't know why I didn't put this piece together before."

His expression coaxed her on.

"I came across an old report." She took a deep breath. "Karlene Swanson was assaulted by a boyfriend when she was a teenager, and she had him charged. Actually, much of the report consisted of a statement made by a bystander, an older woman. I'm not certain, but it seems that her last name was Robinson, and she lived in Evanston."

Kenyon gave no acknowledgment of relevancy.

"Remember," Eve went on, "the fiasco at Wrigley Field on Saturday morning?"

"Starsky and Hutch."

"Yeah." Eve smiled. "The car that rammed into them. The one that Karlene allegedly was driving."

His eyes pressed her on.

"It belonged to a woman from Evanston by the name of Robinson."

Kenyon snatched the radio microphone. "We'll get that address and pay a visit to Mrs. Robinson."

With both hands on the steering wheel, she looked behind her before backing the car out into the parking lot. "Her name is Lilly, Lilly Robinson," she said.

As his partner shifted the car into drive, John Kenyon placed his hand lightly on her shoulder. "That was good detective work."

Eve's smile projected concern. "I should have figured it out sooner."

"Better now than not at all." He gave her his best reassurance, yet he knew all too well what Eve Jensen was thinking: a little late can sometimes have the same results as not at all. He hoped this would not be the case this time.

The familiar streets and sights of Evanston only drew forth from Karlene more apprehension and despair. The realization that she did not know what David Stout would do was sinking in. She tried assuring herself that she would be free to go just as Michael Duran was free to go if the money was still there.

Suddenly, the rows of thousand dollar bills stacked neatly within the aluminum case lost all numerical value. It's worth dwindled into one simple commodity: life. Clearly, it was all that mattered.

Karlene's thoughts turned to Theresa. Was she safe? Had Thatcher found her? Where was she now? Too many questions rushed upon her. She needed to keep focused. She needed to finish this one last task.

Minutes away from finding out her fate, Karlene reasoned once again there would be no cause for David Stout to kill her if the money was found intact. Reason and fact collided head-on, sending a pervasive chill through her. It wasn't intact. She had with careless impetuosity given Thatcher fifty thousand dollars. Would she be killed for just fifty thousand? Would David Stout be reasonable? The image of Aaron's lifeless body answered her question. It would be no more than a business matter: a token of his allegiance to his new boss.

Turning onto Oakton Avenue, her impulse to run eclipsed all other thoughts. Karlene felt a deluge of adrenaline filling her brain, placing each muscle on alert.

Thatcher and company found no one home at the gray Victorian on Monroe Street. Relieved there would be one less person placed in jeopardy, Thatcher, nonetheless, sensed Theresa's growing apprehension.

If the money was still in the upstairs closet, it would indicate that nothing had occurred, that Karlene may still be enroute, that all they needed to do was to wait, and it could also mean that there were still unwanted visitors yet to arrive. The risk was clear.

Gretta wasted no time picking the back door lock. "This is a piece of pie," she said seconds before pushing the door open.

The tall, unruly privet and lilacs surrounding the small backyard successfully hid their entrance. Once inside Thatcher led his troupe upstairs. Holding his breath, he pulled open the closet door. The sight of the aluminum case allowed Thatcher, at least for a moment, to breathe easier.

The black Crown Victoria cruised north on Lake Shore Drive. The busy holiday weekend traffic presented its obstacles, but Eve Jensen was up to the challenge. In Chicago, congested streets and freeways were a way of life.

"John, how many minutes behind do you think we are?"

"No more than twenty." He lied a little. He was certain it was closer to fifteen, but with the little incentive he just provided to his partner, and with her skilled driving, they could make up at least five.

Kenyon was pleased to have Jensen behind the wheel in times like this. He hated city driving, and she loved it, particularly during the chase. She was very good at it. Five years ago when he had requested Detective Eve Jensen as his new partner, he first looked at her driving test scores. They were exemplary.

Contacting the Evanston City Police to request a squad car to stand by, Kenyon provided only the most essential information. Always wary of having unknown personnel involved, his gut feeling told him to hold back a little until he had a better idea what was in the works.

John Kenyon relied on his uncanny ability to anticipate, and to swiftly counter as many times as necessary. His system had worked exceedingly well for nearly thirty years. Perhaps, he thought, they would merely find an elderly woman at home.

Western Avenue North provided considerable adversity. Vehicles of all denominations competed over its four narrow lanes cluttered with unfinished street repairs. The unrelenting parade of defiant pedestrians added to the chaos. Less pandemonium could be found in Pampalona during the running of the bulls.

Out of nowhere a roaring buzz and a whirl of incandescent purple zipped past Jensen's window. It startled even her.

"Jeeeezus," she said, as if her own driving credibility had been maligned. "Where'd he come from?"

They both watched as the Kawasaki ZX-9R guided by excessive hormones zoomed ahead, navigating with pointless abandon between a body shop-bound Chevy cab and a FedEx delivery truck.

"I'd love to pull his ass over!"

Kenyon only grimaced.

Catching his subtle expression, she asked, "What is it?"

"We don't pull them over. We wait until some unfortunate EMT is called to scrape them off the pavement."

Eve Jensen sighed.

Gretta slowly pulled her sunglasses off the top of her head as she stared at the opened case lying on the bed. "Holy Christ-a-roni." It was her version of Hail Mary.

Leaning into her, Flame whispered, "Amen."

Theresa flashed a hopeful glance toward Thatcher. "So, what do we do? Wait?"

Thatcher closed the case as the reality of the consequences converged on him. He wasn't certain what to do. In his previous life, he had always been quick and concise. Having held responsibility for huge written sums of money accompanied by page after page of terms and conditions and definitions and exceptions and penalties, Thatcher had been expected only to place his professional life on the line. The millions in cash enclosed in the aluminum case held the severest of penalties. He had to refer back to his early years with the Bureau to help make a decision: clear out the citizenry.

Returning the case to the closet, Thatcher soberly addressed his troupe. "I think all of you should leave."

The three women stared at him with collective contrariety. It appeared the citizenry didn't agree.

"I have a bad feeling," he said.

"We all leave, or we all stay." Flame was resolute.

Placing her hands on her hips, Gretta concurred. "Fuckin' A."

Theresa nodded in agreement. "I'm staying."

Running his fingers through his hair, he displayed his frustration and concern, "This money is extremely dangerous."

"It's not the money. That's not why we came." Flame waited less than two seconds before jabbing Gretta in the side to encourage the desired unanimity. It didn't come.

"Yeah." Gretta grimaced at her partner. "Whatever."

Another jab to the ribs informed Gretta she had answered wrongly, but there was no rebuttal, of which certainly would have followed if not for creaking floorboards downstairs. It was the sound of someone not wanting to be heard.

Anxious glances flashed back and forth between them before Gretta whispered, "This is just fucking great."

Theresa started for the door. "It's got to be Karlie."

Stepping in front of her, Flame placed her hand firmly against Theresa's shoulder and shook her head. Theresa turned quickly toward Thatcher.

"It's not," he whispered.

Exhaling slowly, and glancing toward Flame and Gretta, Theresa simply asked, "Now what?"

Gretta pounded her fist into her hand. "I got high."

"I got low," said Flame.

Theresa just stared, having no idea what the two friends were talking about.

Thatcher attempted to visualize himself charging the first body to enter the doorway, hitting him hard, hitting him squarely in the chest. He imagined lunging headlong in pursuit of a dislodged weapon. His thoughts ended abruptly, and without the scroll of stunt credits, when a booming voice reverberated up the stairway.

"Amazon!" It was a harsh salutation, followed by an uncertain silence. "I know it's you and your fuckin' squaw pal."

"Shit." Flame cocked her head to one side and looked at Gretta in unguarded surprise. "It's..."

"Wazoo." The two peculiar syllables escaped comically from Gretta's lips as if she had just announced the next carnival act. "All three hundred pounds of him."

Thatcher quickly amended his previous scenario of charging headlong into heroism with a dramatic escape through the second-story window following the three women down an ivy-shrouded trellis. Unfortunately, there was no ivy and no trellis on the gray two-story Victorian.

"Who?" Theresa's own bewilderment and fear of the transpiring events struck her as being tremendously and darkly amusing. She began laughing.

Flame and Gretta stared at her in disbelief.

"We do have a problem here." Thatcher regained their attention. Theresa, covering her mouth, subdued her laughter.

"Sounds like a party up there! Is that you Squaw Bitch?" Wazoo retained his cockiness, yet there was no further movement on the stairway.

Flame answered Thatcher with candor. "A big fucking problem." She turned quickly toward Gretta. "Why is he here?"

Gretta interpreted Flame's intonation correctly. "How the fuck do I know? I just got here myself. Why don't you ask him?"

"Who's Wazoo?" The sound of his name amused her once more. Theresa muffled her laughter. "Sorry," she muttered through her cupped hand.

Thatcher looked toward Flame. "Who is he?"

"He's the Prezo." Interpreting his expression, she added, "President of the Storm Riders." Flame paused to let it sink in before she explained further.

"The Stormies are a bunch of minor-league morons who couldn't make it in South Chicago, so they moved north to make their own little boy's club. They'll do anything to get the attention of the big leaguers."

"Bikers." Thatcher clarified for Theresa.

Flame glanced toward the closet, then over to Gretta. "If they score a million bucks..."

"More like ten." Thatcher interjected.

Gretta looked toward her compadre. "Can you imagine what kind of social chaos a bunch of psycho-pathetic-idiots could create with that kind of money?"

In another time, he would have been amused at Gretta's psychiatric diagnosis, nonetheless, he was encouraged by her sincere concern for society, but it was totally unnecessary. The Mob would make short work of the "little boy's club" of Waukegan.

"What does all this have to do with my sister?" Theresa was no longer amused. She looked to Thatcher for an explanation.

"Not a thing."

Without glancing toward David Stout, Karlene said softly, "It's up ahead."

"Identify the house, but don't stop." Stout looked toward his driver. "Don't even slow down."

Continuing to look straight ahead, she said calmly. "On the left, the gray one, third from the corner."

"I assume there is an alley?"

Karlene nodded.

"Go there," he ordered, "and drive past quickly."

She said nothing as she put on her left blinker. Her racing thoughts united with a singular purpose: survival. Match point was inevitable; she would play the ball.

David Stout was more than just a little concerned as Karlene drove swiftly past Lilly Robinson's car port. He counted at least six motorcycles, and one figure looming among the lilacs.

"It appears there is a party," he announced. "Drive to the front and park."

For Karlene, the unexpected appearance of several large motorcycles parked behind Lilly's house sent chills through her. The apparent reemergence of the bikers Thatcher had told her about was eerie, yet it seemed to complete the cycle of events. It was the sight of the big blue one with the back seat that gave her renewed strength. She had found Thatcher. The sanguinity was short-lived. What kind of danger had Thatcher met? What danger was she delivering? Her heart raced wildly. Was Theresa here also?

Karlene turned to David Stout. "Let's not waste any time."

Jensen remembered recently reading a survey, while waiting at the dentist's office, that reported "shit" as the most often uttered expletive just prior to a sudden, unexpected bout with disaster. The survey went on to say that it was possibly the very last syllable spoken by many of those who tragically didn't survive. She had meant to mention the article to John Kenyon for his non-biased opinion.

At the time, Eve thought it a rather crass and absurd survey, with little factuality. However, as the rear of the FedEx truck in front of her suddenly engulfed her vision, she provided resounding validity to the survey that she had scoffed. Slamming on the ABS brakes with all her strength, the Crown Victoria came to a halt inches from the delivery truck.

Kenyon, as he fell back against the seat, made the immediate supposition that the young man on the sport bike would soon provide an EMT with the gruesome task he had only moments before mentioned to his partner. As he reached out the window and slapped the flasher onto the roof of the car, Jensen carefully swung around the delivery truck.

It was as John Kenyon expected. The once-sleek sport bike had become no more than metal and plastic refuse neatly stuffed beneath the rear of a dilapidated three-quarter-ton pickup filled with tart cherries. The rider was nowhere in sight.

"I don't believe this," Jensen muttered as she stopped the car.

"I'm going to check it out. Call it in." John Kenyon got out of the car.

As he stepped closer to the truck, what he saw astonished even him. The mound of cherries in the back of the truck began to move, and slowly emerging from the over-ripened fruit were the back pockets of Calvin Klein jeans. John Kenyon waited for the other end to rise from the cherries. A few seconds later a whole person was sitting in the pile of smashed fruit.

The driver of the truck was now standing beside Kenyon, too dumbfounded to speak more than a few mumbled words in Spanish. They both watched, along with more than a dozen bystanders who had accumulated around the back of the truck, as the slightly built rider slowly began to remove the bright red closed-face helmet.

The driver and apparent owner of the smashed cherries placed his hand on top of his head and murmured, "Chica."

And, as the helmet dropped onto the cherries beside the young rider, she uttered the word of the moment. "Oh, shit."

Back in the car Jensen asked about casualties.

"Minor."

Jensen was pleasantly bewildered. Creeping their way out of the traffic jam with the flasher on, Kenyon described the events of the last few minutes to the dispatcher.

With her 1978 Bonneville still impounded, Lilly had taken to the streets via public transit. It was slow yet reasonably reliable. From her house it was a ten-minute walk to the nearest bus stop. She didn't mind the walk, except when lugging groceries.

She readjusted her purse strap over her shoulder and picked up the plastic bag of groceries she had set on the sidewalk. Up to now she had always requested paper grocery bags; she didn't trust what appeared to be flimsy plastic, but the cashier assured her the plastic sacks were super strong, and easy to carry. At this moment, with two blocks to go and a half-dozen cans of sweet and condensed milk in the bottom of the bag, she was pleased with the new super strong plastic.

"Lilly Robinson!"

She turned toward the familiar voice, and waved with her free hand.

"Come, stop in a moment." Her friend stood on the front porch and waved her over.

"Oh, Della, I can't. I have to get some baking done for the church social tomorrow night."

"Oh, just buy something at the bakery like everyone else."

Lilly let out a howl. "Della, I've got a reputation to keep!"

"Lilly, you've got time for some iced tea. You come on over."

Heaving a heavy sigh, she agreed. "You know, I insist on fresh lemon with my tea."

Looking toward Gretta, Thatcher said calmly, "Tell me about Mr. Wazoo."

Gretta was succinct. "He's three hundred fucking pounds and he likes to hurt people."

"I know that part," he said.

Flame continued with more useful information. "He probably has two members with him, all with big sidearms. Although, according to Weezer, not one of them could hit the broad ass of a milk cow if it swatted them in the face with its tail." Pausing for a moment, as she looked squarely into Thatcher's eyes, she said, "Still, don't take any chances."

"The Prezo carries a .44 Magnum and likes doin' a Dirty Harry number." From above her head, Gretta slowly lowered her arm in the fashion of aiming a gun. "You know, 'the most powerful handgun in the world' routine, 'it can blow your head clean off.'"

Running her fingers through her hair, Theresa whispered through a curious frown, "Charming character."

Gretta, concurred. "He's one charming motherfucker."

Flame looked toward Gretta, adding, "There's probably one left with the bikes, and one with..."

"The invidious fatass." Gretta, to everyone's surprise, had actually augmented her vocabulary.

"So, what do we do?" Theresa glanced back and forth between her new companions.

"Amazon!" The guttural sound startled them again.

Flame looked toward her partner.

Raising the index finger of her right hand to her lips toward her companions, Gretta turned her head toward the door.

"Mr. Prezo, sir," Gretta began, "what the fuck can I do for you?" She glanced back at Flame and the others. "What'd you expect I'd say?"

"You could've been a little more diplomatic." Flame's voice carried a noticeable edge.

Thatcher just shrugged his shoulders.

Not having gone beyond the top step, the Prezo was obviously being cautious. Thatcher interpreted this as being favorable; it suggested that Wazoo was uncertain about whom he was attempting to rip off.

"It seems," the Prezo began, "you have come into some money."

Flame glared at her friend.

"What?" Gretta's was a bruised defensive tone. "I didn't say nothing to nobody."

"You've been waving that grand around."

Gretta attempted to stare Flame down. "So. Some people saw it. So what?"

"So, now we have a three-hundred-pound shark circling in for the kill."

Thatcher glanced toward Theresa. "Get me a pillowcase." He went to the closet and took a stack of bills from the aluminum case. Facing his companions, he tore off the paper band. "We're going to throw bait to the shark."

Catching on quickly, Theresa shook the pillow free, and held it out like a sack toward Thatcher. He let the bills separate and fall freely into the white cotton pillowcase.

"The Prezo doesn't know how much money there is. He's just guessing the two of you have scored big. Fifty grand should qualify as big." The beginnings of a plan came to Thatcher.

Flame turned toward Gretta. "How did he know we were here?"

"Someone's been following you," Theresa replied.

"Waiting for you to hook up with me," then glancing at Theresa, Thatcher added, "and the woman in the limousine."

Looking at Thatcher, Flame asked, "How did they figure we would hook up again?"

Thatcher massaged the back of his neck. "They were just guessing," he replied as he took the pillowcase from Theresa with his free hand.

Placing her fists staunchly on her hips, Gretta stared dubiously at Thatcher. "So, we just give him the fucking money?"

"You want to arm wrestle him for it, or what?" Flame made her point.

Dropping her hands, Gretta looked back and forth between Thatcher and Flame. "How do we play it?"

"I'll step out with the pillowcase above my head." Watching Gretta and Flame exchange troubled glances, he stopped massaging his neck. "I'll toss it to him." He dropped both arms to his sides.

"Maybe," Flame encouraged, "you should just throw the money to him from around the corner."

"I need to get a sense of who I'm dealing with."

"You're dealing with," Gretta chided, "Jabba the fuckin' Hut packin' a .44 Magnum."

Looking to Flame, Thatcher received the confirmation he expected. "Okay, I toss it around the corner."

"And, you said," Gretta looked at her partner before turning back to Thatcher, "he was just plain shithead stupid."

"He's learning."

Theresa stood by silently.

"Gretta, address the president." Thatcher loosely tied the corners of the pillow case together.

With a touch of sarcasm, "Mr. Prezo, sir," Gretta called out. "My bro's tossing it out to you. It's what you want."

Thatcher moved to the doorway. Grasping the pillowcase firmly in his right hand, he held it out into the hallway.

"Hold it right there!" The Prezo spoke.

Thatcher froze.

"Step out here," Jabba grunted. "Slowly."

"No!" Flame whispered.

In the early years of his first career he wouldn't have done what he was about to do, and as he glanced back at his companions he had little doubt there was nothing else he could do. If facing the heavily armed Jabba the Hut might end this siege without gunfire, he would chance it. Before stepping out into the hallway, he provided a relaxed expression of intrepidity to his companions.

Prezo Wazoo was all of three hundred pounds and then some. His shaved head sported a tattoo of a misshapen swastika, the approximate diameter of a Jewish skull cap. He was an ugly man with teeth missing on either side of his rotting nefarious grin.

Thatcher wondered what Wazoo's intimidation potential could be if he were dressed in a three-piece pinstriped suit and seated at the end of a conference table. Deals would be signed and sealed within moments. The thought amused him, and allowed him to smile as he looked into the hideous face of Prezo Wazoo.

With his .44 Magnum clenched in his thick hand, the Prezo motioned toward the bag. "Let's see what you got there bro. And, no sudden moves. This Smith & Wesson gets real nervous."

Thatcher slowly opened the case. Reaching in he pulled out a fistful of bills.

"That's good, bro." Brown saliva stretched from a single rotten front tooth to a bleeding cold sore on his lower lip. "Put it back, and slide it over here."

Thatcher followed the Prezo's instructions, and slid it fifteen feet across the wooden floor.

"Watch him," Wazoo spoke to his churlish footman behind him as he looked inside the bag. Pulling out a single bill, he studied it carefully, and then looked up at Thatcher. "Who the fuck is Grover Cleveland?"

"The twenty-second president of the United States." It was a polite informative response. Thatcher didn't consider it necessary to mention Grover's second term four years later.

Wazoo handed the bill to his associate. Thatcher watched the second Storm Rider suspiciously inspect the money.

Tapping his leader on the shoulder, he said, "This was made in 1929."

Wazoo tossed a dubious and malignant stare in Thatcher's direction.

Thatcher shrugged his shoulders. "Grover's been dead a long time." He watched the second Stormie shove the bill back into the pillowcase.

Wazoo released his stare and turned quickly toward his assistant.

The smaller, yet equally malicious, biker suggested, "Maybe this old money is worth even more."

Thatcher was impressed by the biker's insightful conclusion. He had not considered the antiquity value, perhaps fifty cents or more on the dollar. That in itself was a handsome bonus, if, in fact, it could ever be collected.

Wazoo turned his attention back to his captive. "How do I know this is all of it?"

Dryly, Thatcher replied, "Do you think we shook down the Mob, or what?"

The huge, ugly man smiled. "You know," his voice became gravely earnest. "This is the most powerful handgun in the world..." The .44 slowly rose.

Instantly recognizing the ungracious gesture, Thatcher readied himself.

"It can blow your head clean off..."

He wondered if he should have been more polite. He wondered if he could drop to the floor just at the right moment to avoid gross bodily damage. Strangely enough, he felt reasonably confident.

The barrel of the gun stopped at knee level. "But, I like you." His demeanor turned suddenly jaunty. "So I'm only going to blow off your knee instead of your head."

Assuming Jabba could be taken for his word, Thatcher quickly discerned dropping to the floor would be the wrong strategy. He wondered how high he could jump.

Inside the room Gretta had all she could do to keep Flame from rushing into the hallway.

"We'll buy him a new fucking knee, then we'll find that fat motherfucker, and peel that swastika off his fat head with a dull tomahawk."

Flame screamed with the first gunshot, and before she could move to the door, Thatcher came crashing through it falling at her feet. Gretta rushed the door preparing to smash the first body she saw, while Flame threw herself on top of Thatcher.

Eye to eye with Flame, Thatcher whispered, "I think he missed."

Two more shots in rapid succession ended with the thunderous sound of an immense mass toppling down the stairway.

Thatcher and company had no more plans as they heard deliberate footsteps a few moments later coming up the stairway.

Flame and Thatcher slowly got to their feet. Standing beside Theresa, the three waited motionless for someone to appear. Gretta backed away from the doorway; she had no fondness for the police, yet under the circumstances the city's finest would be a welcome sight.

Theresa gasped and took a step forward. Her heart raced as she stared in disbelief at her identical twin.

"You didn't?" Thatcher's enthusiasm was cut short.

"She only assisted." Strolling into the room, David Stout nudged Karlene forward. In one hand he held a .38 revolver, and in the other the white pillowcase. "I believe there's more from where this came."

Twenty-Two

"How much time do you think we lost?" Jensen weaved to the outer lane.

"Not much."

"We missed the last party." She kept her eyes on the traffic. "I don't want to miss another."

Kenyon wasn't certain anything was going down at Lilly Robinson's house, but if there was, he reasoned, it would be a quick and simple transaction with little spectacle, and without the carnage that up to this point seemed to be indicative of anything having to do with Aaron Henderson.

"There might not be much of a party, if any." He looked solemnly at his partner. "We may not come up with much of anything."

Jensen glanced at John Kenyon emitting the slightest of smiles. "I think we will."

"We'll know shortly."

"I want to file this case closed," she turned serious once again, "but with Henderson gone, and if no one else is killed," she let out a sigh, "I guess that would be enough for now."

Thatcher had always considered himself an excellent judge of character, which allowed him to anticipate the responses of others with reasonable accuracy. David Stout stood before him concealed in cryptic reticence. He had little clue to what might happen in the next few minutes.

"I assumed those three were not associates of yours." Stout was addressing Thatcher.

"No," swallowing a modicum of spit, "actually, I was quite certain I was going to be shot."

"I was under that impression as well." David Stout allowed a brief smile. "It seems the bigger the gun the worse their aim."

"A Freudian connection, perhaps?"

Stout allowed another brief smile. "Perhaps, Mr. Thatcher, you're right."

Thatcher sensed he was not facing an assassin, but rather a businessman with a .38 Special. "I appreciate your intervention. Thank you. I'm sure a second shot would have left me with a considerable hole."

"That would have been a possibility." David Stout lowered his weapon.

Listening to the peculiar conversation, Flame and Gretta exchanged perplexed expressions. Theresa and Karlene paid no attention as they embraced one another.

"Now, in regards to the money." Stout glanced around the room. "I regret that I need to collect the rest. I assume that it is still intact."

Gretta slowly reached into her pants pocket, and touched the crumpled bill with her finger tip.

"I know it seems petty," Stout continued, "but I must have it all. My employer insists." He provided a regretful expression. "If it was up to me," looking at Gretta with a cool gaze, he continued, "I'd say keep whatever you may have stuck in your pockets: a finder's fee." Narrowing into tiny slits, his eyes emphasized his candor. "However, my employer, I regret, is not that generous."

Flame slowly pulled her neatly folded bill from beneath her leather brassiere, then slowly and methodically unfolded it.

David Stout smiled. "That is a wise choice." He turned his attention toward Gretta. "I have very explicit orders to recover all the money, and to do it by whatever means I deem necessary. Mr. Wazoo didn't give me an opportunity to explain that situation."

Gretta quickly pulled the crumpled bill from her pocket. "Christ. Do you know how many fucking toilets I have to clean to earn this much money?"

"Too fucking many." David Stout consoled. Turning his attention to Thatcher, he said, "Please retrieve the case from the closet, and place it on the bed."

Thatcher followed his directions.

"Open it."

He unlatched it slowly and opened it, and then backed away.

"Take the bills from the ladies, and place them in the case." His voice was calm, almost cheerful.

Again, Thatcher followed the directions.

"Redundancy is sometimes necessary." Stout looked from face to face. He watched Karlene as she gave a wary glance toward Thatcher. "Unlike Mr. Wazoo, I don't enjoy killing, but it does become part of my job from time to time." He turned his attention to Thatcher. "I'm sure you have figured out that if my intention was to eliminate all of you, I would have allowed Mr. Wazoo and associates to do that for me."

"Thatcher," Karlene's voice was almost a whisper.

"Yes, Mr. Thatcher." David Stout's eyes narrowed in on him. "I suspect you may have the remainder of the money."

"It's locked in the trunk of the bike," he said.

"I sense that you are a man of good character and loyalty. I will stay with your friends while you go get it. I need not explain the consequences if you do not return."

As Thatcher stepped toward the doorway David Stout added, "Oh, there are a couple obstacles at the bottom of the stairway."

There was a single neat hole above the Prezo's left eye. He appeared to stare vacantly toward the ceiling as dark crimson pooled beneath his ponderous skull. The swastika was streaked with red. His associate lay facedown with a shattered occipital; blood and gray matter still oozed ever so slightly from the jagged opening. He deduced Mr. Wazoo had taken the second shot as he turned to see his partner tumble down the stairs only to follow immediately after.

As a young federal agent he had spent his time in surveillance; there had been few kills, and none resembling the one before him. The FBI had a policy and procedure; the Mob had a different one. The Storm Riders had been expediently assassinated. Thatcher carefully stepped around the mess, trying not to look too long at the lifeless bodies. Wazoo appeared harmless, but no less heinous.

Once outside, he felt the need to take a deep breath. He exhaled slowly as he stood on the back steps. Staring momentarily at the motorcycles parked beside the garage, he stumbled down the steps at the sight of the bright, menstrual red customized Fat Boy parked nearest to the garage. Overcome by the sight of the *Wanderer*, he didn't notice the soles of two boots protruding from beneath the privet as he walked toward the Harleys. Weighing the odds, Thatcher graciously welcomed the kismet-like return of the *Wanderer*.

Thatcher considered the fate of Earl. How did a Storm Rider come by his bike? He reached into his pocket and felt the spare key. Up to now, Thatcher had not believed in predestined events, yet, at that moment, no other explanation came to him. Perhaps Earl was more unscrupulous than Thatcher had anticipated, or he was dead. Still, it was more likely Earl Hoeskema had made a handsome profit selling the *Wanderer* without title to someone who cared little about assuming legal ownership of anything.

He walked rapidly to Earl's blue Electra Glide. As he unstrapped his duffel bag from the trunk rack, a black Crown Victoria appeared. As it approached it slowed down. He noticed the dark-haired woman behind the wheel. Their eyes met only briefly. Placing her detective shield against the glass window, she nodded imperceptibly. Thatcher was startled only by her omniscient expression. The car continued on.

Thatcher quickly secured his duffel bag onto the *Wanderer*, then retrieved the stack of bills from beneath his cap. He held back any expectation of immediate rescue. What was to transpire upstairs within the next few minutes still remained his dilemma, and his responsibility. He hurried back into the house.

Entering the room unwavering, he walked directly to the bed and placed the last of the missing money into the case. Thatcher turned in the direction of Karlene's appreciative gasp. The sight of Theresa and Karlene standing side by side was gratifying. He conceded a fleeting smile.

Flame and Gretta, a few feet a part, assumed nearly identical poses. With their arms across their chests, their weight shifted to their right hips, and their jaws clenched in a disparaging grimace, they seemed to mutually accept a momentary defeat. Clearly, David Stout, with the .38 casually at his side, seemed no less intimidating, and no less in control.

"It's all here." Thatcher addressed the armed, yet seemingly benevolent mobster. "I estimate ten million, or so."

"You seem accustomed to large amounts of money, Mr. Thatcher."

Accepting it as a subtle compliment, he smiled politely.

Stout tossed the pillowcase of money to Thatcher. "If you would be so agreeable as to place this in the case and close it securely, I'll be on my way."

"That would be fucking great."

Flame jabbed her partner in the ribs.

Gretta returned a vexatious frown. "Hey! I'm getting sore down there."

"Then don't make me do it."

As David Stout walked to the bed, he raised his weapon. Dread spread through everyone like a swift, cold current.

"I'm afraid that I will still need some insurance." Looking at Karlene, "You are a bit too unpredictable."

Immediately, Karlene shouted, "No!"

"No? Miss Swanson, really." Feigning sincerity, he continued. "You certainly understand why I would feel much more comfortable in the company of your charming sister."

"Don't!" Karlene's voice was pleading.

His eyes became dark shiny droplets as he looked directly at Karlene. "Let's begin with everyone staying right here, in this room." Stout glanced at Thatcher standing beside Flame and Gretta. "That is understood." David Stout, holding his .38 in a benign display, spoke softly. "I make an effort not to eliminate anyone unnecessarily, but be assured that I will if necessary. Mr. Wazoo and company are evidence of that."

Stout motioned for Theresa to come to him. "You'll be just fine. If everything goes well, as I suspect it will, you'll be with your sister again very soon."

Karlene embraced her sister, "I'm sorry."

"I'll be all right." Theresa grasped Karlene's shoulders and whispered, "Crunch time."

The sisters separated. Theresa turned toward the large man with the case of money and the gun. "Let's go." She looked back at an unusual cast of characters. "What do you say we have cocktails later? Not at Ernie's."

Her effervescence startled even David Stout.

Looking directly at the mobster, she asked, "You won't mind if I drive?"

"I insist."

Eve Jensen continued driving down the alley for several more yards before pulling over to the side. "That was our Mr. Thatcher."

John Kenyon was not one to doubt his partner. After all, he had been the one to teach her the abstruse science of intuition. He was, however, curious as to how she had come to her conclusion. His grin evoked an explanation.

"He looked healthy and fit. I don't have much experience with bikers," lowering her eyes, she said, "as you know, but I'm led to believe their lifestyle does not promote good health and fitness. And, I didn't notice any tattoos." Before she continued, she watched for Kenyon's expression as he considered her deduction. "He didn't have the look of a social outcast," she went on, "although he certainly appeared on the lam."

John Kenyon smiled. "I'm impressed, Detective Jensen."

Eve Jensen attempted to conceal her amusement. "And the bright red motorcycle parked closest to the garage did strongly resemble the description of the one at Wrigley Field Sunday morning." She smiled and added, "Oh, and the bike nearest the garage. I think we found Mr. Thatcher."

"I've taught you well."

Jensen waited for her partner's commentary of what he thought might be taking place at the residence of Lilly Robinson.

"There are six motorcycles parked in back." Kenyon continued. "One belongs to Mr. Thatcher, two others may belong to..."

"...the two female accomplices at Wrigley Field," Jensen interjected.

With raised eyebrows, he added, "That could be."

"And the other three?" Jensen was looking toward her partner for an explanation.

"Members from the social club in Waukegan?"

"I want to drive around to the front," she added.

"Another hunch?"

Eve smiled. "I'm thinking that something seemed out of place when we drove by." She pulled away from the shoulder of the alley.

As they drove along Monroe one more time, Eve Jensen pointed to the black car parked on the side of the street just beyond Lilly Robinson's sidewalk. "Is that a typical car for this neighborhood?"

Kenyon raised his eyebrows slightly. "New Coupe de Ville."

"The Swanson woman has brought David Stout to the money," she said informatively.

"And the Storm Riders have come to crash the party." Turning to his partner, he smiled. "You were right about Mrs. Robinson's uninvited guests."

As they drove past the house all was quiet.

"John, time for backup?"

Kenyon took a deep breath. "I don't want to create mayhem in this quaint neighborhood, or possibly a hostage situation. Let's circle back around and sit tight at the end of the block." Reaching inside his jacket, he unsnapped his holster. "I have a feeling that Mr. Stout could have already taken care of the Waukegan boy's club."

Lilly stayed longer on Della's porch than she had planned.

"Della, why don't you stop by later, after I get the pies out of the oven?" Smiling, Lilly rose from the glider. "You know, I always make an extra pie."

Lilly picked up her bag of groceries by the handles. "You know, these flimsy plastic sacks are plenty strong." She shook her head in amazement. "Plenty strong."

Della took another sip from her tea. "Just the other day..."

"Gotta go." Lilly interrupted. Without looking back as she descended the porch steps, she added, "Della, you stop by around eight o'clock."

David Stout never allowed himself to be overconfident. He was painfully patient: a cautious man with a plan. There was nothing in his world that could be taken for granted. There was no room for absolute trust. Trust occurred only when dominion was achieved, and its price then became reasonable.

As he left Lilly Robinson's house with Theresa Swanson beside him, and The Affiliation's ten million dollars in his possession, Stout felt he had achieved a moment's ascendancy. The Swanson woman would eventually be given her freedom, when the time was right, and Mr. Revelle would soon be given the good news. This was turning out to be a profitable day for David Stout.

Theresa was not without fear, nor was she without anger. As she had told her sister moments earlier, it was crunch time. As she walked beside her opponent, she was remembering Karlene's words from years before. Defense, she had said, doesn't get it done when you're serving the last point, but the chosen moment has to be right, the timing has to be perfect, and the desire has to be overwhelming.

Theresa wasn't one to assume the worst, nor was she one to allow her fate to be in the hands of another. The moment had to be right, and the timing perfect.

Jensen had parked along the opposite side of the street four houses down from the Cadillac. Slouching easily to the level of the dashboard, she watched the front of the Robinson house. Kenyon maneuvered awkwardly out of sight by nearly lying his head on his partner's lap.

"What will the neighbors think?"

"That you're a very lucky man."

"Hmm, could you move a little."

Her quick movement upwards pushed his head into the steering wheel. "Sorry."

Rubbing the side of his head, he asked, "What?"

"We have Stout and one of the Swanson women coming out the front door." Glancing to her left, she moaned, "Oh, shit."

"What?"

"We have an older woman with groceries walking down the sidewalk in their direction."

John Kenyon gingerly rose to a leaning position. Peering over the dash, he watched as David Stout walked casually down the Robinson walkway with the Swanson woman close beside him.

"He looks real cool, John."

"That's good news for the lady with the grocs."

"Grocs?"

"Groceries."

John Kenyon resumed his position below the window as Stout

approached the passenger side door of the Coupe de Ville. "Be ready to get out of sight. Then, get on his tail."

Lilly had picked up her pace since leaving Della's front porch. She didn't want to be baking pies late into the evening. The plastic grocery sack swung by her side in rhythm with the Gershwin melody she was humming.

Lilly was not immediately disturbed by the sight of the man and woman walking down the sidewalk that led from her house. Not caring much for canvassers, she was pleased that she'd been delayed.

Halting momentarily, a glimmer of a smile crossed her face. Karlene had come back sooner than she had expected. All at once, it struck her; something was wrong. It wasn't the same man she had met a few evenings ago. Walking more quickly, she hoped to make eye contact with her friend. As the young woman glanced in her direction Lilly realized that it wasn't Karlene. The hair was too short, and she would never wear overalls.

As she carefully watched Karlene's sister, Lilly switched the groceries to her right hand, and gripped the plastic sack tightly. She began humming a little louder hoping to attract the young woman's attention. With less than twenty feet between them their eyes met. She recognized Theresa's distress. To intervene was Lilly Robinson's nature; to intervene with force was Lilly Robinson's way.

David Stout looked away from the large elderly woman approaching as he stopped beside the Cadillac to unlock the passenger side door. As he pulled open the door his peripheral vision caught sight of an object hurling toward the side of his head. David Stout ducked out of the way, but not in time to escape a glancing blow.

Instinctively and unwisely, he swiftly drew his gun and fired as he pushed his captive into the front seat of the car. As an explosion of sweet and condensed milk splattered the hood of the Coupe de Ville, Theresa screamed.

She could only watch as the old woman tumbled to the grass, and it was in that instant she knew who had just tried to rescue her. Before having time to think she was pushed in front of the steering wheel. The barrel of a gun was pressed against her side.

David Stout jammed the key into the ignition. He started the car. "You wanted to drive. Drive!" The aluminum case rested at his feet.

As Theresa pulled away from the curb a black Crown Victoria veered in front of her several yards away. She slammed on the brakes. Instantly, David Stout swung open the door, and leaning against the top of the window, he quickly put two shots through the rear side window of the black sedan, and then two more into its rear tire. He had no desire to kill a cop. That was never good business. Within seconds he was back in the car; the gun barrel again pressed against Theresa's side.

"Back up!"

Theresa followed the instructions; the Coupe de Ville sped backwards just missing a parked stationwagon. A hundred thoughts raced through her mind, then suddenly, with lucid clarity she could hear her sister's words. The moment has to be right, the timing has to be perfect, and the desire has to be overwhelming. She aimed the rear of the car toward a fire hydrant.

It was the hot metal of the gun barrel against her neck that convinced her that the moment was not right. She pressed firmly on the brakes, the car slowed, and with surprising ease she made a U-turn.

In the rearview mirror she saw a large red-headed man with his hands on his hips standing in the middle of the street while a woman rushed toward Lilly Robinson.

With the sound of the first shot, Karlene raced from the bedroom. In an effort to quickly sidestep the mammoth corpse of Prezo Wazoo, and his lesser associate sprawled at the bottom of the stairway, she tripped and fell. When Thatcher reached her she was kneeling at the foot of the stairs sobbing.

"I've lost her. Oh, God. I've lost her."

Thatcher helped her to her feet. She clung to him.

Flame stepped agilely around the bodies. "She's okay, I just saw her drive off." Standing beside Thatcher and Karlene, she repeated, "She's okay."

From the top of the stairs Gretta called out. "Hey! It ain't over!" As she waited for her companions to look upwards, she glanced down at the late Prezo Wazoo. "It ain't over until the fat man farts!" She was momentarily amused by her spontaneous variation of an old cliche.

Gretta moved swiftly down the stairway. When she reached the Prezo she stepped squarely on his rotund abdomen. Air escaped his lungs in a flatulent gurgle.

Looking down at the corpulent face, she grimaced. "Isn't this the grossest thing you've ever seen?" Gretta squinted with disgust. "He's uglier dead than he was alive." She took three more steps and placed her arm around Karlene's shoulder. "You're ridin' with me. Let's go."

Before Karlene could answer, a brusque voice came from across the room.

"Chicago PD."

The four of them turned to face a large, red-headed detective with a gun drawn. Flame was the first to raise her hands.

"That's right." John Kenyon coaxed. "Slowly. Place your hands behind your heads." He quickly scanned the room, then motioned with his head toward the bodies on the stairway. "It seems we have some fatalities. Anyone you know?"

Gretta, with her hands now behind her head in a familiar shake down fashion, pointed with an elbow in the direction of Wazoo. "The fat one here is the former Prezo Wazoo of the Storm Riders. I don't know the other one by name. And, by the way, we didn't do this."

From behind John Kenyon came the curt shrill voice of Lilly Robinson.

"What do you mean I can't come into my house! This is my house! And, what in heaven's name is going on?"

Within seconds Lilly Robinson was standing in her living room with the woman detective beside her. She was splattered with sticky sweetened and condensed milk. The plastic sack in her right hand was still intact, except for a single small hole that dripped the white sticky milk. Lilly recognized Thatcher immediately, and then saw Karlene standing beside him.

"Karlie girl!"

Karlene rushed to her like a young child. "Lilly, he's got Trese."

Lilly put her arms around Karlene and held her tightly. She then turned toward John Kenyon. "You're the police aren't you?" She didn't wait for a reply. "Get on out of here, and catch that hooligan." She dropped the plastic bag at her feet. "He shot my groceries!"

At that moment, for the first time, Lilly noticed the two bodies on the stairway. "Oh Lord, there's dead people in my house." She squinted to look more closely at the large corpse. "And he's bloatin' already."

Gretta took a step forward. "Hey. We goin' to stand around here like this, or are we gonna get after that motherfucker?"

John Kenyon did something he had never done before. He lowered his gun without having the suspects secured.

"John?" Jensen watched her partner in astonishment.

Holstering his weapon, he inspected the unusual ragtag assemblage in front of him. "I'm assuming that I'm dealing with law abiding citizens, more or less."

"Fuckin' A."

Flame shot an elbow into her partner's ribs, and took on her friend's glare with one of her own. "Don't make me do it again," Flame warned.

Gretta said nothing as she rubbed her side.

John Kenyon was certain that Theresa Swanson could easily become another fatality in a long list of victims connected to Aaron Henderson. He was determined not to let it happen. This desire superseded procedure.

Kenyon addressed the peculiar convocation. "Does anyone have any idea where Mr. Stout may be taking Ms. Swanson?"

One by one, Thatcher, Flame, and Gretta lowered their hands as their expression professed no insight into the mobster's plan.

Eve Jensen looked at her partner. She had been able to lead them to Lilly Robinson's house by a chance, last-minute deduction, but she was now out of reasonable guesses. She had hoped that John Kenyon was not. It appeared that he was.

Thatcher had endured many boardrooms equally shrouded with uncertainty. It was often at these times that a sudden ephemeral clarity would steer him toward a percipient conclusion. His mind was blank.

Still in her friend's arms, Karlene waited intently for someone to speak, for someone to know what to do.

Flame took a step toward the large detective. "There's an old Indian saying."

Immediately moving from Flame's elbow range, Gretta frowned cynically at her partner. "Do we have time for this?"

Karlene moved from Lilly's embrace; she interrupted earnestly. "I want to hear it."

All eyes were on Flame as she delivered her Indian lore. "What goes around, comes around."

Gretta moaned acrimoniously. "Let me guess. Sittin' Bull said that."

Remarkably, the random pieces began falling into place for Thatcher. Recalling the feeling that crept over him minutes earlier when Karlene had stepped into the bedroom, and again moments after that when he had found the *Wanderer* parked outside, he turned toward Flame and agreed, "It is going around."

Flame eagerly awaited the translation of her aphorism as the others turned toward Thatcher.

"What the fuck is going around?" Gretta's patience had expired.

Thatcher looked over to the large detective. "Could he be going back to where it all started?" He saw the vacant stares. "Friday night."

Thatcher watched as Gretta and Flame exchanged quizzical glances. He continued, "It started at the bar in Waukegan."

Silence.

"That's it! That's where he's going!" Karlene shouted as she rushed to Thatcher. Placing her hands on his shoulders, she whispered, "Thatcher, that's it."

Karlene turned toward John Kenyon. "Curtis Lane was recruited by David Stout," she began to explain. "I know that because Aaron and Stout argued over it continuously. But Stout always assured Aaron that Curtis was loyal, but he was, from the beginning, Stout's soldier. He would have done anything that Stout told him to do." She paused to catch her breath. "I don't know why Curtis drove me to Waukegan, but he did it because of David Stout. And that's where Stout is taking my sister right now. I know it. I feel it."

John Kenyon addressed the assemblage. "I need to borrow a bike."

His solicitation seemed strange only to his partner. Jensen attempted to conceal her surprise.

With a flat rear tire, the Crown Victoria was going nowhere soon. Time was extremely important. Kenyon looked toward the one most likely to acquiesce his request. "Mr. Thatcher?" A quick glance toward his partner evoked his adolescent retort. "What?"

Eve could think of nothing to say.

Thatcher slowly reached into his jeans pocket and retrieved the key to the big tour bike. He walked over to John Kenyon and placed it in his hand. "It's the blue Electra Glide."

Kenyon took the key and nodded. He then looked toward his partner. "Detective Jensen."

"You're not considering leaving without me are you?" Questioning a superior in front of civilians was absolutely against her standards of conduct, however, it was her superior who departed from the standards several moments earlier. She was not going to allow him to stand alone against a mobster, or a board of review, even if it meant she needed to mount a motorcycle.

Jensen looked her partner squarely in the eyes. "The Evanston PD will be here any time. I'm staying with you on this one," she declared.

John Kenyon tried to stare down his partner.

"Detective Kenyon," she placed her hands on her hips, "you're the one who suggested that I go riding with Bubba." Pressing her lips tightly together, Eve Jensen suppressed her smile.

"I know Bubba." Gretta interrupted forcefully (she knew a half-dozen Bubba's). "You don't want to ride with Bubba. In fact, I'm not so sure you want to ride with Big Red over there."

Both Kenyon and Jensen stared at the tall, broad-shouldered, tattooed woman in leather.

"What?" Gretta looked back and forth between the two detectives. "Hey, I don't usually work with the police, but hell, this has been one strange trip anyway. So, lady detective, you want to ride with me or what?"

Jensen, feeling peculiarly aligned with the tall biker, stepped over to her. Placing her hand on Gretta's left shoulder, she whispered, "Let's ride," with the anticipation that John Kenyon would reconsider his plan.

Twenty-Three

Theresa kept both hands on the steering wheel. Her eyes scanned the traffic in front of her as they headed west on Main Street. She was fully aware of the gun nudged against her side, yet strangely enough, it was no longer evoking fear. It was simply there: no more intrusive than the seat harness across her chest.

With a relaxed repose, the command was given. "Take US 41 North."

"Are you going to tell me where we are going?" After several seconds of silence Theresa turned in David Stout's direction. "You're wondering if I'm more of a liability than I am insurance." A cool shudder came over her as her words escaped.

"Do as I say. No more talk."

Lilly Robinson, waiting for the ambulance to arrive, paced anxiously back and forth in front of her kitchen window. She had hoped Karlene would stay with her, but she understood why her young friend needed to go after her sister. Family was family. Lilly watched as Karlene and the newly formed alliance gathered around the motorcycles parked in her backyard.

Although John Kenyon had, at times, utilized unorthodox methods, he had never once organized a posse, and he wasn't inclined to do so now. He addressed the civilians.

"This is Chicago PD business."

Gretta gallantly swung her right leg over the seat of her Harley.

John Kenyon knew at once there was nothing he could say to prevent the self-appointed deputies from riding to the Leather & Lace. He would have to place them all under arrest and wait for the Evanston PD to arrive. There was no time.

Gretta called out to Eve Jensen. "You ridin' or what?"

Giving a long glance at her partner, it appeared he wasn't going to alter his plan. And now, neither was she.

John Kenyon wondered how much he would regret not having cuffed the crew-cut blonde in the very beginning.

"First time?" Gretta emitted a playful grin. "It's a hellava lot more fun than havin' your cherry popped."

Eve, now uncertain of her previous proclamation, wondered what she had been thinking as Flame nudged her toward Gretta's Fat Boy.

Flame added, "It feels a lot better afterwards."

"Detective Jensen," John Kenyon confidently, yet somewhat stiffly, mounted the Electra Glide. "You're in charge of these yahoos."

Eve Jensen accepted the last-second revision of her assignment reluctantly as she took her position behind Gretta.

"Three things!" With a passionate zeal Gretta addressed her new passenger. "Keep your feet on the pegs, lean with me, and hold on!"

Eve scanned the motorcycle quickly to find something secure to hang on to.

Flame reached over and placed her hand on Jensen's shoulder. "Hold onto her. Real tight." Flame lowered her voice to a whisper, and tilted her head closer. "If you don't, you might die."

Gretta turned her head to one side. "I never killed anyone."

Noticing a peculiar glance shared by the two friends, Eve asked Flame. "What? What is it?"

"I never got anyone killed." Pulling her shades to the tip of her nose, Gretta peered over them to return a blameless expression to her partner. "He's got a limp: not a big deal."

"He's got a six-inch steel rod in his leg." Flame felt obligated to clarify.

Gretta turned and leaned back into her passenger. "He wasn't holding on."

Jensen grabbed tightly around Gretta's waist, pulling herself firmly against her new associate.

"That's good, but we ain't movin' yet." Gretta turned toward Flame. "Did ya hafta mention the steel rod?"

Before rolling his Fat Boy away from the other two Storm Riders' bikes, Thatcher took a moment to retrieve his cap from the duffel bag. As he put it on, he glanced toward Karlene. She smiled timidly as she bit her lower lip.

"Ready?" he asked her.

With a subtle nod, she answered, "Ready."

As he felt Karlene press against him, he considered the odds. He would have never conceived that Karlene would once again be sitting behind him on the *Wanderer*. It did, indeed, feel as if it was starting all over again.

Having driven carefully, and silently acknowledging directions with no more than a nod, Theresa began to feel a sullen hopelessness settle over her. To subdue the despair, she forced herself to think of other things. The sight of her classroom and the faces of her students came to her as she recalled the morning of the last day of school and the afternoon picnic in the city park. She thought about the first days of summer vacation that followed. Theresa skipped ahead to the autumn colors that would engulf the Paint River in early October, and imagined the brisk walks through the woods with Luke, sniffing and snorting at her heels.

She was jolted back into reality by the sound of David Stout's voice. "This exit."

She quickly maneuvered into the next lane and onto the exit ramp for Belvidere Road.

"Go right."

The song in his head had been a folksy elegy. What it lacked in originality, it lacked even more in melody.

"Leavin' on a JetRanger.

"Don't know if I'll be back again.

"Leavin' on a JetRanger.

"Don't care if I come back again.

"I've seen the crazy and I've seen the insane.

"Now, I'll see sunny days that will never end.

"No more guns or gangsters my friend.

"Don't worry, I'm sure I'll see you again."

Michael Duran couldn't carry a tune, and he couldn't carry out his plan without finishing what he had begun in Crystal Falls.

This revelation of a conscience had startled him as he returned to Solidarity Drive with the Adler Planetarium looming in front of him. He had not waited long before spotting Karlene and Stout making their exit from the building.

Duran, with no plan other than following and waiting, had no idea what he would wait for, or what he would do. He convinced himself an opportunity would present itself.

Michael Duran intrepidly followed the black Cadillac onto Belvidere Road.

The sight of four Harleys cruising north on US 41, unrestrained by speed limits or by available lanes, was not an unfamiliar sight. What seemed peculiar to those who cared to notice was the large red-haired man in an unfashionably, ill-fitting summer suit piloting the big blue Electra Glide.

As he maneuvered the large motorcycle in and out of traffic in pursuit of Gretta and his partner, John Kenyon was beginning to feel less and less in command. He imagined his thirty-plus years on the force colliding head-on into a tidal wave of internal investigations.

He could not stop thinking of the endless stories of how situations had gotten completely out of control, of how close friends had been lost, of how careers had abruptly ended in disgrace. He never imagined that he could be drawn into such a scenario.

The rescue of the Swanson woman and the survival of his associates were tantamount. Kenyon knew that Eve was one of the best. She would have to be at her best. He hoped she had taken time to put on her Kevilar; he knew how she disliked wearing it.

Eve Jensen held on tightly. She was having the ride of her life. She had never conceived it possible to move with such propulsion across Chicagoland traffic, then again, she had never considered the shoulder or the meridian of the expressway to be passing lanes. Her pervading thought was simply setting her feet firmly onto the ground. Yet, oddly enough, shielded by the stalwart woman in front of her, she felt undaunted.

Gretta could not get the image of ten million dollars neatly stacked and tucked into the aluminum case out of her mind. While cruising in and out of the northbound traffic, she had done some laborious calculations in her head and concluded that ten million dollars was the equivalent to changing the sheets on fourteen million beds taking nearly six hundred thousand work days, meaning she would need to work only another two thousand or so years. If there was the remotest chance of stealing away with that aluminum case, or any part of its contents, she would take it.

Flame couldn't help recalling the numerous occasions where she'd found herself entangled in precarious circumstances orchestrated by her best friend. They had survived them all, more or less, each one providing rich fodder for their barroom tales. This time, it had been her fascination with Thatcher, and her obsessive desire to track him down that had cast Gretta and herself in an unrehearsed melodrama of cops and mobsters. Flame wished she could pull her friend over and tell her she had a bad feeling about this one, and to forget the whole thing.

Karlene thought of Theresa. Where had the last ten years gone? Why had she been absent from her sister's life? How could she have let it happen? Leaning against Thatcher, she held on tightly. She closed her eyes and prayed she could make it up to her sister.

Riding through the madness that was Chicagoland, Thatcher imagined the mountain majesties stretched out before him. He wanted to get on with his new life, whatever it was to be. He wanted only to steer his Harley-Davidson into the sunset and ride. He had envisioned tending bar in any of a hundred out-of-the-way little saloons in the foothills of the Sierra Nevada. He wanted to lean on one elbow and listen to meaningless conversations about SOB bosses, bitchy wives, and mooching brother-in-laws. He wanted to watch NASCAR and football games on big screen TVs. He wanted the most technical thing in his life to be tapping the next keg of Schlitz beer. And then, he wanted to ride to the next place.

Michael Duran sat behind the wheel of the purple Geo contemplating the shape of the small car. It reminded him of an Easter egg. He was not controlling his thoughts well.

Michael recalled the Saturday night before Easter, more than two decades ago, when he had sneaked downstairs well past midnight, and bit off the tiny yellow heads of each Rodapeep in his little sister's Easter basket.

Justice had come swiftly and harshly that Easter morning. Young Michael could only watch as his little sister, with the sanction of Mom and Dad, bit off the ears of his chocolate bunny. He had quickly concluded that his had been a foolish and reckless escapade.

As he steered into the pitted asphalt parking lot of a deserted convenience store adjacent to the Leather & Lace, he unequivocally concluded that this too was a foolish and reckless escapade.

David Stout's black Coup de Ville was parked to one side of the biker bar in a fashion suggesting it wasn't going to be there long. Michael Duran, whether he was ready or not, was going to have to begin formulating a plan. The time to act was near.

Theresa was not so unsettled that she didn't consider it peculiar to be stopping at a biker bar on the outskirts of Waukegan. If not for her precarious circumstance, she would have snickered at the name scrawled in purple neon above the entrance.

David Stout briskly ushered her past a collection of large motorcycles on the way to the front door of the roadhouse. His left hand pressed firmly against the small of her back as they walked. As Stout swung open the heavy metal door, the stale, bitter air rushed out to greet them like a sudden gust of wind from over a cesspool. Once inside, it took several seconds for her eyes to adjust to the dim interior.

"Go sit at the bar." His instruction was forceful, yet strangely condoling.

Puzzled by his order, she spun around and looked at him. "This isn't really," her eyes darted back and forth across the room, "my kind of place."

With a subtle nod of the head, he directed her toward the bar. "If you attempt to leave, someone will stop you by whatever means may entertain them." David Stout turned away, and began walking toward the back room entrance. "The entertainment here can be repulsive." Just before stepping into the dark corridor, he looked back at his captive standing in the middle of the room. "And, by the way, benevolence is not served here."

Theresa stared indignantly at David Stout before shrugging her shoulders, and saying, "I'll be at the bar."

As she neared a stool two large bikers in worn jeans and weathered leather vests approached from either side. She assumed Stout's exit into the back was their cue.

Within moments Theresa found herself wedged securely between them at the bar. Neither made eye contact with her as their large, hairy, tattooed forearms locked her in place. They smelled of mildew and Old Spice.

She watched the lone bartender carefully drying glasses with a white cotton towel, and with detailed precision, placing them beneath the bar. He was several years older than the others, dressed in the same biker fashion, with the exception of being neat and clean-shaven with a white apron drawn tightly around his slim waist.

Several other bikers were scattered among the tables behind her. Two waitresses dressed in tight leather pants and small leather brassieres smoked cigarettes, and made small talk beside the jukebox at the far end of the bar away from the clientele.

"Hey, Wanda!" The craggy voice came from behind her. "Get your ass over here!"

"Whaddya want?" Her contrived Texas twang reverberated across the room.

"Whaddya mean, whaddya want?" The craggy voice delivered a menacing intonation.

"I mean, whaddya want?"

Wanda, Theresa determined, was not inclined to take abuse from anyone. Twisting toward the inclement voice, she watched as the oversized and predominately tattooed biker whirled around in his chair. He stared malevolently toward Wanda.

The other waitress standing beside Wanda placed her hands on her hips and returned his stare with equal malignancy. "She means, whaddya want?"

The craggy voice addressed the bartender, "Hey! Weezer."

"Hey, Carl! Whaddya want?" Weezer began wiping the top of the smooth burnished bar.

Weezer appeared as an old archetype, a remote kin to *The Wild One,* Theresa thought, despite not having the slightest resemblance to Brando, then or now. He was short and wiry, and no more than one-hundred-fifty pounds, yet it appeared to Theresa that he held rank over anyone in the bar.

Theresa caught a subtle wink from Weezer to Wanda. Wanda took a long drag on her cigarette. "Yeah, whaddya want?"

"A fucking beer! I want a fucking beer!"

"Wanda!" Weezer barked. "Get 'em a fucking beer! He's beginning to irritate me."

Wanda gave the bartender a smile, snuffed out her cigarette, and went about her task.

As Wanda walked back from delivering Carl's beer, Theresa turned toward her. "Could I have a beer, Wanda?"

Wanda stopped abruptly, and stared for a moment at the soft-spoken young woman tucked tightly between two Storm Riders. "Sure, whaddya want?"

Hoping to avoid a drawn out conversation, she said, "A draught."

The slender waitress nodded and continued on.

Theresa turned back around and stared forward once again. "It is okay that I have a beer?" She spoke to her two bodyguards for the first time. She had meant to keep her tone cordial, but it came forth with a nuance of sarcasm.

The larger of the two turned his head slightly in her direction. "Drink it fast."

His remark sent shivers through her. Theresa reminded herself she needed to rise above her fear if she was to keep a cool head. The realization she was alone and in serious jeopardy was becoming a certainty. Convinced her release wasn't forthcoming, she accepted that her survival was in her own hands.

"I'm in no hurry, guys." She slipped the words out with as much spirited poise as she could. "Hey, you know," she turned toward the one who had spoken to her, "I hate to drink alone."

"Wanda," the other Storm Rider called out, "Two more beers over here. The lady's buying."

A little affability is good, she thought. Now, relax, and think. You'll get out of this, she said to herself.

Wanda arrived with three draughts balanced on a circular tray. "That's three bucks."

Under less critical circumstances, Wanda's erroneous Texas twang would have humored her immensely. Theresa pulled a ten from her bib pocket. "Keep the change," she said cordially.

"Yeah, thanks." Gratitude didn't seem to be one of Wanda's best qualities.

Theresa took a sip from her beer as bright sunlight slashed across the room illuminating the otherwise invisible nebula of dust particles drifting through the stale air.

"Shut the fucking door!" came the chorus.

The light continued to absolve the barroom from darkness, as well as authenticate the need for an air purifier.

"Hey, motherfucker, shut the motherfucking door!" the craggy voice boomed across the expanse of the entire room.

Turning around on her stool, Theresa spotted a disheveled young man in a t-shirt and jeans leaning against the heavy metal door. She watched as Wanda strutted over to him. Theresa sensed this could be her moment, her match point. She glanced about the room, the mobster was nowhere in sight. The timing had to be perfect. Theresa watched and listened.

"These guys here get pissed, and they hurt people," Wanda said as she attempted to shove the young, drunken intruder outside.

Incorrigibly, he resisted.

"Hey, get that dumb fuck out of here!" Weezer was not in the mood to intercede over a beating. He had no particular sympathy for the kid, but he did have a particular interest in keeping the cops out of his place.

Wanda tried one last time to get him out the door. He rebuffed her. Then with a sudden change of direction, she pulled him inside and slammed the door shut.

"Okay, you're in." She let go of his arm. "I'm not responsible from here on." She turned and walked back to her post near the jukebox.

Unlike Weezer, Wanda didn't care if the cops showed up, and certainly didn't mind watching the violent antics of stupid men as long as they weren't directed toward her, or any other woman.

Theresa stared at the young man incredulously. She wanted desperately to get out, and this guy had just fought his way in, and was very likely only moments away from getting beat up. During the chaos, she would make her move. Theresa could feel her adrenaline mounting, her muscles twitching, and her chest pounding.

As his eyes finally met hers, Theresa was startled by his broad omniscient smile.

"Karlie! There you are!" He staggered forward and stopped. "I've been looking all over for you." Astounded, she welcomed the mistaken identity. But, who?

The bodyguards exchanged glances, then simultaneously stared in Michael Duran's direction.

"Karlie, baby," he said cheerfully.

By her wayward expression, Duran could tell without a doubt that this was Theresa and not Karlene. Had he not been so immersed in his act, he would have known right off by the hair and Osh Kosh overalls. He told himself not to panic. He would simply have to lead strongly and coax her into her role.

He staggered a few more steps closer to Theresa. "Karlie," he held out his arms, "come to Michael."

It was a resounding click inside her head. This was the helicopter pilot! She jolted from the stool.

"You son-of-a-bitch!"

Michael smiled; she had taken the role on impressively.

"If you hadn't gone off to get drunk with your goddamn buddies, I wouldn't be in this mess!"

Everyone's attention was drawn toward them. One bodyguard grabbed her by the shoulder. She jerked away.

"I have a score to settle with this son-of-a-bitch." Theresa stepped swiftly toward Duran knowing her assigned associates would be close behind. She would have to brush them back somehow.

Michael Duran was amazed how she was going with the character so effortlessly.

Wanda observed the action with great interest. When the young woman connected with a right hook across the boyfriend's jaw Wanda rushed in. Being beaten too many times by too many men, Wanda was determined to take a stand with this woman, with any woman.

As the two bodyguards, who had momentarily been taken aback, reached for their charge, they were met with a bar stool across the knees courtesy of their waitress. They fell to the floor. Other patrons began to rise to get a better view.

Theresa reached for Michael Duran, and pulled him to his feet. "Sorry," she whispered.

He in turn pulled her toward the door with the two Storm Riders scrambling to their feet.

There were more than a dozen motorcycles backed up to the split rail fence that traveled the length of the sidewalk across the front of the bikers' roadhouse. Each was unmistakably Harley-Davidson. Each was customized in classic gang fashion depicting the traditional sociopathic symbols, as well as subtly displaying a small lightning bolt on the bottom of the front fender.

The insignia of the Storm Riders did not escape Gretta's attention, then again, who else would be at this disreputable dive in the middle of the afternoon? She pressed the kill button, and turned off the ignition. Gretta steadied the bike as Jensen dismounted.

Eve Jensen immediately looked around for Kenyon and the others. Concluding her forces had been caught in the traffic jam Gretta had avoided by detouring through a strip mall parking lot, and around the back of a Marathon station, she decided to step behind a rusted-out pickup truck and wait. It was at that moment the front door of the Leather & Lace burst open. Tumbling out onto the sidewalk was a young man in jeans and a t-shirt pulling the Swanson woman behind him.

Standing beside her Fat Boy, Gretta, without hesitation, rushed toward the door. Side-stepping the two fugitives she lowered her shoulder into the metal door. A split second later the impact sent her reeling. On the other side the two bodyguards staggered backwards, dazed by the unexpected collision.

Eve Jensen, drawing her revolver as she moved quickly toward the Swanson woman and her accomplice, prepared to take aim on the next person exiting the door.

"Chicago PD," she said to the young man, not wanting to be confused with the bad guys.

"That's cool." Breathing hard, Michael Duran said, "The next two guys out that door," he paused to catch his breath, "shoot 'em."

"Over there." Jensen motioned with her head. "Get behind that van and stay down."

Theresa said nothing and allowed Michael Duran to pull her to the van. Gretta, now steady on her feet, saw Jensen's revolver drawn and pointed toward the door. She hurried out of the line of fire.

"Take their fucking kneecaps off," was Gretta's poignant suggestion.

"Get over here," Jensen had a bead on the door.

Expectantly, the door swung open with a tremendous force. The two Storm Riders emerged like two frenzied hornets, the largest one brandishing a .357 Stinger.

"Stop! Police!" Before she could utter another syllable, the long barrel turned in her direction. Eve Jensen, for the first time in her ten-year career, squeezed the trigger of her .32 with the sole purpose of doing great bodily harm.

Jensen's .32 slug exploded the large man's patella. Crumpling to the ground, he squeezed off a single shot. The .357 sounded like a cannon compared to Jensen's .32. Gravel scattered a few yards off to the left of the detective.

The other Storm Rider stood frozen in his tracks. His eight-inch blade dropped to the ground. His hands reached upwards.

The large Storm Rider on the ground held his bleeding knee in one hand. The other hand and the gun were out of sight.

Gretta, now standing a few feet from Jensen, uttered excitedly the most obvious question of the moment. "Where's his fucking gun?"

Eve Jensen now took a bead on the downed man. "Push the gun over here."

The large man only groaned.

"The gun! Now!" Every muscle in Jensen's body was taut, and in the recesses of her mind she was calling for her partner.

The big man's hand and gun slowly emerged from beneath him.

"That's right. Nice and slow." Her voice was steadfast and strong. "Slide it this way."

Gretta was impressed.

As the large handgun slid across the sidewalk and into the gravel parking lot, Jensen changed her focus to the man standing. Swiftly, the downed man moved his other hand from his bloodied knee toward his ankle. From the inside of his boot he pulled out a Snub Nose .38.

"Hey!" Gretta's yell was punctuated by the sound of a gunshot.

Eve Jensen was thrown back from the impact of the slug. She did not lose sight of the man with the gun. She struck the ground hard on her left side, her right hand firmly gripping her gun.

Gretta quickly knelt to retrieve the gun from Eve's hand to defend herself, but before she could reach it a second shot whirred past her head. Gretta fell backwards. She heard a third shot as she lay on her back staring at the cloudless sky.

"Shit," Gretta muttered as she began rolling away like a kid playing tumbleweed. Seconds later she scrambled to her feet and dove behind the nearby pickup truck. Holding her breath, she looked toward Jensen.

Eve Jensen lay still on her back, her revolver clutched in her hand.

"Fuck." Gretta looked in the direction of the Storm Riders. The one that had been standing was now out of sight. On the ground lay the one with the gun. She stared at the bloody hole in the top of his bald crown. Gretta slowly looked toward the detective. Jensen's legs stirred.

"Hey," Gretta whispered loudly. "Jensen." Rising to her feet, she watched Eve Jensen's left foot move. She glanced first at the front door before leaving the cover of the pickup truck to aid the fallen detective.

Eve's eyes fluttered open to the sight of Gretta hovering over her. "I hate guns," she murmured.

"I see the hole. Where's the blood?"

"Kevilar." Jensen extended her hand.

"Kevilar." Repeating the word carefully, Gretta took the detective's hand and smiled. "You're bulletproof."

With the sound of the approaching Harleys, Eve raised her hand, allowing her partner to know immediately she was all right.

Twenty-Four

David Stout, within the security of his private office, was finishing a brief phone conversation with Mr. Revelle when the commotion began. Watching the security monitor as he listened to Mr. Revelle's expression of gratitude over the recovery of the ten million dollars, he witnessed Michael Duran's grand entrance. Settling into his chair, Stout respectfully closed his conversation with Mr. Revelle, and from the monitor he observed the first act of young Michael's valiant rescue attempt. David Stout watched as he reflected upon his triumph.

It was two years ago that Mr. Revelle and The Affiliation recruited David Stout for one of many money laundering operations. Recognizing him as a competent associate well up to the task, they also perceived his worth as a valuable tool to eventually eliminate the Henderson empire. The intent of The Affiliation was to remove the competition one by one, either by absorption or by subjugation.

At the time, David Stout had seen no justification not to work for two bosses, discerning that it was a perspicacious insurance policy for the future. After all, crime bosses were high-risk employers.

Inquiring with a local Realtor about the availability of the old

Waukegan bar, David Stout couldn't have timed it more perfectly. The newly established Storm Riders of which Weezer was the Prezo, had just closed a deal on the establishment. David Stout seized the opportunity, offering Weezer an extremely lucrative arrangement for leasing him space. Who would suspect a biker roadhouse of being anything but a biker roadhouse? He knew the cops would be watching, but not for high tech crime. David Stout had felt exceedingly clever and secure.

Weezer eagerly accepted the offer. Not particularly concerned with David Stout's affairs, he retired comfortably from the office of Storm Rider Prezo. He willingly turned it over to his Vice Prezo, Wazoo.

The Leather & Lace became the official clubhouse for the newly formed Storm Riders, and the headquarters for David Stout's new enterprise. Everyone was satisfied.

Stout watched as the Swanson woman cold-cocked Michael Duran. He laughed to himself trying to imagine, for whatever wacky reason, Duran believed he could rescue the young woman. David Stout grinned with the realization that young Michael had not apparently noticed the switch in hostages in Evanston, and now, because of his lack of observation, found himself laid out flat from Theresa's right hook. It was all too amusing. Nonetheless, David Stout appreciated Duran's unyielding, yet foolish effort. As he watched the monitor, David Stout went over in his head the events of the last two days.

It certainly hadn't gone as planned, due to Curtis Lane's guileless stupidity. Karlene wasn't supposed to be with him on Friday night. More importantly, he wasn't supposed to get himself killed, at least not before the aluminum case was locked away inside the office safe. The unplanned disappearance of the limousine and of The Affiliation's money eventually played into David Stout's hands. It forced him to operate extemporaneously, displaying to The Affiliation his ability to adapt swiftly and deftly to rapidly changing adversity.

With millions of dollars actually missing, Henderson was judged irremediably incompetent by The Affiliation. Mr. Revelle ordered Aaron Henderson permanently dismissed. David Stout was given the contract, and with its completion, the reins of the former Henderson empire under the direction of Mr. Revelle. All was fair in crime and war, of which David Stout was equally adept at managing.

Lane's untimely demise came as no great surprise to David Stout. Curtis despised bikers, and it had become readily accepted that Curtis Lane had provided two Storm Riders with tainted Lysergic acid diethylamide. The LSD launched the two members into a one-way psychotic adventure. Had Stout known the membership had marked Curtis Lane for execution, he would have altered his plan for Friday night. Nonetheless, the sequence of events that followed turned out exceedingly well for David Stout.

Unfortunately, it never occurred to Stout that Duran would follow him to the Leather & Lace. Leaving the Swanson woman with the Storm Riders seemed a judicious move. He paid Weezer $5,000 to detain her for six hours, and then to release her thoroughly intoxicated and relatively unharmed.

Stretching leisurely into his chair, Stout awaited the conclusion to Michael Duran's futile escapade. He didn't expect the scrawny, big-mouthed waitress to intervene with a bar stool. Nor did he expect Michael and Theresa to ever make it to the door, let alone exit through it.

Rising from his chair, he reached inside his jacket for the holstered .38 Special, once again thinking he would have to handle it. He watched the monitor as the two big bikers rumbled toward the door in pursuit. When the massive duo bounced off the door, Stout wished he had allowed Aaron to shoot the smart-ass pilot after all.

David Stout reached the front of the bar as the first shot was fired. He instantly knew that it wasn't a large caliber, typical of the Storm Riders. The thought of Michael Duran with a gun astonished him. With the retaliating blast from a .357, Stout immediately surmised it was over, and it was only a matter of having the mess swiftly cleaned up. It was the third and fourth shot coming from something other than a .357, that caused him to stiffen.

The reappearance of only one Storm Rider announcing that "some bitch shot Maxie deader than shit," convinced David Stout it was time to take the money and run.

With his gun drawn and his eyes constantly surveying the surroundings, John Kenyon's first action was to go to his partner.

"I'm all right, John." She manufactured a semblance of a smile as he knelt beside her. "I promise, I'll never complain about wearing it again."

"What do you think we have here?" he asked.

"Another dead Stormie," Gretta droned.

John Kenyon glanced toward the corpse laying on the sidewalk near the door. He saw the Smith & Wesson in the gravel.

Turning wide-eyed to his partner, he said, "You took a .357 mag?"

"No." Sighing unevenly with severely bruised ribs on her left side, she replied, "He had a .38 or something in his boot. I can't believe I missed it."

"Yeah, but you didn't miss his fat head," Gretta complemented. "Fucking nice shot."

"Saved your tattooed ass." Flame now stood beside Gretta. "By the looks of it, you've been rolling around in the gravel."

"I don't know how many we have inside, but it seems they're staying inside." Jensen began to get to her feet. "Or, leaving by the back door."

"Easy, partner." John Kenyon helped her to her feet.

She sensed his gratitude for her staying alive. "I'm fine, John," she assured him as she touched her bruised ribs.

Those club members who died well before turning fifty were the angry ones overwhelmed by their own capacity for violence. Being stupid and intoxicated, of course, was widely suspect as well. Weezer had not grown old within the throngs of biker clubs by being intoxicated and stupid. Nor did he allow his anger to supersede his common sense.

With Wazoo and company missing, with Maxie laying dead on the front sidewalk, with David Stout apparently preparing to close up shop for awhile, and with five thousand dollars in his safe, Weezer concluded that it was time to empty the safe and hit the road. His '49 Hydra-Glide was parked out back.

A craggy voice boomed over the chaotic noise. "Let's get that bitch!"

The sound of scuffling chairs and tables followed. Every Storm Rider was on his feet, muscles taut, jaws clenched, and eyes focused on the door. Carl and three others stormed the door as Wanda lit a cigarette.

"Fucking idiots," she said to her friend. Wanda glanced over to Weezer and recognized the signs of an early departure. She blew a plume of smoke above her head and nudged her friend. "Judy, the ol' man's packin' it in." Wanda motioned toward Weezer.

Judy crushed out her cigarette in a nearby ashtray. "Shift's over."

The large Storm Rider in front of Carl suddenly halted at the door. "I ain't got the gun."

His revelation spread quickly through the ranks; Maxie had the official clubhouse gun, and that was laying somewhere in the parking lot. Carl immediately looked over toward the bar. Weezer was nowhere in sight. There were ten seconds of profound silence before Carl slapped the shoulder of a fellow Storm Rider.

"Hey, let's have another beer. It's on me." Carl began walking toward the bar.

"What about Maxie?" came a whisper from the ranks. It was Maxie's accomplice who had escaped with only the loss of his folding Buck knife.

The craggy voice boomed once again. "Take 'em a fucking beer!"

Karlene immediately noticed the purple Geo parked across the street as Thatcher veered into the parking lot of the Leather & Lace. It gave her a peculiar sense of assurance that Theresa was all right. She then saw Michael Duran and her sister crouched behind an old rusted van.

"Over there!" Karlene pointed wildly in their direction.

Thatcher steered his bike toward the van. Karlene didn't wait for the Harley to come to a stop. Her unexpected departure nearly left Thatcher and his Fat Boy sprawled in the gravel. Upon regaining control of the *Wanderer*, he watched as the sisters, with arms outstretched, ran to one another: a Hallmark card commercial.

The twins, embracing one another, jumped and danced around in a circle as they had more than a decade before when they had won the conference championship in the third game 20–18.

Michael Duran approached Thatcher. "You must be the infamous Thatcher." He held out his hand.

Thatcher hit the kill button, leaned his bike into the stand, and grasped the outstretched hand. "The pilot."

"Yeah, the pilot."

Smiling, they took a moment to watch the dancing Swanson sisters.

Now standing behind the rusted pickup truck ten yards from the front entrance, Kenyon glanced across the parking lot toward the black Cadillac and asked, "Any sign of Stout?"

"No." Jensen brushed herself off. "Do you think he's still here?"

"His Caddie's here."

Eve Jensen inspected her revolver before reloading. "So, do we walk in the front door?"

"Fuckin' A!"

Flame jabbed her partner in the ribs. "She's kidding."

"We keep the front entrance secured," he spoke primarily to his partner, "and we wait. I suspect the Waukegan PD has been alerted by a passerby."

"Maybe not," said Flame. "This isn't the most upstanding part of town. The place across the street is empty."

"Gunshots ain't too big a deal around here," Gretta added. "And, except for the hole in his head, it ain't so unusual to have somebody sprawled on the front sidewalk."

John Kenyon addressed Flame, assuming she was more likely to take direction. "I need you to call this in."

"Eve," Kenyon spoke confidently, "I want you to cover the front." He turned his attention to Gretta. "I want you with me."

Gretta punched Flame in the shoulder. "Get this, Detective Big Red needs my backup."

"He needs to keep an eye on you." Flame started toward her bike. "I'll make the call." Looking back at John Kenyon, she said, "Watch her real close."

Kenyon nodded.

With his Coupe de Ville parked in front of the building, Stout promptly concluded simply walking out the back door was the only option. He holstered his .38 Special and armed himself with an Uzi. Picking up the metal case filled with money, he left his office for the last time.

The dark storage room, with its rows of stacked cases of beer and booze, concealed Wanda and Judy as they passed a joint back and forth to the opening chords of "Freebird" coming from the juke. David Stout walked formidably to the rear exit.

It seemed good fortune was still on his side. Just outside the screen door Weezer was haphazardly stuffing stacks of tens and twenties into his saddle bags. A getaway vehicle was no longer in doubt. David Stout liked the old biker, but he needed his bike, and didn't have time to negotiate. He stepped through the door with the Uzi raised.

Weezer looked up, startled. Staring into the bore of the lethal weapon, the old biker slowly raised his hands. He never suspected he would be taken out so easily. After a brief silence he spoke.

"We can both get out of this." Weezer's voice showed no fear. "This here bike is no cinch to ride, if that's what you're thinking." He could see David Stout analyzing the probabilities. "Suicide clutch, shift on the side."

Stout immediately determined the old biker was right. He lowered his weapon. "Okay."

Weezer started the old Harley and threw his leg over the seat. "Get on."

As John Kenyon approached the rear corner of the building the sound of a Harley engine rumbling to life stopped him momentarily.

"That's an old one," whispered Gretta. "Late forties. Panhead." She knew she was right, because she knew Weezer always parked out back, and she knew he rode a '49 Hydra-Glide.

Pulling his 9mm semi-automatic from its holster, he reminded Gretta to stay behind, and to stay close. He emphasized behind.

"Yeah, whatever," she replied.

As he leaned cautiously around the corner of the building, Gretta attempted to do the same. With his new associate pressing against him, Kenyon stepped back abruptly, pushing Gretta back on her heals. Turning in her direction, Kenyon raised his left hand with his palm out, and said, "Stay!"

She mumbled something about not being a fucking Rottweiler as she watched him raise his gun to shoulder level.

Easing around the corner of the building, John Kenyon watched as David Stout, holding an aluminum case in his left hand, mounted the rear of the motorcycle twenty yards away.

"Chicago PD!"

Kenyon took a bead on David Stout, certain that Henderson's former right-hand man was carrying substantial fire power. Peering down the barrel of his Smith & Wesson, he watched the right arm of the mobster swing over the top of the old biker's head. As soon as he spotted the automatic weapon he squeezed the trigger. The 9mm slug struck Stout's left shoulder. The aluminum case dropped to the ground. The momentum of Stout's right arm was momentarily halted with the impact of the bullet. Kenyon called out for Stout to drop the weapon.

There was no choice. Without the money, David Stout knew he would be taken out by The Affiliation. Swinging his weapon into position, he intended to kill or be killed. It was the way of his profession.

As the barrel of the Uzi began its descent, Kenyon fired one more time. His shot went high. The 9mm slug struck below the base of the skull shattering the cervical vertebrae, and severing the spinal cord just inches below the brain stem. David Stout collapsed, falling backwards from the motorcycle.

Weezer accelerated with the sound of the second blast, and as Stout tumbled off the back, the Hydra-Glide swerved into the alley. John Kenyon had no desire to shoot anyone else. Lowering his gun, he watched the old biker disappear down the alley.

Once again, the patriarchal biker escaped to ride another day; this time with five grand in his saddlebags. He imagined Willie Nelson singing the refrain, "On the road again..."

Eve Jensen heard the gunshots from her post behind the rusted pickup. She was torn between holding position and going to her partner; Jensen held her position. Glancing across the lot toward Thatcher and the others behind the van, it seemed apparent they hadn't heard the shots. At that same moment, Flame pulled in behind the van. Reinforcements would arrive soon. The waiting became easier.

A couple minutes later a city police cruiser with flashers on veered into the parking lot; it appeared to be a maneuver familiar to the Waukegan PD.

Jensen held up her badge. The cruiser pulled up behind the pickup. The lights went off as both officers exited.

Flame stood close to Thatcher and the others as the Chicago detective talked with the two police officers. As if Jensen's departure around the corner of the building was Flame's cue, she nudged Thatcher. "Hey." Nodding in the direction of the two officers, she said, "Let's go see."

Thatcher knew curiosity was overwhelming her. There was no doubt Flame wanted to know what was happening on the other side of the building, as well as what her road warrior partner was into.

"Hey!" She slugged him hard in the shoulder, "the Boobsy Twins will be just fine."

Thatcher took the punch without flinching.

"I'm checking it out," she said as she strutted past him.

"Flame."

Twirling around without breaking stride, she threw her hands into the air. "If you're worried about me, come along."

His own curiosity pulled at him. By the time Thatcher caught up to her, one of the officers had already begun his interception.

"I'm going to have to ask both of you to stay back. This is a secured area." The young officer did his best to deliver an authoritarian demeanor. In a way, it reminded Thatcher of himself many years ago: exhibiting authority, and hoping for the best.

Flame wasn't impressed, and didn't hesitate to assert herself. "I'm going to have to ask you to get out of my way, or try to cuff me."

The challenge had been made. Thatcher paused, took off his cap, ran his fingers through his hair a couple of times, and put his cap back on with the bill forward. He watched with interest.

For the young officer, it had already been a long day: two domestic disputes involving a knife and a crowbar, three car accidents (one with a messy fatality), shots fired at a local playground, and now this. The officer was in no mood to tangle with a defiant biker lady with a bad attitude.

"You could be arrested," he warned.

"That's fucking fine. Arrest me when I get back."

Watching as Flame swaggered away, Thatcher turned to the officer. "Undercover."

The officer shrugged his shoulders and assumed his vigilance of the front entrance.

Peering around the corner after the second shot, Gretta had spotted the aluminum case laying on the ground. The sight of it sent shivers down her spine. As the detective lowered his gun, Gretta raced toward the case.

Kenyon, wary that someone else might emerge from the back door, called out, "Get back!" He followed swiftly after his wayward partner, with his gun once again raised ready to aim and to fire.

Gretta's only thought was of the stacks of thousand dollar bills packed inside the metal case. As she bent over to pick up the case, she glanced only briefly at the lifeless body staring toward the sky, but it was long enough to see the head wasn't securely attached to the neck. Cringing and stepping back, she didn't have time react to the sound of the screen door swinging open. A large tattooed forearm caught her around the neck.

"Gotcha, bitch." She recognized the voice.

Carl had wandered back after drawing several beers for his troops. He had been curious as to Weezer's whereabouts after noticing that the safe door was ajar. Having watched the shootout from just inside the door, he was in a perfect position to grab Gretta, and snatch for himself what he thought was the booty from Weezer's safe.

"Fuck you, Carl."

He let out a growl. "You know what this is stuck in your fuckin' ear?"

"It's too hard to be your pecker." She felt his grip tighten as she resisted being pulled into the back of the building. "Hey dumb fuck." Gretta spewed the three syllables effortlessly. "That detective over there can shoot a fly off the end of your teenie weenie."

Carl and John Kenyon were already engaged in a staredown. With a quick forceful lunge backwards Carl could have pulled his hostage through the back door, but he could not resist the showdown with the big cop.

"Drop your weapon," Kenyon's voice was clear and unwavering. "Then, let the woman go."

Carl whispered into her ear. "Did you hear that Gretta? He wants me to drop my gun and let you go."

"I'm not deaf, asshole."

He continued whispering as he stared at the large cop several feet away. "I want you to tell him to put the gun down and back off. Can you do that in a convincing manner?" He squeezed even harder. Carl was enjoying the moment.

"Sure." Gasping for air, she continued, "I can do that, if you ease up on the throat."

She felt his grip loosen. Gretta twisted her neck back and forth creating a little more clearance for her head to move.

"Detective Big Red," she winked at Kenyon, "this here is Carl. He wants me to tell you to drop your gun and back off."

Recalling Pasco and Smits at Wrigley Field, John Kenyon readied himself. He was certain Gretta wasn't going down without a fight.

"But, I'd rather you just shoot him." And, with that she jerked her head down and away from the gun barrel, while pushing up with her hands against his forearm.

John Kenyon had one brief moment to squeeze off one shot. He hesitated and the shot was lost.

Carl renewed his grip on his hostage and pulled her closer to him. He backed up through the doorway. Gretta did not struggle. She was saving her strength for later.

Kenyon could only watch as the biker and his captive disappeared into the building. Lowering his gun, he leaned back against the building. This could be that one day, he thought, out of thirty years he was going to regret the most.

Eve Jensen appeared from around the corner. "Stout?"

"Dead." Kenyon turned slowly in her direction.

"I've got two Waukegan patrolmen at the front. Nothing has happened." She recognized the look. "What's wrong?"

"Gretta." Running his hand over the top of his head, he stated, "She's inside."

"How?"

"Whatever's in that metal case, money I assume, caught her attention." Taking a breath, he confessed, "She was by me before I could do anything."

"To stop her," blending humor with consolation, Jensen remarked, "you would have had to shoot her."

"I thought about it."

She couldn't help seeing the weariness in his eyes. "John, we'll get her out."

"Someone snatched her right in front of me from the back door." He looked at Eve, and lamented. "I had one shot." Shaking his head, "It was too close," he said.

Jensen stepped closer. "We wait it out?"

Looking toward the ground, he said, "It's a feeling Eve. I don't think we have time. Gretta isn't going to be an accommodating hostage."

"Then, we go get her." Surprised by her own disregard of protocol, she added, "You make the call. I'm there."

"I can't let you go in there." It was his paternal tone. "It's too risky."

"John, if it's too risky for me, then it's too risky for you."

Kenyon wanted to fix it right away. He wanted to rush in Eastwood style and get Gretta out, but he had already strayed way too far from procedure. Common sense told him to wait. His gut told him to go get her. Common sense settled over him.

"It's too risky. We wait," he said despairingly.

TWENTY-FIVE

JOHN KENYON WAS MOMENTARILY STARING PAST JENSEN TOWARD the corner of the building, trying to figure out the next move. One hostage had simply been traded for another. This was turning out to be a bitch of a day.

"Shit," he murmured.

"What?" She watched as her partner rotated his lower jaw usually indicating his TMJ was acting up. Migraines usually followed.

"It's the other one," he said.

Jensen turned slowly and casually toward Flame. Thatcher was close behind. She saw Flame scanning the area for her friend.

Stopping several feet short of the detectives, Flame asked, "Where's that dumb-ass blonde?"

Eve Jensen glanced quickly toward Kenyon who was seemingly preoccupied massaging his jaw.

"This one's yours," he mumbled.

Turning back toward Flame and Thatcher, Jensen waited for her to take a few more steps. She was certain Flame wouldn't accept the news very well. She was equally certain the only way to prevent Flame from going after her friend was to cuff her to Thatcher. As unfair as that was to Thatcher, Jensen considered it the best option. She casually moved her left hand toward her hip where she kept her handcuffs.

Unfortunately for Jensen, Flame had seen that maneuver before.

"So where is she?" Staying her distance, Flame didn't wait for a reply. "Where's Gretta?" Sliding her sunglasses to the top of her head, Flame stared at the detective and said, "She's inside, and she's in deep shit."

"We're going to get her out." Jensen raised her right hand in a calming gesture, and spoke slowly. "We're going to get her out."

Lowering her right shoulder, Flame charged the detective. It happened so quickly that it caught Jensen off guard, pushing her back into her partner. Flame was past her in a flash.

Thatcher looked at the two detectives with empathy, then shrugged his shoulders. "It seems she's going to get her out now." Although his cavalier response implied his confidence in the dynamic duo's capabilities, it didn't efface his concern.

Sprinting to the back screen door, Flame stopped, and peered inside. Gingerly opening the screen door, she slipped inside.

Flame entered the dimly lit building like a cat burglar, crouching along the side of the west wall moving stealthy in and out of the stacks of beer and liquor cases. The scent of marijuana, although a common backroom odor, caused Flame to move even more cautiously. She didn't want to startle a couple Stormies getting high.

From the barroom jukebox, the Allman Brothers Band justified a "Ramblin' Man," and from behind a stack of liquor cases a freshly lit cigarette disclosed company nearby. Standing still, Flame listened for the slightest of sounds. Several seconds passed before she heard a muffled smoker's cough. She was certain it was a woman.

"Gretta," she whispered.

There was no response. She said nothing until she heard a boot scuffing the wooden floor a few seconds later.

"Gretta," she whispered again, a little louder.

There was more scuffing followed by a cough. Flame heard whispering a few feet away from among the stacked cases. There were two.

"Hey, you a cop?" came a woman's voice.

Flame waited several seconds. "No. I'm looking for Gretta."

"She's up front."

Flame tried to place the voice. "Who's this?"

"It's Wanda. Is that you, Flame?"

"Yeah, who's with you?"

"Judy's here."

Gretta was haphazardly tied to a chair. She had already freed her right ankle, and was working on her wrists. Bleeding from the mouth, and with one eye nearly swollen shut, she expected more to come.

Women were not highly regarded among the Storm Riders, and women with attitude were knocked around whenever possible. In Gretta's case, it took two determined members to take on the tall, broad-shouldered blonde they all called Amazon.

Carl was now the bartender, once again drawing beers for his companions. Gretta wondered when he was going to get around to mentioning that a mobster was laying out back with his head nearly blown off, and that there were cops at the back door and the front as well. She watched as the Stormies raised their glasses to salute Carl's miraculous recovery of the booty that Weezer had attempted to embezzle from the Storm Riders Motorcycle Club.

Carl had not bothered to open the aluminum case. That was probably all for the best, Gretta figured, although she was tremendously curious what their reaction would be to a true fortune. Yet with Weezer gone, she doubted that anyone present had the capability of accurately calculating its total contents.

Deciding it was time for Carl to report the actual situation, she shouted. "Hey, ass wipes!" Her mouth ached. "Hey, you motherfucking morons!"

The newest Stormie recruit stepped away from the others. He took three steps toward Gretta.

"Shut the fuck up!" Yelping belligerently, he hoped to impress the others. Newcomers were always looking for ways to exalt themselves among their peers.

Gretta recognized him through her one good eye. "Shut the fuck up," she mimicked through a crooked smirk. The left side of her mouth was still swelling from Carl's right hook.

A large hand reached out and shoved the bantam-size recruit in Gretta's direction. "Give the bitch another whack. She's startin' to piss me off."

"Yeah, come on over here Leo, and give me a whack." She chortled. "I should have broken your fucking arm the other night." She watched his approach. "How's that arm feeling, Leo? You know, the one with the pomegranate."

Leo was glaring through glazed, drunken eyes as he stood over her. Gretta was not going to miss this opportunity. As he reared back his right fist, Gretta swept her right leg across the side of his left ankle. As he tumbled to the floor, she promptly stood and swung the chair around and set it down on top of him with the rear rung pressed against his throat. This is too easy she murmured to herself. When he began to squirm she pressed the heel of her boot into his groin.

"Leo, this was too fuckin' easy." Staring down at her victim, she went on with the insults. "Leo, you fight worse than you arm wrestle." Gretta let out a howl. "Looks like I can take you with both hands tied behind my back."

Having gotten everyone's attention, Gretta addressed her audience. "Hey, you fuckin' morons, did Carl happen to mention who he ran into out back?"

Leo was gasping for air. Two of the Stormies started toward her to rescue their diminutive recruit, whose face was beginning to turn an ashen gray.

She jammed her heel forcefully in his groin. His muffled scream momentarily halted their approach.

"Who do you think shot your big guy out front?"

"Get her off him!" screamed Carl.

As they rushed her she yelled, "The fuckin' heat!"

Gretta felt herself flying through the air. The chair, breaking her fall, splintered apart as she slid up against the jukebox.

Amused at first by Gretta's swift disposal of Leo, Flame discerned she had watched long enough at which point Gretta went airborne. It was time to intervene. She wasn't going to allow her partner to go down alone. Flame sprinted from the back room. As she passed by Leo, who was still gasping for air on all fours, she caught him on the side of the head with her right boot. He collapsed to the floor.

The two members who had thrown Gretta through the air were bending over her, preparing to pick her up off the floor for another toss. Lowering her shoulder, Flame blindsided them headlong into the jukebox. The "Ramblin' Man" came to an abrupt sojourn somewhere along Highway 41.

"Who you supposed to be?" Gretta asked, as Flame pulled her away from the two Stormies who were still sprawled on the floor.

"Sarah Connor," making reference to Gretta's favorite movie, "coming to terminate these motherfuckers."

Gretta rose to her feet. The shattered chair fell away in pieces. "That's just great." Gretta squinted at her friend through her one good eye. "But, she had some bad ass help."

Hurriedly grappling with the rope around Gretta's wrists, she announced, "We got backup!"

"I hope so." Gretta watched one Stormie rise gingerly to his feet. "Now these guys are really pissed."

As the largest biker reached for Flame, she snap-kicked him in the groin. He staggered backwards into the other, and fell over the top of him.

"I didn't know you could do that." Gretta pulled her hands free.

"Makes you want to give me a little more respect, doesn't it?"

"Fuckin' A, Sarah." Gretta smiled through her swollen, lopsided mouth.

"Hey, that's a good look for you." Flame grimaced at her friend's grotesque face.

The Dynamic Duo turned to confront the others who had not yet made a move to leave the proximity of the Pabst tap. All four nervously leaned back against the bar as Carl slowly walked the length of the bar with Weezer's .357 acquired from the opened safe. He leveled it in the direction of the two women.

"This isn't good," whispered Gretta.

Carl stopped at the end of the bar near the entrance to the back room. Slowly he moved the gun sights back and forth between his two targets. "Who should I shoot first?"

"Carl," Gretta began.

Flame glanced at her. "Eaaaasy," she whispered.

"Stick it up your ass, and blow out your brains."

Flame did not take her eyes off the barrel of the gun as she jabbed her partner. "I hope he shoots you first."

Carl turned toward his small hoard. The two near the jukebox were now upright and stepping rapidly out of the way. Carl was not known as a crack shot, in fact, there was not a Stormie in the place not holding his breath, with the exception of Leo who was out cold. Carl suddenly tilted back his head and howled, then set the gun down on the end of the bar. There were sighs of relief all around.

"I'm going to do this with my bare hands," he said as he started his approach.

"You've got a better right jab," Flame whispered. "You hit him high, and I'll kick him low." Glancing at Gretta, she inquired, "You can see, can't you?"

"I can see." She leaned close to Flame and whispered. "I can see Wanda crawling on her hands and knees."

Wanda scurried to her feet and snatched the .357 from the end of the bar. The scrawny blonde waitress pointed the gun at Carl. "Freeze!"

Everyone looked in the direction of the small, squeaky voice, except Carl. He froze.

"Freeze?" Gretta looked at Flame. "That's our backup?"

Wide-eyed, Flame took a step back.

Gretta returned her attention to Wanda and the large chrome revolver. "Holy Jesus!" Gretta stared at the wobbling barrel pointed in her direction. "Hold it steady, woman."

Carl turned slowly around and howled like a cornered animal. Without hesitation he rushed the little waitress with the big gun.

Wanda, having no intention of firing the gun, bent over quickly, and slid it across the floor past the charging Storm Rider and toward the waiting hands of Sarah Connor. Flame scooped up the huge gun, pulled the hammer back, and leveled it in Carl's direction.

"Freeze!"

Gretta stared at her partner. "Freeze?"

"I've got the fucking gun. I can say freeze."

Carl stopped a few feet from Wanda. For several seconds there was only silence. No one moved.

"That's right! Freeze you motherfucker!" Gretta added.

Flame scanned the room, looking for the slightest movement from anyone. No one moved, particularly Leo. "Okay, guys. We'll be leaving now."

She kept the gun leveled at Carl, who only now began to turn around to face the barrel of his own gun. Wanda disappeared swiftly into the back room. Flame figured she and Judy would be out the back door within seconds.

"Back behind the bar, Carl." Flame motioned with the gun. "Draw up some more brewskis for the deviants." She was more than ready to turn these moronic misfits over to the police.

Shrugging his shoulders and turning toward the Pabst tap, he walked casually along the bar. "Hey, who wants a beer?" he called out. Then, reaching beneath the bar, he brought out a glass in his left hand, and in his right he hastily raised a small caliber pistol. He fired once before Flame could react.

As Flame squeezed the trigger she heard Gretta groan, and from the corner of her eye she saw her friend twist around and drop to her knees.

Flame's target had been his sternum; the shot went high. The .357 slug struck Carl just above the right eye, popping the eyeball from its socket and shattering the back of his skull into tiny shrapnel splattering the mirror behind the bar with blood, bone, and brain. The big man collapsed in a heap. The remaining contents of his cranium began oozing out onto the floor.

With great apprehension, two of the six Stormies near the Pabst tap leaned over the top of the bar to check on their fallen member.

"Holy fuck!" said the tallest. "That's two in one day."

"Wazoo ain't gonna believe this shit," said the other.

Twenty-Six

KENYON AND JENSEN, WITH WEAPONS DRAWN, HAD CAUTIOUSly made their way to the back door of the Leather & Lace. With the sound of gunfire, Eve Jensen turned to her partner.

Kenyon said only, "Cover me."

"John, I'm quicker. You're the better shot."

John Kenyon pulled open the door. "After you."

Once inside, the two detectives swiftly worked their way toward the front of the building. Scurrying foot steps from behind a row of beer cases announced an escape. Both detectives froze, and waited. As two unidentified women hurried past, Kenyon motioned his partner to continue on.

Neither Wanda or Judy had missed a stride until they ran head into Thatcher at the back door. Keeping his balance, he watched as both women careened off the door jamb and tumbled to the ground. Judy found herself face to face with David Stout's corpse. Staring into the gore, Judy screamed. Wanda, sprawled out beside Judy, screamed. Thatcher undauntedly stepped into the dark building.

"Woman down!"

Thatcher shuddered with the urgency of Flame's voice. Hurrying through the shadows, he collided with a stack of empties. As longnecks scattered across the wooden floor, he watched the two armed detectives burst into the bar, one after the other.

Kenyon and Jensen, with their guns leveled, scanned their respective sides of the room.

John Kenyon's voice boomed. "Chicago PD!"

The six remaining Storm Riders, with the exception of Leo who was now only beginning to stir, raised their hands.

"I've got it," Kenyon said.

Lowering her .32, Eve immediately joined Flame who stood undaunted above Gretta with the revolver still leveled in the direction of the Stormies. Eve located the wound quickly: a small neat hole from a small caliber just below the right clavicle. There was a clean exit; the bleeding was minimal.

"You'll be fine," Eve said matter-of-factly.

"Fuckin' A," Gretta concurred.

Watching from the doorway, as Kenyon gingerly took the large handgun from Flame's trembling hand, Thatcher sighed with relief. He went to kneel beside Gretta opposite Flame and Jensen.

"Look at this," Gretta said to Flame before turning toward Thatcher, "he finally decided to join the fun."

Glancing back between Flame and the detective, she asked, "Can I get up now?"

Flame placed her right forearm under Gretta's good shoulder, while Jensen put her right arm around Gretta's waist to support her right arm. As Gretta rose to her feet, she looked over to Thatcher.

"Where the fuck you been, anyway?" Pressing her left palm against her wound, she waited for his reply.

He removed his cap and wiped the sweat from his forehead with the back of the same hand. "Staying out of the way."

Gretta rolled her one good eye. "No shit."

Flame looked austerely at her wounded friend. "You should try that for once in your life." Keeping her eyes locked on Gretta, Flame went further. "You wouldn't have a hole in your..."

"I wouldn't have a hole in my shoulder if you were quicker on the draw."

Eve Jensen looked in Thatcher's direction.

Shrugging his shoulders, he put his cap back on, and said to the detective, "They'll work it out."

John Kenyon had holstered his own gun and held the .357 in his left hand as he walked behind the bar. Side-stepping a small gelatin blob, he ordered the remaining Storm Riders to sit down at the largest round table with their hands palm down on the surface. They did so quickly, and without question.

Within seconds a self-appointed spokesman, without lifting his hands from the table, slowly rose from his chair. Cautiously eyeing the large detective emptying the remaining cartridges from the Smith & Wesson onto the bar, the spokesman poignantly presented their disclaimer.

"We here didn't have nothin' to do with this shit. We'd just been mindin' our own business, and drinkin' a few beers."

John Kenyon looked over the collection of disheveled outcasts. Pushing the aluminum case aside, he leaned forward against the bar and uttered, "Whatever," before beckoning for Thatcher.

Thatcher stepped away from the feuding duo and walked behind the bar toward John Kenyon.

"Mr. Thatcher, you and this metal case have been through a lot together." Kenyon pushed the aluminum case in his direction along the top of the bar. "Open it for me."

Catching it as it veered off the edge of the bar, he rammed his knee into the open door of Weezer's massive antique safe. With the case under his right arm, he rubbed his knee with his left hand. As he knelt on his one good knee with the case balanced on the other, he looked up at the big detective. "It's just a few thousand thousand-dollar bills."

Dryly, Kenyon remarked, "NBA signing bonus."

As he opened it for the detective, he heard a high gasping voice cry out.

"Kill 'em all!"

Above the sound of chairs and tables tumbling across the floor and scuffling feet, Thatcher heard a voice yell out, "Fire in the hole!"

His peripheral vision caught John Kenyon drawing his gun as another voice roared, "Grenade!"

Kenyon had no time to fire.

With the case spread open on his knee, Thatcher stared at the money with a curious thought that it might be the last thing he would ever see. At that moment, as if on a predestined trajectory, it fell onto the stacks of money with a definitive thud. His brain recognized it within a millisecond, yet it felt an eternity before he could react.

Slamming the case shut, he fell backwards. And, like a last second Brett Favre shuffle pass, he pitched it into the open safe. As he hit the floor he saw the charging figure of John Kenyon lowering a massive shoulder toward the safe door, and like a defensive end diving franticly for Barry Sanders, Kenyon careened off the safe door and crashed to the floor beside Thatcher.

Moments after the safe door slammed closed, a deafening explosion shook the entire building. The seconds that followed seemed like hours. Thatcher opened his eyes, not remembering he had closed them. Being quite certain he was still alive, it wasn't until he recognized the singed fragments of Federal Reserve Notes fluttering down on his chest that he was certain what had just occurred.

The Chicago detective stirred and slowly pushed himself up on all fours. John Kenyon carefully picked up a bill that, except for it crispy corners and charred surface, was still intact.

"Tell me," John Kenyon began as he moved gingerly to a sitting position. "How much was it?" Now leaning against the bar cabinet, he looked down at Thatcher. "I need a figure to put in the bazillion reports I'm going to have to write."

"The equivalence of working a forty hour week for two centuries." Glancing at Kenyon, he added, "Cost of living notwithstanding."

From outside came the squawking amplification of a megaphone. "This is the Waukegan Police. This building is surrounded!"

✦

Still looking at the ceiling and contemplating the worth of being in one piece, Thatcher did not notice Flame scampering toward him on her hands and knees. Suddenly, he found himself smothered in passionate caresses.

With scraps of singed money in her dark hair, Flame fell on top of Thatcher and kissed him hard on the mouth. When she felt him stir beneath her, she released her hold momentarily.

"Is everything in the right places?" she asked solicitously. "I mean, I'm not hurting you?"

Before he could answer, she kissed him again, more softly.

"I thought you were..." she murmured. "How?"

Pointing toward the opened safe, he grimaced. "Quick deposit."

Eve Jensen appeared at the end of the bar with her right arm supporting Gretta. "John, my God, it was a grenade. How?"

Nudging the safe door closed with his foot, he announced, "They don't make 'em like this anymore." The resounding clink of the safe door closing emphasized the proclamation.

Gretta looked squarely at John Kenyon. "Gimme your gun." Catching Flame's disparaging look with her one good eye, she countered with, "What?," and glanced between the big detective and her companion huddled beside Thatcher. "I wanna put that little bastard out of my misery."

Flame got to her feet. "If you would have broken his fucking arm the other night," Flame reminded her, "he couldn't have tossed his goddamn pomegranate."

Resolute, she replied, "I still wanna shoot 'em." Gretta brushed off shredded fragments of money from her shoulder with her one good arm. "Isn't there a reward or something for recovering all this money?"

"Take all you want." Flame selected an intact charred bill from a nearby chair. "I bet it's worth as much as your VISA."

John Kenyon slowly came to his feet as the Waukegan PD entered the front door. "We're out of our jurisdiction, Detective Jensen." He waited for her subtle smirk. "Let's get out of the way."

"Anyone got a smoke?" Gretta looked back and forth between the others.

"Not since September 1982." Kenyon thought a moment. "It was a Tuesday."

"So, you're sayin' you don't got one?"

Flame exhaled loudly.

"I want the three of you at my precinct tomorrow at eleven," Kenyon informed his ragtag posse, "and don't plan anything for the afternoon."

"Detective Kenyon," Eve addressed her partner. "I'll advise the two Swanson women and Mr. Duran of the same."

John Kenyon looked down at Thatcher, who was now sitting upright on the floor. "Mr. Thatcher." Offering his hand, he carefully pulled Thatcher to his feet. "I'm making you personally responsible for these two yahoos until then."

"I'll do my best," he replied as he stooped down to pick up his Cubs cap. Slapping it hard against his thigh to knock off the singed fragments of once-legal tender, he looked sternly at his two friends.

Flame grinned, "Don't let me out of your sight."

Epilogue

THE CORN FIELDS OF IOWA WERE AS THATCHER EXPECTED: flat and green, dissected by straight, unrelenting highways. The sight of a lone oak tree could excite the senses. It was the northward jaunt to the Black Hills that provided the long awaited reprieve from the sameness of the Great Plains. Then came the slow climb into the rolling grass-covered foothills of Wyoming, and ultimately the ascent toward the majestic grandeur of the Rocky Mountains.

Crossing the Illinois state line a week earlier, he had assured himself he would return to call on Flame and Gretta, to drink a beer to their adventure, and to once again attempt to absorb their intricate simplicity. Crystal Falls he would visit in October, and share a crisp autumn afternoon with Theresa and Karlene. However, as he watched Old Faithful rush toward the late afternoon sky, and felt its warm sulfurous mist against his sunburned face, he knew it likely would never happen. Yet, the thought of it gratified him in a way that even the spectacle before him could not.

THE END